DARK HORSES

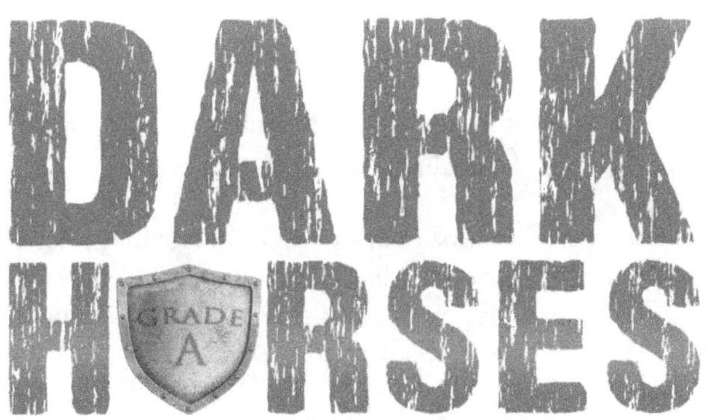

Blood Brothers #5

MANDA MELLETT

Disclaimer

This is a work of fiction. Names, characters, businesses, places, events and incidents are either the products of the author's imagination or used in a fictitious manner. Any resemblance to actual persons, living or dead, or actual events is purely coincidental.

Warning

This book is dark in places and contains content of a sexual nature. It is not suitable for persons under the age of 18.

ISBN: 978-1-912288-01-4

CONTENTS

PROLOGUE
Two years ago

They say, if you save a life you're forever responsible for the person whose life you saved."

My eyes close briefly in exasperation, letting out the words with a frustrated sigh. "I didn't save her life." A bonding session between brothers, as usual, rapidly evolves into a light-hearted argument.

Nijad sits forward and points at our older brother Kadar, the emir of Amahad, "For once," he grins, "I agree with him. You might not have literally saved her, but you watched over her while she was at risk." Breaking off he shrugs. "Without you, she could have died."

"Hypothetical, and in this instance, wrong. It was just a precaution."

Kadar shakes his head. "Irrelevant, brother, the intention was there. I reiterate. If you save a life, you take on that responsibility."

"Utter rubbish. That particular quote has come from the movies, no culture will lay claim to it, not even ours." As Arabs, we might have numerous sayings attributed to our heritage, but would certainly not own that one. "Just think about it. Any doctor, lifeguard, fireman… their lives would be ruined by the complication of looking after everyone they've saved. No one would ever apply for the job, let alone volunteer."

"Your only interest in her at that time was that of a medic?"

I nod emphatically. "Yes."

"Bullshit, brother."

"You're talking crap, Kadar."

As my younger brother chuckles, I direct my next comment to him, "For fuck's sake, Ni. It was the only reasonable thing to do."

"You're talking out of your arse again, brother. Something drew you. Whether or not you had any obligation to her, she owned you from that point on."

But while I shake my head in denial, I can't stop myself reflecting on his words. *Was that really the point where it all began?*

CHAPTER 1
Jasim

Feeling like bashing my head against the nearest available brick wall, and ascribing the ability to keep a tight rein on my temper to nothing other than my lifetime of diplomatic training, I only just stop myself rolling my eyes. When Bates pauses for breath, I take my opportunity to step in, trying to explain once again, this time using the simplest possible terms I can find.

"Dungeon monitors…"

Bates interrupts *yet again*, his hands waving dismissively. "Your club, Club Tiacapan, can afford to pay for monitors, hell, you've got six figure membership fees. Here, I can't afford to pay for any more staff than I already do; security on the door and the bar staff. Sure, we've got one monitor, but there's no money for any more."

I suppose I should be grateful Bates has approached me for advice having at last recognised that there have been too many accidents and incidents of abuse at his underground, and poorly, run BDSM club in Soho. Being the founder and now part-owner of one of the most exclusive clubs in the UK, with the reputation of being one of the most respected in the world among those serious about the lifestyle, I'm well qualified to give my opinion. But if all the man is going to do is raise excuses why he won't act on my suggestion, what I'm doing here is a complete waste of effort on my part, if not on his. But for the sake of the unsuspecting who play in his club, I feel bound to stay.

As he rattles on, telling me for a second—or is it third time?—all the reasons why it's impossible for him to take on board my ideas, I allow myself a moment to enjoy the juvenile joke of what his name would be, were he to go by his full surname on the floor instead of the simpler Master B. There's little reason to wonder why.

"Bates," I now use a voice I seem to have borrowed from my older brother, the emir of Amahad. The one he uses which makes the even the roughest desert sheikhs quake in their boots. It has the desired effect on the man I'd given up precious time to meet with tonight, and he at last stops his tirade. "We don't pay our dungeon monitors. Those who have gained Master status at the club take their turn at overseeing the scenes and making sure all play is conducted in a safe environment. If, as we've already discussed, you added training and mentoring to the services you offer here, you'll likely find the right kind of Dominants who'll want to give something back and won't expect a penny for it."

As Bates goes to answer, probably to refute my suggestion—the man has already told me he wants to improve the reputation of his club while rejecting every single proposal I've so far offered—there's a knock on his office door. The club owner seems almost relieved at the interruption, and eagerly calls out permission for whoever it is to come in.

The bouncer, who appears to be Bates' sole member of security, enters. He shuffles a little as though embarrassed. "Sorry to burst in like this, boss, but there's a woman downstairs and I don't know what to do with her." He's a big man, about my height, standing at least six-foot three and heavily built. On the surface, it looks like they'd be few people who would cause him any problem.

Bates frowns. "A member? Someone looking to join?"

"No, nothing like that. It's a girl." As he wipes his hand over his sweaty face, I notice he seems frazzled. "She's been mugged and assaulted in the alleyway between this building and the one next door." Still appearing flustered he continues, "She's injured, but refuses an ambulance, doesn't want the police called, and is afraid to leave in case her assailant's still out there. She managed to get away, but he took her handbag." He looks down and then back up, "I offered to get her a taxi, but her purse must have been in her bag and she's got no money."

Both Bates and I rise to our feet. Whatever the deficiencies of his club, both he and I are Dominants, and the idea of a woman attacked and hurt calls to our overriding protective instincts.

"How badly is she injured?" My background in medicine spurs me to ask.

The bouncer shakes his head. "She's obviously taken a nasty blow to the head, but beyond that she won't say. Look, I'm sorry to disturb you, Master B. I know you're in an important meeting, but I didn't know what else to do."

"Is she able to manage the stairs?" As the bouncer indicates he thinks she can, I turn to Bates, "Bring her up here, I was a medic in the army, I can take a look at her, see whether we should insist she goes to hospital or not. Unless, of course, you'd prefer your own first-aider to examine her?"

The club owner's brow creases, which makes me wonder whether he's even got a member of staff with that qualification, then consider he's probably realising it's not good advertising to have someone bleeding in the club's reception. My thoughts are confirmed as he decides and instructs, "Yeah, that's the best idea. Bring her up discreetly, Al. Jasim, it would be useful if you could check her out. Thank you."

As Al disappears on his errand, the owner of Tops and Tailends turns to me and shrugs, "I doubt you have these problems. Being on a busy street leaves us open to all sorts wandering in. We've had to boot away many a drunk before now. In your location you won't have so much foot traffic passing by."

No, we certainly don't. Never. Club Tiacapan is situated in a secluded mansion on the outskirts of Hampstead Heath to the south of London. The two organisations couldn't be further apart either in locale or clientele. As I think about the differences, I ask myself again whether I've wasted my time coming here tonight. My instincts suggest nothing I've said will be acted on. If I'm wrong and changes will be put into place, that's all to the good, keeping BDSM play safe is a goal I'm happy to help achieve. But if Bates has just been going through the motions, considering improvements his members have asked for without any intention to follow through, there's a lot of more appealing activities I could have been taking part in this evening.

My fingers tap on the table in front of me as I study the man I'd come to meet, and then my attention is drawn to the door as it opens for the second time.

It only takes a split second before I'm on my feet, my hands going out automatically to steady the girl who's entering. *Fuck, she's young, she barely looks in her twenties.* She's got almost jet-black hair, reaching down to her waist, a lithe figure, not overly endowed, and a clear complexion that's marred by blood running down the side of her face from a nasty gash on her forehead. Her eyes are wide and staring, and she's shaking like a leaf.

Pushing gently on her shoulder to encourage her to sit on the chair I'd just vacated, I notice Al's carrying something in his hand. Recognising what he's holding, I nod my appreciation at his foresight in bringing up a first aid kit with him. "Thanks."

Now I turn my attention to the girl, who's clearly in shock. Her body is trembling and her face is very pale. "Water?" I suggest to Bates.

"Does she want anything stronger?" He seems eager to help.

"Not until we know what we're dealing with." I crouch down in front of her, bringing myself to her height so I don't scare her any more than she already is, and slowly reach out my hand. I wait for her eyes to meet mine, then, using as gentle a voice as I can, speak to her. "I'd like to look at your wound. Clean it up and see how bad it is. Is that alright?"

Taking her small dip of her head as permission, my fingers touch her chin, and gently I turn her head. As I look at the blood coming from her temple, relieved to see it's no longer flowing freely, I suspect that it's not as deep as I first feared. Still, I've got to check whether it needs stitches.

Opening the first aid box, I'm pleased to find it well stocked and that antiseptic wipes are to hand.

"This might sting," I tell her, as I open the pack, "Are you sure you don't want to go to A & E? I've got my car here…"

There's a flare of something unreadable in her eyes as she replies adamantly. "No." Then she remembers her manners, "But thank you for helping me."

"No worries, sweetheart. I was a medic in the army, so qualified to provide first aid treatment at least." I talk partly to reassure her as I start to clean the wound. "Can you tell me what happened?" She winces, the cut smarting as I touch it. "Sorry."

"I'll call the police."

"No." Throwing a horrified glance toward Bates, she tries to justify her refusal to involve the authorities. "He'll be long gone now, and it was too dark to see anything of him. Please, I don't want to go spend half the night at the station when I've got no answers to anything they'd ask."

She's seems so determined, and really, if she can't give a description, what could they do? But it does seem odd she doesn't want to report what happened. *Who is she? And why doesn't she want to seek proper help?*

"I'll get that water."

As Bates disappears on his errand, I take the opportunity to study her. She's on edge, her fight response absent, and if I'm any judge of character, an insistence on dialling nine nine nine would have her running. Although inside I'm seething that anyone could even think of hurting a tiny slip of a girl like her, I force calm into my voice, "Okay, no police. But, sweetheart, to treat you properly, and make sure you haven't any serious injuries, I need to know what he did to you. Tell me what happened, and we'll take it from there. If I'm satisfied I'll be able to treat you here, we won't need to be making any phone calls."

Her eyes flick to mine, and another small dip of her head shows she agrees with my bargain. In part, as well as needing to hear her story, I'm hoping that talking will help take her mind off the pain I'm undoubtedly causing, however soft my touch. While I continue to gently wipe away the blood, she commences to tell me her story.

"I was out for the night with some girlfriends, it was supposed to be girls' night out, but I'm sure you know what those can be like. Good intentions and all that." She attempts a sheepish grin, "It wasn't long before our joking and laughing attracted attention. Some blokes sitting near us bought us a few shots. They were nice enough, and well, my friends, they sort of hooked up with these guys, and decided to go on to a club. I didn't fancy it. I wasn't feeling in the mood to make it a late one. I decided to go home."

"Go on," I encourage, as she breaks off, her face tightening again as she remembers.

"I was heading for the tube, walking along the road outside this place. I could already see the illuminated Underground sign, when suddenly I was pulled into an alley." She pauses, and swallows as she forces herself to relive her ordeal. "It was so unexpected I didn't react at first. A man grabbed my bag off my shoulder—and I couldn't hold onto it. I was angry, thinking he'd got what he wanted and was going to run off. Stupidly, it crossed my mind that in my heels I'd never catch him." Another moment of silence, and she bites her lip. Her voice starts to shake, "But that wasn't all he wanted." She gives a full body shiver. "He pulled me further back into the alley, his hand was over my mouth and he seized hold of my coat like he wanted to tear it off."

As she stops talking, I've cleaned all the blood. I'm happy she doesn't need stitches, and a couple of butterfly plasters will keep it closed. But what worries me most is the enormous bump on her head. She must have clouted hard for it to have come up like that. "Tell me the rest, sweetheart," I encourage, needing to know exactly what happened so I know what to do next, my rage almost like a wild beast I'm having difficulty keeping contained.

"I elbowed him, hard, as hard as I could, but it wasn't enough to do anything except make him angry. He pushed me hard against the wall, and that's when this happened." To show me what she means, she starts raising her hand toward her forehead. I catch it in mid-air, to stop her hurting herself, noticing how cold her fingers are.

"Did you pass out, sweetheart?"

"I don't know, I was stunned. If I did, it could only have been for a second or two. He," her voice starts to break, "He pulled me up, and I think he was going to, to… rape me."

I'm sure that had been his intention, but I don't think he did. She'd be far less coherent had he gone all the way. But it had gone far enough to badly shake her up. Pulling back, I stare into her eyes, set deep in her face making them seem large, although tears now make them glisten. Her makeup, carefully applied for a night on the town, emphasises and draws my attention to the dark orbs. My main reason is to check the dilation of her pupils, but I can't ignore the fact that they're almost the same dark brown/black of my own and have visible flecks of gold and a reddish tinge toward the centre.

Beautiful eyes which roll as she answers my unspoken question, "But he didn't, of course," there's a touch of spirit in her voice which was missing before, "I'd be a complete mess if he'd done that."

I note the deserved pride now she's remembering how she'd fought her assailant off. "How did you escape him?"

"Luck." She shivers, "pure luck. My coat was undone. As he pulled it, I slipped my arms out. And ran. Luckily someone was coming in this… club?" I realise she doesn't know where she'd walked into and in the circumstances, don't think it's right to enlighten her as to exactly what type of establishment this is, so I nod to confirm it this indeed a club, though I very much doubt it's the type her friends were planning on visiting tonight. "Well, I tailed him and followed him through. The bouncer wasn't impressed, and I think I'd have been chucked straight back out, had it not been for this." She points to where the blood had been on her face, now all cleared away, and the cut neatly fixed up with steri-strips.

"What's your name?" I ask, realising I've been remiss in not asking before.

"Janna. Janna Stevens." She says it in a way she's hopeful I might have heard of her, but the name means nothing to me. Only a slight disappointment shows on her face, so if she's any kind of celebrity, she must be a small one. An actress, perhaps? A small role in one of the soaps I don't watch? It's impossible to say.

"I'm Jasim," I tell her. She can't have failed to have noticed my olive coloured skin, so much darker than her own. Though paler that it used to, be since I no longer spend time in my home country. As she holds out her hand to shake, I take it, again noticing how cold she is. As the room is on the warm side, it must be shock.

Seeing me staring, she lowers her eyes, and the Dominant inside me twitches. This is no time for that though, and anyway, she's far too young. I concentrate on the signs I should be looking for. Her memory of her attack seems clear, no gaps and nothing forgotten. Her speech isn't slurred, and her answers to my questions have come fast and are coherent. But that possible brief loss of consciousness still worries me.

I ask about the symptoms I can't see, "Have you got a headache? Feel nauseous? Dizzy? Any ringing in your ears? Tiredness?"

"It's two in the morning. I've had a long day, so yes, I'm tired," she replies with a self-deprecating smile, one side of her mouth turning up. The rearrangement of her features shows she's quite pretty, though not in classical way, a model's face, one with character, rather than beauty. "And my head's thumping, but then, I did hit it hard."

Tilting my head to one side, I consider her answers. Enough to worry me. Pushing back my hair that's flopped down over my forehead, I ask, "Is there anyone I can call to come to get you?"

"No." She answers too quickly.

Taking her apparent youth into account, I wonder whether she's got family who could be worried about her, "Your parents?"

The look she gives me is comical. "I'm twenty-two, and if I did still have parents, I'm a bit old to have a curfew, don't you think?"

She's the same age as my little sister, and I'd worry about Aiza if she was out alone on the streets of London in the early hours of the morning. But what do I know? Except, while she's not quite as young as I'd expected, she's still eleven years younger than me. Meanwhile, the medic in me is concerned. Having run through her symptoms, I don't like the idea of her being left alone tonight, As I'm wondering how to phrase it without causing undue concern, I'm saved by Bates walking in through the door carrying a bottle of water.

"Sorry I took so long. There was a problem on the floor that I needed to sort out. Here, pet, do you want this?"

While she gives him a grateful look, I delve back into the first aid kit and find paracetamol at the bottom. I take two from the bottle. "Take these, they'll help with your head."

As she washes down the tablets with a mouthful of water, my eyes are drawn to the way her throat works and the sleek slenderness of her neck.

"What's the verdict, Sheikh?" As Bates gives me my title, her eyes open wide and she sinks back on the chair, making me wish he hadn't given away my rank. Her reaction shows she seems in awe of it, and the camaraderie we've just been building disappears in a flash.

I answer his question, trying to ignore both the effect the designation had provoked, and the flutter of unexpected disappointment inside me, "She's got a cut on her head, but it's not serious. However, young Janna here might have concussion." I emphasis her age in part to remind myself. "You got anyone at home who can watch over you?" The latter I address toward her, while wondering whether there's a boyfriend in the wings, even though she'd indicated there was no one to call.

She shakes her head, then gives a little groan, causing me to suspect her headache is worse than she'd admitted. As does the way her fingers go up to rub her temples, carefully avoiding the bump. "No, I live alone." Her eyes flick sideways, and I suspect she's told me a lie. *Why?* "It's alright, I'll get a cab and go back. I'll be fine. Thank you for everything you've done for me." Then her face twists as though she's remembering her money's been stolen.

Before I can speak, it's Bates' turn to discourage her. "I had Al go look in the alley. He found these." He passes her a handbag and a discarded coat and his eyes flit to me.

Ignoring the coat for the moment, she takes the bag from him with a pleased smile, and rummages inside, her face falling as she does so. "He's taken my purse, keys. And my phone. Everything." She looks again, opening side pockets and examining them, then shakes out the empty bag as though to see if there's anything he could have missed. A lonely tampon falls out. With a flush of red, she pushes it back in.

"Was there anything in there with your address on it?"

Her face goes blank, as though she's mentally cataloguing what she had with her. Her eyes widen, "Yes, I had a letter from my bank."

"Well then, you can't go home. He knows where you live and has your keys." I spell it out for her, in case she hasn't put two and two together. "You'll have to stay with a friend. That would be better anyway. You shouldn't be alone tonight, not with the bump you've had. If you give me an address, I'll drive you there and explain what care you need. Just in case."

Another shake of her head, "Not possible." She might only be twenty-two, but there's a presence about her, an independence at odds with her age. Does she mean she's got no friends, or none she wishes to impose on?

"What about the friends you were with tonight?"

A slight quirk of her mouth. "From the way they were behaving I think they'll be otherwise engaged tonight."

At last I stand, stretching as muscles protest the crouched position I'd held for too long. I pace the room, my hand brushing back my hair as I think. I can't let her go home, not when her attacker has her address. I could pay for her to stay in a hotel, but then she'd be all alone. Now it's me who glances Bates' way, but know he'll be no help at all. And I'm not at all sure I'd want to leave her with him.

It's late, I'm tired. And there's only one solution I can come up with. "You'll have to come home with me, then. I'll watch over you, make sure you don't have concussion, and tomorrow I'll get you back home. You'll need to get your locks changed, but you're in no state to get that sorted tonight." And, despite the fact she doesn't want to report it, I'll have a quiet word with my friends in the police to make sure they include wherever it is she lives on their rounds.

CHAPTER 2
Janna

This man, *this Sheikh*, is suggesting I go home with him? Aren't sheikhs super mega rich or something? And haven't they a reputation for kidnapping any woman they want? Or have I just been reading too many romance novels? While he's been studying me, in the same detached way as anyone in the medical profession would, I've been examining him too. And shit, is he handsome. He's got an aquiline nose, slightly pointed chin covered in designer stubble, dark hair well styled, but long, just touching his shoulders. And his eyes, well, all at once I understand the saying, a girl could easily drown in them.

Now I come to think of it, his suit does smack of money. As he stands, I'm able to see it fits as though it was made for him—it can't be off the rack—and outlines a figure I suspect is well muscled. His shoulders are broad, his jacket tailored to show a trim waist. A stark contrast to the other man beside him who carries a middle-aged spread and who's giving off a vibe I'm not certain I like. Now if it was him offering to give me a bed for the night, I'd turn him down without a second thought.

But Jasim? *Sheikh* Jasim? He's got trust and integrity written all over him, or is that wishful thinking? Was that blow to my head harder than I thought? Could it be screwing up my sense of self-preservation? I don't know him from Adam, but I'm tired and sore, and I just want a bed. Can I take a chance and accept his kind offer? *Can I be certain there's no ulterior motive?* While it's not something I'd normally even contemplate, I know at least one of my friends will probably be ending up in a stranger's bed tonight. Where's the difference?

I've precious little alternative. I can't go home, being in no state to face the inevitable interrogation tonight. Maybe by morning I'll have concocted some credible story about how I've ended up with a head injury. I can't imagine telling them what actually happened. Christ, they'd have a field day with that. My first taste of freedom, and just look at how it ended. They'd never let me forget it.

Telling Jasim there was no one to look after me wasn't the first untruth I've told tonight. Even before I'd left the house I'd used manipulation to get my own way, and gotten hurt as a result. God, I'll have provided them with enough ammunition to keep me grounded me for another six years. The longer I can delay letting them know, the better it will be. And maybe, with luck, the lump on my forehead will have gone down by morning, and they'll never have to know.

That I find the intriguing sheikh attractive is probably what influences me most, and the words come out of my mouth before I've seriously considered all the implications. If I wasn't so shaky after being attacked and groped, if my head wasn't hurting so much or fatigue threatening to overwhelm me, maybe I'd have thought twice before saying to a perfect stranger, "Sheikh, that's a generous offer. If you really think it's necessary and you've a spare bed, I'd like to take you up on it."

"Jasim," he corrects, before pulling out a business card. "I know you don't want to bother your family or friends for a bed, but please, give them a call or text and let them know where you'll be staying. My motivation is simply to make sure you've not got any lasting complications from your injury, but you don't know me at all. Bates here will vouch for me, of course."

Bates seems bewildered by the direction the night has now headed, and offers up another suggestion, "Perhaps one of the girls here could take you home with them?"

And impose on a complete stranger? I open my mouth to tell them I don't want to do that, then close it, realising that's exactly what I'm proposing to do. My hand touches the bump on my head as though I could tell it's responsible for my lack of inhibition tonight. I'm normally more careful that this. Strike that, correction, I'm never allowed to be anything but.

The thought that my protectors would be horrified I was going home with a strange man decides me. My one chance of freedom, and I'll take it. And if I end up in his bed, well, I know enough to understand it certainly wouldn't be rape. He intrigues me; this man with his faintest of accents, his title, and the darker shades of his skin tone. If I walked away from him now, I would never know what I might have missed.

"I'll text my friend, if I can borrow your phone." My decision is made. And oh, yeah, Mara would be over the moon to know I'd gone home with a man. Hell, she'll laugh her head off, it's so unlike me. And she's probably in God knows whose bed at the moment herself, and won't even read my message until morning. But soon enough, if I disappear off the face of the earth. *Don't sheikhs keep women as slaves?* Heaven help me, but that idea carries no revulsion, just ignites a tingling between my thighs. *Shit, Janna, you're in trouble here, girl.*

I send a quick text to a memorised number while Jasim finishes up the conversation which I'd interrupted with my entrance, a series of 'I'll be in touch' from him and a half-hearted, 'I'll think on what you've suggested' from his companion. Then, seeing they're saying their goodbyes, I get to my feet. A wave of dizziness goes through me, and I sway. A strong arm comes around me, holding me up.

"Sorry." Is it tiredness, or have I really hit my head too hard?

Sharp eyes scrutinise me, then with a last look at Bates, Jasim draws me along with him, "Let's get you home."

As he leads me to the door and down the stairway, I lean on him for support, but inwardly admit I'm enjoying the comfort of his muscular arm around me. Instead of taking me out of the main entrance that I'd come in by, he takes me to another door and we descend a set of stairs leading down to a basement carpark and then he directs me across toward an expensive looking car, a four-door saloon. Opening the passenger side, he helps me into a soft leather seat and I'm encased by the luxury. Leaning my head back, I close my tired eyes.

After hearing the driver's door shut, the car starts to move so silently I hadn't noticed the engine starting, only realising we're on our way when I feel the slight vibration as we leave the garage.

"Quiet car," I comment, already half asleep, lulled by the movement.

"It's electric," he replies. My last conscious thought is to idly wonder whether he drives it because he cares about the environment.

It's probably very stupid and naïve of me, but I'm completely unaware of my surroundings or where he's taking me as we drive through the quiet of the late night, or more to the point, early morning London streets. I'll likely look back on my actions tonight with a more critical eye and blame my out of character actions on the fact I'd banged my head. At the moment though, our brief interaction, the way he cared for me so gently and competently, is making me trust him, and I believe he's got nothing but my best interests at heart.

The smooth movement of the car, and the silence of the man beside me lulls me into a deep sleep, and I don't wake until we're pulling up in another underground car park, and he's opening my door.

"We're here."

Opening bleary eyes, it takes me a moment to remember who he is, and what's happened tonight. And it's only now, for the first time, I get a sense of unease. *Where am I? He could have brought me anywhere.* Wherever it is, I'm not going to find out sat in the car. I swing out my legs and strong arms are quickly there to help me to my feet; it's lucky there's someone to hold me, still half asleep, I'm feeling a bit weak.

Once again holding me close to his side, he leads me over to where there's a lift waiting. Inside, he takes out a card and swipes it. The lift begins to rise, the motion making me lean on him even more. I'm so close I can smell the expensive aftershave he uses, and underneath that, a masculine perfume all his own. It must be intoxicating, as it makes me feel lightheaded.

With a slight jolt, the lift arrives at its destination, and when the doors open, I find myself in the foyer of an apartment bigger than any I've ever been in before. Without wasting a moment, he presses his hand to my back, and encourages me into a well-appointed sitting room, floor to ceiling windows revealing a view extending for miles. Realising this must be the penthouse suite, I feel overwhelmed by its ostentatiousness, but don't have long to admire the luxurious furnishings or comfortable looking sofas, before he takes me through and down a hallway, and into a bedroom.

It's immediately clear that it must be his. The dark leather-bound bed, covered in black satin sheets, screams masculinity. A comfortable wingback chair sits under a window, with a book lying open on the seat. Clothes are already set out, hanging on a vast wardrobe door doubtless in preparation for the morning.

My senses return to me. I fancy this man, felt the attraction almost from the moment I stole my first real look at him, but that doesn't mean I have any intention of sharing his bed. It had been a nice fantasy, not a real desire.

"Um." At a loss for words, I point at the bed, knowing my body has gone stiff.

"I'll sleep on the chair," he explains, understanding the reason for my hesitation immediately. "I need to stay close, to keep an eye on you." In a gesture I've already noticed must be one of his characteristics, he brushes back his hair, "My housekeeper's spring cleaning, and the guest rooms are all stripped. I don't feel like making up another bed tonight."

The housekeeper? How the other half live! It must be wonderful to not have to clean your own room. I must still be out of it, when the most ridiculous thing comes out of my mouth, "It's not spring."

He laughs, the first time I've heard his amusement, it's a deep throated chuckle, and one which sends tingles down my spine, "Spring, autumn. I just let her get on with whatever she wants. When she decides it's time to do a deep clean, there's no stopping her." He turns me to face him. "The bathroom's through there." Indicating an open door, he continues. "Make yourself comfortable and get into bed. I'll leave out one of my shirts for you to wear. Unless you want to keep that on?"

That being my skimpy dress I wore not for comfort, but for a night out with the girls. With its tight bodice, it would be awkward to sleep in. "Thank you. A shirt would be great."

"Right, you get yourself sorted, and I'll go into the lounge for a while."

With that he leaves me alone. I do the necessary, and finding the shirt he'd left out, take it back and change in the bathroom. He's got a selection of new tooth brushes, and a range of soaps and feminine creams and face wipes, suggesting I'm not the first female visitor he's had in his flat, and I don't understand why that thought disappoints me. Staring at my reflexion in the mirror, I gently brush at the strips over my wound. Even pulling down my fringe doesn't hide them. *Shit. I'd hoped to conceal it.* Sighing, knowing I'm unlikely to get away without any explanation, I briefly think of the trouble I'll be in come morning. But there's nothing I can do about that now. *They're going to flip.*

At last I return to the bedroom, and with only a slight hesitation, slide underneath the smooth silk covers. The bed's comfy, the pillow cradles my head perfectly, and I'm almost asleep before I finish the thought that I'll not be able to sleep in a strange room.

A hand is shaking me. "Janna, wake up."

Bloody hell! *Is it already morning?* I don't feel I've slept very long.

"How you feeling? Is your headache worse or better? Can you look at me, pet?"

The events of the night before come rushing back to me, along with the realisation I'm in a sheikh's bed. The thought makes me want to giggle, but I suppress my mirth, restricting myself to a simple reply. "My head's feeling better."

"No double vision or dizziness?"

Huh! He's just woken me from a deep sleep, what does he expect? "No, I'm fine."

Gentle fingers take my wrist. *He's feeling my pulse.* Suddenly I want his hand to touch more of me. He could trace my arm, up to my shoulder and down to my...

Moving his hand to my face, he lifts my eyelids and stares into my eyes, pulling away when I blink to avoid the harsh light.

"Go back to sleep now." At his quiet instruction I gather he's just doing what he'd said, waking me to check I'm alright. But the command in his voice has me obeying. Turning on my side, I close my eyes as he switches off the light.

And this time the nightmare hits. I'm back in the alleyway, fighting my assailant off. The difference, this time, is I can't get free. I scream for help, but it's futile. In the cacophony of the London evening there'll be no one able to hear me. I punch out with my arms, only to have them held firmly...

"Hush. You're having a nightmare. It's to be expected, pet. You've been through a lot tonight." He holds my hands in one of his, the other he smooths across my forehead, in the same way my mother used to when I was a child. He's sitting next to me, the warmth of his body coming to me through my bedclothes and the shirt that I'm wearing. Brazenly, I snuggle into his side, and now it's my hand that imprisons his.

"Stay with me?"

"I'm here, pet. I'm sleeping on the chair. I'm not far away."

I want him to be closer, need the comfort he gives me. "No, please. Hold me."

I feel him tense with reluctance, "It wouldn't be proper."

"Please." I inject unashamed begging into my voice, as I'm scared at the thought of the dream returning. "I don't want to feel alone."

At last he relaxes, his release of tension suggesting he's going to give in. "Shift over a bit then." I move, and he settles beside me. "Turn over." Again, I obey, and he pulls me toward his firm and muscular chest. We're spooning, but I'm under the covers and he's on top. "Try and go back to sleep. I'll keep the monsters at bay."

I close my eyes, but sleep evades me. The truth is, I've never slept in a man's arms before. Rather than relaxing me, his closeness excites me, sending sensations to parts of me that have been dormant before.

"Child, don't move like that." His amused voice rumbles in my ear.

Embarrassed, I find I've pushed my bum into him, and even through the bedclothes I can feel something hard pushing against me. *He's aroused.*

As I still, he continues, "Sorry, pet, but a beautiful girl in my bed will do that to me. To any man. Now go to sleep, child."

Child? Why does he keep calling me that? Despite his compliment, there's no way I want him to see me as someone too young, too innocent for him. I protest, "I'm not a child, Jasim."

"You're not quite a woman yet, though, are you?"

My body floods with embarrassment as there can only be one meaning. *How does he know? Is it stamped on my forehead?* I have no rebuttal. I'm got all the right womanly parts, as he must be able to see. Is this where I should flirt with him? Show my attraction? I've watched others do it enough before. From observing, I know all the right moves. It's just that I lack the confidence to pull it off, and would probably make a fool of myself. *He's a sheikh for God's sake.* He could have any woman he wants.

As I try to convince myself of the reasons he wouldn't want me, I notice his breathing has slowed, the measured rise and fall of his chest against my back telling me he has gone to sleep.

CHAPTER 3
Jasim

I leave her sleeping in my bed. After the shock of the attack the night before, and the resultant head injury, what rest she can get will do her the world of good. As I recall her description of the mugging, I grasp my mug of tea a little too hard. If her attacker hadn't been left holding an armful of coat, giving her that momentary window of escape, she could have been raped. There's not much to her, it wouldn't have taken much of a man to overpower a girl of her slender build. I put down my drink before it breaks, my hand shaking with barely concealed rage. To even call her assailant a man is doing a disservice to the male half of the human race. No woman should ever be forced. It would have destroyed her.

I don't need to be a Dom to recognise her innocence, it's written all over her face. And I certainly shouldn't have to remind myself how young she is. Fuck, if someone of my age came on to my baby sister I'd be talking to him with my fists. But hell, when she'd pushed against me last night, it was all I could do to resist taking her into my arms and divesting her of her purity once and for all. Thank Allah she's going to be out of my apartment and out of my life as soon as she awakes. She's woken a beast inside me, and I'd be lying to myself if I tried to pretend it's only a protective instinct that she's aroused.

Didn't she know how close she'd come to playing with fire as she rubbed that cute arse against my cock? I let out a huff, dismissing the notion she'd intentionally taunted me. Whether consciously or not, the result was the same. But I won't give in to temptation. No, tonight I'll go to Club Tiacapan and find an experienced woman to play with, and one who'll let me fuck all this strange attraction, along with the frustration I can't do anything about, out of my system.

"'Morning."

Lost in my thoughts I hadn't heard her get up. As her gentle voice brings me out of my reverie, I turn to see the object of my desire dressed just in my shirt, and a wave of possessiveness floods over me. *She looks right in my clothes.* And how wrong that thought is. At least she's decent, my shirt is long and covers her down to her thighs, but I can't prevent my mind wondering what, if anything, she's wearing underneath. Quickly I swing back around, leaning with both my palms flat on the worktop, fighting to get myself under control. My very evident hard-on is the last thing she needs to see.

After clearing my throat, I answer her, "Good *afternoon*. I let you sleep in, as you seemed to need it. How's the head feeling today?"

She puts her hand to her injury, as if only just remembering it's there, so I guess it can't be paining her too badly. Then her face falls, as what I've said registers. "Oh heck, what time is it now?" Her eyes flick around the kitchen as if seeking out a clock.

"Half past one. Sorry, did you have somewhere you needed to be?" I feel guilty, I hadn't given a thought to what she had planned for today.

She shakes her head and nervously bites her lip, her youth too apparent as she replies, "No, but they'll be about to send out search parties by now."

"They?" Again I wonder whether she's got family who'd be missing her. But she turns away, clearly not going to expand. She's fidgeting, making me speculate whether she's uncomfortable in my presence, and rethinking her agreement to stay with me last night.

"Want a cup of tea?" I try to inject some normality into the situation that's probably strange for both of us. Her first time in a stranger's bed, and mine to sleep with a woman without wetting my dick.

Another shake, "No, I better get going. I'll just get dressed and get out of your way."

With that, she turns to go back to the bedroom, but before she goes through the door swings back around, "Er, thank you, Jasim. For letting me stay last night. I'm really grateful."

"It was no trouble." I wave my hands, dismissing her gratitude. She nods, her head bobbing awkwardly, and the flush on her face suggests she finds the situation a little embarrassing. I find it bizarre, normally a woman leaves my bed looking satisfied. But then, I've never had someone the age of my baby sister in my bed before. As she starts to walk away, I remember she still needs my help and call out after her, "I'll give you a lift when you're ready to go."

She stills, and then gives another nod, presumably remembering she's going to have to do the walk of shame in last night's clothes. Unless she wants to get on the tube with just a torn dress and dirty coat to cover her, she doesn't have any option but to accept my offer of a ride. A spare toothbrush, I can supply. Replacement women's clothing, I can't. Of course, I could call a taxi and give her the few quid to cover her fare, but I won't. For more than one reason, which I don't stop to examine, I want to spend a little longer in her company, and also, to see where she lives. And, perhaps, to discover who the mysterious 'they' are.

She gets ready quickly for a woman, and soon we're in my car driving across London in an easterly direction, our progress slowed by the heavy traffic that's always an issue this time of day. She guides me at last to a side road off Hackney's Mare Street, an area now up and coming, having shrugged off its previously poor reputation. While initially dubious coming to this renowned rough part of town, my mind's put at ease when I discover the houses are well maintained. Even I wouldn't mind parking my Tesla here, though perhaps not the Ferrari. She points out a parking space, and I pull the car up.

I go around to open her door, and she places her fingers in mine as I help her out and then glances up at the house we've parked outside, as if watching for prying eyes. Then politely she shakes my hand, thanks me again and says goodbye. It's a dismissal, and a clear indication I'm not going to be invited in to satisfy my curiosity, nor will any plans be made to meet up. The regret I feel is unexpected. Why should I worry whether I'll see her again? Surely, the affection I feel for her is only that she reminds me of my sister, my concern totally that of a brother? *That's all it should be.*

Getting back into the car, I wait until I see her walk into the large house, the type typically divided into flats, not even knowing which one would be hers. Tapping my fingers against the steering wheel, I delay starting the engine, unable to understand my reluctance to leave this area, and this woman, behind. Glancing up, I notice she hasn't gone inside yet, she seems to be lingering on the doorstep, key in her hand. Just as I'm wondering whether she's given me a false address, and am thinking about challenging her, she at last fits the key to the lock and disappears inside.

Well, that's it. Ships that pass in the night and all that. I doubt our paths will ever cross again. Why does the thought cause an emptiness inside me? Shaking off the odd feeling, trying to convince myself it's easier this way, I put the Tesla into gear, and make my way out of the side street, and enter the fray of the London traffic again.

Avoiding the embassy—I've no diplomatic duties today—I make my way across to the modern office area of the rejuvenated Docklands, and to the glass and steel building that houses AmaOil, the headquarters of the company I'm president of, and which I manage on behalf of my homeland. Having at last discovered oil under the sands of the southern desert of Amahad, I have taken on the responsibility for getting contracts set up, so when we finally manage to extract the liquid gold and it starts flowing from the pipeline into the containers housed at the Amahadian port in the north, we have buyers set up to take it and process it for us. It's a mammoth task, but one with potential multi-billion pound returns for both Amahad, and the neighbouring countries of Alair and Ezirad.

Thankfully, appointing contractors for all the steps, negotiating with OPEC and deciding whether to throw in with them, or go it alone, can be done remotely, as I have absolutely no desire to ever make my home in Amahad again. My late father, Emir Rushdi, had ruled country and home with an iron rod and outmoded ideas, culminating when I was complicit in kidnapping an innocent business woman for crimes her father committed. While that surprisingly resulted in an incredibly happy marriage between my younger brother and said abductee, the fact such archaic punishment was even considered, let alone followed through, was the final straw which broke this particular camel's back. I turned away from my country, and made a permanent move to England. Which gave me the opportunity to concentrate on my BDSM club, originally conceived as an outlet for my own preferences for play. Since its inception, the club has become a resounding success and provided a strong return on my investment.

While my elder brother's accession to the throne has resulted in much needed reform in Amahad, it's still not sufficient to call me home. But I haven't abandoned my country, contributing what I need to from these prestigious offices and working as my country's ambassador to the UK, as well as heading up our oil operations.

But today I'm not going to the offices to work. No, I've a meeting this afternoon that I'm very much looking forward to. Exiting the lift with a smile on my face, I enter my office to find my younger brother and his wife already waiting for me.

"Ni!" Walking forward with my hand outstretched, he clasps it in his, and then hugs me to him. It's been a month since I last saw him, when I made an obligatory brief visit back home just after the birth of the latest addition to our family, my nephew, Ra-id. Son to my older brother, Emir Kadar and his English wife Zoe, he's well named, Ra-id translating to leader, which he'll one day become. I'd stayed less than a day before returning to the UK.

"No hug for me, Jasim?" Cara chuckles softly, and I swing around to greet Nijad's beautiful wife, letting my brother go and crossing over to her in an instant.

I kiss both her cheeks, then embrace her tightly, remembering that if it wasn't for her belief in Nijad, his name would never have been cleared of a heinous crime. Our family has much to be grateful to her for. As well as restoring Nijad's reputation, she also played a significant role in discovering the oil lying under our sands.

Releasing her, I take a step back, holding her at arm's length while I examine her face. Her scars have almost completely disappeared now, her skin all but flawless and smooth. "You're looking really good." I speak the truth, she is. And it's clear to see she's become comfortable with herself. I can't help teasing her, "Done any hacking lately?"

Her face drops as she pretends to scowl, "Ni won't let me."

"I'm surprised he can stop you." A growl from behind me suggests he's not always successful. I bark a laugh, and then get down to the hospitality. "Come, sit. Nijad, Cara, what can I get you to drink?"

"Just something soft, please, Jasim. We've got plans to go to the club later."

Nodding, I press the intercom and put in a request to my personal assistant, then join my brother and his wife sitting on the comfortable leather couches I use for the more informal meetings. "How's Zorah?" I enquire, asking about my niece, their young daughter.

"She's great. Doing well. I don't like to be away from her, but now she's nearly a year old—a year, can you believe that, Jasim?—I felt able to leave her for a few days."

"And Cara's been longing to go to Club Tiacapan." Nijad's grin implies she's not the only one.

I can understand why. Nijad, like me, is a Dom, and he introduced his wife to the lifestyle when he'd quickly found she was his ideal submissive. Only in the bedroom though, she's got him twisted around her little finger outside of it. It was I who'd set up their own private dungeon in their palace in Zalmā, the desert city.

"Cara's longing to try the suspension rig. She's kept on ever since she heard about it," Nijad continues. He doesn't sound put out about that.

"Has Kadar given you any tips?" My older brother might be emir, and as such needs to keep his proclivities quiet, but he's also a Dom, and a master rigger.

Nijad jerks his chin, "I've been practicing Shibari, and yes, he's given me some pointers."

"Ha! I'm looking forward to seeing you tied up in knots, Cara."

Her eyes twinkle mischievously, "And I'm looking forward to seeing you in action, Jas." I exchange a glance with my brother, and raise my chin at his quick warning frown. I'll make sure to refrain from my more extreme activities tonight.

My assistant appears with a tray, I thank him. When he leaves, I lean forward, my hands on my knees, "You've never played in public before, Cara. How do you feel about it?"

Her trusting eyes go to her husband, "Ni will take care of me. And, of course, he's vetted my clothing."

"You won't be seeing my wife naked, if that's what you're expecting."

Of course, I wasn't. And I wouldn't want to. She's as much as a blood sister to me as Aiza.

Nijad puts out his hand and picks up his glass, and after taking a sip, he gives me a stern and appraising look. "When are you coming back to Amahad? And I don't mean just for a flying visit. It doesn't look good, you know, your staying away. Kadar worries about the impression it gives. He wants you to come back. And for longer than you did last time."

"You, of all people, know why I left, Nijad. I vowed never to go back." I suppress a shudder at the thought of those long gloomy hallways in the palace of Amahad in the country's capital, Al Qur'ah. The place where I was born and raised, until sent abroad to be educated and had come to understand how outdated my view of the world was. The obeisance and deference shown to me by virtue of my accident of birth, my privileged life, while there was poverty and suffering around me. The extravagant displays of wealth, while in the south of Amahad, my countrymen starved, eking out their meagre living from the parched desert.

Inhaling sharply, Nijad shakes his head, "Times are changing. Kadar's plans for an elected government are coming to fruition. A vast proportion of the wealth from the oil fields will go the desert tribes. New hospitals and schools are already in the planning stages…"

"My home is here, Nijad. I've got the club and my work." As always, I find myself shifting awkwardly at the thought of paying a visit of more than a few hours to the country that stifled my youth. Oh, I spent much of my time away, schooled at Eton and then Oxford. But when I was home… Rushdi had been hard on his sons. Never bending, always controlling. He might be dead, but it's my fear that his influence lingers on.

"I'm not asking you to move. Just to show your face." Nijad shakes his head in frustration.

"Kadar's put you up to this?" Nijad gives nothing away, so I continue, "He doesn't need me now that he's got an heir." As second son, I had always been the spare. For years Nijad, neither heir apparent or next in line, had been free to live the life of a playboy until the incident that almost destroyed him. I, on the other hand, wasn't allowed so much freedom, called back to learn the affairs of state. Until I escaped. And now, even with my father buried, I remain reluctant to be drawn back inside that web.

I stand and pace, thinking of Amahad, the country I hate and love, almost in equal measures. However, it's my heritage after all, and while my head might think otherwise, the blood that flows through my veins retains a desire to return. And it concerns me that my absence may be having a detrimental effect, something I'd not previously considered. It's not as if I need to search for an excuse. It's not stretching the truth to say I need to visit the oil fields, to oversee the work done on the ground that, so far, I've only directed from afar. I admit it looks bad, the second son who's abandoned his roots.

Surely I can spare some time? It's not as if I'll be held prisoner, and won't be allowed to return. I can trust my brother, the emir, not to keep me there by force, can't I? Of course, he's got the power to do that if he wanted to. But Kadar wouldn't stoop so low, would he? I glance quickly at my sister-in-law. *Kadar condoned Cara's kidnap.*

Nijad and his wife are murmuring to each other, giving me much needed time to think. My steps take me to the window, and I gaze out over London, at the heavy rain clouds threatening, the coats people are wearing showing colder weather has already arrived. With winter on its way, it's an appropriate time to go back. I'm Arab after all, the sun will restore me.

I didn't expect to be swayed, hadn't thought I'd agree, but seeing Nijad and Cara, talking about my niece and nephew, a sudden bout of unexpected homesickness washes over me. Until I spoke, I wasn't sure I'd made the decision. "I'll come."

My brother comes up alongside me and slaps me on the back, his open eyes showing my acquiescence was unexpected. His hand settles on my arm as he turns me to face him. Pleasure beams from his eyes. "You won't regret it, Jas. It's time you came home."

"Only for a month or two." I rush to assure him my return will have a time limit. "And I'll need to make sure everything's running smoothly here first."

"Jon will watch over the club. And I hear Devil's coming back for a while. It's good timing, brother."

My lips turn up in a cautious smile, he's right, the two other owners will keep Tiacapan running in my absence, but, "There's never a good time, Nijad. Although you're right. If I'm ever going to get closure, I need to move on. I need to return. Understand though, this is where I'm making my life now. This," I point back around and out of the window again. "This is my home. Not Amahad. Whatever you and Kadar think, I'm never going to live there again. Not for good."

"You might find yourself nice Arab woman."

Even though I see that he's teasing, I toss him a glare. His reference to a pure and untouched native the last thing I want. "Don't go there, Nijad. Just don't. You know me, you know my lifestyle choice. Taking an innocent virgin to my bed? Someone who doesn't share my desires?" I step toward him, almost in his face, "If you've got any plans to set me up, you can drop them now. You and Kadar might be happy shackled to one woman, but I'm wired differently to you."

"Jasim, I didn't mean…"

"You mentioned it. I'll take it you meant it as a joke. Now drop the subject, else I'll change my mind. If the two of you are plotting to set me up I won't step foot in Amahad."

The thought of me with a naïve woman is a joke. So why do I immediately see a vision of Janna Stevens in my head?

CHAPTER 4
Janna

"Where the fuck have you been?"

I knew it. As soon as I step through the door, Mickey is waiting for me. And it had to be him, didn't it? He's the most protective out of all of them. "I, er…" Although I'd had the whole journey to concoct some sort of story, I hadn't been able to concentrate with the enigmatic sheikh sitting by my side.

He's not even giving me a moment to get my thoughts together. Storming up so he's right in my face, he starts, "And don't think of saying you were with Mara. I've been blowing up her phone since early this morning. Where have you been, Janna? And I want the truth."

Shit. I didn't expect her to drop me in it.

My thoughts must have been plain on my face, as he continues, "Oh, she tried to cover for you, but there's just so many times you could be 'on the loo', 'brushing your teeth', or 'just popped out for some milk'."

"Mickey, you weren't too hard on her, were you?" He can get overbearing at times. It's alright him berating me as if I was an errant child, but I don't like the thought of him taking his ire out on my friends.

"Of course not! But in the end she told me the fucking truth and told me about that asinine text you sent her. You left her around midnight and went off alone. And ended up with some man. And fuck it, Janna. What the hell has happened to you?" Now he breaks off his tirade, and looks at me properly for the first time. He reaches out his hand, and gently turns my head, "Fuck, I knew something had to be wrong. How did you get that? What did that bastard do to you?" He touches the bump and cut on my forehead, and I wince and move away.

"Jesus! *This* is exactly why we watch out for you, girl. Now tell me *what the fuck happened to you!*" As he raises his voice, another man appears from behind him.

"What's happened? Fuck, Janna! You fall or did you get hit?" Ben's noticed my wound a lot quicker than Mickey. "Joe, get out here, man. Janna's been hurt."

Oh, shit, now there's three of them. Might as well get this over with. "Who else is here? Is it everyone?" I sound waspish. I can't help it.

Ben's voice confirms he's present when he yells out, "Liam, Rory! The wanderer has returned."

"Hey, girlfriend! They're all here! And now you're in trouble!" A female voice this time, Sunny, Mickey's sister and Rory's long-term girlfriend laughs, but throws a look of sympathy my way.

Mickey's arms are folded over his chest. At his sister's words he shakes his head, and his taut features don't relax one bit. "Yeah, she's in trouble. Whatever she's done, she's worried us sick. You better have a good story, Janna. We were about to report you missing to the police."

My head, which had been feeling much better, now starts to ache again, and that's probably what makes me snap, "I'm twenty-two years old, I'm a grown woman. For fuck's sake, I don't have to report my every action to you!" My eyes flick round the five men glaring at me, "If I want to stay out all night, that's my prerogative. And anyway, I told Mara I was with someone and I was safe."

"She told us that, yes. But wasn't particularly forthcoming about who you were with." Mickey's not giving up.

I throw up my hands, "Just leave me alone." I try to brush past them to go up to my room, but I've got five angry men to get past, and they're not moving out of my way.

Ben's hand comes out and takes hold of my arm, "Not so fast, darling. Not until you explain, this."

This being the wound on my head.

I inhale and exhale loudly. God these over-protective males frustrate me at times. Knowing they won't stop badgering me until they get the truth, I might as well get it over with now. I'd hoped to avoid a confrontation, but any chance of that disappeared when Mara was unable to provide a good back story, though she had covered up for me as best she could from what Mickey had said.

Oh well, at least they're all here, I won't need to explain more than once. Letting out another deep sigh, I give in, waving toward the sitting room, "Okay, I'll tell you what happened." They'll only concoct an even worse tale if I don't tell them at least some of the truth. I lead the way in, and take my normal seat at the end of the three-seater couch. *Christ, they're going to flay me alive.*

Mickey takes his place beside me, Ben next to him. Rory and Liam take the armchairs, and Sunny plonks herself in her customary fashion on Rory's lap. Joe pulls up the pouffe, the leather footstool almost collapsing under his weight, his long legs folded so his knees are to his chest. When we're all here, we usually gravitate to this seating arrangement.

I take a second to glower at them in turn, in the vain hope that going on the offensive will offset their anger, "What I do is *my* business. If I get into trouble that's down to me."

"So, you have got into trouble?"

Of course, that's the bit he focuses on. "Oh, for God's sake, shut up, Mickey. Else I won't tell you anything at all.

I'm here, I'm alright. That should be enough. Can't you keep your nose out of it, just for once?"

"We promised your mother..." Ben drops in their normal justification, but this time I shrug it off.

"I was six*teen*. Ben, Sixteen. Six bloody years ago. I think I've grown up some since then and should be able to look out for myself."

Pointedly nodding toward my forehead, Rory butts in, "Obviously not."

"And you've never made a mistake? Got yourself into any hassle that wasn't your fault?"

He's unrepentant, "I'm not you."

No, he's not. And for some reason, they think I'm special. I lean back in the comfy seat, resting my head against the cushion. I know six pairs of eyes are upon me as I try to restrain my temper, knowing their concern comes from the right place, even while it's immensely annoying. Six years ago, my parents had had a car accident. My father was killed instantly, my mother lived only long enough to elicit a promise that the group would look after me. And by group, I mean band. A precocious but gifted guitarist, I'd joined Anarchy Rules a year earlier, when I was just fifteen. My parents didn't like the idea at first, but agreed after giving the five other members, all male, a strict vetting and instructions to be hands off themselves, and keep all other males away from their sweet baby girl.

When my parents died, with no relatives around to take on a sixteen-year-old teenager, they kind of adopted me. And had taken my parents' message to heart.

All I'd ever wanted to do was play guitar. As far as I was concerned, I was living the life of Reilly, becoming a full-time musician once I'd left school. I was doing what I loved, touring, trying a hand at recording, and working to make a success of our band. That I was chaperoned on dates at first didn't concern me—most of the boys I'd met seemed a distraction from my music in any event. During the evening I normally found myself composing songs in my head or new riffs, and too preoccupied to listen to conversations going on around me. Some dates they didn't even need to chase off, my habit of zoning out putting them off without trying.

It wasn't hard for me to be a good girl, living by the rules I'd been set. Surprisingly slow to mature, despite the companions I had in my life, and having more than once walked in to see one or other of the guys in action with a one night stand, I'd never felt any stirrings of my own sexuality, or the need to have a personal life. That is, until recently. Now I've started to become restless, feeling an increasing need to break out of the comfortable cocoon surrounding me. Last night was the first time I'd pushed at the boundaries. And look at what could have happened.

Maybe they're right, and I'm not safe to be allowed out alone.

Then, if I don't make my own mistakes, how will I ever learn? Being a member of Anarchy Rules has become my whole life. But what if it's not enough for me anymore?

"Janna," Mickey growls, he's getting impatient.

"Okay, okay." I sit forward again, "I was wrong, alright? Look, I went out with the girls like I told you, but they wanted to go clubbing, and I didn't. I was making my own way home."

"Why didn't you call one of us?" Joe's glance encompasses the other four men's nodding heads.

"Because I'm twenty-two years old!" I snap, "I'm not a child. I should be able to get back here alone." Four identical looks of incredulity are thrown at me, accompanied by growls of refute. Yeah, well, by the state of me, perhaps they've got a point. Taking a deep breath, I proceed to give them a blow by blow account. Rory and Liam, our Irish twins, clench their fists when I speak about the attack.

The former so irate he prods Sunny to move to the floor, while he stands and paces the room. "He threw you against the wall? Stole your stuff? Did you report it to the police?"

Shaking my head, I swallow, "I didn't get a good look at him, so no, I didn't report it. What good would it have done? He left the bag, but took everything in it. I'm sorry guys, he's got my keys and my address."

"Fuck!" Mickey's cheeks glow red as he sucks in air through his teeth, "Fuck, Janna. We need to get the locks changed. And you're not going to be left on your own until we do."

At this I don't object, I certainly don't want my attacker paying me a visit.

"So you went to hospital? Is that where you've been? A & E?" Sunny's mouth turns down as she continues, sympathetically, "The waiting times are horrendous. You've probably been there all night."

She's offered me a way out, but I'm too honest to take it. However overbearing they are, it's not in me to lie. "No. I refused to go to hospital."

I'd tried to avoid it, but there's nothing else for it but to explain exactly what happened. They listen, and one by one jaws drop and eyes widen.

"You went into Tops and Tailends?" Mickey says disbelievingly, before getting to his feet then looming over me, one hand resting on the arm of the settee as he speaks right into my face, so can I feel his warm breath, "You know what the fuck kind of place that is?"

It's true I'd seen some rather weirdly clad people entering, but hadn't had time to look around, "No, I didn't get a chance to find out. There was a stairway just inside the entrance, and a security chap took me straight up to the manager's, or owner's, office. Bates, I think he was called."

"Thank fuck for small mercies! Hang on. You met *Bates?*" Mickey swipes back his long hair, which has fallen over his shoulders, "Have you any idea of what the fuck you were getting into? What in hell's name made you go in there?"

"Wait. What?" I shake my head, surprised they think I had a choice. "I ran to the nearest place, Mickey. I had a man after me. I wasn't going to stop to check what sort of business it was. I was lucky that somewhere was open. What are you talking about?"

Liam's laughing, the bastard, his loud chuckles starting the others off. I look around, waiting for someone to enlighten me. Sunny's looking as mystified as myself.

It's left for Joe to let me in on the secret, "It's a BDSM club, darling."

BDSM? "I, er…"

"Bondage, Domination, Submission or Sadism, and Masochism." Rory clarifies unnecessarily. "Have you any idea what goes on in there?"

I can feel my face burning. I've read books, of course I have, so I'm pretty sure I could guess, and don't need him to draw a picture. "Well, I didn't go inside, and I didn't even stay very long. Just long enough to be patched up." I don't know why I feel the urge to touch the steri-strips, but I suppose it's to emphasise what happened. "Wait." It's just dawned on me. "How do you guys know of that club?"

"We're not the ones who have to explain," Mickey growls, "It's you that needs to tell us what the fuck went on when you got inside."

I glare at the tone of his voice, but don't remind them again I'm an adult.

Reaching forward to the coffee table, Joe picks up the makings for a joint, then sitting back, starts to roll it. "So, what happened then? If you didn't stay there long, why the bloody hell have you only just come back?"

And now I have to explain exactly who took me home. And of course, cause a predictable eruption about me going off with a strange man.

"For fuck's sake, girl. Of all the stupid things you could have done, that comes right at the very top." Mickey had retaken his seat, now his clenched fists are bouncing off his thighs, "You went home with someone you'd only just met and who you knew absolutely fuck all about? Why the hell didn't you ask for some money, get a cab, and come home?"

I just stare at him, and then look around at the look of censure on everyone's faces. Put like that, it does seem like I acted pretty crazily. But this scene is exactly what I'd wanted to avoid. "I told Mara. I sent her a message."

"You told that bitch? She was probably drunk and in bed with a man she'd picked up," Ben scoffs. Hmm, seems I'm not the only one aware of her reputation. "She knew who you were with? Why didn't she tell Mickey when he asked? We've been going out of our minds." I feel a twinge of guilt that I'd worried them so much by telling Mara it was a secret. Ben leaves his seat, and comes to crouch in front of me, covering my hands with his, "What happened, Janna? Did this sheikh touch you? Did he… Were you forced…" His fingers stroke my hands, and the fallen look on his face makes me want to reassure him.

"He was a perfect gentleman." I put his worries to rest quickly, "He didn't touch me at all. Except when he woke me up to check I didn't have concussion." I didn't think it would be helpful to mention he'd spooned behind me most of the night, or, that if he'd seemed at all willing, that I might have allowed things to go further. Which would be farther than I'd ever been with any man before. It's a strange confession for someone my age. Not only has there not been anyone who's come up to my over protective guardians' very high standards, it's only recently that I've started being interested in what it is that makes the women the guys bring home scream with such delight. Oh yeah, I hear it all from my room.

"And he was a real-life sheikh? What was he like? What's his name?"

Trust Sunny to grab hold of that part. I grin, "Yeah, he is. Sheikh Jasim, he's called. He's obviously very rich. But, normal with it, if you know what I mean? I wouldn't have guessed he's got a title until the other man used it." I remember him offering to make me a cup of tea earlier with no airs and graces.

"Was he good looking?" Her eyes are gleaming.

Christ, yes! I shrug, dismissively, "All right if you go for that type, I suppose."

Mickey's looking at me carefully, I'm not sure I'm fooling him.

Rory's tapping his fingers against his nose, "Jasim. Sheikh Jasim." His eyes open wide, "Fuck, no. *Sheikh Jasim.* Jasim fucking Kassis. Tell me you that wasn't who you went home with?"

My own eyes crease, what is he talking about? "He didn't tell me his surname, so I don't know."

Mickey looks across at Rory, tilts his head to the side, "There can't be many Sheikh Jasims that would be having a meeting with fucking Bates now, can there?"

"And that's what's worrying me." Rory nods back at him, before his eyes settle on me, "Please say you're not going to see him again." He sounds worried, but I put him at ease.

"I'm not going to see him again," I parrot. But have to ask, "Why?"

Joe lights the joint, sweet smelling smoke wafts my way, making my nose twitch, but I don't feel it's the time to remind him I don't like him smoking inside. He inhales, then lets out more of the disgusting vapour. "Because, sweetheart, he owns the most exclusive fucking BDSM club in the UK."

My jaw drops. Jasim? Not only is he into a lifestyle I can't even begin to imagine, but he *owns* a club? No wonder he wasn't interested in me. God. Overcome with embarrassment, I wish the ground would open and swallow me as I remember just how innocent and naïve I must have seemed to him. Dropping my head into my hands, I try to hide my blushing face. And not the least of my thoughts, is just how the other group members are quite so au fait with the type of establishment we've been discussing. Deciding it's probably best I don't know, I stay quiet on the subject. Peering through my fingers, I see Sunny looking at me. Her brow is creased, and as she opens her mouth I wonder what she's going to contribute.

When she speaks, she surprises me. "Hang on, guys, this could be just the opportunity you're looking for." It's the last thing I expected her to say.

Rory reaches forward and tugs her back onto his lap, "What you talking about, hun? You thinking of getting entrance to his club?" His eyes light up as if he's considering the idea.

She punches his arm, "No, I'm not. You know I'm not into that." She stares at him until he gives a rueful nod. "Let me go a mo, and I'll show you." She slides off again, falling to her knees and crawling over to the coffee table, and fumbles about underneath on the low shelf where we toss old mags and newspapers. "It's here, somewhere," she mumbles to herself. "Ah, yes. I knew I didn't throw it out." She backs out with a bridal magazine in her hands.

"What you got, woman?" Rory points to his lap, and she returns to him. His eyes narrow as he sees the name of the mag she's holding, and his eyes flit to his twin's. Uh oh, trouble in paradise? Is Sunny getting ahead of herself?

Completely oblivious to her boyfriend's reaction, Sunny flicks it open to the centre spread, "Look, it's the venue you were looking for."

Rory stares at the open page, his mind obviously working, if the myriad of expressions crossing his face are anything to go by. He taps his fingers to his lips, then indicates the page, which the rest of us have yet to see. "Sunny might have something here, you know?"

"What you talking about, bro?" Liam gets up and goes to sit next to his twin. Not for the first time, when they're next to each other, I notice for anyone else it would be hard to see any difference between them. It's only the years of experience that enables me to easily tell them apart. He takes the magazine out of his brother's hand.

Sunny nods at the page, and then explains to the rest of us, "You know what you've been discussing? Finding a backdrop for the video for your next album. You know, what we've been spending all those hours tossing ideas around? You wanted somewhere unique. Somewhere different."

"You can't get anywhere much different than a real-life harem in an Arabian palace, can you?" Liam's eyes spark with interest.

Passing his joint to Ben, Joe sits up straight, "Chuck that over here, Li." After he's retrieved the magazine that landed on his head, he studies the page and his eyes light up with interest. "You know, you could be onto something here."

"Give us that." Ben pulls it away, and Mickey looks over his shoulder. "I see what you mean, it's just the sort of thing we've been talking about. But going to, where is it…" he pauses to read the text, "Amahad, wherever the hell that is… First there's the cost to consider, then we've got to persuade the top man to let us film in his fucking palace."

I'm thankful that Sunny's at least removed the heat from me, but for the life of me I can't see the connection between the man I met last night, and the article in the magazine. Leaning over Joe's shoulder, I read the headline, *Exciting New Hen Party Venue*. I continue reading how the ancient harem in an Arabian palace has been converted to cater to such events.

Either Mickey's sister's gone mad, or she's planning her future.

But then she enlightens us, "See what it says here?" Sunny's now perching herself on her brother's knees and pointing half way down a page, "*Jasim* Kassis is the middle brother in the Kassis family. And if he's got up close and personal with Janna, he might just be able to get us permission."

I stop being a spectator at that, "There was absolutely no up close and bloody personal involved. And I hardly know the man enough to ask him such a huge favour. I don't even know how to contact him again."

Rory's eyes are gleaming as he stares across me, "You wouldn't be asking for much, Janna. Just for him to use his connections to get us access for a couple of days, maybe a week or so. We've got the songs down pat, we wouldn't need long. Come on, babe, use your feminine wiles for once."

"Sexist or what? And I thought you wanted me to hide my wiles." I glare at him. Talk about a double standard.

"Not asking you to get down and do the dirty with him. Just get us permission to film in the harem."

"Hang on a minute, Rory. I'm not sure the budget will stretch to that." Mickey's hand's toying with his long hair, loose at the moment, and reaching way past his shoulders and down to his waist. "We've got a film crew to get over to Amahad, as well as us and all the equipment. I thought we'd be filming somewhere in this country."

"Tight bugger," Joe butts in. "We've got money allocated for this. Remember, we planned for it to be a professional effort, make a big splash and help us get known? Come on, man. Live a little."

"We deserve some success after all these years. Our previous YouTube vids have brought in some new followers, but they were cheaply made amateur crap. Speculate to accumulate, man." As Liam speaks, Rory slaps him on the back.

And then all of them turn and look at me. My heart rate increases. I grasp they're giving me the excuse I need to make contact with him again. A shiver runs through me at just the thought. And then the practicalities hit me, and I remind them, "We didn't exactly exchange contact details. I don't have his phone number, or know how to get in touch. I went to his flat, but there's no way I could find it again." He'd passed me his business card, but I'd left it in Bate's office. I remember putting it down after I'd called Mara.

Joe snatches back the joint and takes a long drag, he stares at the glowing tip for a moment, "Babe, it says here he works at the Amahadian Embassy, and heads up AmaOil. And Bates must have the information about how to get in contact with him at his club. There must be a hundred different ways to reach him. It will be no problem to find out. And," he points the joint toward me, "You've got the perfect excuse. You want to thank him for helping you."

CHAPTER 5
Jasim

Entering Club Tiacapan I feel, like always, as if I've thrown off the shackles of the daily grind and that, just for a little while, I can leave the real world to go fuck itself. My sense of pride in what I, and my partners, have achieved swells through me as I make my way across the main room, hearing sounds of pleasure and pain as the members enjoy their proclivities in a safe and secure environment. Anyone with the money can play here. We have senior politicians and judges, CEOs of major companies of both sexes and with whatever leanings. Who cares if a crown court judge likes to be submissive in his or her free time? To let go of all that pent-up stress if just for a while? No one gives a damn. Not here.

And it's not only the rich and famous who come to play. There are little known, but well used, membership options for those who deserve it, and for those who pay it back to the club in other ways. A construction engineer involved with our recent extension, or Diamond, a girl with such deeply ingrained submissive tendencies that it would be nigh on criminal to deny her a safe place to play.

Then there's a number of operatives from Grade A. As two of my co-owners are also partners in the security firm, any of their staff can join for a greatly reduced membership fee. It leads to a healthy balance of Dominants and submissives, and others with varying kinks.

Heading to the bar I find, as it seems nearly always, Master Ralph. He makes his money on the stock exchange, by day staring at screens and calculating odds and having millions pass through his hands. By night he comes here to play, and to tend bar, finding enjoyment in simple interaction with like-minded friends.

"Master J! Looking like a good night."

Turning my back to him, I lean against the bar and survey my kingdom set out before me before saying over my shoulder, "It is that, Master Ralph."

"All dungeon monitors are on duty." In his position at the back of the room, Ralph has a clear view of what's going on. "And your brother's here! Was good to catch up with him, and to meet his lovely wife. He's taken a leaf out of Master K's book I see."

Moving my attention to the suspension rig which takes up most of one wall, I see Nijad binding Cara, preparing to hoist her into the air. In comparison to most, and to my relief, she's very modestly dressed, with all the important parts covered. As I watch, I see my brother expertly attaching carabiners to the ropes he's bound her with, getting ready to raise her up. Even from here I can sense his wife's complete surrender and utmost trust in her Dom as illustrated by her winsome smile, her open mouth, and her closed eyes. Nijad's standing tall, his back ramrod straight, pride in his sub on plain view. Feeling pleasure on their behalf, that my investment, my club, has given them that, the opportunity to play and experiment with equipment not readily available to them elsewhere. And now Cara's high into the air, and turning slowly as she hovers above the ground. She'll be deep in subspace by now, everyday concerns and worries left far behind. And Nijad's full focus will be solely on her.

"They've got a private room booked."

"I know, Ralph. And I think they'll be needing that soon," I chuckle, as I turn back to the barman. "Give me an orange juice, will you?"

"Playing tonight?"

"I might very well." My cock's been half hard since I dropped Janna off, and I need something to clear my head and get her out of my mind. My eyes scan the room, taking in the familiar equipment and then alighting on the available subs, seated off to one side. Just when I'm thinking of who I might approach, a meaty hand slaps me on the back, almost splashing the drink I've just picked up out of my hand.

"Jon, you bugger! Might have guessed it was you." We exchange man hugs, and then I pull his wife in for a hug. "Mia! I haven't seen you in a while."

"Thought I'd wait until I stopped breastfeeding my daughter. Leaking boobs wouldn't be a good sight in the club."

I can't stop the grin coming to my face, "This *is* a kink club, sweetheart. Ouch! Jon, man, can't you control your wife? Mia, you know what happens when you're violent."

Mia's eyes have opened wide, "I barely touched you."

Jon's chuckling, "Doesn't matter, Mia, love. See that spanking bench over there? I reckon that's got your name on it."

As he points to it, I'm amused to see his wife's eyes lighting up. Yeah, they'll be having fun and making up for lost time tonight. As Jon lifts his chin, signalling his intention to bag the free bench before anyone else does, I touch him on his arm, "Jon, it looks like I might be going back to Amahad soon."

His eyebrows rise, "Another quick in and out?"

"Not this time. Longer. Perhaps a month, maybe two."

"Didn't expect that." He knows my aversion to going back home. Tapping his fingers on his chin, he realises why I've told him. "You want close protection?"

"Might need it. I'll be travelling to the oil fields." I'll have Amahadian guards when I go into the desert, but will feel more comfortable with the anti-abduction skills that the experts on Jon's team can provide. Particularly when at the back of my mind I have the niggling worry my elder brother might employ methods the last emir might have used to force to get me to stay in the country. He's got many options. He could rescind my diplomatic status, revoke my passport... I suppress a shudder at the thought of what, to me, would be worse than death. Yeah, an independent bodyguard might be needed to protect me from my own family. I trust someone from Grade A to have the resources to get me out of the country whatever happens.

I watch as he contemplates what I've told him, then slowly he nods, "I'll speak to Ben. Let us know your schedule and I'll sort something out."

"Thanks, mate." And with that, I let him go, my mouth quirking as he leads a protesting Mia over to the spanking bench. Her complaints on her part all a ruse, her brattish behaviour to wind up her Dom.

"Master J?" A seasoned submissive comes running up to me. I watch her boobs as they almost bounce out of her corset. Hmm, her approach is a bit hurried, but maybe I could play with her tonight? And punish her for approaching a Dom uninvited.

I feel myself starting to grin as I consider an appropriate chastisement, and take a second to compute what she says.

"There's a telephone call for you."

Damn, I'd misread why she'd addressed me, "Thank you, Angel." Leaving the main room, I go to my office out back. No one, not even me, takes a mobile phone into the club. It's not unheard of for me to get calls here, but also not common. Usually, my staff would deal with anything that comes through. It must be important. Or strictly personal.

Sitting down in my comfortable leather chair, intrigued, I pick up the old-fashioned handset that's connected to the landline. "Kassis."

"Er, is this Sheikh Jasim?"

The uncertain and breathy female voice surprises me, and I'm not immediately able to place it. "Speaking."

"Er, it's Janna. Janna Stevens."

And just like that my cock's fully erect. I lean back to give myself more room to ease it, but I doubt she's ringing up to give me phone sex. More's the pity. Unable to see her, to have her relative youth flaunted in my face, or to betray my inappropriate reaction, I allow her voice to excite me.

"How's the head? Everything okay?"

"My head is fine. Thank you for helping me."

"My pleasure." And it certainly was. Thinking back, I'd enjoyed every minute ministering to her, *sleeping beside her*. Too much. Whatever she's calling for, I know I mustn't see her again. There's only so much temptation a Dom can take when faced with such an obvious sub.

"What can I do for you?" I prompt her, when there's silence at her end of the line.

A sound as if she's taking a deep breath, "I'm calling to ask a favour. A very big one, I'm afraid. I don't quite know how to ask you…"

As her voice tails off, I wonder what request she's going to make. Is she going to ask for membership to the club? Racking my brain, I try to remember if I mentioned I was an owner? But if I hadn't, how did she know to contact me here? Bates. She must have got in touch with Bates and he told her who I was. Would I allow her to join? Could I stand it? Seeing her corrupted by somebody else? Someone in the right age bracket? Mentally I run through possible Doms, but come up with none other than myself. And I'm definitely not suitable. For a start, I'm far too old.

"I didn't tell you anything about me." She's speaking again, and I realise I've been distracted.

Ah, so now she's going to tell me she's into kink. I'd never have guessed it, she seemed far too innocent and unworldly. Perhaps it's an excuse to see me again?

"You want a membership to Club Tiacapan," I sigh, wondering how I can dissuade her. Seeing her lithe body tightly laced into a corset would be far too much temptation for me. Just the thought starts my cock throbbing painfully. Though her hair's dark, her skin is fair, a lovely contrast. I start to imagine it pinking up under my hand. Shit, I can't possibly have her playing here and keep my hands off without losing my sanity. I'll have to discourage her.

"What? *No!* That's not my scene at all." Her indignation comes down the line, showing me that, while I've got the reason for her call all wrong, she's denying her nature. I sigh with relief, and swallow down my regret.

"What favour are you asking then?" This call's dragging on, but I find I don't mind that. My hand goes to my crotch and I finger my stiff dick.

"I'm in a band, I don't know if you've heard of us? Anarchy Rules?"

"You sing?" I hadn't thought about it, but now she's said it, I can see her doing that. Something sweet and melodious. Strange band name for that type of music though.

She gives a gravelly laugh, I squeeze my cock harder, "You really wouldn't want to hear my singing voice."

No, I'd prefer to hear her screaming my name, if I'm totally honest. I murmur something insignificant, it encourages her to go on.

"I'm a guitarist. We play rock."

I wonder whether it's a girl band. Fuck, others like her on stage? Making a mental note to find out where they're playing, and balancing the phone between my ear and my shoulder, I jot the group's name down on a writing pad. And then I think of another possible reason for her call.

"Sorry, Janna, we don't have live bands playing here." We couldn't afford to. Taped music doesn't have eyes and ears that could see or hear all the wrong things and threaten our members' anonymity.

"No, I'm not asking for that. Jasim, the guys I play with have asked me to contact you. It's a bloody cheek as I barely… I don't know you at all, really."

Guys. There goes my fantasy of an all-girl band. Then I have to suppress a growl at her use of the word play, and then remind herself she's not using it the same way I do.

"Go on, Janna," I encourage her. "Just spit it out."

"We're planning to make a video, to coincide with the release of our next album."

"You can't film in the club." I'm adamant about that. Not even when it's closed.

"No, no. Look, I'm making a hash of this, but I'm embarrassed to ask." Her frustration and self-consciousness make me want to put her at her ease.

"Janna, you've slept in my bed." And why did I have to remind myself of that? "There's nothing to be embarrassed about. Just come straight out and say whatever it is you want to ask me. I'll either say yes or no." *And no will probably be the answer.* Placing the heel of my hand hard to the base of my cock, I try to will it to go down.

"Your brother's harem." Her voice has dropped to a whisper.

Her mention of that surprises me. My first thought is that it's not Kadar's special place any longer, he's rescinded his ancient rights to the place. In fact, his wife, Zoe and Cara have renovated it and are offering the place as a destination for hen parties, of all things. It's only just getting off the ground, but they've taken a few bookings so far, and from what I heard, it's already showing signs of being a success. Then my brain catches up. Shit.

"You want to have your hen party there?" *Is she going to get married? Was there a man waiting in the wings, even while she was lying beside me?* The memory of her giving no indication of that serves to deflate my cock. I don't like cheaters.

"No, no. Definitely not." Her hasty denial elicits a sigh of relief, but leaves me annoyed that the thought bothered me at all. "The thing is, Jasim, the guys have seen pictures of the harem, and think it would make the perfect backdrop to the video we want to make for our next album. And other locations nearby, we could go out into the desert or film at a souk." Her voice sounds excited, and I picture her envisioning the exotic locations.

Choking back my immediate dismissal, and the thought of the horror I'd see on my older brother's face were I to suggest it, I take a minute to think before replying. Unexpectedly, Kadar had agreed to the outlandish idea of hen parties, and one of his main aims is to attract tourists to Amahad. In view of what I believed was a rather odd change of use for the harem, I can't summarily discount that he might welcome the publicity. I slip on my businessman's hat.

"What kind of following do you have? I'm afraid I haven't heard of…" I consult the writing pad, "Anarchy Rules." Kadar wouldn't go for it if they were just starting out. However much I might want to help the girl I'd treated as a medic.

"Okay. That's fair. I'll tell you something about us. We've been around a few years. I joined them seven years ago."

"Shit, you must have been young!"

"Fifteen." She laughs down the line. "A child prodigy they'd have you believe, but I think a precocious brat is probably nearer the truth." And the thought of her being a brat starts my cock throbbing again.

Ignoring my body's unwanted reaction, I urge, "Go on."

"Well, we started off like everyone else, playing in local pubs. But we've become somewhat known. Now we've moved onto clubs and bigger venues. We've got quite a large following, and make just enough to support us. There's six in the band in all, four of us are original members, two, the twins Rory and Liam, joined three years ago. Rory replaced one of our original members. Sorry, I'm rambling. You don't need to know that." She pauses, presumably to get her thoughts together. "We've done music vids before, the last one got over a hundred thousand hits on YouTube. But it was amateurish, and we want to do this one right. We've got a film crew in mind, and have been searching to find the right location."

A hundred thousand visits for one video not well produced. It's easy to understand how, done right, they could improve on that. The idea intrigues me, and I begin thinking how I could sell it to Kadar. He'll want more information, I open my mouth to start to ask her to send me a few tracks so I can judge for myself, or the link to the video, but different words come out of my mouth.

"Have you got any gigs lined up? I'd like to come and watch you play before I make any decision about forwarding your proposal to the emir." Fuck, why did I suggest that? My idea of fun is not being in the midst of a heaving throng of rockers headbanging the night away. I must have been at Uni the last time I did that. Not that I have anything against rock music, I'm just too old to go to a live gig. Which reminds me, too old for the likes of her. And it will probably be far more gentle than the gigs I used to go to, and would bore me to death.

"Oh, Jasim. That would be wonderful. We're actually playing tomorrow, if that's not too soon?" And the enthusiasm in her voice tells me I can't disappoint her.

I ask her for details of when and where, and write them down. Perhaps I could send one of my younger friends instead? Preferably a happily married one. *And why should their marital status concern me?*

But I would like to see her again. To watch her in her element, doing what she obviously loves. A vision comes to me of her in a beautiful white virginal dress, strumming along at the back of the band, the other members tolerating her as she adds a bit of eye candy for the men. If I see her like that, among youngsters of her own age, surely that would put some sense in my head and squash this unwanted attraction?

Then I think of the band. *Is she sufficiently protected? Do they take care of her?*

And do the members take care of all her needs?

I suppress my growl at the thought, and temper my voice so I'm able to respond politely. "I'll be there. And I'll look forward to it."

Ending the call, I sit back in my chair, my cock hard as iron. What is it about this girl/woman? And why does she affect me? And why do I, a Dom, seem to be unable to control myself even at just at the sound of her voice?

CHAPTER 6
Janna

My hand is shaking as I press the key cutting me off from Jasim's deep commanding voice, having to squeeze my thighs together to ease an unfamiliar tingling, almost like an itch I'm desperate to scratch to get some relief. My underwear is damp, purely from the short conversation. I might be inexperienced, but I recognise the symptoms. *He's turned me on.* And he's not even in the room.

Nobody's ever had this effect on me. I've read some books, seen the words describing things I'd love to try for myself that have evoked similar reactions, but no actual man has interested me enough to excite my body this way. Is it that I know he's a Dominant? He must be, he owns a bloody sex club for a start. My eyes fall on my Kindle, loaded on there and hidden from prying eyes is my secret obsession, hundreds of romance books featuring Doms and their subs.

How would I have felt if I'd known that when I'd met him? Would I have called for a cab and come home? Or would I have found the nerve to offer myself to him? I'd told one more lie when I said I wasn't interested in his club. In truth, I'm intrigued.

I'd insisted on privacy for this call, and had escaped to my room, luckily, as my face feels hot and flushed. Now I'm standing, my phone held to my lips, realising how crazy I am. *Merely his voice has made me wet.* And how darn embarrassing is that? This smouldering candle I hold for him is an impossible dream, but oh, so difficult to extinguish. I try to think sensibly. He's a frigging sheikh after all, a prince in his own land. And so sexually experienced as to be totally out of my league. *I'd thought I'd turned him on.* I must have been wrong. When I felt his hard dick press into me, he must have been thinking about someone else. His sub, perhaps. My heart skips a beat when I think of him with another woman, dominating her, commanding her…

I'd thought I'd never see him again. And now I'm going to. Tomorrow night. Shit.

A knock on my door. "Yeah, what is it?"

"Everything okay, babes?"

"Hi, Sunny. Yeah. It's fine. Come in." She's still my best friend, even though we're going to have to have a difficult discussion soon. The way she's been acting recently has become increasingly worrying. But now's not the right time.

I give her a smile as she comes in and jumps on my bed, the elderly springs creaking. She looks down in disgust, "Don't know why you don't replace this, Jan. It can't be comfortable to sleep on."

"I like it just fine," I say, absently, "It's moulded to my body shape."

"Thank fuck you don't have a man."

Well, yes, there is that.

"Did you get through?" She pulls herself up until she's kneeling, her eyes bright and alive. "What did he say?"

"Janna? You speak to the sheikh?" It's Mickey's voice yelling up the stairs.

Sunny rolls her eyes at her brother's impatience, making my lips curl as she doesn't seem to recognise she's just as bad. "You coming down?"

"Yeah," I smile at her, "I'll tell everyone together."

I follow her downstairs where the others have congregated, waiting to hear whether I've had any success with the call. I flop myself down on my usual seat, reaching forward to nab a piece of pizza that they must have had delivered. I take a bite.

"Well?" Rory looks impatient. "Did he say no?"

Chewing and swallowing, I must admit the look on my face isn't encouraging. I'm still trying to work through why Jasim affects me in such hitherto unknown ways. Fidgeting to get myself comfortable, I abandon the pizza slice, lean forward with my clasped hands on my knees, and let them out of their misery. "He didn't say no."

At their combined and varied exclamations of pleasure, I raise my hand, "He didn't say yes, either. He wants to come and hear us play. See whether we're good enough, I expect. He'll be there tomorrow."

Mickey's arm snakes out around me, and he places a kiss on the top of my head, "Babe, you did fucking well there, even to get him to agree to that. And that's a great gig for him to come to. It's a good venue, it'll be packed to the hilt. We'll just have to play at our best."

"Yeah, that crowd's easy to get wound up. Janna, you'll just have to do your thing and impress him." Thanks, Ben, put it all on me, why don't you?

Joe also sits forward, "We get a good mix there. I'll encourage the girls and get them screaming for more." As our front man, most of how we play the crowd is down to him. Especially when there are a lot of women in the audience. He's an arrogant bugger, but girls seem to go for his type. And he's a good-looking son of a bitch too. Part of the reason for us going more visual, none of the band would get kicked out of many beds.

I glance at Mickey beside me, his long straight dark brown hair has a tinge of natural red highlights when seen under the lights, and as our drummer, his muscular body, covered by a sheen of light body sweat, is accentuated by the sleeveless vests that he wears and normally discards at some point during the show. Rory and Liam, bassist and saxophonist, are always a draw while, Sunny sits on the sidelines, knowing she's the one who'll be taking one of them home. *Which reminds me of that necessary conversation.* And Ben, well, Ben's our token blonde, and plays guitar too, usually sticking to rhythm, though he's well able to take over lead. He just leaves that to me, it's what I do best.

"Do we need to alter the playlist?"

"How old's this sheikh?" It's Ben who's answered Li's question with one of his own.

They all look at me. "Early thirties, I think."

Mickey tuts, "We play like normal. Our new stuff interspersed with covers of oldies. He doesn't like it? That's up to him. What's more important is that he sees the reaction of the fans. And if we alter want we do, we'll change the dynamics of that."

"I agree." I don't want to shake it up, some of my best solos are already part of the set.

"Right. Any re-stringing done tonight, guys." I roll my eyes at Mickey's unwanted suggestion. My guitars couldn't be better maintained, but he started the band, so he likes to boss us around.

"Got enough spare sticks, man?" Rory teases him, not letting him get away with it. Mickey tends to give it his all, and it's not uncommon for a drumstick to go flying off into the crowd.

"Fuck off!"

"Hey, fellas," Sunny stands and stretches, "You treat this like it's something out of the ordinary and you'll cock it up. You guys are all great, you deserve your success. Play as you normally do and you'll have all the panties you need thrown at you."

I make a face.

"Or boxers." She points toward me, not wanting to leave me out. I cringe, yup, that's happened. And proposals of marriage. Or other more unsavoury offers.

On that note, and as it's late, I decide to go to bed. Sunny follows me out. She hovers just in the doorway to my room.

"Janna, we've been friends a long time. I've done something to upset you. I can tell."

I really don't want to get into this now, but when will be the right time? "It's none of my business what you get up to." I try to sound dismissive.

She invites herself in, closing the door behind her, and sits down. "It's Rory and Liam, isn't it?"

I shrug.

"I don't with both of them together if you're worried about that."

Rolling my eyes, I tell her, "I wouldn't care if you did. But something's going on, Sunny. And don't try to deny it." I pause, trying to find the right words, "They might be difficult for most people to tell apart," I know they style their hair alike on purpose, "But I can see the difference. And you must certainly be able to too."

She pouts and repeats, "I've not been with them together at once."

It's a partial admission, "The other night you were with Liam. I saw you take him into your room."

Now she looks down at her hands, "I'd hoped you'd missed that," she mumbles. "Look, Liam found a girl, Rory fancied her. Liam brought me home."

"And took you to bed. Fuck, Sunny! Have they got identical cocks so you can't tell the difference?" I tuck my hair behind my ears to give my hands something to do. When she simply smirks at my question, I guess she's not going to answer it.

"Are you and Rory finished?" I worry about the effect on the band and the complicated relationships within it. She's the drummer's sister, and if Mickey was to find out what's going on I don't give much for Rory and Liam's chances. "Look, if you're ending it with Rory, either commit to Liam, or leave them both. You can't play them against each other."

"They don't mind."

"Sunny!" It comes out more sharply than I intended. "We're just about to launch a new album, we could make the big time. Apart from the effect it must be having on you… You're my best friend, my sister. We've lived together for seven years. I worry about you, babes. It just doesn't feel right."

She looks thoughtful, "Honestly? You're saying nothing I haven't already thought of. The last thing I want to do is to be responsible for breaking up the band."

"I thought you loved Rory."

"I do." She protests.

Closing my eyes, I shake my head, how can you love someone and go off with his brother? Whatever she thinks, it's never going to work.

"It's not cheating, they know."

"They're taking advantage. What, so Liam is your consolation prize when Rory wants to get his dick wet elsewhere?"

"That's harsh."

It's the truth.

I've said my piece. I'm not going to say anymore. As I turn away, I hear the door opening and closing. Rolling my head back on my shoulders I let out a sigh. Bloody relationships. Perhaps I'm lucky I don't have to worry about them. I'd never want a man who couldn't commit to me, and only me. Christ, what a mess. And if anyone else spots what's going on, I only hope I'm not around for the fallout.

I drop onto my bed, thoughts aplenty going around my head, not the least what will I do if Anarchy Rules falls apart? For the first time in my adult life, I start to think about other options might be open to me. To be honest, I'm lucky the band's stayed together this long. What would it be like to do something different? While previously that thought would have horrified me, now I find it a challenge. What else could I do?

Determined to put my altercation with Sunny out of my mind, knowing it's up to her to decide where her relationships are going, I make no further comment when I see her the following morning. The day passes like any other except for that flicker of excitement inside me when I think about seeing the handsome sheikh again. Helping to push my friend's issues to the back of my mind are thoughts of Jasim which intrude as I go through the routine of boring household tasks and doing my washing—pointedly leaving out the few shirts and pair of jeans Mickey's tried to sneak in to my wash. Mickey, Sunny, and I actually live here, it just seems that the others do too, often crashing when we've all come back from a gig. But while I'm always happy to put Sunny's clothes in with mine, as she does the same for me, I made a point early on that I might have boobs and no cock, but that doesn't mean I'm uniquely qualified to do the laundry. Or vacuum. Or dust. To give him his due, Sunny and I have got Mickey fairly well trained in that respect.

For seven years this has been my life. Getting ready for a gig comes naturally to me. When it's time I shower, straighten my hair, and put on what has evolved into my standard uniform, knowing my fans will expect it. As I pull on my top, I feel myself starting to slip into my stage persona, a process that will be complete as soon as I pick up my guitar. For now, the adrenalin starts buzzing, my nerves getting frayed. But all that will be focused into energy once I start to play.

We head off to the club, arriving an hour before the gig starts. Now earning more money we've roadies to set up for us, but I like to check where they've positioned my guitars. Mickey sorts out his drums making tiny adjustments, and Joe and Ben check out the mics. Then it's time for a sound check. Travis checks it out from the back, and Tim, working the mixer, reacts to his thumbs up and thumbs down and other hand signals that they've practiced over the years.

Then, all set, we disappear out the back and partake in our favourite tipple, ready to make our entrance when we're announced. It's all so normal to me, just like any job. I'd gone through the motions on autopilot, only remembering at the last moment that there's going to be an extra person in the audience tonight. *Will I notice him?* Or will he be just one of the crowd. *He's tall, he might stand out.* Or he might be hidden by the lights. I shiver with cold, or is it anticipation?

With butterflies tingling, I respond to our call, walking out onto the stage and picking up my Strat.

And like that, I'm in character. The house lights dim, then spotlights come up on the stage, finding first Mickey who gives a four beat. Then a light comes on me and I let out a blistering riff, my solo entrance to one of our own songs. More lights come on, Rory lets that bass fly, Liam warms up with the sax, Ben strums out the rhythm, then we all stop.

Joe takes centre stage, and howls out the start of the song.

The crowd goes wild, jumping and roaring. And singing along. I nod toward Ben, it's a good audience tonight, many are regulars already familiar with our playlist.

Our first set's a blast, the audience enjoys it. As promised, Joe plays to the women, flirting away. I can see he has his eye on one girl at the front and won't find it surprising if he disappears later on tonight. Whether he'll take her home or just see to her around the back of the club is anyone's guess, but I've learned not to go looking for him if he goes out of sight. Yuck, I've been treated to far too many intimate views of my fellow group members over the years. Nope, don't want to go there again if I can avoid it.

We take a fifteen-minute break, time to pop to the loo and to down another drink.

"Have you seen him, yet?"

"Sorry, Mickey, no. Can't see much from up there. He's not at the front."

Liam taps my arm, "He definitely said he'd come?"

I raise my shoulders. "Sounded that way to me. But you never know, something else might have come up." I frown, "He's a busy man." *Is he at his club? Unable to pull himself away from a sub?*

"Hey slackers, time up!" Ben's waving us over and we're back on stage.

We play through some oldies and then a favourite of mine, our cover of AC/DC's Whole Lotta Rosie, I love the guitar solo that leaves me all but exhausted. Another couple of our own songs, and then Guns 'n' Roses' Sweet Child of Mine. Now Ben steps forward and we play off each other. I'm having such a great time I've totally forgotten we're supposed to have an addition to our audience tonight. I'm playing to the crowd, hyped by their energy as they get wound up by ours. It's a symbiotic relationship between band and audience, each feeding off the other.

Mickey's thrown off his T-shirt; he might be like a brother to me, but even I can appreciate his muscles working as he hammers at those drums, sweat glistening in the lights as his pectorals flex. He throws back his head and beats down hard.

Liam's making that bass sing, Rory's keeping up with the sax, then leads into his solo, giving it everything he's got. Ben's gritting his teeth in concentration, Joe's clapping in time before taking up the vocals once more.

I come alive on the stage, I own it, it's mine.

It's the end of our set, but not the end of the night. The music comes to a halt, Joe's vocal's fade away. The crowd roars for more, stamping their feet and shouting. We give them a moment, then Mickey hits those drums, counting me in again and for the encore we ramp it up another notch.

CHAPTER 7
Jasim

I must have changed my mind a dozen times about whether or not to come tonight. It would have been easy enough to refuse to present Anarchy Rules' case to my brother. I don't owe this girl anything. Or I could simply ask for their tapes. Or look them up on YouTube.

But as I finish with my business for the day, I decide to go along, if only to confirm what I hope I've convinced myself of. That this girl means nothing to me, and never would. It's just my memory playing tricks with me, that night and her softness up against my hard cock.

She's too young, and as far removed from my lifestyle as it's possible to get. And she can't have anything to offer me I wouldn't be able to find anywhere else. Seeing her again, seeing her innocently playing her girly music, will probably kill my desire stone dead. I'll go, get her out of my system, and hopefully, if the gig doesn't end late, come back to the club and find a sub to play with. Someone able to cope with my tastes. Yes, I'll go, get her out of my head. If the band's good enough, there could be mutual benefit if

Kadar agrees to hire out the harem. If not, well, I'll have to let them down gently. And having seen them play, I'll have fulfilled my commitment.

I've worked late, not having seen any point in getting to the gig as it starts. I only need to hear a few songs to make an assessment. As such, I have difficulty finding somewhere to park, ending up a couple of streets away. The car park and roads around the club are jam packed. Perhaps they are good enough to attract quite a crowd, unless there's something else on at another pub.

I can hear the music from outside, loud heavy rock thumping. It stops me in my tracks, it's not what I expected at all. I push through the doors, and pay my entrance fee, being given the once over by an enthusiastic bouncer wearing a shirt with Anarchy Rules blazoned across the chest. I must pass sufficient muster, as he waves me on through. I go past the cloakrooms, and then into the club.

The band's up on the stage. Here at the back I can hear, but not see them clearly. The crowd's leaping and jumping, the atmosphere electric. Even after only a couple of minutes I can hear how talented all the musicians are. But I want to get closer, I need a visual.

I start pushing my way through, my height and build helping ease my path. The crowd seems good-natured, enjoying their evening out, and I don't have much trouble getting to the stage. And as soon as I can see, I stop dead in my tracks, my eyes widening at the sight in front of me. As a searing guitar solo rips through the air, the guitarist steps forward, taking centre stage. A spotlight falls on her as she gyrates and grinds in time with the music she's playing. My mouth falls open as I gaze on in disbelief, hardly recognising the shy, innocent girl who had shared my bed that night.

Janna's wearing a red satin corset, decorated with black lace, her small breasts accentuated by the garment. Her legs are encased in skin tight black leather jeans, with high heeled boots which come up to her thighs. Her eyes close as she picks for the high notes, her instrument held over her crotch and her plectrum strumming in an almost erotic display. The way she's dressed, the command in her posture. She has the audience under her dominion, and in the palm of her hand. She controls the crowd like a dominatrix, using her guitar in place of a whip.

"Fuck, she's hot!"

Despite the volume of the music, I pick out appreciative comments out from the men standing around me, and I suddenly get the urge to push them all from the floor. *They've no right to leer. She's mine!* What?

It's hot and stuffy, my brow's getting sweaty, and as I wipe my hand over my forehead I realise my cock's throbbing and hard as rock. I'm no different from those surrounding me, she's affecting me the same as every other man here. There's a magic about her, a presence on the stage that blows me away. She looks ageless and wanton, but also someone money couldn't buy. She's untouchable, unless she wants to be touched.

"I'd worship at her fucking feet."

"Fuck, look at that hot mouth."

The coarse comments continue, making my ears blaze. And then the spotlight pulls out, highlighting the rest of a band. The sax player steps forward and carries the tune on. But my eyes ignore him, focusing only on Janna. Suddenly the room feels airless, I'm finding it hard to breathe.

And then the music ends, the drummer finishing up with a last final beat. The crowd roars for more, but it must be the last encore. As the band members step away from their instruments, waving to the crowd, for the first time I take a look at the rest of them. They're all striking looking men, from the drummer who's casually swinging his arm over Janna's shoulders and making me burn, to the bassist and sax player who look so similar they have to be twins, the rhythm guitarist is smiling and grinning, and the vocalist is preening in front of the women who are crowding the stage.

But Janna looks tired. Oh, no one else seems to notice, but I do. I want that fucker's hand off her, I want her in my arms. I want to protect her from the lewd men trying to get near her. I want…

She's too young for me.

Watching as they leave the stage I make two decisions. The band is good, there's no questioning that. Certainly talented enough that there could be mutual benefits in letting them film in the Palace of Amahad, so I'll contact Kadar on their behalf. And the second is, whatever this strange attraction to this girl/woman I have, it will never be acted on. She's not, and will never, be mine. And that is that.

But fuck me. The sight of her tonight stirs something inside me, and I feel the beginnings of a smile on my face. She's playing a role. It's clear not one of the men around me understand who she really is. No one knows, except for me. *They think she's a Domme.* I know better.

Softly huffing a laugh, I make my way through the throng that's now heading back to the bar as the entertainment is over. It's easier now the way's clearing as I head in the opposite direction, toward where the band members disappeared. Reaching a stage door, I find there's a group waiting, and Janna and her band are chatting to their fans. I stand at the back, my eyes fixed on her face. I see fatigue lines on her forehead, and again wonder why it only seems to be me that sees it. She's dead on her feet, but still acting her part.

Suddenly her eyes look up and meet mine. Then drop to the floor under the intensity of my gaze. Now she's pushing her way through, and coming to my side.

"You came." It's a statement, and there's pleasure in it. Her voice gentle and sweet, so at odds with her clothes.

"You look tired." It's not perhaps the best opening, but someone should care for her.

My words have surprised her, and she brushes it off with a laugh, "It's draining," she explains, and it's clear to see she gives her all to the crowd. And they're giving nothing back, still wanting more of her.

"Janna, can I have your autograph?" A burly, tattooed man tries to push between us, but as his eyes meet my glare, he takes a step back.

"Mickey, this is the sheikh," Janna pulls at the drummer's sleeve. When she gets his attention, he waves above his head, and two men approach, wearing Anarchy Rules shirts. They begin corralling the band's admirers away, and I take it they're roadies or something.

Once a space has cleared, the drummer reaches out his hand, "Mickey Carey," he introduces himself as he tries my grip with his fingers. We come out about equal. "Come on back, we can talk."

He taps his colleagues on their shoulders, and one by one they disappear through a curtain. I'm led down a short corridor, and into a tiny room. Janna puts down her guitar and throws herself wearily on a well-worn couch with a loud sigh.

"Fuck man, that was a good one!" The bass player takes a towel, rubs it over his face, and then drapes it around his neck. "Anything to fucking drink in here?"

One of the men wearing a band shirt says, "I'll get some beers from the bar." Noticing me standing there, he raises a quizzical eyebrow, "Do you want anything?"

"Thank you. A beer would be great."

Janna looks up surprised, "I thought Arabs didn't drink?"

It's a reaction I'm used to, so I toss her a grin, "When in Rome and all that." Neither I nor my brothers are teetotal, except when we need to be in our homeland.

"So, you're Sheikh Jasim?" The vocalist approaches me, "Joe Bradshaw."

Another man looks up. "I'm Liam Hamilton, and this," he breaks off to put his arm around his mirror image's neck, pulling him to him and ruffling his hair, "This is my younger brother, Rory."

Rory thumps him in the chest as he breaks free and growls, "By two fucking minutes," I take it it's an old joke, as he doesn't wait for his brother's reaction and continues to me, "Pleased to meet you, man. And this here's Sunny. She's mine." Sunny presses into his side, and nods at the sheikh.

My attention returns to Janna in time to see her stiffening. *Does she fancy him? Is she jealous?* But somehow, I don't think it's that.

"Ben Price," the last man introduces himself, and is the first to ask, "What did you think of the set?"

I hadn't heard much as I'd arrived so late, but it had been enough, "You're good." It's sufficient answer for now, and the praise elicits smiles all around.

The beers arrive, and for a few minutes we busy ourselves grabbing bottles and opening them. I take a swallow, the chilled lager a welcome relief from the heat of the room I'd just come from, and give them a few moments to wet their throats, realising if it had been hot for me, it must have been doubly so for the band.

Janna drains her bottle, then rests her head back. She's looking at me quizzically.

"You play well, Janna. I must say, I'm very impressed." I nod toward her, then turn my head to address the rest of the band, "You all do. You've got an energy and vitality on stage. You are very visual. I can see how a music video would work."

"In the harem?" Mickey gets straight to the point, and his posture suggests he speaks for the group.

I appreciate his directness, "The decision will have to come from my brother, the emir. But for my part, I'm happy enough to recommend it to him." A chorus of

'That's great' and 'Thanks mate', comes to me, and I shrug it off. "Tell me how I can reach you, and I'll contact him when I can."

As Mickey hands me his business card, I slide it into the pocket of my jeans. It's then I notice Ben, the rhythm guitarist is looking at me, his brows creased. I turn to face him.

"You don't look like a sheikh, man." He's shaking his head.

Giving a chuckle, I know what he means, my jeans and leather jacket were worn to blend in. My normal Armani suit would have stuck out like a sore thumb. And I'm here without security tonight, enjoying being incognito. "Looks can be deceiving." And as the words leave my mouth, I can't prevent myself from throwing a look toward Janna, and raising my brow. She catches my expression, and her cheeks go bright red.

It seems no one has noticed our silent exchange.

"Well, I for one am fucking glad that you came tonight, er, Your Excellency. And owe you thanks for helping Janna the other night." Reminded of my title, Mickey seems at a loss as to how to address me.

"Just call me Jasim," I tell him, while knowing I'd like to hear the word Master out of Janna's mouth. Then I remember my resolve. "And it was my pleasure to help a woman in distress." I turn to the woman in question, "Are you fully recovered now? No lingering headache?"

"I'm fine, thank you Jasim." A lingering pinkness still tinges her cheeks, as though she doesn't want attention drawn to herself.

"Well, we're about to pack up and spilt. Jasim, can I have a word with you? I'll walk you to your car?"

It's Mickey, the drummer who's dismissing me, but that's fine. The sooner Janna gets out of here and gets some rest the happier I'll be. I nod at them all, "I'll be in touch as soon as I can. Kadar's a busy man, so don't be surprised if it takes a few days."

"Just grateful you're going to put our case forward." Ben's the first to shake my hand, the others follow suit. Then as Mickey holds the door open, I precede him out.

"Where are you parked?"

"Couple of streets down. You pull in quite a crowd."

In the light of the carpark I see pride flush his face, "Yeah, this is one of our favourite venues. Been playing here on and off since we started. They're a good lot here."

"You get any trouble when you play?" Is Janna exposing herself to danger?

"Not often. Some get a bit rowdy, but Janna and Joe know how to play it down. We vary the set, take some of the energy out if it's riling them up too much. And if it's a new place, well, we don't go back."

We're just making polite conversation, he hasn't yet got to the point. Suddenly he stops, he draws out a packet of fags and offers one to me, I dismiss it with a shake of my head. Smoking is not one of my vices. Holding a flame to the tip, he lights it, and it glows orange in the late-night air.

"I see the way you look at her." Now we're getting to the gist of it. "She says you didn't touch her."

"She's telling the truth."

He sucks in and blows smoke out, "Look, Jasim. I know who you are."

Casting a glance his way, I wonder in what capacity. "I work on behalf of Amahad."

"I'm not talking about that."

Oh.

"Look, let's be men about this. You own a BDSM club. And I've seen you at others."

Regarding him more closely, I wonder if I'm noticed him before, but I don't recognise him. Mind you, he might look different wielding a whip. "Dom?" I query.

His quick nod tells it all. Again he takes a long drag, I wait to hear him out. "She's not in your league, Jasim. Fuck, yeah, she's submissive, though she doesn't know that."

I have to stop him there, "I have no interest in Janna, Mickey. I assure you. Yes, I saw she was sub material as soon as I met her, but she's too young for me. And too innocent." The dip of his head at the last bit confirms what I'd expected. Wondering how much of a lie I'm telling him, I make my position plain, "I helped her, that's all. I didn't, and have no intention of, touching her. Or of even seeing her again. I wouldn't have been here tonight if you hadn't wanted something from me."

My answer seems to have reassured him, but his eyes come to meet mine, "No offence, mate, but I worry about her. I've looked after her for a long time. She's my responsibility."

Half of me is jealous that he's so close to her, but something tells me there's nothing sexual between them. The other part is pleased she's got someone looking out for her.

"That's me, over there." I point to the Tesla, "I'll be in touch, Mickey. Just as soon as I can."

His eyes are still narrowed as he flicks the butt down a drain, but then he gives a nod. "Just so we understand each other."

I don't use words for a response, just steel my eyes. With a final nod, he turns and walks away.

CHAPTER 8
Janna

When Mickey returns my brow creases and I glare at him suspiciously, knowing from the way his eyes won't meet mine that I'm right to be concerned about why he wanted to speak to Jasim. It was about me. Me. Anything else he'd have said in front the band. It's certainly not the first time he's interfered in my life, and the burning inside tells me I've reached the end of my tether, and I won't be putting up with it any longer.

He, and the rest of them, need to let me stand on my own two feet. And I need to start standing up for myself and demand some independence. Sure, it was great to have these men watching out for me when I was still in my teens. After the loss of my parents I appreciated their protective and guiding hands. There's no denying they've been useful dissuading a few of the more unsavoury element from getting too close. But I've grown up now, I'm a woman, no longer a young girl in need of their stalwart protection. And that means it's past time that they stop controlling me and my life.

Allowing me the freedom to make my own choices and mistakes is not going to be easy for either them or me. For my part, I've become comfortable with them making decisions for me, and on theirs, well, they still feel an obligation to keep me away from the harsher side of life and keep me from getting hurt, protecting me not only from physical, but emotional harm as well.

Despite my anger bubbling inside, I can see Mickey's looking tired as I suspect we all are. When we're playing to a crowd as responsive as this one had been tonight, we give our all on the stage. Thinking rationally, now is perhaps not the right time to start the conversation I want to have with him and the others. Tempers could flare easily, and things let slip that are best left unsaid. Biting back my frustration, I know it would be better to go home and to bed, sleep on it and then approach them tomorrow.

Biting my tongue, I consider the familiar pattern of the ways we all come down after the buzz and excitement of the gig, it always follows the same pattern. One of the guys will take me home, then they'll go on to chill in their own individual ways. Mickey and Joe might find a girl and fuck it out of their systems, Liam and Rory will probably get lost in a drunken haze, with or without Sunny, and Ben, well, he might do either or both. I've been with them a long, long time, and while they think they shelter me, I'm not stupid. Once deposited in my room with a book, they believe I live in ignorance of what they get up to, when in reality I'm just turning a blind eye. Up to now, I've been content to read as my way of coming down from the evening's high.

But going to bed like a good little girl is the last thing I want to do this evening. I feel restless, with an unfamiliar tingling inside of me. Dressed in casual clothes, Jasim had blown my mind, the attraction I'd felt for him when he'd taken me home increasing ten-fold, and the look in his eyes had showed he wasn't unaffected by me. Why, for once in my life, couldn't I be allowed to have some freedom to explore what there could be between us? Even if, at the end of the day, it might end in heartache. Wasn't that all part and parcel of growing up?

Why are they allowed to let their hair down, while making sure I stay put in my room? The unfairness and knowledge that Mickey's probably chased off my sheikh leads to me lacking my normal good humour.

Drinks finished, sweaty t-shirts exchanged for clean ones, clothes packed away, I stand when the others do and pick up my bag, looking around to see if there's anything I've missed. At least nowadays the roadies will have loaded all the gear into the van, including my precious guitars.

"All ready to leave?" Mickey asks cheerily. "Here, Janna," he tosses his car keys at me, "You're okay to drive back, aren't you?"

For Christ's sake! And it's that that makes all my good intentions fly out of the window. He won't be coming home tonight, he'll be off with some girl. While he's probably frightened the only man who's ever interested me away. Suddenly I'm not able to take the diplomatic route and let it ride until the morning. I turn on him, not wanting to wait a moment longer to find out whether my suspicions are right.

"What did you say to the sheikh, Mickey?" I snap.

Mickey's eyes flick guiltily away. Fleetingly, I think he's going to lie and get ready to call him out on it, when with a sigh and a quick glance at the others, he gives it away. "He's not for you, babe."

Never have I felt more like stomping my foot, "I didn't suggest he was. But that's not up to you."

"Babe, we've told you the kind of man he is."

"Mickey. Just listen to me. I'm sick to death of you controlling everything I do. I'm not a kid anymore."

"We promised your mum…"

"Ben," I swing around on the man who's adding his support, and to the wrong party in my opinion. "Do you really think she'd approve? Look, frigging hell, I'm not talking about Jasim. I'm talking about my *life*. You never let me have one. You wrap me up in cotton wool and it's starting to suffocate me."

"Babe," Mickey's hand touches my arm, his long hair swings down and feathers across my skin as he leans down to talk to me, "We," he points to himself and then indicates the others, "We know what men are like. We want to protect you from that." It's at that moment Joe comes back in, zipping his fly, and by the satisfied grin on his face I don't think he's been for a slash. It emphasises the freedoms they have, which are denied to me. It makes me see red.

Angrily, I swipe his hand away, "I'm well aware of how you lot treat women," I scoff, nodding pointedly at the vocalist. "I've seen it often enough."

"Janna, we're looking out for you. Nice boy shows an interest, we'll be right behind you."

"And that's the frigging point!" Now I'm snarling, but I can't help it. "A *nice* boy? What's that, in your definition? And I know you'll be fucking behind me. I've been there, remember?" On my first date, I'd turned to find all of them in the bar, eyes on me at all times. They'd followed me into the cinema. Hell, the guy I was with got so nervous he took me home at ten o'clock. And that set the pattern for dates after that.

I'm not normally so confrontational, but Mickey's actions tonight have riled me. I play a major role in this band. Joe and I control the audience, they trust me to do that. But that's the limit of the faith they have in me.

Heaven help me if I decide I want to try my luck with a man. They've no right to keep interfering. Mickey's attitude is just too much, how dare he warn someone away? He's gone too far, and now I need to bring things to a head. Taking a deep breath as I look around me, I say the words I doubt they ever expected to hear.

I'm deadly serious as I voice my threat. "Back off. Or I leave Anarchy Rules."

The expressions on their faces would be amusing had I not issued such a serious ultimatum. And the one on mine shows them I mean every word I said. Let them eat that. I stare at them all while my warning sinks in. When no one answers, I swing my bag up on my shoulder, toss my hair back, and walk to the door, pausing only to say, "We going home then?"

I've stunned them into silence. They follow me out. There's none of the usual camaraderie as we go to the car park at the back. Avoiding the looks of hurt and dismay on their faces, I get into Mickey's car and drive it back home where I go to my lonely bed. The emotions of the evening make me burst into tears, and I bang my hand against the pillow in frustration. I'm ashamed to admit I cry myself into a restless sleep.

I feel trepidation when I leave my bedroom the next morning after a long night which had seen me tossing and turning, my declaration ringing in my ears. Had I been wrong? Whichever way I looked at it my only conclusion was that I'd been right. It's time I made a stand. Everyone breaks out from their family at some time, and this dysfunctional group happens to be mine. Unless they allow me more freedom, their oppression is going to destroy me. My attraction to Jasim, the catalyst for my decision. If I want a man, why shouldn't I go after him? Without my family vetting my every move.

"Morning, babe." Sunny's perched on a stool by the kitchen counter, a mug of tea in her hand. Nodding at her in greeting, I busy myself flicking the switch to boil the kettle, and putting a tea bag in a cup. "You got them riled last night. It was all Rory could talk about. You wouldn't do it, would you? Leave the band high and dry?"

Swallowing down the sarcastic comment, *oh, it was Rory's turn then,* I drown the tea bag and then take it out, opening the fridge and pouring milk into my drink before I answer. I take the stool beside her. "They'd be fine without me. Ben's good enough to take over. He hides at the back, but he can handle lead just fine."

Her mouth turns down, "You're the draw for the band, you know that, don't you?"

I give a little shrug, shaking off her implied compliment, "No more than Joe. You know he gets the girls screaming."

"But it's you the males want to see."

Pushing back my hair, I refute it, "It's the music. Anarchy Rules would still survive if I left."

"But would you be able to survive without Anarchy Rules?" A new voice breaks in.

Turning to greet Rory, I take a moment to consider his question, and then give an honest answer. "I don't know. But it feels like it might be time I found out." Though I don't actually have much of an idea what I'd do instead. But if they ignore my ultimatum, I know I owe it to myself to try.

Crossing over to his girlfriend, Rory places his mouth on hers, and gives her a full kiss, his tongue delving deep. I don't miss the way his fingers trace discreetly over her breast, making her squirm in pleasure. *Now that's what I want. A man who so clearly desires me.* And if I stay with the band I don't see any chance of me experiencing that.

At last releasing her lips, he looks up and stares across at me, "The music's important to you, it's all you've ever wanted to do."

He's right, it's all I've ever known. But it doesn't mean I couldn't do anything else. "I could go into producing. Do a solo album. There's loads of things I could do."

"You could marry a rich sheikh."

I play punch Sunny's arm. Under the circumstances, I don't believe her comment is useful.

Thankfully ignoring what his girlfriend said, Rory gives me a cheeky grin, "But you'd miss us." He's right and I can't deny it. I would miss them.

I inhale, then sigh, "The answer's simple, Rory. If you lot don't want me to go, stop suffocating me. Let me have a life *and* the band."

I feel a presence behind me, and arms surround me, pulling me back into a strong muscular body, "Babe, if that's what we have to do to keep you, then we'll try to back off." A feeling of relief comes over me, it seems Mickey's been giving this some thought. But as his words sink in, my initial glow of elation fades, words come cheap.

I have to test him. "And what if I wanted Jasim?"

"Oh, babe," Mickey lets me go, then comes around the other side of the breakfast bar. Resting his elbows on it, he leans forward and looks into my eyes. "Janna, he's too much for you. He's too old and experienced. And he knows it."

I knew it! "That's what you told him."

Mickey's eyes gaze steadily into mine. "I admit that's what I'd been meaning to say, but he got in first, Janna. It wasn't what I told him, but what *he* told *me*."

My mouth drops open. I don't want to believe him, but the earnestness written all over his face shows he's probably sincere and telling the truth. I turn away to hide the tears pricking at back of my eyes. Of course, a sophisticated man like Jasim wouldn't be interested in a nobody like myself. I was stupid to think that for a moment.

"Janna…"

I don't turn back to face him, "Just leave me be, Mickey. I'm going to my room, there's a riff I want to work on."

No one tries to stop me and nothing more is said as I leave the kitchen. In my bedroom I pick up my guitar and lose myself as my fingers fly across the strings, working on a break that had been going around my head for a while, sliding up and down the fret board trying to get it just right. It's the escape that I choose and, as usual, I lose myself in my music and, for a while, try to forget all about the handsome sheikh who'd so suddenly come into my world, and who had left it just as abruptly. Leaving me with only fantasies running through my head of what might have been. *Too young and too inexperienced for him.* Yeah, right.

I'm playing through my headphones, so don't hear a knock on the door. The presence looming over me startles me and I drop my pick, swearing as I try and locate it on the floor. I glare up at Joe.

"I did knock," he shrugs, apologetically.

"Frigging hell, that was my favourite. Now where the hell has it gone?" I put aside my guitar and slide down to the carpet on hands and knees, feeling with my hand where it might have gone. Finally, when I find the plectrum just under the bed I sit back up, happy again. "Well, what did you want?"

Reaching out his hand, Joe helps me to my feet. "Mickey's had a call from your sheikh."

"Already?" My eyes narrow in surprise.

Joe shakes his head and grins, "Babe, you've been in here for hours. I arrived about twelve and it's now half past four."

Christ! I've lost the entire day. Mind you, that's not unusual. Then I realise what he said. Ignoring the reference to *my* sheikh—that's not likely to happen—I ask, "What did Jasim say?"

"Mickey sent me to get you, he wants to tell all of us at once."

"Everyone's here?"

"Yeah, you're the only one missing."

"Well, what you waiting for, then?" I lead him out of my room, and into the lounge, then take my place on the couch. Mickey is standing, his hands clasped behind his back as though he's about to give a presentation. He smiles as I sit down. *Good news, then.*

"I've heard from Sheikh Jasim. And the short answer's yes." His grin broadens showing he's chuffed with the news.

"Yeah!" Joe's exclamation of pleasure contrasts with his wide-open eyes. It seems he didn't think it was going to be that easy.

"Great!" Rory and Liam high five each other.

"Fucking brilliant!" Ben fist pumps the air.

As various appreciative calls ring out, my face beams. If I divorce my thoughts of the sheikh from the opportunity for the band, I can really see some good coming out of this. From the pictures, I'd seen it's a fantastic venue for us to use, and will give a unique flavour to our music vid. After this morning's clearing of the air, if they really give me some space, I'm happy to throw all in with Anarchy Rules. And this is about the best news we could have.

Mickey raises his hand, "Pipe down a mo, there's something other things you need to know, and, Joe," he nods toward the vocalist, "Some logistics we'll have to work out."

"How we can afford to get out there with the film crew for a start," Liam butts in, "We need proper support on this. Can't have the best venue in the world and cock it up using cheap camera and sound."

"If you give me a moment?" Mickey glares at the bass player. As he lets us know there's more to come, he starts grinning again, pausing before telling us the rest, "Sheikh Jasim's come up trumps. He's flying back to Amahad in about four weeks' time. If we can make the arrangements, we can go with him, and take all our gear and equipment on his family's jet. That halves our travel costs as we'll only need to make arrangements for coming back home."

Another round of pleased exclamations.

"Jeez, Janna. You did good when you met that man." Ben thumps me on the back.

"You didn't say that at the time," I shoot back at Joe, who has the grace to look sheepish.

What does it mean for me? Excitement bubbles inside me. We're going on his private jet, and I'm be seeing him again. Then my mouth turns down, as I remember with dismay the rejection he sent via Mickey. *Does he really see me as little more than a school girl?* Should I really feel pleasure at the chance to see him again? Wouldn't it be better to put him out of my head? If I'm travelling to the same country as him and on the same plane, wouldn't that only be rubbing salt into the wound?

Realising my conflicting thoughts have resulting in me zoning out of the discussion going on around me, I make an effort to pull my attention back.

"We've got gigs lined up."

"Yeah, Joe. That's what I meant about needing to get our end sorted. We'll put our heads together and see what we can shift or cancel. We'll just have to work it out. But for now, let's fucking celebrate!" Mickey's beaming like a loon.

And me? I'm not quite sure what I'm feeling.

CHAPTER 9
Jasim

As the middle of three brothers, I often believe I'm comprised of traits from them both; my elder brother's considered and measured way of approaching the world, and my younger brother's more relaxed slant. Usually able to apply the relevant aspect of my personality to situations as required, I focus on my work and on my diplomatic duties, keeping my private life, those times when I can relax and metaphorically let down my hair, separate from the everyday grind. My life is partitioned into neat little boxes, my work and my play. And I never have them open at the same time.

I've become expert at keeping the two halves of me apart. Never have I let thoughts of a sub intrude into my working day, but by night Club Tiacapan is my luxury, my escape from the responsibilities of the job I do on behalf of Amahad.

Segregating my life means I have no distractions and that allows me to concentrate when making multi-billion pound deals. And rarely, if ever, do I make an error.

Until now.

Why is it I feel like I've made the biggest mistake of my life? As the day draws closer when I'll be returned to the land of my birth, why is it at times my heart beats faster in equal measures of anticipation and dread? I'm a Dom and a sheikh, in both roles known for having strict control over myself. But over the past weeks, my power to exercise that hegemony has been shredded to pieces. And the source of this perplexing state of affairs is really no mystery.

My concentration has drifted during important business meetings, my thoughts interrupted as the vision of Janna dressed as a Domme and commanding the stage comes into my head. Acting completely out of character, more than once I've had to ask for someone to repeat a question and then had difficulty forming the answer as I dream about divesting her of those deceiving clothes, stripping her naked and bringing her submissive side to the fore. Despite my best intentions and my expectation I'd simply forget her, she seems to have taken up residence in my mind, and try as I might, I can't get her out.

What seemed like a sensible offer to make, now seems a miscalculation. My own thoughts on the woman, consolidated by my discussion with the drummer, only confirmed what I'd originally surmised. She's attractive and alluring, but so wrong for me. I'd assumed time and play with faceless subs would clear her from my thoughts. That when I saw her again, she'd make no further impact on me. But what do they say? That absence makes the heart grow fonder? Not only am I unable to forget her, I'm eager to see her again.

Disturbed and disgusted with myself, there have even been times when I've had to stop myself picking up the phone to contact her, just to hear her soft voice. The small hours of the morning are the worst, those moments between sleep and wakefulness when my weakness summons her to my mind. Once, at three am I weakened, resolving to call her the very next day, unable to go any longer without making contact. I'd even concocted some excuse I'd use, something about making arrangements for the flight.

But fate stepped in and saved me early the next day, in the form of a phone call from my baby sister Aiza, reminding me all over again that Janna's her equal in age, and just as innocent. A mental rap around my head to bring me back to my senses and stop me making such an ill-advised call.

I'm a Dom, an owner of a BDSM club. I shouldn't be getting myself riled about one woman, and particularly one I can't have. Maybe that's the attraction? That she's out of my reach? I feel like a dirty old man lusting over a girl so much younger.

By day I manage the oil business on behalf of Amahad, involved in matters of diplomacy spending my time working out of the embassy, or my offices in the Docklands. My nights are spent at Club Tiacapan, but even there it seems I'm almost forcing myself to go through the motions. Finding when I play, although I give one hundred percent attention to the fulfilment of the sub I'm with for the evening, often I've been coming away unable to find satisfaction myself. Most telling, I've had no inclination to make use of the private rooms for quite a while, my cock not interested in anyone else. That little girl has got me twisted up. That I constantly remind myself to remember what I am, and how far removed that is from the man someone like her needs and deserves, seems to have negligible effect.

Tomorrow I leave for Amahad. Tomorrow's the day I'll see her again. Looking down at my hands, I'm surprised to see they're shaking with barely suppressed excitement at the thought of seeing her again. A desire to know whether my memory is deceiving me, hoping time apart will make me view her with fresh eyes and divest myself of the thrall she holds over me. And the dread that it won't.

Tonight, like almost every night, I enter the club and head for the VIP area. Jon's there, with his wife Mia. On the outside, it appears that I act as normal, successfully hiding the confusion that's buried inside. I greet my friends warmly, making a polite enquiry about their baby which causes Mia to launch into glowing reports of how she's thriving, while her husband looks fondly on, his head nodding in agreement. I'm pleased for the pair, at one time having a child seemed an impossibility for them. Their life might not be the one I hanker after, but it seems to work for them.

It's not long before Mia leaves us, asking permission from her Dom when she sees a member who's a Crown Court Judge at the bar. Jon laughs as he sends her off, supplying an explanation, "Mia wants to get some details correct about court procedures for her new book." He points his hand, "Master Simon agreed to talk to her."

I smile, "She's asked me about the oil business before." Even an erotic fiction writer likes to get her background facts right.

With an indulgent smile toward his wife, then a more critical one for me, Jon picks up his whisky and takes a sip. Noticing I'm keeping to water for now, he asks, "You playing tonight?"

I shrug, not having made up my mind, but wanting to keep my options open, "I'm not sure yet."

He replaces his glass on the table, and then looks up. "What's on your mind, Jasim? You've been out of sorts for a while. It's not like you. When was the last time you did a demonstration?" When I don't immediately respond, he continues, "We've a few new members, some aspiring Doms and Dommes. They could do with you watching you."

Annoyed that he's noticed, my mouth turns down in a frown. I'm one of the club's sadists, my tendencies as a Dom are toward more extreme play with one of the more masochistic subs. While not inclined to wield my whip to inflict lasting injury, leaving marks with the lash or cane which will remain for a few days gives me the satisfaction I crave. And my expertise lies in knowing when to stop before it goes too far, reading the reactions of, and the tiniest signs of discomfort from a submissive's body, and putting that above anything they might have agreed to in the prior negotiation. Even a sadist Dom holds onto the overriding aim of making the experience fulfilling for their play partner, giving them just what they need, rather than what they think they want. It takes experience and practice, and having been on the receiving end of any implement used.

BDSM attracts all sorts, many people come to the club believing they'll be wielding a crop or flogger as soon as they start, not realising they need instruction as to how to use the implements properly, including an education on what body parts to avoid. I usually don't mind an audience when I take a sub for the night, or object to taking the time to explain what I'm doing, and the various signs I'm watching out for. And, of course, we have sessions where our wannabe Doms or Dommes go under the whip themselves. Which can weed the real ones out from the sheep.

Jon's got a point. I haven't done any displays for a while, I seem to have lost the inclination. Not that it matters, each of the Master Doms are more than happy to take turns mentoring new members—which is what I'd been trying to explain to Bates when I'd gone to his place. But asking myself why I've lost interest is a completely different question, and one I'm currently unable to answer. I own the fucking club, surely I can get all my needs catered to here? Oh, for fuck's sake, I'm lying to myself. I know the truth, and that there's one unsatisfied desire that will never step through the doors of Tiacapan. And that's the real reason she's so wrong for me. A sadist and a virgin? That sounds like the start of an extremely bad joke.

Jon's still waiting for a response. I take another sip of my water, and before I answer, wave to Diamond, one of our most experienced subs, and ask if she could bring me a brandy. When she brings it, I follow the rules and hand over one of my two wristbands. I might be the club owner, but I do the same as everyone else. Drinks are limited when playing, and if I use up both bands, I won't be allowed to take part in a scene.

Jon's eyebrow has risen, I usually play sober.

"I'm not feeling it, Jon."

An intense look, and he widens his eyes, then barks a laugh. "Bit of a sorry state of affairs, if the owner of a kink club has lost his appetite for kink."

One corner of my mouth turns up, "I'm sure it's not permanent, but I've got a lot on my mind."

"Going back to Amahad," he nods, "I know you must have mixed feelings about that. And it's tomorrow you leave." Brushing his hand across his face, his mouth purses, "I'm not surprised your head's not in the game tonight."

He's given me an easy out, and in fact, one which is valid. I'd left Amahad before my father died, my last official act in that country to take part in an abduction as punishment for a crime, retribution swift and brutal. An innocent woman, stripped of life as she'd known it. That Nijad and Cara's marriage had turned out a success was a miracle. That I'd been part of what could have been disastrous, unbearable. I'd left my country and its primitive views on vengeance behind and had never looked back.

And now I was to return. Not just for a flying visit of a few hours like last time. I'd promised a number of weeks.

I lift my chin toward Jon, "You know how I feel about the country." Before he gave up working in the field, he'd been my bodyguard for some time, and knows at first-hand how brutal some of the Amahadian customs can be.

"Now your brother is the emir, he's made a lot of changes. It's not as bad as it was in your father's day."

At his offered reassurance, I nod and agree, "But how far have those changes seeped through to the tribes?"

"Abdul-Muhsi is dead. He was a root cause of many of the problems."

I spare a brief thought for the man who'd almost caused the death of Zoe, now Kadar's wife and mother of his son. "I'd spit on his grave if he had one." He'd been buried in the desert, where he'd fallen, only a shallow smattering of sand and stones covering a rotting body, which by now had probably fallen victim to vultures. A fitting end for such an iniquitous man.

A jerk of his chin shows his accord with my statement, then he makes a swift change back to the current situation. "I've assigned your protection. He's already in place."

"Sean?" Thinking of the errant sheikh had made me remember the close protection officer who'd almost fallen at Abdul-Muhsi's hands."

"No," Jon shakes his head adamantly. "He's no longer on active service. He's going to be working with Devil."

Now it's my turn to raise a brow, "Jason? I heard he's back." Jason Deville is Club Tiacapan's silent partner, and he also part-owns Grade A. But it's been years since he returned to the UK.

"Yeah, he's setting up a new team. Don't ask me what he's up to, he always plays his cards close to his chest."

"Will we see him here?" I've always thought it strange he bought in, but has never come to the club to play. Mind you, it's been a solid investment. Despite our sky-high membership fees, we're always having to turn people away.

Jon lifts his shoulders, "Perhaps. It depends how long he stays."

"Tell him to get in touch." I've always liked Jason, or Devil, as he likes to be known. He's a man who prefers living on the edge. A distinctive looking man with a scar splitting his face.

"I will do. Anyway, it's Ryan I've sent out. He's familiar with Amahad, having worked there a few times, and was getting itchy feet in the office." Looking up he grins, "He jumped at the chance."

Ryan's a tall muscular ex-Special Forces man who doesn't have a lot to say for himself, but when he does, you listen. Like many of Grade A, he's a Dom and a member of this club, taking advantage of the reduced membership fees. Yeah, he'll do fine. I tell Jon so, and for a moment we discuss the arrangements he's made. My bodyguard has gone ahead to get the lay of the land, and will be there to meet me tomorrow when I land.

Mia returns and kneels at Jon's feet, a smooth and practiced move as she folds her limbs and bows her head. Her master reaches out his hand and smooths her hair, and she rests her cheek against his leg. Total trust and devotion, the love between them almost palpable. My gut clenches, realising I've never known anything like that. Oh, I can always find an anonymous sub who will kneel for me, but that emotional connection is always missing.

But, I remind myself, such devotion comes with ties and responsibilities. And those ties are things I've never desired or needed.

"Well, we're going to go now. Need to get home to relieve the babysitter."

And that's it right there. That's the very reason I don't. How could anyone want so much commitment? Such loss of freedom? The answer is far beyond my comprehension.

I stand as they leave, but then retake my seat. There's a restlessness inside me, which makes it impossible to relax. Knowing it wouldn't be right to find a sub when I'm unable to focus, I partake of my second drink, and then a third, putting my disquiet down to the impending return to the country of my birth. And then I leave and go home. Alone. And attempt to shrug off the strange feeling of emptiness as I walk through the front door. It's the impending return to my home country that's got me tied up in knots. Not anything else.

Like most things in my life, international travel is made easy by my position and my wealth. Being able to use the family's private jet makes getting through security is a doddle, likewise I don't really notice as my baggage is whipped out of the boot of the car and into the airport to be taken to and loaded on the plane without me lifting a finger. Being so used to the ease afforded to me by my position in life, I'm aware of the delays and long queues at baggage drop off other travellers' face, and know how lucky it is that I've never had to experience them.

Making my way to the executive lounge I again question the wisdom of sharing the plane with Anarchy Rules. At the time it seemed expedient, why not bring them along when there was the room? But that was before I'd been plagued with thoughts of their guitarist, and had hoped I would have had more success in putting the girl out of my mind. Now I wish I'd never invited them. Part of me is longing to see her again, and the rest of me is hoping she'll be less than I remember. If she isn't, all I'll end up doing is torturing myself with something I can never have.

Oh man up, for fuck's sake. You're a Dom, you should have more control that this. Walking into the lounge, I see my guests have arrived. I tell myself it's a good thing I don't immediately see Janna, but the pang of disappointment betrays me when I observe she's not with the rest of the group. As I stride over to them, I curb my impulse to ask where she is. And then give myself a mental slap. It's better to believe I don't care.

"Mickey." I greet the drummer with a nod. "You made it okay?"

"Yeah, no problem, man. Must say, I could get used to this." He waves a glass of the free champagne in toast.

"Everyone here?"

He looks around him, and nods. "Yeah, we're all here. That's our film crew," He points with his glass, "Blake Hawkin's the gaffer, that man with a clipboard is the grip, Eli Marshall. And that's Sally Cartwell who works the camera. Travis and Tim, here, they're our roadies. You met them at the gig."

Politely I shake everyone's hand, trying to remember everyone's names while attempting to stop myself from looking around for the missing band member. I'm trying hard to resist but's on the tip of my tongue to ask whether she's not coming, and attempting to convince myself I'll be relieved if she doesn't, when out of the corner of my eye, I see the door to the Ladies opening, and Janna steps out. She's dressed for the climate of my country, in a long flowing pale pink dress that reaches just below her knees. It makes her look so feminine and beautiful as it swirls around her. Her hair is captured in a plait down her back, and my cock starts to swell at the notion of holding onto it as she's on her knees in front of me and my cock is entering her from behind. *For fuck's sake!*

"Now we're all here, let's get to the plane." My voice is sharper than it should be, my impatience aimed at myself, rather than the ones who'll be my travelling companions today. Immediately, I berate myself and bite my tongue, I shouldn't have spoken so sharply, but my diplomacy seems to have fled.

As Janna approaches, I turn my back on her, unable to prevent myself being so rude, knowing my expression would betray my true yearnings should I meet her face to face. And there is no way I can trust myself to speak to her without my voice giving me away. Leaving them to follow on, I stride toward the walkway that will take us to the jet, my arousal tenting the front of my trousers. Keeping my distance will be the only remedy to the immediate and unwanted reaction just the sight of her has caused. My mind knows she's not for me, my body hasn't gotten the memo.

As we ascend the stairs to the plane, I make the only resolution available to me. If I unable to control myself and fight this highly inappropriate reaction, I'll spend as little time as possible in the capital city where Anarchy Rules will be filming. As soon as I can, I'll take myself off to the desert city of Z̧almā, a two-hour helicopter journey away.

Yes, hundreds of miles of desert should be enough distance between us. Surely it should.

CHAPTER 10
Janna

The last four weeks have passed slowly, my mood swinging between excitement, impatience, and trepidation as I counted the days until I could see Jasim again.

There's certainly been some changes following our heated discussion and my threat to leave the band. Having hit home hard, Mickey and company have accepted the idea that maybe they have been smothering me, have admitted I'm no longer a child they need to watch out for. While they'll never back off completely, they certainly have given me more freedom than I've ever had before, and while I can see they're uneasy breaking the habit and lifting their sanctions, they've agreed not to stand in my way if I want to go out with a man. And have promised not to give any more Spanish Inquisitions, and leave me to decide who's right for me.

Which would be great, were it not for the just one slight problem, there's only one man who I'm interested in. The sheikh who haunts my dreams, the man for whom I play my music. Who consumes all my thoughts, leaving no room at all for anyone else. It may just be a silly infatuation, but as the day approaches when I'll see him again, I become determined to use the opportunity to blast his invalid objections away.

My age shouldn't make a difference. An internet search reveals he's only eleven years older than me, yes, an age gap, but not too significant. My innocence? Well, I've got to lose my virginity sometime. And what better way than with an experienced man? I'm not looking for a lifetime commitment. I'm just looking to explore and take further what started that night, when he lay behind me, and I'd felt the evidence of his attraction.

But there's one big drawback. How do I get a man to notice me when I've no knowledge of how to make my interest known? What practical experience have I got of flirting? Absolutely none at all.

My reflection smiles back as I carefully apply my makeup, critically examining the mascara I've just put on. The lines I've heard the boys use on the girls they pick up won't work on him, they have a rather more direct approach than any I could use. A woman has got to be far more subtle. But even I know a man's first turned on by what he sees, so this morning I'm taking care with my appearance, gauging that I've been successful achieving the look that I want by the appreciative whistles of rest of the band.

I can't wait to see Jasim. *I wonder whether he's been thinking about me?* As we climb into the taxis that will take us to the airport, guiltily I realise the real reason for us going to Amahad has become lost among my hopes of seeing Jasim and persuading him to take that first step with me. *He'd called me a girl.* I want to become a woman. With him.

When we arrive in the airport lounge that only the most moneyed people use, I can't get excited by the amazing facilities there. Instead my eyes search to find him, soon realizing we'd arrived first. Jittery with anticipation, butterflies swirling in my stomach force me to escape to the loo, nerves not about the flight, but about the man I will be meeting for just the third time and who I want to impress. At last, when I exit the facilities my eyes light upon him.

During the weeks waiting for this moment, I'd made myself believe I'd built him up in my imagination, remembered him as being more than he was. But when our eyes meet briefly before he abruptly turns and starts walking away, my pulse beats frantically. He's even more desirable here in the flesh than as a recollected vision in my mind. So tall, his natural build already putting him head and shoulders above most of the passengers, his carriage and bearing regal, like the prince that he is.

My heart skips a beat, my lungs forget to draw in air, and a tingling runs from my head to my toes. *I feel alive.* As if I've been sleepwalking, and have now woken up.

But he ignores me, as though I mean nothing at all.

I'd prepared so carefully, my dress chosen to be modest, yet show off my curves. My hair carefully braided, my makeup light, but enhancing my eyes. The effect understated, yet flattering. I'd dressed as a woman, not as a young girl. But it had made not the slightest impression on the one man I wanted to impress.

My steps falter, my prepared welcome dies on my lips. As my companions follow him, I make my legs work and trail along behind, angrily wiping a stray tear from my eye. *He doesn't want anything to do with me.* How stupid I'd been to dream about him. Of course, he doesn't reciprocate my feelings. Had I really believed with one glimpse of me he'd understand what he'd been missing? Jeez, how frigging ridiculous I'd been. Berating myself, I climb the stairs after the men.

Oh, I hadn't thought I'd change his opinion that I was too young and naïve instantly, but it would have started with a few friendly words, and that would surely have given me an opening to my make interest known. He's afforded me no chance to even speak, he's offered me nothing at all. *He's acting as if I don't exist.*

And now he's talking to Mickey and Joe, pointing to the seats down the plane. He's sitting at a table with them, and there's no place for me.

Suddenly, a hand is touching my arm, "Hey, Janna. Come sit over here. With me. Hey, you joining us, Sal?"

I'm unable to speak, feeling cold and alone. Following Sunny to the couch she's indicated, I seat myself beside her, shifting over to clear a space for the camerawoman. I nod to her, not knowing her particularly well, and then turn my attention to Sunny. She's got herself two men, and I can't even get one. For the first time, I don't feel like criticising her. Perhaps she should take all she can get. Life's too short for regrets. I inhale sharply, and apply that thought to myself, narrowing my eyes, as I glance down the plane. *I'm not done yet, Jasim.* I want him. I won't let this stumble at the first hurdle put me off.

"Not like any plane I've ever been on." Sunny's looking around excitedly at the tables and couches which make it look more like a lounge bar. The furnishings all plush and comfortable, the last word in opulence. Trying to shelve for the moment my thoughts of the man I desire yet who seemingly has no interest in me, but remaining slightly distracted, I simply nod.

"Nor like one I've been on either." Sally's eyes open wide, and she nods at Blake and Eli sitting on a similar couch opposite. "Squashed up against the seat in front in economy is normally more like it." Stretching out her long legs, she adds, "Mmm, I could get used to travelling like this."

"Better get un-used to it," Blake calls over, his face creasing, "Unless we decide only to work with millionaires."

"The chance would be a fine thing," Eli grumbles.

A flight attendant approaches, her uniform smart, a jacket buttoned to the top. "Good morning, ladies, gentlemen. We're going to be taking off soon, so can I please ask you to fasten your seat belts?" Helpfully, she indicates where the restraints are concealed under the cushions. "We should have a smooth flight today, and I'll be serving drinks once we hit cruising altitude. If you want to look at the menu, I'll take your food order then as well."

She hands over folders with the Kassis family emblem embossed in gold leaf. "Choose whatever you like, the chef is well prepared today. If you prefer something that isn't listed, please just ask and I can find out if it's available."

Moving off to see to the others, she leaves us alone. We all flick open the menus, and I feel my eyes bulge. It's more what you'd expect from a very expensive high-end restaurant.

"Wagyu beef? I've always wanted to try that!" Sunny's eyes have gone wide.

Beluga caviar has caught my eye, even though I don't have much appetite, "They don't do things by halves, do they?"

"Black truffle mushrooms," Sally's going down the list of starters.

"Fancy lobster or sushi? They certainly don't stint on feeding their guests." Sunny points down at her menu, running her finger down the page, and flicking through the various offerings.

Though I'm still feeling shaken, Jasim's reaction, or rather lack of it, making me feel like I've been knocked off my feet, I smile and put my hand on Sunny's arm, "Do you think the chef would make me cheese on toast?"

"What?" She turns to me incredulous, "With all this here, and you're wanting cheese on fucking toast?"

"Okay, I'll go posh them. Welsh Rarebit."

She lifts off my hand and pretends to punch my arm, "Be serious woman."

As she and Sally laugh, I focus on what she said. Woman. She sees me as a woman. Why can't he? I glance to the front of the plane, where Jasim is deep in animated conversation with the drummer and vocalist. They look like they're excitedly telling him their plans, he's just nodding in presumably the right places. Well, Jasim, I've got two weeks and sufficient resolve to last for that time. I *will* make you see me. I'm determined on that.

I think of the costumes I have packed for the vid. Having played gigs for years, I know how to play a crowd, and especially what to wear to turn the male element on. *No, Sheikh Jasim, you might not have appreciated my dress today, but you'll have no defense once I get out my black leather bra and boy pants ensemble, not forgetting my whip and chains. Hmm, I've been around men long enough to know not many can resist that. You've issued me a challenge. And I accept.*

We're in the air now, the takeoff so smooth I barely noticed. As I watch England fall away beneath us and we start to level out, the flight attendant reappears for our orders. Feeling more composed, I order the truffles and the steak, while Sunny goes for the caviar, and also decides to try the beef. Well, why shouldn't we take advantage of everything that's on offer?

While the film crew makes their selections from the mouthwatering choices, my eyes flit again to the front of the plane, Jasim's facing away from me, but I can hear his deep laugh at something Joe has said.

I'm not going to sit here like an obedient little girl.

Making a quick decision, I undo my seatbelt and stand, stretching to get the kinks out of my neck, tension having made my muscles stiff. I nod to Sunny and Sally who seem to be getting on like a house on fire, and wave to show where I'm going, then make my way along the centre gangway.

There are only three seats around the table, but that's never stopped me before. I tap Mickey on the shoulder. When he looks up with a smile and pushes his seat back, I plonk down in his lap. Familiar arms come around me, and his chin nuzzles the top of my head.

"Doing okay, hun?"

"Just peachy. Some flight this is, isn't it? Better than economy when we went to Germany last year."

"Just a bit." Joe's grinning, his appreciation of this mode of travel gleaming from his eyes.

I turn to Jasim, my intention to thank him, but his eyes aren't looking at me, they're fixed on the arms that are holding me tight. *Now that is interesting.* I've lived with Mickey since my parents died, he and the other guys are all like brothers to me. The thought of anything sexual between us would be akin to incest. *But perhaps Jasim doesn't know that.*

Mickey pats my back, "Here, jump up a moment. I need to take a leak."

As I rise, Joe holds out his hand, and I relocate onto his lap. A low growl sounds, then Jasim abruptly stands and walks away without saying a word.

"What's up with the sheikh?" Joe asks, his mouth dropping open.

"I have no idea," I say, innocently. Hoping the explanation that comes to me is right. *Jealousy?* I can work with that.

But I don't get a chance during the rest of the flight. There seems to be an office at the rear of the plane, where Jasim holes up. Hmm. Is he trying to avoid me? *He may think he's won. But it's only the first round. Game on.* There'll be plenty of time for me to pin him down when we arrive. My interpretation of the signs is that this attraction isn't all one sided. What other than envy could have made him leave in such a rude way?

The food, when it arrives, is delicious. Even at high altitude, the chef obviously knows how to prepare it perfectly. If I'm right, and Jasim was jealous, that gives me a place to start. I begin feeling happier, and in the end, I'm able to eat so much my stomach is full to busting. The plane droning on, my appetite satisfied, I feel my eyelids drooping. Looking around at my companions, I'm not the only one who overindulged in the unexpected gourmet lunch, nor alone in taking the opportunity to have a doze.

The flight continues smoothly, and at last we're coming in to land, the change in engine noise alerting me. Looking out, I see we're dropping toward a runway which appears out of nowhere from the desert beneath us. I've been abroad before, but never to a destination as exotic as

Amahad. As the plane touches down, the ground shimmers in the heat. Now, at last, Jasim must emerge.

But my plans to renew my efforts to seduce the sheikh on the way into the city immediately come tumbling down.

A stairway is wheeled over into position before the engines are even switched off, and behind it emerges a convoy of vehicles, the first a limousine flying the Amahadian flag. Out of the following black SUVs descend guards in uniform, and a man wearing a more casual shirt and tie, with a visible gun in a holster comes to the foot of the stairs. Outriders on motorcycles sit waiting to escort us. And finally, there's a large van, presumably to carry our gear.

The stewardess holds us back as we go to get out of our seats, indicating we should allow Jasim to exit the plane first. Watching out of the window, I see the soldiers standing to attention and saluting him, bringing home to me his elevated status in this country. The Caucasian man openly wearing a weapon greets him at the bottom of the steps, shaking his hand, then with his palm on Jasim's back, leads him quickly over to the limousine, his eyes scanning in all directions as though looking for possible threats. Once Jasim's safely inside the car, the soldiers seem to relax their stance, and we're given the signal to descend, and are directed to the other vehicles.

Hmm. We might have accompanied him on his private jet, but we're obviously not grand enough to be offered the spare seats in his roomy limousine.

Before I get into one of the SUVs, I turn and check Tim and Travis are supervising the transfer of our equipment into the van provided. I'm always anxious when I'm away from my precious guitars. I've had the Strat since I first learned to play—a present from my parents—and the Gibson Les Paul I treated myself to a couple of years ago. When I see Tim's taken charge and is carrying a case carefully in either hand, I relax and get into the car. *Okay, Jasim, round two goes to you too. But you can't hide forever.*

It's not long before we're heading into what I learn from the commentary of the English-speaking driver is the capital city of Amahad, Al Qur'ah. The sun blazes down from an unbroken sky of brilliant blue, making the white of the buildings stand out as we leave the desert and approach a more built up area. At first, the buildings are squat and obviously residential, and then we're driving past a colourful souk which I just itch to explore, and after that, more modern office buildings. As we head up a palm tree lined boulevard I crane my head forward to look out of the window as the palace comes into sight up ahead of us. It's huge, much bigger than I had imagined.

I give Mickey a nudge, "Hey, look at that!"

Joe, sitting in the front because of his extra-long legs, speaks over his shoulder, "Impressive, isn't it?"

Sunny gives an unladylike whistle.

Rory, Liam, and Ben are in the car behind us, but I suspect they'll be just as impressed. The film crew are in a third vehicle behind.

Up to this point we've been following the limousine, but once we pass through the gates to the palace, it goes on up ahead, and our vehicle turns off and drives around a perimeter road. I sigh quietly, *it was never going to be easy, was it?* But slowly the thrill of arriving seeps through my disappointment, and I look up in interest as we pull up outside a row of houses built backing on to the high surrounding walls. The driver gets out, and comes around to open the doors.

"This is where you will stay." I take my first proper look at the robed man who speaks good English, but with an accent. I feel a bubble of excitement as it brings home to me that I really am in a foreign land.

He's pointing to the house, and the adjacent one, "The three adjacent residences are allocated to you."

"Our equipment?" Joe looks around for the van which should have been following us.

"It has been delivered to a storeroom for you. There's a small hall where you can set up and practice if you like. And tomorrow you will be afforded a tour of the harem.

My name's Ahmed, and I will be your guide while you are here." He nods back toward the palace entrance. "Feel free to explore the city, just keep to the well-lit areas at night. Al Qur'ah is a tourist destination, so you'll be quite safe in the main part. There are restaurants, a casino. Everything you could want."

The driver's pride in his city goes over my head. I'd only focused on one thing he'd said. *The harem.* Those provocative sounding words trigger a reaction inside me, as I begin wondering what would it be like for a sheikh to kidnap me and secret me in his own personal hideaway, keeping me for his pleasure. A sheikh called Jasim. *Oh shit, Janna. You've got it bad.*

CHAPTER 11
Jasim

I successfully evaded her throughout the flight by forcing myself to remain in the plane's well-equipped office, needing somewhere alone where I could hide the burst of rage that had affected me when I saw her companion's arms hugging her tight. *It should have been me holding her close.* I couldn't let my thoughts betray me, so removed myself from the situation.

I can't trust myself around her.

At last, the torturous journey and its temptations has ended. Ryan's waiting to greet me as I step off the plane, and other thoughts thankfully push the woman to the back of my mind. I'm in Amahad and with very mixed feelings about coming home.

While Kadar will have provided security for me, having my own English bodyguard as my companion grounds me, and reminds me I've still got one foot in either camp. Jon will have briefed him, and he'll know my views well, together with my concerns. I know Kadar isn't my father, but if I've been tricked into coming here, if any attempt is made to forcibly keep me in this country, Ryan will get me away. Abduction can work in more than one way. Part of me knows my fears are irrational, but they reflect the intensity of my belief there's no way I could ever make Amahad my home. However much my brothers might wish me to do so.

Ryan welcomes me, then after presumably assessing there's no immediate threat, he quickly ushers me inside the limo.

"Sheikh." He greets me formally. "Are any of your companions coming with us?"

I eye up the empty seats, and shake my head. "No."

He waits for no explanation, just says a word to the driver, and the limo starts to move off.

Noticing the way he greeted me, I don't want any distinction from him, "No formality, Ryan. Call me what you do in the club."

He chortles, "I'm not going to call you Master."

I laugh back, "Jasim will do." I grow serious, and give him a sharp look, "Have you sussed out what's going on? Whether there's anything I don't know about why they want me back?"

A shake of his head. "Nothing more than has been said. Kadar's emphasized it's a statement to the country who think you've deserted them. A chance to show you're doing excellent work, albeit from abroad."

"And my brother's got no nefarious plans? Nothing's going on behind my back?"

"If the emir has, I haven't been able to pick anything up. And I've been staying in the palace, enjoying your brothers' hospitality. They've not let anything slip."

Many Grade A employees have become close to the royal family, having previously laid their lives on the line to keep us safe, Ryan amongst them. It doesn't surprise me that they've extended the hand of friendship to him. Only a few months earlier he'd played a part in my older brother's wife's rescue. "I'm relying on you," I begin, and then pause to brush back my hair, "I can't stay in Amahad. I'd suffocate, Ry. Any hint of my unwilling detention, and I expect you to have my back."

"You can rely on me, Jasim. Kadar wants you to use the palace security, but seems to have no issue with putting me in charge. I'll get you out of here, if necessary. My reading of it is they want you to stay as long as possible, but wouldn't resort to using anything other than verbal persuasion. And if there's a sniff of that changing, I'll get you away. It's my job."

Normally a man of few words, Ryan has reassured me. To anyone else my fears would be unrealistic, but then other people haven't experienced my father's rule, and the Amahadian ways. If Ryan thinks I'm overreacting, at least he keeps it to himself.

For the rest of the journey we sit in silence. Driving on into the city, and especially as we approach the palace, I again start to feel uneasy, wondering about the ploy to get me back, still having suspicions that now he has me here, Kadar won't allow me to leave. Has my brother something up his sleeve to entice me to stay? He wouldn't resort to actual incarceration, would he? Of course not. But as kidnapping isn't unheard of in our family, I'm not ready to let go of my suspicions just yet.

And as the limousine comes to a halt at the main palace entrance, where two men are waiting to greet me, I relegate my second thoughts about the wisdom of my return to the back of my mind. Ryan nods as he leaves me, knowing this is a private reunion.

"Jasim." The unexpected tone of that voice, that one heartfelt word, smashes my foreboding into smithereens and gives me a sudden and unanticipated feeling of being home. An emotion I hadn't expected to feel. Unlike the cold greeting my father would have given me, Kadar, my older brother is stepping forward, sentiment making his eyes glisten as if he's holding back tears. His robes waft around him in the warm breeze as he walks forward and envelopes me in a full body hug, his mouth pressing against first one cheek, and then the other. I'm held tight for a few seconds, an embrace which expresses how much I've been missed.

"Welcome, brother," he tells me, when finally, he eases his hold, but keeps his hands on my arms. "You look well, but pale. You need some sun on your skin."

"And you, Kadar. You look well also. Fatherhood must agree with you." His warm welcome was not what I would have predicted, and so totally different from the one I would have received from the last emir.

A smile softens his naturally stern expression, "It certainly does, Jasim. My child gives joy to me every day." Just looking at him it's easy to see how marriage to the woman he loves has transformed him. The woman who almost sacrificed her own life to save his, her unselfish action earning her the respect of the tribes.

"Good to have you on Amahadian soil, Jas."

"Nijad." I clasp my younger brother to me, then release him. "It's not been that long…"

"You were here for just a few hours last time, brother. Hardly enough time to say you'd even been home."

"You know my problems, Ni. And you, Kadar. When father was alive…"

"But he's alive no longer." Now Kadar interrupts. "His influence is gone. Amahad is moving forward. And we need you to help us proceed on that journey." He pauses, and then his next words blow all my fears out of the water. "We'd prefer to have you here, Jasim. I won't deny that. But I also can't refute the tremendous work you're doing for us in London. Having you, in that position, working for Amahad is extremely beneficial. Wherever you're based, you remain a son of Amahad."

I nod, well aware of the responsibilities I can't shelve, however much I might want to do so. Even though Kadar now has an heir, should anything happen to him, I would be named regent.

"Come." Kadar stands aside, and indicates the way into the palace. "We need to speak with you, and bring you up to date on what's going on."

I laugh, Kadar hasn't changed. I've barely got my feet on home soil and he wants to talk business. "Where are my lovely sisters-in-law? And my niece and nephew?" I glance around, surprised they're not here ready to greet me.

"Time enough to catch up with them later, we've a family dinner planned."

But for now, I'm the meat that's going to be grilled. Typical. With a slight shake of my head, I follow them into the palace and down corridors that have been familiar all my life. When Kadar leads me into the emir's office, I falter on the threshold, memories of unpleasant meetings with my father echoing in my head.

"Jasim, you're letting the family down."

"Jasim, you disrespect our country with your manner of dress."

"I hold your fate in my hands, Jasim. You do what I say."

Another shake of my head to try to clear the memories, and then I take that first step, into my past. Realising I've closed my eyes, I open them, and this time view the changes. The desk's still the same monstrosity from another age, but on the leather clad surface sits the equipment of the twenty-first century, an open laptop and two screens, and underneath a PC tower. A router sits to the side with lights flashing, Then I notice the conference table has been replaced with a more modern type able to accommodate wires and laptop chargers in front of each of the seats.

My eyebrows rise at Kadar's modernisations, and a small smile plays at my lips at the thought of the coarse desert sheikhs sitting around, laptops open in front of them, gnarled fingers tapping at keys. The technology shows me time hasn't stood still and, rather than taking a step back, Amahad, like myself, has moved forward. The transformation helps ease a little more of the worry that I hadn't been able to shake.

"Here." Kadar indicates a smaller table, one with comfy chairs around it, a coffee jug and cups already in place. As I take my seat, he pours out refreshment.

The first sip of the thick sweet coffee makes me appreciate not everything about my Arab home is bad. I've missed the bitter tang on my taste buds, the West just can't make the same drink that our Eastern country can.

Nijad's mouth has turned up, "This brings back memories." He waves at my suit, purchased on Saville Row, and then indicates his robes. "Nothing's much changed, has it, Jasim?"

I'd taken to western dress to offend my father, and hadn't seen reason to change just because I'd stepped foot on the Amahadian sand. But already I feel the shackles of history falling from me, so I throw my younger brother a bone, "If my robes are still here, I might wear them when I go to the desert." They'll certainly be more practical.

Kadar raises a brow, and exchanges a look with Nijad. It might not seem like much, but it would be a momentous step for me to take, and would be a sign that I'm no longer making a protest against my heritage. He nods, then lifts his own cup.

"Jasim, first, this harem business. I was intrigued by the suggestion. And I agree with you. If the band's as good as you say, it will be good publicity for us."

I'm glad he sees the benefit in it. Interested about the modifications to the harem, I enquire, "How's the hen party business going, Kadar? Has it got off the ground?" I can't resist chuckling, it seems such an unlikely venture for the royal family to have become involved in.

The emir considers for a moment, "You'll have to ask Zoe and Cara about the details, but we've hosted a couple of parties so far and the venue seems to have been well received. Like any new enterprise, it needs time to take off and we must be able to reassure people there's no terrorist risk. But we're working on that." He pauses, to give a smile, "And next month we've got Vanessa's party booked. But of course, we won't be getting a penny for that."

I chuckle, a few months ago it would have been impossible to imagine Sean Cooper, an employee of Grade A, Master Dom of Club Tiacapan, and a man we all called friend, unexpectedly becoming a parent and now planning to get married. The consummate bachelor, or so we'd all thought. Hosting his fiancée's party was the least Kadar could do to repay him for his contribution to the country.

"I still can't believe Sean's walking voluntarily into the marriage trap," I tell them, speaking my thoughts aloud.

Nijad gives me a sharp look, "Only because you haven't found the right woman, yet, brother. When you do, you'll understand."

"Not likely," I respond quickly with a smirk, "I prefer variety. And I've got a choice, unlike you." Nijad had been forced into marriage, and Kadar had had to marry the woman the country had chosen for him. The fact that both delight in their partners is a matter of chance, and not a little luck.

"I could find you a wife. A nice virgin." Kadar's grinning at me, "I could dictate that you marry."

A threat the old emir would have made, but one I hope my brother wouldn't follow through on. "Fuck off."

My response makes both men laugh.

"It's good to have you back, Jas."

I nod my thanks toward Nijad, realising with surprise that it is satisfying to be home. Home. It's been the first time for many years that I've given the palace a description approaching anything like that. It gives me cause to wonder whether I was wrong to suspect some kind of entrapment. I refill my coffee cup, taking a moment to enjoy the sweet nectar. And then to get to the point.

"Kadar," I wait until I've got his full attention, "What gives, brother?" As he shifts as though he's uncomfortable, I know I'm on track, "I could have made this visit at any time, but why was it so important to ask me back now?"

"How are the negotiations going with OPEC?" he counters.

"Fine," I reply shortly, my brow creasing, "But it's still not been decided whether we're to be part of that group. Kadar. Don't stall."

His eyes flick to Nijad, and then back to me, "Okay, Jasim. Yes, I particularly needed you to come home." He brushes his hand across his short beard, "We've received information. After the attempt to sabotage the oil fields, Amir Al-Fahri's going down a more diplomatic route."

My eyes widen, "Information from who? And what exactly was it?"

The emir's eyes scan the room, as if making sure we're alone. I know the room will have been routinely swept for bugs, but his unease signals what he is going to say will be of utmost importance. I watch as his hands go to his ghutra, smoothing down the sides, his unconscious action helping him come to a decision.

"We had Danielle Smith in custody?" His voice rises at the end, as though posing it as a question. I nod, showing I've kept up to date with information sent through the diplomatic bag, the contents unopened even by British Security. Danielle, the mother of Sean Cooper's child, died in prison in Amahad before she could be questioned by the British Secret Intelligence Service, the CIA, or any other interested party.

Kadar allows me a moment to digest the name, and I glance at Nijad, to see him staring at me intently.

"Her death must have been a relief to Sean." Vanessa, Sean's fiancée had killed the son of Amir al-Fahri, the world's most renowned terrorist, and Danielle Smith had been the sole witness. With Danielle's death, there was no one who could implicate Vanessa in the shooting.

There's a moment of silence, and then it sinks in. I smack the palm of my hand against my forehead, "You arranged it." I don't look at my brother as I speak, but do raise my eyes just in time to hear his response.

"It had to be done." Kadar waves his hand in dismissal, but those five short words are sufficient to confirm she had been killed to keep her quiet.

The world thought her secrets had died with her, a fight between inmates, a shanking no one could have prevented. But now I'm reading between the lines. I look at each of my brothers in turn, and quickly reach my own conclusion. "You interrogated her first."

Their nods are all the confirmation I need. I stand, walking over to the windows, looking out at the glorious garden outside which should be wilting under the hot sun, but instead is blooming, irrigation pipes hidden under the paths keeping it well watered. *This* is why I didn't want to come home. It's not the view, which reminds me how we squander the country's precious water on keeping plants alive so the wealthy can look at them. No, that's bad enough, but the fact that my brothers were responsible for having a woman debriefed—and probably quite brutally— and have kept the resultant information to themselves, before ordering her death. Something my father would have done.

I feel a hand on my shoulder.

"Brother, if we'd let her live, al-Fahri would have found out about the true circumstances surrounding the death of his son. And that would have planted a huge fucking target on Sean's fiancée's back. And, on ours. Vanessa has value to the world, Danielle had none. And what if he decided to take Kadar's son in retaliation? I would put nothing past him."

"Who are you to judge someone's value? It's something our father would have done without flinching," I tell him, through gritted teeth.

A mirthless laugh is huffed behind me, "Believe you me, I flinched. I fucking felt sick. But as a Dom I had to protect a sub, even if she wasn't mine to protect." My older brother's voice is filled with self-doubt, and at once I recognise the pain he's feeling, and that my reaction, *my comparison to our dead father,* is only adding to it. Our father wouldn't have felt one iota of remorse.

Turning my back on the garden, I consider what I would have done in his place. Vanessa is the sub, and soon to be wife, of a friend to Amahad, a man who took bullets to protect Kadar's wife. He's right, any one of us would do anything to keep a sub safe. Would I commit murder in an analogous situation? As a theoretical question I find it impossible to answer. I shiver, grateful down to my bones I'm not the emir. I look toward him, "I'm sorry, Kadar. I'm looking for ways to prove this place hasn't changed, where instead I can only find improvements for the good. Forgive me. While you might have taken the same route as our father, your reasons for doing so hold merit. Unlike his."

Kadar stands, and lifts his chin toward me. "Thank you, brother."

"Now, can we get back to the important part? Leaving aside how we obtained it, the information Danielle had is what's important for us to discuss, Jasim." Nijad's hand is encouraging me back to the table. I take my seat, unbuttoning my jacket as I do so.

"Okay. Hit me with what you've got." If they had found out something that would affect me and my work, the quicker I know about it, the sooner I can deal.

Kadar's nodding, his fingers steepled under his chin, "Al-Fahri's attack on the oil fields was little more than a test of our security in the desert. He knew all along he might fail. The direct attack was a distraction." He pauses to take a breath, "Unfortunately we have discovered his real ploy is to discredit us. He's fabricating documents as we speak which will put doubt on the amount of oil under our sands, and those of the adjoining countries of Erizad and Alair. The information will be leaked by 'reliable sources'."

I smooth my hands down my face. *Damn.* "That's not good news, Kadar. My negotiations are in a sensitive stage, and heavily depend on oil being there in significant quantities. If there's any distrust or hint that we've been untruthful, it could set us back years."

"That's why we need you back, brother. You work with the right people, with governments eager to buy our oil. You've made the contacts, and people value your opinion." Sitting back again, Kadar's dark eyes stare into mine, "We need you to be visible, to publicise the truth from the very region. Hiding back in London, it could be presumed that you are being kept in the dark about all the facts."

I might not like living in the country, but my roots are in Amahad, and would do anything not to see it harmed. Or caught up in red tape for years. "And you see that taking…?"

"One, two months at the most." As Kadar keeps to the original timetable, I feel myself starting to relax, and when he adds, "I wouldn't want to keep you away from all those subs at your club for too long, else you might forget how it works." And as he waves down toward my genitals, I give a genuine laugh.

"Brother, he's got his hand for that." Nijad adds slyly, as though recognizing the atmosphere has lightened.

It's good to be back in the company of my brothers again. Or that's how I'm starting to think, until Nijad opens his mouth again. He sits forward and puts his hands on his knees. "So, she's pretty, isn't she?" His words are accompanied by a teasing expression on his face.

My younger brother's abrupt change of subject has me floundering, "Who?" At this point, I genuinely don't know what he's talking about.

"Oh come on, Jasim. The girl, the guitar player for Anarchy Rules." Kadar shakes his head, "Not sure I'm a fan of the band's name."

My eyes narrow, "What do you know about the group?"

Nijad shrugs, "We watched a couple of their YouTube vids. They're good."

Even better live, I think to myself. And immediately I recall Janna in her Domme costume and my prick starts to stir.

"Is she why you agreed to plead their case? I can see the attraction," Kadar jokes.

I need to nip this in the bud, and fast. "Stop right there, both of you. She's the same age as Aiza, far too young to attract me. She's innocent, too."

"Innocent?" Nijad's brow rises. "She didn't look it on film. But I can see why you wouldn't be interested, of course. She's obviously a Domme."

"She's no Domme," I scoff before I can censor my words, "She's an out and out submissive."

My younger brother doesn't miss a trick, "And how the fuck do you know that?" He's grinning, the bastard, "And she's only what, eleven years younger than you?"

"She's barely out of fucking school!" I retort.

"Hmm," Kadar's looking at me with interest, "It's like that, is it?"

"Like fucking what?"

Nijad chuckles, "You like her."

I feel like stamping my foot like an irate child, "I don't *like* her. And anyway, I'm going to Z̧almā in the morning. I'll have nothing to do with her while she's here." As Nijad continues to look at me suspiciously, I continue, "I'm here to work, not to babysit a child."

Kadar shakes his head, "Not tomorrow. I've got meetings set up for you in Al Qur'ah before you head to the desert city. No, we'll need you here for a week at least. And, as you brought them here, I expect you to oversee this Anarchy Rules crowd getting settled in the harem."

"I didn't sign up for that."

"You arranged this, brother." Kadar's tone has changed, "They wouldn't be here if you hadn't spoken, vouched, for them. I expect you to do what I say."

Looking into his face, I see it's the emir that has spoken. I swear under my breath as Nijad huffs a laugh. Don't they know what they're doing to me? They're putting temptation directly in my way. Now I've got to man up and be strong enough to avoid it.

CHAPTER 12
Janna

It feels more like we're on holiday. After sorting ourselves out and settling into the more than adequate accommodation we'd been offered, we decide to wander down into the city to see what Al Qur'ah has to offer. Arranging to meet up again later, Blake, Eli and Sally go off on their own leaving me, the rest of Anarchy Rules, and Sunny to explore. It's not long before we find it's an amazing place, full of colour, exotic sounds and aromas. I fast fall in love with the souk, and could spend hours there browsing the various stalls and probably spending more than I can afford. Unable to resist, I buy myself a beautiful headscarf, the delicate designs simply too hard to pass by, and, thankfully, Mickey pulls me away from the jewelry on display, before I give into temptation.

The palace is just on the outskirts of town, so all the shops and tourist areas can be reached on foot. Rory and Sunny want to see the beach, so we head toward the dunes leading down to the sea. The sun is dipping toward the horizon, more comfortable now as the heat of the day begins to cool as night falls. When the sky darkens we head back to town, noting a busy casino along the way and deciding to visit it another time. Finally, hungry after the journey and our explorations, we find a restaurant that's geared toward tourists, and are able to pick food from the menu that's written in English as well as Arabic.

The only downside is that there's no alcohol on offer, but Joe had already checked out the fridges where we're staying, and had found them well stocked, so after we've eaten, we make our way back.

We must have been out for hours, it's late evening by the time we return. The flight, our walking tour, and delicious meal where I'd again eaten far too much, have taken their toll. I have one glass of wine, then take myself off to bed, leaving the rest of them to enjoy themselves.

After a quick run through the shower, I get ready for bed, adjusting the air con so it's a comfortable temperature, and cracking open the window to let the unfamiliar sounds and aromas drift in. In the distance, I can hear some sort of night bird calling, and faint shouts can be heard from the souk, which seems to run on into the night. There's music playing somewhere, but nothing I can identify.

My eyes close, but my brain can't seem to quiet. Now I'm in bed, my tiredness flees and I'm wide awake. I toss and turn, knowing the time difference means I'll need to get up four hours earlier than normal. But even that thought doesn't make me sleep. And predictably, my mind goes to the sheikh who ignored me today.

Remembering the look on his face when I sat in Mickey's lap I wonder, had it really been envy, or is that just wishful thinking? There had been something he hadn't liked, that was for sure. Is it that he just he doesn't understand the overfamiliarity between us? Mickey has looked out for me since I was sixteen, treating me exactly as he does his sister. Yet, to an outsider, maybe it had been inappropriate for me to be so close to a man who isn't a blood relation.

Oh, how amazing it would be if I'm right and Jasim returns my attraction to him. He's like no man I've ever met before. Just being around him excites me in ways I've never felt.

Writhing to try to get comfortable in a strange bed, my body remembers what it was like to have him spooned behind me, holding me through the night after my ordeal. The memory of the attack might have faded away, but I can clearly recall every moment of my time with Jasim in full technicolour. The image of his chiseled and oh so handsome face comes to my mind, his slightly thin lips, his aquiline nose, and shapely chin covered with a short neatly trimmed beard, all framed by that luscious dark hair are etched on my brain. And his eyes, oh, his eyes. So dark, and flecked with gold. Mmm mm.

My pulse starts to quicken, my skin becomes flushed. I can feel myself getting wet, just thinking about him, imagining those large but attractive hands caressing my body. What would it actually feel like to have a man's hands on me? My own fingers trail to my breasts, imagining Jasim touching me there. My nipples grow erect at just the thought.

My other hand wanders down, slipping inside my sleep shorts, touching myself. My clit is already pulsing, needing relief. Trying to imagine something I've never felt, another person touching me there, I circle my fingers around, sliding along my slit and collecting the slippery moisture and using it as lubrication. I strum faster, my heels dig into the bed. It's *his* face I see as I come to my peak, my muscles going taut as I go over the top.

Stuffing my other hand into my mouth I suppress the slight cry my self-satisfaction elicits. But I feel no relief, my attempt to gratify myself unsuccessful. I'm feeling less fulfilled than if I hadn't touched myself at all.

Sitting up, I plump up the pillows, my fist hitting them hard in frustration. I've seen a lot of men over the years, men who've flirted with me, who'd made known that they wanted me, but none that made me feel I wanted to make the effort to break out of my protective custody and take them up on it. Not until I met Jasim. Is it that he's a powerful sheikh, his unattainability that attracts me? Or that he's the one man who doesn't react to me.

Just go to sleep, Janna. Easier said than done.

Eventually I do drift off and, not surprisingly, have exotic dreams flavoured with the new and different sights I'd seen the night before, and one where a mysterious robed sheikh steals me and takes me away to his harem. In my dream, the sheikh, of course, wears the face of Jasim.

I wake to the loud sound of bird song, and light streaming in through the gap in the curtains. Stretching, I let out a wide yawn before glancing at the clock to see it's already nine o'clock. Christ, I'm still tired, and no wonder. It would only be five am in England. Still, the quickest way to adapt is to go with the flow, and try and force my traitorous body to believe it's later and I really need to get my lazy self out of this bed. How is it, that a bed that feels so uncomfortable when you're trying to go to sleep, becomes the cosiest you've ever slept on come morning?

It's obvious, by the time I've traipsed downstairs, that my companions are no wider awake than I. In fact, they seem worse.

"What time did you go to bed?"

Mickey's looking particularly worn-out as he replies, his usually neatly brushed hair still knotted from the night, "Half past five," he replies, sheepishly.

"Yeah, we got talking, you know how it is." Joe takes out a packet of cigarettes, and offers one to Mickey, the only other smoker among us. Joe swears smoking gives him that sexy rasp to his voice, despite the amount of times I tell him it will also give him lung cancer.

"I hope you're going to take those outside," I tell him, through pursed lips.

"Yes, Mum," he replies with a laugh. Joe and Mickey disappear out the back door into the tiny yard that sits between the house and the palace wall.

I flop down on the nearest chair. "What time are we going to the harem?" I can't wait to see where we're filming, that exotic sounding place that so far, I've only seen pictures of. I'm looking forward to seeing whether it lives up to my imagination.

"About ten." Ben comes over and sits beside me, his hand touching mine, "How you doing, kiddo?"

Inside I seethe at the use of the pet term, but calling him out on it will only make him tease me. I long to shake off this image they still have of a young girl. If they don't see I'm a woman, how can I expect Jasim to? I do what I always do, I ignore it. "I'm fine, Ben. Eager to get started."

Giving my hand a final pat, he links his fingers behind his neck, "After we've seen the harem, we thought we'd check out the sites where me might do some shooting to start with, find the best back drop."

The door to the house opens, and the film crew step in.

"Hey, good timing. We were just talking about scouting locations." Ben nods as he greets them.

Sally's eyes brighten, "Do you think we'll be able to film at the souk? We went there last night and it was amazing."

"We'll have to ask Ahmed about the local customs and whether we'd be allowed to." He refers to the driver cum guide who dropped us off yesterday. He nods as Blake indicates the kitchen, a silent request for permission to make a drink. Eli wanders off with him.

"What time is he coming to collect us?" I ask, reaching down to idly scratch at an itch on my leg. Shit, it's an insect bite. I make a mental note not to leave the window open tonight.

"Ten."

"Anyone else want coffee?" Eli calls out.

"I've already had one, thanks." The others join me in echoing my refusal.

"It won't be long before Ahmed's here." Ben's consulting his watch.

I'm seem to be the better organised, dressed and with my normal smattering of light makeup on. "I'm ready," I tell him.

He's obviously not. "I'd better go and get these knots out of my hair."

"Want me to do it for you?" It's something I've often done, envying his thick curly hair which reaches down past his shoulders, while mine is completely straight. When he nods, I reach down to my bag, extract a comb, and start teasing out the tangles. Living around these men I often do such things for them. Sally comes over and watches, seeming bemused by my task.

Joe and Mickey come back in as I'm finishing his hair, making no comment as it's a sight they've seen many times. Travis wanders in with Tim, and they start discussing sound systems or something of that ilk. Sunny comes down, Rory's arm around her, and Liam's not far behind. Looking around at them all, I feel smug that at least I got a few hours of sleep last night. Everyone else certainly looks worse for wear.

"Did you empty the fridges?" It's hard to keep the grin from my face.

"Almost. Hey, shift ya butt, let me sit down." Sunny gives me a prod and ends up sharing my chair.

There's a knock on the door, Ben's closest so opens it, and Ahmed steps inside. We're lounging over all available seating places, and from the look on his face, he's not impressed. He tuts with his tongue, and then a professional mask shutters his features.

"If you're ready," he announces in his clipped English tones, "I'll take you across to the harem now."

It's the moment I've been waiting for. I'm the first to stand up. "Come on, you lot. Let's get this party started!"

There's a few grumbles and moans, but mostly supressed as underneath the hangovers and lack of sleep everyone's as eager as me. What started as an idea from pictures in a bridal magazine is about to become reality. Following Ahmed, band and film crew are led around the outside of the palace to an ancient doorway in the back. He unlocks it using an out of place looking modern key pad and the door, which looks a thousand years old, incongruously slides open along metal rails.

Standing on the threshold, my eyes open in amazement. We're entering by the garden entrance, flowering plants abound and colourful parrots squawking as they fly around the trees. To me it's an incredible sight. "Do they stay in here?" I ask our guide, eyes wide, my hand shielding them from the sun as I try to track the birds overhead.

"They're free to fly away, but we feed them and encourage them to stay," he replies.

"Wish they'd bloody bugger off," Tim mumbles, not too quietly. "Be hell if we're trying to record out here."

I hear it as beautiful bird song, he's obviously only hearing squawks.

Ahmed regards him thoughtfully, "Inside the harem it's quieter. Can you film and add sound later?"

Tim shrugs, "They can mime," he points at us, "But it's never as good as capturing sound at the same time. Gives it more of a studio feel, as no one can ad lib."

"We'll manage," Mickey pats him on the back. "And if we're playing out here, the birds might get frightened away.

"Or squawk louder." Tim's not convinced.

"Come." Our guide leads the way around the raised flower beds, allowing us to stop for a second and admire the impressive fountain, water playing and landing in a pool with a fascinating mosaic on the bottom. It's a welcome cooling scene in the heat. I'll be glad to get into some shade, the temperature here is approaching unbearable as we're heading for the hottest part of the day.

After pausing at the fountain, Ahmed at last leads us on through huge glass doors which slide open at the touch of a remote, arched windows reaching from the roof to the floor on either side of them. It's my first look inside the harem, and, in this instance at least, the camera hadn't lied.

As expected from the pictures in the magazine, there are bedrooms dotted around the outside, their doors concealed by drapes which make them blend into the scene. In the centre is a huge bathing pool, shallow, but as I walk closer, I see a mosaic even more impressive than the one we saw outside on the bottom. It's a sea scene, with fishes, mermaids, Neptune, whales, and all manner of creatures, the colours bright and shimmering beneath the water. Ripples are caused by what is presumably a modern filtration system, and there's a smaller fountain playing in the middle.

"How deep is it?" Joe asks, stepping forward, stretching out his hands to the water.

"About thirty centimetres," Ahmed informs him.

Joe looks around, his face becoming animated. "We could stand in it and play."

Mickey laughs aloud, "All right for you, but where shall we put my drums?"

"Could be done with a platform." Travis seems like he's bought into the idea.

"Isn't there a danger of electrocution?" I ask, not sure how it would work.

"Hey, live dangerously, babe." The arm Rory doesn't have around Sunny's shoulder, slips over mine as he hugs us both to him. "With the radio mics and pick-ups there shouldn't be any problems."

As Blake and Eli discuss practicalities with Sally, Ahmed coughs, making us aware of his presence, and begins to point out features we'd missed. One intrigues me, a doorway that now leads to the staff quarters, used to be the sultan's entrance, and a hidey hole above, where he'd sit and look out on his concubines, choosing which would be brought to his bed that night. And of course, my mind has to go there, and the thought of Jasim sitting hidden, pointing down as he selects me, sending a shiver of anticipation down my spine.

It's at that moment the great golden doors at the opposite end to the garden entrance swing open, and in walk two women, Caucasian but in Arabic dress, and behind them are two men, one in robes, and one in a tailored suit. My mouth drops open as I recognise Jasim, not having dared hope that I'd see him today. The other man, I notice quickly, must be his brother. He looks too much like him to be anything but.

The women step forward, entering at a faster pace than the men. The first one to reach us holds out a hand in welcome, "Hi, I'm Cara. And this is my husband, Nijad. You've met his brother, Jasim, obviously. And this, here," she pulls her female companion up beside her, "This is Zoe, wife of the emir and designer of the harem. She knows everything about it if there's anything you want to ask." Waving her hand, she draws our attention to the renovations which have been completed so carefully. "She's a genius, as you can see."

A broad grin crosses Zoe's face, and she fists her hand and bumps it on Cara's arm, "Says the hacker to the landscape gardener," she says in a musical joking voice.

"Shush!" Cara admonishes her in a stage whisper, "You're not supposed to tell anyone that!"

"Financial wizard?" Zoe offers instead.

"That will do," laughs Cara.

My eyes had been captured by the short and amusing exchange between the two women who are clearly good friends, now they take in the men, just in time to see Jasim quickly turn away. *He'd been looking at me.*

I feel myself flushing red, and hope it will be blamed on the heat. Nijad, standing next to Jasim, could be his twin. Their facial features are almost identical, though his hair is hidden beneath his headdress. The only difference I can see is that Jasim has a designer beard, and his brother's clean shaven. As I stand comparing them, Nijad's eyes flick to me, and he leans over and says something to Jasim and laughs. I can see the tension in Jasim's body from here. I wonder what amused Nijad, but upset his brother.

Then, at last, they come forward, into the harem. Two of them is too much, it's sensuality overkill. Despite their similarities however, I feel no attraction toward Jasim's brother. He's married to the gorgeous woman in front of me, for one thing. But as the man who'd featured in my dreams comes approaches, he certainly does have an effect as I feel my traitorous nipples peaking through my thin top, and the closer her gets, the more my breathing quickens.

Nijad is the first to speak, his chin drops and lifts as he gives us a small bow. "Welcome to the Palace of Amahad, and to the ancient harem. I trust you are happy with your accommodation? And that you find the harem as suitable for your purposes as you had hoped?"

As Tim mumbles something about bloody parrots under his breath, Mickey speaks for all of us, "You've made us very comfortable, thank you, Your Excellency. And this," he pauses, and indicates our surroundings, "this is exactly what we were looking for. It seems to have everything."

Jasim's looking around the harem as if he hasn't seen it before. "Are there enough electrical sockets for you to use?"

It's his brother who answers him, "Zoe made sure of that. She calculated most of our guests would be bringing hair dryers, straighteners, chargers and so on. Getting electricity to this part of the palace was a major endeavour, so I suspect it's more than sufficient."

"We haven't gotten around to checking details like that out yet, but you've answered one of our questions, at least." Blake nods in appreciation.

Travis steps forward, his iPad in his hand showing the storyboard we'd agreed on back home. "I think we can add to our ideas from what I've seen already. I'd like to take some time just to roam around, flesh out our thoughts." Our roadie has stepped up to be our director. It seemed a good fit, he spends all his time watching the band, directing the lighting and adjusting the sound. While we play our music, he creates the visual effect. Tim's doubling as the sound man, and with the gaffer, grip, and Sally the videographer we should have a good team. As Sally looks around she keeps nodding, as if she's seeing features she appreciates.

"Has our equipment arrived?" Blake starts taking an interest, "I want to check out the lighting. Depending on where you want to set up, Trav, we might need a reflector. The sun's very bright coming in through those windows." He waves his hand toward the outside.

The men's voices wash over me as they discuss the technicalities, it doesn't bother me much, I just need to be told when to play and what they expect me to do at the right time. While Nijad is listening intently, interested in how it's going to come together, I find my eyes glued to Jasim who seems as distracted as me. Instead of looking at the crew, he seems fascinated with the mosaic in the middle of the pool. Taking a breath to fortify myself, I move to stand beside him.

"It's wonderful place, Jasim. Even better than we expected. Thank you for arranging it." Breaking off, I do a full circle, indicating I'm taking it all in, "The makeover has been done so well, there's still such an atmosphere of magic here." I can't help it; my eyes are drawn to the sultan's peep hole.

Jasim's followed the direction where I'm looking, and he stiffens, "Barbaric practices in ancient times," he states, his brow creasing, "not so romantic, I assure you. The sultan would have many wives and concubines, some kidnapped against their will. Are you imagining starry-eyed beauties awaiting their summons?" He shakes his head dismissively, and continues without giving me time to answer. "That might be how Hollywood portrays it, but that wasn't the case. No, more likely they were waiting in dread and plotting their escape."

My lips turn up, "Spoilsport. What if they wanted to be here? To be kept for their master's pleasure?"

His eyes flare, something I've said affects him. "Whatever," he says, indifferently, "Feel free to imagine it that way."

"It's hard to do anything else," I respond, "Amahad is such a magical country."

He swings around, and barks a short laugh, "Oh, it has a mystique alright, you're correct about that. Now, if you'll excuse me, I have matters to attend to." The way he speaks is imperious, he's turned into the sheikh. However contemptuous he seems about his homeland, it's clearly influencing him. Turning away from me, he catches the attention of his brother, and jerking his head, indicates he's going to leave.

And then he's gone, the enormous harem door closing behind him with a loud ringing clang. He seems to take the air out of the room with him, and all at once my pleasure in this place fades.

CHAPTER 13
Jasim

I had to leave, had to get away. She was standing so close to me, I could smell her perfume. Not something that comes out of an expensive bottle, but something that's all her. Coconut oil—probably some type of suntan lotion—some flowery shampoo, and an underlying scent that's pure woman. *But she's not a woman. She's just a girl.*

And the words she was saying? I couldn't stop myself imagining me calling for her to be brought to me as a concubine for the night. And when she spoke about women being kept for their master's pleasure, I immediately started imagining me mastering her and had to get out of there before my swelling cock betrayed me. Damn Kadar for making me see her again. Whatever he fucking says, I'm going to the desert city. Today.

But however much I want to make an escape, I should have known my older brother would have other ideas and thwart my plans. He hadn't been joking when he said he needed me to spend some time in the capital.

First, he'd arranged meetings with Rais and the desert sheikhs, though why I should meet them here and not closer to their homes, I have no bloody idea. And then there are meetings to sit through with the financiers, and state dinners, welcoming a lost son of Amahad home. A week passes before I can even think of repacking my bags, seven long days spent trying to keep out of her way. One hundred and sixty-eight torturous hours torn between visiting the harem and seeing her again, and equally long nights pleasuring myself, my own hand providing me with little satisfaction but hopefully enough to give me the strength to stay away.

Once, I saw her coming down a corridor, animatedly talking to one of her friends. I'm ashamed to say, using my vast knowledge of the palace, I'd dipped through a concealed door and had hidden myself. Something I'd not thought of doing since my childhood when avoiding my father and, after his passing, had never thought I'd need to employ such a ruse ever again.

Nijad knows, the bastard, he can see right through me. He keeps making unhelpful suggestions that I should check up on the band. Luckily Cara and Zoe are both interested, and have kept us updated with the filming, so there's been no need for me to intervene. Still, Nijad keeps poking at me; he doesn't understand why I'm holding back when he realised how she affected me, sometimes I think he can read my mind. Similar in looks we might be, but there I like to believe any resemblance ends. He married an innocent, and has ended up extremely happy. Not in the least envious of my brother's good fortune, I try to get him to stop trying to push us together. What is his pleasure, would be a prison sentence to my mind.

It's on the eighth day he comes to find me.

"Brother." Nijad walks into my suite and pulls me in for a hug, kissing me on both cheeks. "It's feels right, you being here. Are you settled?"

Tossing a glare at him, I answer, "As well as I can in this mausoleum of a palace. Fuck, Ni. Don't you remember how fucking badly we wanted to get away?"

Throwing his headdress on to a chair, he goes to the sofa and sits, legs outstretched, his ankles crossed, arms stretched out wide over the back. He regards me for a moment, "You know I do. But I was forced to come back."

I take a seat opposite him on the other sofa. I'm only too well aware of the circumstances that brought him home. I'd been there. "Do you regret it?"

"How could I?" His eyebrows rise. "I'd never have found Cara. And, brother, believe me, meeting her meant the three years I was banished to the desert was worth it. And now we've got Zorah." His face softens as he refers to his daughter, "I never thought I could feel as at peace as I do now."

Peace. Was does that feel like, I wonder? I shrug. "That way of life isn't for me. I own a BDSM club for a reason."

"Just because you're a Dom doesn't mean you have to spread yourself around."

"You know my preference as to how I like to play, Ni. It's only in a kink club I can find a woman to match my tastes. And there's not many I go back to, and none with any strings attached."

He shakes his head, and his lips purse, "I feel sorry for you, Jas. But don't cut yourself off. Cara's a sub, you know that. But she's all I want and need. She's *my* sub."

"As Zoe is Kadar's," I agree. "But I'm different than you, Ni. You know what I'm like."

"That I do." His eyes darken for a moment. "We shared the apartment in Paris."

I feel my cheeks heating as I wonder whether he's remembering when he was arrested, and the police had found a cupboard containing my toys. He'd accepted ownership of them when questioned, leaving me thankful for that. Being accused of such a violent crime, it was the least of his concerns at the time.

We sit quietly for a moment. It's rare we're ever in the same place at the same time, and even rarer that we can take a break from our busy lives. We were so close at one time. Near enough in looks that people think us twins, even though there's eighteen months difference between us.

"So, the woman."

I look at him sharply, "What woman?"

"The guitarist. Janna. She's good you know, I've been watching her play. She's got a real presence about her. She commands the stage."

I nod, "I know. I've seen her in action." But not here. I've successfully managed to avoid that. And now he's gone and put that memory of her dressed as a Domme strutting her stuff on stage back into my mind. Just what I didn't need. "She's not a woman, she's a girl." I say, airily, hoping he'll get off the subject.

He sits forward, his hands on his knees, his head cocked a little to one side, "So are they all, Jasim, until you make them one."

I flick my eyes toward him, expecting to see amusement on his face, but he's completely serious, his dark eyes, identical to my own, staring at me intently. I bark a laugh, "For goodness sake, Ni. She's the same age as Aiza. What the fuck would you say if a thirty-three year old man was sniffing around our baby sister? By Allah, you don't even like Hunter anywhere near her."

To my surprise, he opens both his palms and holds them toward me, a gesture of nonchalance. "Aiza could do worse than Hunter. It's Kadar who's overprotective. He thinks she should still be playing with dolls."

"And so she should!" I exclaim, tutting. "She's barely out of nappies."

"She's a grown woman."

"She's a girl." We're back to that argument.

One side of his mouth turns up as he repeats, "By your definition, she's a woman."

My eyes open wide, "What the fuck? Hunter? I'll fucking kill him."

Ni gets to his feet, and turns to look straight at me. "No, you won't, Jas. She's been playing around for years. Why do you think she rarely comes home? She's a woman who's been educated in the west. And she takes up every opportunity that affords her. She's no innocent. Not anymore."

I run my hands through my hair, unable to process the information he's giving me. It seems impossible. My baby sister? Fuck! I lift my head, "Does Kadar know?"

Now Nijad laughs, "Of course he doesn't. He's blind to everything she does, unless it's living out the role he's got planned for her in his head."

And if he did know, he'd be furious and certainly want to kill anyone who'd dared to touch her. "I thought he had her lined up to marry Rami, son of Asad, King of Alair. To unite our countries. Rami won't want her if he knows…"

"Oh, brother, just listen to yourself." Nijad interrupts, "That was our father's plan, not Kadar's. And anyway, there seemed to be a spark between Sheikh Rami and Aiza at my wedding without any prompting. I wouldn't be surprised if that came off without any meddling from ourselves."

I shake my head, "He won't want her if she's not a virgin."

Nijad looks at me incredulously, then snorts. "Can you hear yourself, brother? You're giving values to Rami that you're dismissing yourself."

"I own a kink club!" I throw at him, "I need a woman who knows what she's getting herself into. Who understands my needs."

"Rami's a Dom. I've met him in clubs in Europe before now. And he's the same age as me."

"Fuck!" It's my turn to stand. I pace the room, trying to sort everything out in my head. If I'd known more of Rami's background, and that he's not even two years younger than me, would I still have wanted him as a husband for, what I'd naively assumed was, my virgin baby sister? Would I still have supported our family encouraging the relationship? Part of me says I would, and what does that make me? Someone with double standards and more akin to my father than I'd like to admit.

Picking up his headdress, Nijad prepares to leave. He takes a step toward the door, but then turns back, once again he gives me a piercing look, "I know you, Jasim, almost as well as I know myself. You're acting out of character. You like this woman, Janna, that's why you're avoiding her. And the way she looked at you that first day in the harem, a blind man could see she likes you too. That kind of recipe would have had you acting before, not running away as if your life depended on it."

"Yeah, but the recipe is all vanilla. And that's a flavour that doesn't appeal to me."

"You won't know for sure, unless you try a taste." He stares at me for one more moment, then, with his signature shrug, opens the door and leaves.

I sit back down, folding my arms over my chest. Since when had my younger brother grown the balls to challenge me? It used to be the other way around. Leaning my head back, my mouth turns up. Nijad's changed over the past few years, almost beyond all recognition. Four years ago, our relationship was smashed to smithereens, and I barely spoken to him up until a year ago, after I helped to clear his name. Those three years in the desert would have broken another man, but Nijad was pulled back from the brink by the woman who believed in him, the woman who became his wife. And what had I been doing in the intervening time? Working my way through most of the subs in London, and further afield. And I'm still not ready to be tied down, and doubt I'll ever be. I like that side of my life too much to give it up.

Whatever this strange draw to Janna is, it will disappear when I get home and back to the club. What's making it worse is that here, in my homeland, I'm restricted as to what I can do. As brother of the emir, my every move is scrutinised and examined. No, the only action I'm going to see until I return home will have to be a continued close relationship with my own hand. Just like how I indulged myself when I was a teenager. Nothing much changes here in the palace.

Janna, is most definitely out of bounds. She'd expect and deserve more than the one night stand I'd be able to give her. And it wouldn't be fair of me to indulge her sheikh fantasy, I'd be holding myself back. I'm not even sure I could do that. What is vanilla sex, anyway? Placing my hands on my knees, I try to remember. Have I ever had sex without any play? Fuck me, but I can't remember.

Another few days of a semi-peaceful existence pass, and then I'm thrust into her presence again. Though it's frustrated Kadar, I've stayed away from the harem and the filming that's going on, but he can't complain as I've been working hard at the job he brought me here to do. And when he asks, I just tell him, Anarchy Rules has everything under control, they've got my number should they need anything, and anyway, what do I know about making a film? Zilch. Bugger all.

Even Nijad, thankfully, stops trying to push me into the arms of a woman I'm trying to avoid. Any nefarious planning about finding me a mate seems to be given up as a failure. The day is fast approaching when they'll be able to make no more excuses and I'll be free to escape to the desert city, and put myself a few hundred miles distant from the woman who insists on appearing in my dreams. And fuelling the activities of my hand.

Then, the morning before I'm going to make my getaway, the phone rings. I answer with no feeling of dread, no precognition that, once again, my plans are going awry.

"Hello?"

"Good morning, Your Excellency. Sorry to disturb you, but it's Joe here, with the band."

"Good morning, Joe. What can I do for you? And call me Jasim, please."

"Thank you. Could you possibly meet us in the harem? We've something we want to run past you."

I glance at my watch, and mentally run through my schedule. It's not what I want to do, but my morning's fairly empty and while I could fabricate an excuse, I don't normally lie. "I can be there in an hour if that's any use?"

Having agreed that would be perfect, he ends the call. Hmm. Is it too much to hope that *she* won't be there? Probably.

Sixty minutes later, having tried to mentally prepare myself to see her again, I push open the large golden doors and step inside, my eyes widening at the transformation since I was last here. Lighting rigs have been set up all around, there's a stage area that's been erected, and cables running everywhere. The band members are grouped around a screen, animated and making comments, pointing and gesticulating, but obviously pleased with what they're watching.

I clear my throat to get their attention as I make my way across.

"Hey, Jasim. Thank you so much for joining us."

"No problem." I point to the screen where I can see, and hear, what I assume is the completed video playing. "Is it done?" I sincerely hope so. If it is, she'll be out of my life and I'll never have to see her again. Perhaps then I'll be able to get my life back on track.

And it's Janna who swings round, her face open and smiling, "Not quite, Jasim. We've had some ideas and need some help to move forward. You said we should come to you if we wanted anything."

Feeling my breathing quicken with just one look at her face, I ignore it, waving my hand in encouragement. "What do you need?" I address my question to all of them, not just to her.

Mickey steps forward. "We've completed what we need to do here. But we want to add some elements in, something authentic. We could use CGI, but…"

"It wouldn't be the same." The look Janna tosses him suggests they've already been over this.

"Okay," I start again, "What is it you want?"

Now it's Rory's turn. "Camel racing, horse racing. Something that has the sand of the desert flying up and robed men riding."

"Chasing a woman." Janna adds with a grin.

"And capturing her. Sweeping her up onto horseback." Liam finishes, his eyes glazing over as though he can see it happening in his mind.

I start to get a bad feeling. "And the woman would be…"

"Me," Janna states proudly.

Shit. I didn't need that image in my head, and the inevitable reaction of my body has me slighting widening my stance to hide it. I turn half away to give myself a chance to think. What they're asking isn't impossible, but only the desert sheikhs and their warriors ride like that. Could I ask them to come to Al Qur'ah? And transport the horses here? Or use the ones in the palace stables?

Rais. Rais would be up for it. And quite capable of literally sweeping a woman off her feet and into his arms. *But he's a widower. Her age might not bother him, her inno-*

cence a gift. No, on second thoughts Rais is a very bad idea.

"Your brother mentioned you were going to Z̧almā, and that the southern desert would be the place to get the best shots."

I sigh deeply, I might have known Nijad would have had his hand in this. And there I'd been thinking he'd given up. "I'm going to the desert to work, I'm afraid I won't have much time to set something like this up."

Joe looks disappointed, but isn't ready to give up. "Wouldn't you be able to at least make some introductions? We can take it from there."

They don't know what they're asking. They'll need interpreters, security. Health and safety isn't much cared about in the south, so someone will have to watch out for her… them, I hastily correct myself. But how can I refuse? Despite what I've said, my agenda's not written in stone, as Kadar and Nijad both know. Part of my visit is to be seen, for the tribespeople to know that the second Kassis brother hasn't totally deserted them. And as I think on that, I know Kadar will think that it's an excellent plan.

"We'll need to arrange transport. There's a lot of people to take."

"Oh, no, we're not all going," Mickey looks like he's telling me good news. "Only Janna and Sally. We don't need to do sound. We'll stay here to wrap up, and to start clearing all the stuff."

Fuck. I scratch my chin as I wonder how the hell I'm going to get out of this. Shaking my head doubtfully, I summon up the first excuse I can think of, "There's not room on the helicopter for both of you and your equipment.

"I won't take up much space," Now it's Sally who blasts my last excuse out of the water, "I've only got a handheld camera and tripod, that's all I'll need. We'll do all the editing back home."

Double fuck! I'd planned on flying myself, and it's a four seater. Who am I kidding? There'll be plenty of room. Kadar's tasked me with making sure Anarchy Rules have everything they need. Would that extend to arranging for them to film in the desert? Shit. Knowing him, it probably would.

"I leave tomorrow," I try one last approach, "If you've not finished here…"

"We've finished." Mickey speaks for them all. "While Janna and Sally have gone, we'll do the rest of the editing and with the other camera, do some other backdrop filming. We want some footage of the souk."

"And the sea." Rory butts in, Sunny's standing in front of him, her back to his chest. His head's resting on hers, and his mouth nuzzles her hair. It's a touching tableau, and a strange feeling comes over me, realising I've never had a relationship like that with a woman. What would it be like to have Janna in my arms? Not just for sex, but for comfort and company? That I've even asked myself the question reminds me again just how dangerous it would be to spend time with her.

"As I said before, I've got a strict timetable to adhere to when I get to Ẓalmā, I don't, I was just going to play it by ear, "I won't have time to do anything more than get in touch with one of the tribes and arrange a meeting for you."

Janna's eyes have narrowed. Somehow, she knows I'm lying. *Have I a tell I don't know about?* "That's fine," her answer's dismissive, "that's all we can ask."

Feeling I've been backed into a corner, I can't see any way out. I'd hoped to put hundreds of miles between us, and now I'm going to be forced into her company again. There's no point appealing to Kadar, and if he finds I've refused their quite reasonable request, I could expect a tongue lashing. Which I'd rightly deserve, being unable to offer a rational explanation. Backed into a corner, I say the only thing left to me. "We leave in the morning. Meet me at the helipad at ten o'clock.

CHAPTER 14
Janna

After agreeing on the time and place to rendezvous with him tomorrow, Jasim turns and goes to the large golden doors through which he'd entered, seeming to follow his usual practice of wanting to get away in a hurry.

Hmm. Something had told me he'd been lying, grasping at any excuse to put us off. Does he really dislike me so much that he wants to stay away from me? In the few times I've met him recently, he seems a totally different person to the one I'd met all those weeks ago. Then he was friendly, light-hearted, a far cry from the persona he presented first on the flight, and yet again today. He's gone so cold toward me. The man I've just spoken to would never have tended my wound, nor slept beside me in bed.

I might not have experience with a lover, but male companionship is almost all I've known over the last seven years of my life. And spending so much time around men, seeing them at their best and their worst, I can often read them like one of my books. If any of the band members were acting this way, I'd have it out with them and get to the bottom of what's going on, examining actions rather than words. Of course, his indifference hurts me. But that doesn't stop my body traitorously betraying my feelings whenever I'm around him. My pulse starts racing as soon as he appears, my legs feel weak, and my nipples push at my bra. Is he really so immune to me? I could be over-thinking it, but I do wonder whether he's fighting an attraction that he doesn't want to feel. Do his original objections still hold sway? Well, of course they do. He's given me no chance to eradicate them. I'm driving myself crazy not understanding his behavior. I want to rediscover the Jasim I first met.

As the doors clang shut behind, him I decide that I'd rather end up making a complete fool of myself than miss the chance to be with the only man who I've ever felt the least bit of interest in. Next time I won't let him run away. I'll try a direct approach. If he's battling with himself because of what I believe is a stupid hang up about the age difference between us, I'll make him understand that doesn't matter a damn to me. If confronting him doesn't work, then I'll just have to accept this dark brooding sheikh is out of my reach. But if I don't make a last ditch attempt to make him understand this is not an infatuation of a girl, but the very real sexual desire of a woman, I'll regret it forever. I doubt there are many men like him in the world, and by that, I mean someone who I'd find so appealing on every level.

Why, oh why, did I have to get hung up on such a complicated man? Or is that just par for the course when you're a woman?

Sunny's looking at me strangely, "You're fixated on him, aren't you?"

Looking around quickly, I make sure no one else has heard, and pull her over to a quieter part of the harem, "Is it so obvious?"

"That your tongue's hanging out whenever you see him?" She laughs. "I'd say so." Then, as she sees the concerned look I throw toward the band members still congregated around the screen, she adds, "Don't worry. Men are the last to be able to fathom a woman's emotions."

"Have you sorted out your own situation?" I try to switch attention from my predicament.

She looks down at her feet, "Yeah, well, I'm thinking about it." She glances over to the twins.

At least she's giving it some thought.

Placing my hand on her arm, I give her a squeeze. "You know I'm here if you want to talk about it?"

A nod, then she changes the subject, bringing it around to me again. "What are you going to do about your sheikh?"

"Confront him." I sound determined.

Nodding with approval, she gives me the confirmation I didn't know I was looking for, but am glad she offers. "I think you're right. He's holding himself back. How does the saying go? He who doth protest too much?"

I snigger. "Something like that. And if that's the case, somehow in the desert I'll get him to admit it."

She gives me a hug. "I wish I was going with you. I'd kick him in the butt for you. You're a gorgeous woman, Janna. It's time you got yourself a man. If it goes well, I'll be on your side getting them to come around." She nods over at the band, and then turns back, "Tell you what, if it doesn't work out, we'll go out on the town when we get home and I'll help you bag a decent one."

She makes it sound as though we can just pick a man up at a supermarket. I grin, and hug her in return. It feels good to have someone who's got my back.

"What you two gossiping about?" Sally wanders over to join us.

"Men."

"Can't live with 'em, can't live without 'em." She sounds so serious, both Sunny and I burst out laughing.

"You got anyone, Sal?" I probe.

"No. Never found the right one. Oh, I've put a few through their paces, but there was always something missing." She lowers her voice and adds conspiratorially. "One of these sheikhs would do for me."

She's not having mine.

We spend the next hour hilariously discussing the ups and downs of the opposite sex who drive us to distraction, but who we can't do without. Sally's a laugh and cracks me up with some of her observations. While the distraction helps keep Jasim to the of my mind, I remain convinced that I'm going to give it one last try, and this time be upfront about my feelings toward him.

At the appointed time the next day, Sally and I are ready and waiting, equipment and rucksacks by our side, standing in the shadow of the palace a short way from the helipad, keeping out of the direct heat of the sun.

Having spoken to Cara I'd found that, in the desert, the people are not so cosmopolitan as they are in Al Qur'ah, which calls for more conservative clothing. The sheikha couldn't have done more to help us, so now, together with a selection of modest western clothes, we've also got traditional Arab dress, some of which I'm wearing. A pretty pair of loose silk trousers known as shalwar kameez, and a thaub, or long tunic, in a lovely matching pale green with intricate embroidery. Cara also suggested a hijab, to keep the sun off my hair. The clothing is loose and comfortable, excellent for the temperatures here. Sally has decided to stay loyal to her western heritage, wearing light cotton trousers and a long-sleeved tee complete with a wide brimmed hat.

Punctual, as I expect, Jasim doesn't keep us waiting, and my mouth drops open when he appears. Gone is the civilized man in a well-tailored suit, in his place is an imposing native of Amahad, wearing gleaming white robes and a headdress secured by a black agal. The snow coloured thobe and keffiyeh enriching his olive skin. He looks different; wild and untamed, mysterious, charismatic, and alluring.

If I was tempted by the man before, I'm completely enthralled by him now. Divested of his cultured trappings, he has the appearance of a man who would take any woman he desired and make her his own. Whatever her initial protest, he'd soon overcome her objections and have her begging for more. A shiver runs down my spine, my nipples predictably start to harden, and my clit begins to throb. Licking my lips, I find I've been staring at him.

So intent on drinking him in, I almost missed the flare in his eyes when he sees me in the dress of his country. But I don't fail to spot the speed with which he turns away and with just a gruff lift of his chin indicates the helicopter. He strides toward it, not having made any attempt at verbal greeting.

"Christ, Janna. He really doesn't want us along for the ride, does he?" His impoliteness hasn't skipped Sally's attention.

"Well, we're getting what we want." I mean the opportunity to film in the desert, as any chance I could have of getting what I really desire starts to fade into the distance. I'm starting to think any approach I could make will just be a waste of time. "Let's just go along with it, shall we? I'm excited to see the desert city. There's another palace there, you know?" His boorish behavior has done nothing to dampen my arousal. Trying to have a normal conversation with my nether parts pulsing is not particularly easy, but I try nonetheless. "Perhaps you can get another backdrop there?"

"Good point." Sally starts talking about using natural daylight, filming at dusk to get the setting sun and all the technicalities that go along with that. In other words, not a lot to hold my interest, or capture it from the man who's taken the pilot's seat.

A guard opens the rear door for us, and we get into seats. Jasim at last gives us some attention, passing over two sets of headphones, and telling us how to use them.

His brother appears, and stands by the pilot's door. He nods at Jasim's clothing.

"Don't say one word, brother," Jasim warns him.

"Wouldn't fucking dare," Nijad replies, as Jasim flicks some switches, his concentration turning to the craft he's about to get into the air. "You remember what you're doing? It's been a long time since you've flown."

Oh, shit. I'd been so caught up in the man, I'd forgotten I've never been in a helicopter before. I certainly hope he knows how to fly. As Sally and I cast nervous glances at each other, Jasim barks a laugh, "Of course, I do, Ni. Now fuck off and let me get out of here."

"Got this for you." Nijad chucks a package onto the passenger seat of the helicopter.

Distracted by working the controls, Jasim simply nods in acknowledgement.

"Let me know if you need anything. I can fly down. Feel free to use the royal suite and make use of *all* the accommodations."

Now Jasim turns sharply and glares at his brother. "I'll be fine, Ni. Now get lost."

I suppress a smile at the easy relationship the brothers have, and then have no time to do anything as the rotors start to turn and we lift into the air. Now I have to concentrate on trying to keep my stomach in place, and prevent bile from rising. It's a peculiar lurching sensation I've never experienced before.

A quick glance toward Sally and I see her face beaming, "I love helicopters." She speaks into the mic, allowing me to hear her through the headphones.

I reach for her hand, feeling uncertain, "Complete virgin here," I confide, to explain my nerves.

When I hear a loud strangled snort, I realise Jasim's overhearing everything we're saying and as blood rushes to my cheeks, I know it perhaps wasn't the tactful way to describe that this is my first flight. Sally's oblivious to my unintentional double entendre, and starts chatting excitedly, pointing out the landscape below. Luckily, she's an easy companion, happy to talk and content with mumbled exclamations, which I seem to be putting in the right places, leaving me free to contemplate the man behind the controls. Yesterday's conversation with Sunny and Sally in the harem had allowed me to get to know her better, and today I'm quite happy to class her as someone who could become a good friend.

Conversely, Jasim is a poor companion, he doesn't join in the conversation at all. When he speaks, it's in Arabic and he's obviously in contact with ground control or whatever the equivalent is here. Being all but ignored isn't something I'm used to, and it starts to annoy me. As the two-hour journey continues, annoyance turns to anger. By the time the helicopter starts losing altitude, I'm seething. This rude, obnoxious, and closed-off man is not the person who'd taken such care of me back in London. What the hell has got into him?

It makes me only more determined to find out.

When the helicopter lands, Jasim steps down. He starts to walk away, then at last remembering his manners, turns back and offers his hand to help us both out. For me it's just a casual touch, dropping his hold as soon as my feet touch the ground. Then he beckons a woman forward.

"This is Lamis. Please, go with her and she will show you where you'll be staying. I will leave you now. I will attempt to make the arrangements you've asked for, and will contact you when I have done so." His formal clipped tones make me glare at his retreating back.

Lamis greets us with a wide smile and dip of her head, "Ladies, welcome. I am personal maid to Sheikha Cara. The sheikha wishes you to have comfort. Please to come with me."

Sally thanks her, her eyes gleaming with excitement as she views the admittedly romantic looking palace we've arrived at. Picking up her rucksack she hoists it over one shoulder, and her camera bag over the other, and sets off to follow the woman.

I start to do likewise, but then falter. "Sally," I start in a whisper, "Go ahead and get settled, I'll come and find you soon."

She looks around, "What? You're not coming?"

"Go." I give her a little push. "There's something I want to do."

After giving me a strange look, with a shrug, she offers to carry my bag as well, and starts following Lamis, while I pick up a run and chase after the robed man.

Jasim's just entering the palace when I catch up with him. His long strides are taking him further away, so to get his attention I put my hand out and touch his arm. Swinging around as though ready to defend himself, he pulls back when he sees it's just me.

"Miss Stevens," his eyes narrow, "What are you doing?" He sounds haughty.

Why the hell isn't he using my first name? His formality rekindles my anger. My fingers tighten against his sleeve, "I want to talk to you." I'm hoping my tone conveys I'm giving him no choice.

He looks down at me, in my flats he's over a head taller, "I don't believe there's anything we need to discuss. I informed you I'd help by facilitating what you have asked for. I believe I'm quite clear on your requirements."

And I don't think you've got any idea what I need.

I'm staring into his face and see that flicker in his eyes which always gives him away, and the darkening of his olive-skinned cheeks. *He's not disinterested in me.* I know that look. I've seen it before, many times. But previously only on the faces of men whom I had no reciprocal feelings for. This time it's different. It makes me more determined to fight and make him listen to me. He's drawn to me, but he's running away.

"I believe we do have something to talk about," I state firmly, my hand still gripping his arm, unwilling to let him escape. "Give me five minutes, please, Jasim."

His palm covers my fingers, gently applying pressure until I open them. Once he's set himself free, his feet shift, and at first my heart drops, as I think he's going to continue to walk away. Then, abruptly, he seems to come to a decision, and lets out his breath on an exasperated sigh. "Come then. Five minutes. Follow me." His robes billow around him as he leads the way into the palace, leaving me to trail behind him.

I spend no time admiring my surroundings, just blindly try and stick with him so I don't get lost in this large palace, struggling to keep up with his longer strides, thinking I'll need a map or a guide to find my way back. As last he walks down a smaller hallway, and opens the door to what appears to be a private sitting room that's not furnished formally, but for comfort. He waves me to a chair, I remain standing.

He cocks a brow toward me, "Well?" As I take a second to summon my thoughts, he prompts me again, "You've got my attention. What is it you want to talk about? I'm a busy man, Miss Stevens. I can't spare you much time."

He looks intimidating, and again there's that use of my surname. Once more it makes me see red, and possibly more direct that I'd otherwise be. Taking in a breath, I almost spit the words, "You're avoiding me, Jasim."

An imperious look, "Am I? I thought I'd arranged for Anarchy Rules to film in the harem as I agreed. And brought you here to the desert, to complete your project, just as you requested. I don't see there's any more I can do."

Waving my hands dismissively, I agree, knowing he's purposefully misunderstanding me. "You did. But I'm talking about me, not the rest of the band."

"I'm afraid I'm a busy man, Miss Stevens. I really don't have time to make small talk."

My hands bunch at my sides, and while I've never believed I'm a violent person, in truth I feel like hitting him. He's being so arrogant, but there's something else going on, I'm certain of it. "What is it with the formality? I thought we were friends."

He opens his mouth, then shuts it. Then gives a shake of his head, "Then you thought wrong. I was happy to help you when you were hurt. And there's mutual benefit to be gained by allowing Anarchy Rules to film in Amahad. My part is now played. There's nothing more between you and I."

But his eyes flick sideward. *He's lying.*

I take a step closer, he takes a step back. His face is flushed, his breathing appears laboured, and he doesn't seem to know what to do with his hands. At last he folds his arms over his chest, as though cutting himself off from me.

I decide to go for broke. "You want me, Jasim. And," I swallow, admitting something I've never had to confess before, "And I want you. I'm here for the taking. I'm offering myself to you. Why don't you take the opportunity?"

I've stunned him. My outright confession, without any sugar coating, comes as a complete surprise. He unfolds his arms, stretching them out straight as though to ward me off. I move closer, catching a waft of the soap he must use, and underneath that, the smell of a man. It's a heady mix, affecting me so deeply it boosts my confidence.

"I don't know what game you're playing." He's recovering quickly.

"I'm not playing a game."

And now it's his turn to move forward, his hands reaching out to grip my arms. "Oh yes, you are, little girl. You're playing with fire." He pushes me, forcing me backward until my back is up against a wall.

"I'm not a girl, I'm a woman," I spit at him. There's that age thing again.

One side of his mouth turns up, "Oh no you're not, not yet."

Oh, he's talking about his other objection. There's a simple answer, "So make me one," I challenge.

Flecks of gold flare in his dark eyes, and for a moment I think I have him, but then he releases me and turns his back, "I can't do that."

"Why the fuck not?" My rage is returning. "What's stopping you, Jasim?"

CHAPTER 15
Jasim

What's stopping me, she's asked? At this moment very little, I'm holding onto my control by a thread. One more push and she'll have me over the edge. My cock's pulsating, my balls throbbing with need. The woman I want is right here in front of me, begging me for what I'd give anything to be able to grant her. I can't even look at her now, my limit has been reached.

"You're eleven years younger than me."

"Age doesn't matter."

I swear under my breath. Is she going to come back with an answer for everything? "You're a *virgin*."

"What's that got to do with it? There's got to be a first time…"

"And your first time should mean something."

"Who says it won't?"

Now I swing back around, my hands fluttering to emphasise my point, "I'm not the man for a happily ever after. I don't even do relationships, Janna. If I took you it might just be the once."

She shrugs, "So?"

"So?" My hands rip of my headdress, my robes, worn as a mark of respect to the people of the desert, are annoying me now. Putting them on today seemed to heat the blood in my veins, to remind me of my history and my heritage. And the centuries in which men of my kind stole women to rape and pillage, to keep as our own. Right now, I'm feeling less like a civilised ambassador for my country, and more akin to an untamed warrior of the east. "So," I force myself back to the present, "You should save yourself for someone who wants to give you the world. Who'll worship at your feet."

"I never took you for a romantic."

She's not listening. I need to make it plain. "You know fuck all about me." Once again, I advance on her, my hands taking hers and holding them over her head. My body presses up close against her, at this moment I don't care that the evidence of my attraction is pushing against her stomach, leaving her in no doubt the spark she feels is mutual.

"I've a sister your age," I start, but then, remembering Nijad's revelations, conclude perhaps defending her innocence on that comparison no longer holds merit. "You're too young for me, Janna. And your innocence chills me." There, I've admitted it.

She shrugs, "I'll go find someone to fuck, and then after I've got that out of the way, and I'm no longer a virgin, then you'll want me?" There's a sneer on her face, so I know she's just thrown that out there to wind me up.

But it hits the mark, a primitive rage makes me growl, "You won't be doing that."

"You're saying I can't have sex with you, but neither can I have it with anyone else? That doesn't seem fair." She pouts, and sucks her bottom lip into her mouth, biting down on it.

Allah give me strength. Just that sight makes me grind my hard cock against her. "I'm an owner of a BDSM club, sweetheart. Do you even know what that is?"

She tests the strength of the hold I have on her, but can't pull away from my grip, "Of course I bloody know."

"You've watched that film, or read that book." Everyone has, and a fuck lot of good that did for my lifestyle. Equating play with abuse.

"And others. It intrigued me, I read more."

And just what did she think?

I press harder against her, "It's not a pastime for me, sweetheart, it's the way I live my life. I'm a Dom."

"And I'm submissive."

She knows? Oh, fuck me. She's handing herself to me on a plate.

It's getting harder and harder to refuse. How the fuck do I make her understand? "If I'm the one to take your virginity, I'm going to hurt you."

As much as she can when I've got her so trapped, she gives another shrug, "It might not. Sometimes it's painful, I know, but…"

"Oh, I can make it hurt." It's my turn to sneer.

Her gaze falters, and she looks away before looking back, "I don't think you'd hurt me."

"You don't know who or what I am. You can't even imagine in your wildest dreams." I tell her exactly what I am. "I'm a sexual sadist." I pause to let that sink in before adding, "Nijad's got a dungeon here, I installed it for him myself. I could take you there now, have you under my whip, do all manner of things to you that *I* would enjoy." The tone of my voice suggests she probably wouldn't. Though, it's highly unlikely I'd be able to carry out my threat, it would break the Dom inside me. I only play with those who like the bite of pain, not those who are innocent and have no idea what they're letting themselves in for. Abruptly releasing her hands, I step away, moving across to the windows and looking out. After giving her a moment to let my words sink in, and the necessary time to compose herself after my revelation, I speak again. "I'll get someone to show you to your room."

But she's full of surprises, "How do you know I wouldn't like those things you want to do to me?"

"Believe me, I know."

"You have no idea." I hear her footsteps on the tiled floor, "If you showed me, I might enjoy it."

"And if I want to spank you? To clamp your nipples? To take you in the arse?" I'm being crude on purpose, she's got to know what she's asking for. "To have you under my whip? To put my mark on you?"

She's so close now, I can feel her breath on my neck, "Your words are turning me on, Jasim. I want to try all of that."

By Allah! This can't be happening. How much can a man take? It would be out of the realm of all possibility to hope she'd enjoy the same proclivities as me. She doesn't know what she's speaking of, what she's suggesting she'd let me do. I didn't think my cock could get any harder, but it grows engorged with more blood at the thought of her fair skin being marked by my hand. Could it be possible? Or is she just intrigued by a sheikh, seduced by my robes, agreeing to anything just to get into my bed?

"I'm not for the likes of you, Janna." If she only knew how difficult she is making it for me to turn her away. "Leave, now. Please." *Leave before I lose what little sanity I'm hanging onto.*

I hear a rustling sound behind me, and hope it's her walking to the door. Carefully schooling my features so I don't betray how much the thought of taking her the way I want to take her excites me, I turn back around.

Oh fuck. She's taken off her tunic and trousers, and is standing in her underwear, her arms held out to her sides. Once she sees me looking, she tilts her head to one side, a small seductive smile on her lips, "Take me, Jasim."

"Get dressed," I growl.

Her mouth drops open, a red flush spreads from her face down her body.

"Clothes on, now." I can't form proper sentences, the sight of her, open and vulnerable has demolished all my restraint. *I'm lost.*

She waits for a few seconds, but I don't speak again. Awkwardly, she reaches down and collects her clothes, modestly turning her back to me while she puts them on. Once she's covered her nakedness, I let out a sigh of relief.

Her hands flutter when she once again faces me, and her voice sounds so small it cuts me to the quick, "If you can get someone…" she angrily swipes at a tear that's fallen down her cheek.

"Come here."

"What?"

"Come. Here." She takes a step toward me. And then another. Once she's within reach I thrust my hand into her luscious hair, today left loose and hanging down her back, tangling it around my fingers, using it to tug her into me. With my other hand I grasp her waist, pulling her tight into my body. And then I let myself go.

My mouth crashes down on hers, weeks of pent up frustration making it impossible for me to be gentle. When she doesn't let me in immediately, I bite down on her lip, taking advantage when she gasps and opens, allowing me entry. My tongue invades her, making my cock jerk in envy, and as I get my first taste, I need to make a determined effort not to thrust my hips against her, else I'll come in my pants like a teenager. She lets me lead, following where I take her, our teeth gnashing together and I just can't get enough. We might only be touching with our mouths, but this is some of the most erotic foreplay that I've ever experienced. Her unique taste enthrals me.

I control her completely, and she allows me to take charge, instinctively giving me what I need. My nostrils flare as I inhale her scent, her little sighs are the most arousing sounds I've ever heard.

Desperate to touch her, my fingers bunch the material at her waist, moving it up and out of the way until I'm touching the bare skin of her back. I can't resist sliding my hand downwards, into her underwear, feeling the smooth surface of the orbs of her arse. Fuck, she's absolutely perfect.

She moans, and I need to pull away and take a breath, the sound vibrates through me and will trigger a release if I don't get put some space between us. Reluctantly, I let go of her hair, remove my hand from her pants, and then smooth both my palms down the side of her face.

Her eyes are closed, her face is flushed, her breathing, like mine, coming in pants. Her mouth is still open, lips reddened from my abuse. And it's then, I know, I haven't the strength to run anymore.

"One last chance, Janna. I don't do relationships. I play, I fuck. I leave. I can offer you one night. And that's all."

"I'm not looking for a happily ever after. I just want you. To know what it's like." She's got an answer for everything. And she's saying the words I want to hear.

I've told her. I've warned her. "Then you're going to get what you're after. There'll be no going back."

Her eyes open, and there's a catch in her voice. "Are you going to get it out of the way, now?"

"It?" My brow creases.

"My virginity," she puffs out her breathless explanation.

"Fuck no, I'm not Christian Grey." And it's her turn to look puzzled, so I expand, "The gift of your virginity is the greatest you can bestow on a man, and I'm not going to take it lightly. The time is not now, and the place is not here. No, I'm not going to *get it out of the way*."

"Are you turning me down?" Now she sounds younger, the confident woman being replaced by the girl.

I brush back some hair which has fallen over her face, smoothing it behind her ear. "No. I'm done turning you down. For better or worse, and whatever regrets might come later, you've caught me." I force myself to think with the right head. "Janna, I'm going to give you some space. Time we both need. An opportunity for you to really consider what you're agreeing to here." I take a deep breath, "I'm a sexual sadist, Janna. That's who I am. Underneath the trappings of civility, I'm a monster." My hand reaches out and touches the soft skin around her eyes, "I'll want your tears, and your fears. I'll push you to your limits and then beyond."

Instead of disgust, trust is beaming out at me.

"Go Janna, think on it. And we'll take it from there. Come back with any questions you might have." It's killing me to turn her away, but I'd be wrong to push her now. My dick is not in agreement, wanting just to sink into her soft depths. I might be cockblocking him, but I'll take what I can. Leaning forward, I brush my mouth against her soft lips, a gentle caress.

Now her eyes narrow. "Isn't this just you pushing me away again?"

I shake my head. "No pushing, no more running. I'll be here," I promise her. "But this is a grown-up thing your stepping into, Janna. I want you to go into it with your eyes open. Once you give your body to me, there'll be no turning back."

"Will I have a safeword?"

So at least she knows as much as that. Again, I smooth my hands down her face, "As your Dom I'll push your limits, I'll read your body's reactions. But Janna," I pause, not knowing if she'll understand, "if you can't take what I want to give you, we'll both be disappointed. I'm not saying you should never safeword out, it would be wrong to do that…"

"But I shouldn't do it too early." She *does* understand. At least on some level. "But I won't know unless I try."

And there's much truth in that.

I put my hand on the small of her back, and electricity snaps through me, going straight to my dick. If I don't get her out of here soon, I'll be ravishing her on the nearest flat surface, despite my best intentions.

"Sweetheart. You need to leave, now. I'm not trying to get rid of you, I truly have another meeting." Ryan will be waiting for me in Nijad's office, which he's kindly letting me use.

"But we are going to finish this?"

"Finish?" I raise my eyebrows, "Sweetheart, I'm intent on planning where to start." I give her a little push toward the door. "Trust me."

Her eyes gaze up into mine, and must see the sincerity there. She's won. I'm going nowhere now I've admitted defeat. After a moment, she gives a little nod, and then walks, albeit reluctantly, to the door.

The air is tinged with her arousal, and the faltering of her steps shows it's every bit as hard for her to leave, as it is for me to see her walk away.

The moment she's gone, I adjust myself in my robes, grateful that the traditional clothing hides a multitude of sins. And, in this case, my extremely sinful thoughts. A niggling doubt at the back of my mind reminds me I intend to corrupt her, this innocent woman who's never even known a man's touch before. And soon my desire to get down and very dirty with her is going to be fulfilled. I've lost all compulsion to push her away. A better man might do so, but I've never pretended to be one.

Having brought myself under control, well, as far as a sheikh with thoughts of defiling an innocent can, I proceed to the office allocated to me.

The Desert Palace has a different feel to the Palace of Amahad, Nijad's modernisations mean staff who meet me along the way greet me with a simple '*Yawm jayid*', wishing me a good day, instead of bowing themselves almost in half as I approach. The atmosphere is light, helped by the brightness within the palace, sunlight streaming in through the windows. While I find the atmosphere in the palace in

Al Qur'ah oppressive, here it feels like a weight has been lifted from my shoulders.

Or is it an easing of mind that I, at last, have decided no longer to fight with myself. To give into temptation.

Trying to put Janna and my developing plans for her out of my mind, on reaching the office I open the door and step inside, not surprised to see my allocated close protection officer already waiting for me.

"Ryan," stepping forward I shake his hand, and pull him in for a brief hug. "It's good to see you."

"And you, Jasim."

I indicate a seat to him by the table where refreshment has already been set up, and then sit myself opposite, taking a second to admire the colourful gardens outside the window. Getting flowers to bloom in the desert is a major endeavour, and even now I see gardeners constantly working. But here the gardens are treasured by the residents of Zalmā, and are open to all, and not just restricted for the pleasure of the Sheikh of the Southern Desert, that position currently held by my brother, Nijad.

I fill my cup with thick and sweet coffee, and offer the pot to Ryan who shakes his head.

"Sorry, Jasim, I've never developed a taste for it."

"I know what you mean, I've been living in the West for too long. I do enjoy it, but the longer I'm here, I remember my fondness for latte." I pick up the cup, take a sip, grimace, then get down to business. "So, what's your opinion? You've been to the oil field?"

Ryan nods and sits forward, his hands clasped between his knees, "There have been no terrorist attacks since Amir al-Fahri's last attempt, and security has been stepped up. The tribes are eager to protect their investment, so there are warriors from the tribes bolstering military presence."

"And the pipeline?" Ryan's initially spoken about the operation to drill for oil in the desert, but that's only the start of it. Once we extract the liquid gold, we've got to transport it to the coast. And that means several hundred miles of pipe to be laid under the sands.

"That's more difficult. As each section is finished, it needs to be maintained and protected. They're doing what they can with men patrolling the length, and remote monitoring of course, but of course, it will always be a weakness."

"What's your proposal?" I take another sip, it doesn't taste much better than the first.

His hands loosen, and he sits back, "You've worked remotely, haven't you, Jasim? Have you an interest in seeing the operation on the ground?"

Kadar had called me back so I could make myself visible, show the tribespeople while I might live in London, I've got their best interests at heart. And to convince our investors of the considerable amount of oil we'll be able to extract from below the sand. Now I'm here, I discover I'm eager to see what I've only read about from afar. I've no hesitation in answering him, "Yes, I want to see the oil-field, and perhaps visit the latest section of the pipeline."

As my bodyguard, Ryan's one aim is keeping me safe. He nods slowly, "From what I've seen while I've been here, I don't think there's any risk in you letting yourself be seen. But I'll take every precaution, of course. I'm working with Nijad's security, and with Hunter. The team from Grade A are thick on the ground." Grade A have provided specialists to help protect the oil fields, monitoring possible threats and liaising with the locals.

"I want to get up close and talk to the workers." I fix my eyes on him.

He shrugs, "Of course. I'll work out a schedule for you."

I can leave that to him. "And, the other matter?" The thing I've been thinking about since my meeting with Janna.

He cracks a rare smile, "Yeah, since your phone call last night, I've managed to put something together. You still want it done fast?"

I'd wanted it completed quickly to get Janna out of my hair. Now, my reasons might have changed, but it's even more imperative there's no delay. "Yes, as soon as possible."

"I've spoken to Rais, he's up for it. His tribe are intrigued, and ready to play their part. Sheikh Fadi's based close to the palace and wants in as well."

"Can they do it?"

Another shrug, "Child's play, apparently. A few of them are up to take lead, but I think Rais might want to play that part himself. He sees himself in the starring role."

I suppress a growl; no fucking way is Rais getting near my woman.

When Ryan leaves me alone, my eyes alight on something. The package Nijad had strangely thrown into the helicopter had been brought in and placed on my desk. Curious as to what he'd sent with me, I tear it open.

Had I opened it earlier I would have been furious. Now though I throw back my head and laugh.

CHAPTER 16
Janna

Wow. Just wow. My head's spinning as I walk away from Jasim. How he'd been summoned I'm not too sure, but a security guard is waiting for me outside, and explains in quite good English that he'll take me to my accommodation. Gratefully following him through the ornate corridors of the palace, I reflect I hadn't much expectation of the outcome when I'd challenged Jasim, but I had never dreamed it might go the way that it had.

If I can believe him, he's planning to take my virginity, and then initiate me into the way he likes to have sex. While my first thought is only of pleasure, there are a few doubts niggling at the back of my mind as to what exactly I've signed on for and whether I'll be enough for him. I've read, a lot. And there's no denying what's always turned me on is a woman giving herself over a man's care, letting him take her to her limits. And that Jasim is quite clearly prepared to do. And perhaps beyond. *What exactly is he intending?* A shiver of anticipation runs through me, the slight tinge of accompanying fear sending a feeling of arousal heading south. *Whatever it is, the thought of him taking charge is turning me on.* Not that I've really been turned off since first meeting Jasim.

When the guard stops in front of a door, indicating we've reached our destination, I thank him distractedly, and walk inside. It seems Sally and I have been given a luxurious suite; a central sitting room, with bedrooms off to either side. Sally is sitting at a table, helping herself to food from a buffet which has obviously recently been delivered.

She looks up when I enter, and hastily swallows her mouthful of food. "Hey, how did you get on? Did you catch up with your sheikh? I know that's what you were running off to do." She smiles knowingly.

As I'm having difficulty processing what occurred myself, I don't feel like rehashing the conversation with her. My answer is friendly enough, but concise and dismissive, "Yes, I did. We cleared the air."

Cleared the air? Set it on fire more like.

It seems my answer's sufficient for her, she resumes stuffing her mouth with what appears to be delicious looking food, "Mmm. Come try this. It's fantastic."

My appetite for food seems to have diminished in proportion to my desire for Jasim, which has ramped up to an almost unbearable level. *What's he planning? And when? How long will I have to wait?* He said losing my virginity should be special. *Just how is he going to go about it?*

To attempt to be sociable, I go and sit with her, and despite my lack of hunger, take a pastry and place it on a plate. My fingers toy with it for a moment.

"Did the sheikh say anything about when we'll be able to start filming?"

"No, we didn't discuss anything like that." The reason behind us coming here had been the last thing on my mind.

"It's great, isn't it? Exotic. I wonder if they'll be able to make it play out the way we had planned."

Shaking my head, I respond honestly, "I don't know, but no one has said it won't work."

"Hmm, desert sheikhs and tribesmen on their horses." Sally licks her lips, but whether to clean up after eating her food, or if her mouth's watering at the romantic thought, I can't be sure.

We hear nothing further that evening. A guard comes to offer us a tour of the grounds, and then we eat dinner in a small dining room all by ourselves. When I retire to bed, it's hard to stop my thoughts racing.

When morning comes, I'm still weary, having had little sleep.

Breakfast is delivered, and while we're still eating, a knock sounds on the door. I go to open it, and find the English bodyguard who I remember had been there to meet Jasim off the plane.

"Hi, I'm Ryan. I'm a Close Protection Officer. Jasim's bodyguard."

Nodding to show I'd recognized know who he was, I step aside to allow him to come in. His eyes flick to Sally, and he gives her an appreciative nod. She preens in response. Hmm.

"The scene you want filmed," he starts, his voice deep and low, "it's been set up for later today. Sheikh Rais, the leader of the desert sheikhs, has agreed it can be staged near one of his encampments." He dips his head toward Sally. "You wanted it at sunset, I believe? To get the best light?"

Her eyes light up. "I want the sun setting over sand dunes. Are there any there?"

Ryan chuckles. "More than you can shake a stick at."

She's fidgeting, as if already excited. "I'd like some time to choose the right spot. Perhaps do a practice shoot?"

"Hey," I butt in, "I'm the one who'll be running my butt off in this heat. I only want one take."

"Spoilsport." She pouts, flicking her long blond hair over her shoulder, but then she grins, "Just get me some time to set up the camera. I'll need to know exactly where to position it to get the best shot."

Ryan's taking it all in. "It's all in hand. You'll be leaving at midday. It's a couple of hours Jeep ride from here. There'll be plenty of time to get organized. Rais's men will be on hand to give you advice." He turns to me. "Lamis, who you met yesterday? She's Cara's maid when she's in residence here. She's going to bring along a selection of clothes."

"I brought something with me that would be suitable." I'm not sure why I'd need more.

With a slightly cagey look, as though he knows something I don't, Ryan shakes his head. "Yeah, but you want to look authentic, don't you?"

I give a little shake of my head. "Okay." I agree, maybe Lamis will come up with something I haven't thought of wearing. It couldn't hurt to see what's on offer.

But though we wait all morning, Lamis doesn't appear. Gathering up some fresh shalwar kameez and thaub, I go and dress in the light trousers and tunic that I'd originally planned to wear, and make myself ready for the journey. Surprisingly, Sally dresses the same, the light blue she's chosen complimenting her fair complexion. Before she puts on a hijab, she ties her long hair into a bun.

When I grin at her, she looks at me and shrugs, "When you're in the desert, look the part."

The guard comes to collect us, and yet again leads us through the winding maze of corridors and out to the front of the palace. I take a moment to admire the façade, it's an incredible building. Ryan approaches, and sees my looks of veneration.

"Some parts are over a thousand years old," he tells me. "It's an impressive sight, isn't it?"

It certainly is, and so much history here. "Is there a harem here too?" I wonder out loud, and am surprised when Ryan gives a belly laugh.

"There certainly is," he replies, the words stammered out through his chuckles.

I feel my face flush, his amusement making me wonder whether it's that part of the palace that's been converted into a dungeon.

And then every other thought flees my mind as my sheikh appears, his robes billowing around him in the hot desert breeze. Immediately, I squeeze my legs together in a vain attempt to ease the ache there.

He spares me a nod, and his lips curl a little, but though he's acknowledged me, he doesn't come over. A parade of Jeeps turns up, as if summoned by an invisible signal. Ryan goes to join Jasim in the first, Sally and I are directed to the second.

There's no road to follow, as we weave our way over the sand. Our driver speaks decent English, and as he makes yet another turn on what I only see as unbroken terrain, he explains he's avoiding patches of quick sand.

"How do you even know where to go?"

When he points to the GPS I feel stupid, and disappointed, expecting him to tell me it's his innate instinct and mystical knowledge of the desert. But then feel somewhat vindicated, when he explains, "Quick sand isn't marked, but I know what I'm looking for. See?" I follow where he's pointing, but can't see anything different in the ground. "There's a patch of quick sand there."

Suppressing a shudder, I'm glad it's him driving.

We pass a herd of gazelle, see vultures hovering in the air, but there's not much variety in the scenery except for dune after dune. There's so much sand beneath us, broken only for a fleeting period where the ground becomes hard packed and rocky. The purr of the engine and my lack of sleep the night before, makes me doze off. I'm woken when the Jeep comes to a halt, and it appears we've arrived.

The driver opens our door. As I step down onto the baking sand, I see Jasim's already out of the vehicle in front, and is walking forward to meet one of the fiercest looking men I have ever seen in my life. He's even taller than Jasim. Sally and I look at each other, and exchange nervous smiles.

Jasim and the stranger approach us.

"Sally, Janna. This is Sheikh Rais, leader of the desert sheikhs."

I can see why, no one would want take him on to challenge him for the title. But the big man's face softens when he gives us a genuine smile, "Welcome to my desert home."

He takes our hands in turn, bowing over and placing a kiss on the back, his rough exterior seeming to hide an amorous side beneath.

Jasim shoos him away from me, putting himself almost protectively between us.

Rais raises an eyebrow, and gives a smirk, then his arm gestures with a flourish behind him. "Come, take some refreshment, and then we'll go out to the site I believe will suit your needs."

My attention is drawn to what appears to be a large tent standing slightly apart from about twenty or thirty others which together make up a small settlement surrounding an oasis. The sight of the palm trees giving a welcome flash of green. Noting the ill-concealed curiosity of the tribespeople, and acknowledging them with a smile, I follow Sally and the men and enter the big black tent, immediately seeing it's set up for meetings with a dais at the back. Now, however, there's a low table with cushions around it, and fruit drinks in jugs with various snacks set out around.

While we eat and drink, Sally quickly overcomes her apprehension of the ferocious looking sheikh, and starts asking him questions.

"Is this all your tribe?"

Quickly he shakes his head, "This is one of our bases. Many of the Hami, my tribe, are nomadic."

"And horses? We asked for horses?" her mouth turns down as she realizes what's missing.

Rais laughs, "They'll be here shortly. Do not worry about that."

The sheikh seems happy to answer when she gets back onto the theme of how they eke a meagre living from the barren looking land, and my interest perks when she starts asking about schools and medical care.

"The money from the oil will help provide mobile teachers and doctors," Rais tells her enthusiastically, pointing to Jasim, "And that's down to you, Sheikh, to make sure that goes smoothly."

I hadn't realized what Jasim did for a living, so listen intently as he updates Rais as to where he is in negotiations with OPEC. Wow, I knew he was a diplomatic, and an owner of a BDSM club, but I hadn't appreciated he also was responsible for the country's oil industry.

Our discussion is interrupted when we hear more vehicles arriving, and voices shouting outside. Rais indicates we should finish our drinks—some delicious fruit concoction— and follow him. We step outside into the heat to find men are already busy unloading horse boxes; there must be thirty animals in all. A makeshift corral is hastily assembled, and the animals herded into it. Rais explains they're accustomed to moving horses around, as tribes often race against each other.

"I hear your champion got beaten. At Kadar's wedding?" Jasim nudges his friend, who quickly spins around.

"Fucking biker from Arizona," he snarls. And then as quickly grins, "Never thought I would see anything like that. Left a bad taste in the mouth."

Not understanding what they're talking about, I watch the men sorting out the horses, admiring their efficiency in doing so. Suddenly it hits, me all these large beasts are going to be chasing after me. Hmm, I hope they know what they're doing. I swallow rapidly at the thought of them running me down. *I hope they've got good brakes.*

A woman appears from behind one of the other Jeeps. As she approaches me, I recognize Lamis. She gives a dip of her head to Jasim who responds in kind, then, shielding his eyes, glances up at the sky. Seeming satisfied, he then nods toward myself and Sally.

"Lamis, can you take Janna and help her prepare?" Without waiting for her agreement, he turns to the videographer. "Sally, Rais and I will take you to the site so you can set up the camera. Times getting on now, the horses will be getting prepared and we can plan how exactly this will go down."

I'd rather have gone with Jasim, but I have my part to play, so after allowing myself a lingering glance full of longing as he retreats with Sally, I follow Lamis into a tent. It's clean and tidy inside, and someone has obviously recently vacated it to give me a private place to change. Not that I think I need to do so, but Lamis is pulling garments out of a bag.

I wave down at my clothing, "I thought this was quite adequate?"

The maid has an unreadable smile on her face, "The sheikh suggested you wear. Will look good for camera." As I wonder what Jasim knows about filming and what will look good on screen, while thinking what do I really know about him as I didn't even know about his involvement in the oil business, she shakes out a snowy white dress. It's silk with a long light and almost sheer train which will billow out behind me as I run. The sleeves are full, and pulled in at the wrists. It's a parody of a Western wedding dress, with a flavor of Arabic.

Almost afraid to touch it, I reach out my hand, pulling the material through my fingers. It must have cost a fortune, the embroidery so ornate, and there are little crystals sewn into it which will catch the light of the sun. It's beautiful, the likes of which I've never even been close to before, yet alone worn.

"It's amazing," I breathe.

"You put on? I help." Lamis fiddles in the bag again, and brings out a white boned corset which laces up the front.

I step back, never having worn something like this before. "I don't know, how will I run in something like that?"

"You will," she pronounces confidently, and with a twisted grin I agree that she's probably right. I'll be running for my life if the horses of hell are after me.

The final thing she produces is a pure white silk thong. Well, at least that must have been cheap, there's hardly any material there at all.

"Come, I prepare you for your sheikh." Taking my hand, she leads me behind a curtain where there's a bath prepared with scented petals floating on the top. *Prepare me for my sheikh?* I chuckle, seems she's really getting into this.

And this seems a bit daft, I'll only get sweaty again after tearing across the hot sand. "Talk about getting in character," I say with a laugh. "This is all make believe, you know. It's not real. They're just going to film me."

Lamis giggles, "You get in…" she breaks off and taps her hijab, "Right head?"

"In the right mood." I translate, to her happy nods.

In the mood, yes, definitely. She's clearly expecting me to get naked, and discreetly turns her back while I divest myself of the clothes I choose so carefully this morning. When I'm hidden under the water, she turns back, and before I can protest, is washing my hair with a jug, using a perfumed shampoo that smells absolutely glorious, even if I can't work out what the scent is. I let her administer to me, feeling utterly pampered. And when she holds out a fluffy towel, forget my modesty and stand up, letting her wrap it around me.

She gives me some oil, and offers to rub it in, but I don't want another woman's hands on me, even if this is her job. I take it from her, and do it myself. I don't know what's in it, but it makes my skin feel as soft as silk and has another exotic perfume that I can't quite place. Its heady scent is acting like an aphrodisiac and I breathe deeply, trying to clear my head. A flush warms my skin, which must be down to the temperature of the air, the tent providing protection only from the sun's light. When I've finished she passes me a robe which I wrap around myself.

Finally, she does my makeup, my eyes ending up alluring, outlined in black kohl. If she can get a close up, Sally will be delighted with the effect. Then Lamis shows her other expertise, braiding part of my hair so a long plait lies down my back, leaving the rest free so it will stream out behind me as I run.

At last, having pulled on the thong, I put on the corset, and Lamis laces me into it. Not the most comfortable garment in the heat, but when I put on the dress the shape it gives me is amazing. My small breasts are pushed up, and my slight waist emphasized, the dress flowing down over my hips.

Lamis steps back to admire her handiwork, "Beautiful," she breathes, "fit for prince."

Before I can question her strange statement, the flap to the tent opens. "The sun is beginning to set. It is time." It's Rais, himself who's come to get me. His eyes blink when he sees me, and a smirk comes to his lips. His fierceness makes me nervous. *Is he going to be the one scooping me up?* I glance around to see Jasim, but he must be out with the film crew. I leave a beaming Lamis, and step out into the early evening light.

Fuck, why did I agree to this? I've enjoyed all the pampering, but now I've got to run across the desert, chased by thirty or so horsemen, and be swept up into an unknown man's arms. Hell, I hope he knows what he's doing. What if he drops me and I get trampled beneath flying hooves? Bloody hell, it seemed simple in the planning, who did I let talk me into this? Sally. That's who it was. Damn her for her flipping filming ideas. We should swap places, if only I knew how to work a camera.

I turn to Rais, walking by my side, "Who's going to be in the lead? Who will be picking me up?"

He looks down, his smile enigmatic, "Not I," he refutes, but doesn't expand. When he leads me to a Jeep, and helps me inside, expertly gathering my skirts so they won't trail out of the door, it seems the time for conversation is over. Whichever of his men it will be, I hope he's a good rider.

I'm hit by both the ordinary and the extraordinary when we've driven only a short distance. Here, in the backdrop of dunes with the sun just behind, is Sally behind her camera, adjusting the tripod and calling out instructions. And then, there are the horses, stamping their feet and flicking their tails in the early evening light, a variety of colours, greys, bays, and one such a dark brown it looks almost black. Each man is in full ceremonial robes, scimitars in scabbards clanking against their boots. As the horses toss their heads, their bridles jingle. They're a frightening bunch, almost making me believe this is real. It's an ageless sight, one that could have come from any number of centuries past.

Unnerved, I look around for Jasim, but still I can't see him.

"Wow. Fuck! You look bloody fantastic." Sally approaches, holding a light meter up toward me, "Hey, I'm really going to be able to do something with this." She indicates the dress I'm wearing. "Christ, it's going to sparkle. And your face. I'll need to zoom in and get a close up of that." She pauses for breath, then points to a spot by a rock, "That's your starting point. It's simple. When I give the signal, all you've got to do is run, as fast as you can, in a straight line in that direction." She waves to show me which way I should go.

All I've got to do? I roll my eyes, then glance warily at the loose ground, "What if I fall?"

She chuckles, "Oh don't worry about that. I'll make sure to catch it on film. Would add authenticity. Just get up and start running again."

Open mouthed, I turn to her, I had been joking. I didn't really want to go head first into the ground and split my head open on a rock. And there's enough of them lying around. What if the horse stumbles?

"I just run?"

"Yeah, and one of the riders will swoop down on you and sweep you into his arms. He'll carry you away and I'll stop filming then."

"The sun is dropping." Rais has come up alongside, and Ryan is with him. Again, I look around for Jasim, but he's nowhere in sight. Isn't Ryan supposed to be his bodyguard and at his side to protect him at all times? I feel my stomach drop, I'd wanted Jasim to see me in this dress, if the very male looks of appreciation Ryan's giving me are anything to go by, I'm probably looking the best I've ever done in my life. Maybe he's not even come to watch. Oh, well, it's not to be, and he promised we'd be together when the time is right. Looking around, we wouldn't have much opportunity to do more than suffer torture in each other's presence. There's not even a tent where we could steal a kiss. No, he's probably got more important things to do, like staring at oil coming up from a well.

And then all thoughts of the man I want go from my mind as I hear men mounting up and realise my cue to start running will come soon. The sun sinks below the horizon fast here, we've only time for one take, and I mustn't mess this up. Nervous, I start bouncing on the balls of my feet. *What the hell was I thinking of, volunteering to do this?* It'll be great, they said. A virgin running over the sands, escaping from the horde of Arabs chasing after her. Fantastic footage they said. Yeah, great, my life put at risk for a few seconds of film.

Sally prods me in the back, and points to the rock. "Show time," she grins.

I feel lonely as I walk to my mark, some way in front of the horses so she can get some shots of me running before they come into sight. It might be make believe, but suddenly it feels real, as though I'm not an actor on a film set, but a woman being genuinely chased by a sheikh to take for his pleasure. A woman wanting to escape her fate of being abducted and stolen. *I'm just getting into character.* My fear of the unknown has my heart in my mouth.

Shouldn't we have had a practice run? I decide on the spot a future career as a stuntman is not on the cards.

"Okay, Janna?"

As I turn and nod, Sally calls out, "Three, two, one. And GO!" And now it's too late.

I pick up the long skirts of my dress and start running, as fast as I can and harder than I've ever run in my life. I'm running through the desert, my feet in soft ballet shoes hitting hot sand in the shadows of the dunes which are turning a brilliant gold in the light of the setting sun. My feet pound the ground, my lungs start heaving. And then I hear the thundering of hooves behind me, and the expression of terror on my face is not at all fake.

The sounds get closer, the lead horse must be nearing me. In a flash, I become conscious this has all happened so fast I've had no practice and no idea how this is going to work. How will he take me? Will my arm be wrenched from my socket? Will it hurt? I can only hope the rider knows exactly what he's doing.

Frightened for real, I redouble my efforts as if there could be any chance I'd be able to outrun my pursuers, but the horse is much faster. So close now, I swear I can feel it's warm breath on the back of my neck. Then I get a glimpse of dark horseflesh beside me, then two arms come around me and I'm swept up and into a stranger's lap.

An involuntary scream escapes me, startled from me by shock. But I'm safe, I wasn't harmed, and now the filming will stop. But the horse doesn't. I wait for my captor to pull back on the reins but, if anything, he's urging the horse to go faster. The sounds of the other riders behind us are fading away, and the beast I'm now riding is continuing on, its speed not even faltering. The hooves continue hitting the ground, so fast I can't tell one hoof beat from another.

We're heading away from Sally, away from the rest of the men. A glance behind shows me we've left them far behind. *This wasn't the plan.*

I start to struggle, "Stop, stop! Please, stop!" I'm terrified. Who's got me? And where is he taking me?

I push at the strong arms holding me, try to pry apart the hands holding both the reins and me tight. "Stop! Let me down."

My struggles are getting frantic when I feel warm breath by my ear. "Shush. Stay still, I've got you, I won't let you fall."

I still. That voice…

"Shush," he repeats, "It's me."

It's Jasim.

CHAPTER 17
Jasim

When I decide I'm going after something, I'm all in and there'll be no turning back. Neither do I hang around. Why waste time? Life's too short, as they say. I'd let down my guard and allowed Janna in, perhaps for the first time ever letting a woman seduce *me*. Now it's a matter of when and how, and not if.

When I'd arranged that they'd be filming today, the very day after they'd arrived in the desert, it was only so she could do a quick turn around and take her pretty little arse back to Al Qur'ah as quickly as humanly possible, so I didn't have to cope with temptation placed in front of me every day. That, of course, was before she'd made her intentions so clear, and I'd decided the gift of her virginity was going to be mine to take.

Once my brain had caught up with my cock and dismissed the objections that had made me keep my distance, I had no desire to delay my gratification. If I couldn't keep away, if she insisted I'm be the one to initiate her, there was only one decision remaining to me. How I was going to make it special. That once in a lifetime event she'd never be able to repeat.

It was a source of amusement that she'd set up her own abduction; I just piggy-backed on the plan she already had in motion. When I'd kissed her, I'd known then no other man was going to have her in his arms, however briefly. No, it would be me who'd be chasing her, capturing her, and taking her for my own. I was going to make her every fantasy come true.

With wry and unsuppressed laughter on their part, I enlisted the help of Ryan and Rais, the only ones in on my plan, though clever Lamis I think had seen through me. And like a well-oiled machine, everything came together without a hitch. Of course, being a rich prince of the desert has its advantages, including having enough money to ensure clothes can be bought and delivered at the speed of light. Choosing carefully for my enjoyment, I arranged for her to be dressed as a virgin ready for defiling tonight.

I'd stayed out of sight, hidden behind a vehicle, but from my vantage point able to watch as she strode onto the makeshift set, her white train flowing behind, the breeze in the air making it come alive. My breath caught in my throat at my first glimpse of her face. She's so fucking beautiful, the clothing I'd dressed her in so much more complimentary and flattering than the clothes she nor-mally wears on stage. I'd provided everything she's wearing. Every fucking item. And I can only hope Lamis per-suaded her to wear them all.

I'd seen the flicker of fear as she started to run, thirty horses stamping their feet, ready for the off, making her nervous, her anxiety making my heart speed up.

And now, the time has arrived for me to play my part.

Wrapping my keffiyeh carefully around my face, so only my eyes can be seen, I quickly mount the stallion Rais has provided. Raising my arm in the pre-arranged signal, I dig in my heels, and the powerful beast leaps forward. Although she's been given a head start, we're upon her in little more than seconds. Balancing myself with my legs, I lean over and grasp her in my arms, swinging her up until she's sitting in front of me. I'd learned to ride in my youth, and such circus tricks formed part of my education.

Behind my scarf I smile to myself. She doesn't know yet she's been captured by her sheikh. Her perfume surrounds me, the aphrodisiac oils I'd told Lamis to use. But she needs no fake enhancements, her natural aroma is enough on its own. Her long hair flares out behind her, whipped by the desert wind and, as I scoop up the train to prevent it tripping the horse, her dress sparkles in the embers of the dying sun. I'm becoming impatient and can't wait to take her so carefully chosen clothing off.

She's on the saddle in front of me, my swollen cock pressing into her cute arse. Her lungs are heaving, panting from the run and the shock. I sense she's scared as we leave the others behind, so quickly I seek to reassure her. The way she relaxes immediately at the sound of my voice, leaning back into my arms, trusting me to take care of her, causes my gut to clench with some unknown emotion

The light's fading now, and we've covered a great distance, everyone else left far behind. I pull gently on the reins, and the dark bay stallion I'm riding slows, reducing our speed from gallop to canter, and then to a trot and quickly, so Janna doesn't get bounced and jostled, to a steady walk.

As the wind rushing past us reduces to a gentle breeze, I squeeze her gently, "Are you alright?"

"Huh, now I've got over the shock." She tries to turn in my arms, "Why you, Jasim? You frightened me to death! I thought I was being kidnapped for real. Why didn't you tell me what was going on? And where are we going?"

Her movement has unsteadied the horse who begins to prance, it's one of Rais's racing stallions, not one I'm familiar with and though I'm a good rider I'm two up on an unknown mount. "Stay still, habiti." The Arab endearment shocks me as it falls from my lips, but strangely, it sounds so right, "Just sit still and let me keep you safe." Though there are few horses that can better me—I was riding almost before I could walk—I'm not willing to risk my precious cargo.

When she turns to face front again, I answer her question, "I'm giving you something special. Something you can look back on and remember for the rest of your life." *When I'm no longer around.*

"It's going to be tonight." Her voice sounds breathy as she catches on fast.

"Yes, unless you've changed your mind. I'm not going to force you if you've had second thoughts." She'll be able to tell my mind's set, with my cock nudging against her that I'm making no effort to hide. But I wouldn't be a gentleman if I didn't give her a way out. Not that I'm feeling very gentlemanly at the moment. I suppress the growl that comes to my throat at the thought of her turning me down now.

A violent shake of her head affects her whole body, again making the horse dance, "I haven't changed my mind."

I breathe a sigh of heartfelt relief, "Then relax, habiti. Tonight, I lead and you follow. Relax and enjoy, and leave everything to me." A slight stiffening of her body suggests that she's understandably nervous. "I'll take care of you. Good care of you."

The horse settles and plods on, now going over rock, audible hoof beats echoing into the night.

"Where are we going?" she asks again after a few more strides.

"Not far," I tell her, seeing the lights appear up ahead in the distance. I pull the horse to a halt. "Look up." I lift her chin so she's looking at the sky, peppered with stars.

A little gasp as if for the first time she sees the beauty of the firmament, away from the city it can be seen at its best. "It's amazing. I've never seen anything like it before."

"Beautiful. Like you." My lips find her neck and graze across her skin, and she trembles in my arms. Squeezing my legs, I encourage the horse forward again.

"Is that where we're going?"

She's spotted the lights. "Uh huh." I confirm, still kissing her neck, sneaking a taste of the salty tang of her skin. Then I raise my head, "I promise to give you a night you'll never forget."

"Jasim…"

"Shush, relax and enjoy."

The lights draw closer, and soon we're upon them. I pause so she can take in the sight, smiling to myself at her gasp. It's an elaborate tent, ornate with velvet trimmings, even on the outside. Another thing money can buy. Together with the men to set it up at short notice and the guarantee of their discretion.

A man approaches us, and takes hold of the bridle. Putting my arms around her, I help her dismount, and then swing my leg over the saddle and drop to the ground. "*Shukraan,*" I thank the man who leads the horse away.

"Come." Taking hold of her hand, I lead her inside the ostentatious tent, decorated like something out of the Arabian Nights. Concealing the plain black canvas, the sides are adorned with tapestries, a low wide divan is set up at the back, with silk hangings around it. Low lighting is provided by lanterns hanging from the apex, and there's a low table surrounded by cushions, and sitting on that, gold plates and a jug. And, looking very out of place, an ice bucket containing champagne and two flutes.

As she stands open mouthed, I go to the bottle, expertly opening it so it only makes a slight pop. I pour some into each glass, and once the bubbles settle, hand one to her. Raising my own, I give her a toast, "To us. To tonight."

She takes the champagne almost absent-mindedly, holding it but not drinking. She's gazing around. "This? All this? Why…? How is it here?"

I grin, "I had it brought here."

It takes her a moment, "For me?" she squeaks.

"For you." I agree.

"You needn't have done that."

Seeing she's not going to sip her drink, I take it from her, loving the bemusement in her eyes. "I wanted to make this special."

Now she raises her face, looking into my eyes, "Anywhere would be special with you, Jasim."

Fuck, I hope I can live up to her expectations.

I take a moment to study her, Lamis appears to have followed my instructions to the letter, every one of them, which is greatly appreciated by my cock. I'm a man, I'm a Dominant. The ride through the desert has awoken my marauder's blood. I can't wait. I take a step back and give one instruction. "Take off the dress."

The deepening of my tone surprises her. Her eyes flick to mine and I try not to blink. Pleased when, without my having to repeat myself, her hands go to her back. She fiddles for a moment, her lips pressed tightly together. Then she turns around with a little apologetic smile, "Can you unzip me?"

With pleasure. Slowly I slide down the zipper, the soft material floating to the ground as it parts. Covered only by the barely-there thong, from the rear, her backside looks naked. I close my eyes for a moment, as my balls start to pound with aching fullness.

"Turn around." I instruct.

Now I'm able to see the corset I'd chosen, and the way her breasts are pushed up over the top. My hands itch to touch them, but force myself to remember this is no well-trained sub, I'll need to go slowly. I reach out my hands, touching her biceps, and pull her toward me. As she raises her face, I lower my head, and take her lips with mine.

Last time I ravished her, now I try to be gentle, applying slightly more pressure until she opens and lets me in. I plunder her carefully, mating my tongue with hers. She sighs and then moans, the same sounds as last time and having the same effect. Letting go with one hand, I reach down and surreptitiously grasp the root of my cock, squeezing it hard for a few seconds, until I bring myself back under control. This isn't for me, though I know I'll enjoy it. Tonight has to be all about her. I can only give her this one time and an experience that will stay with her forever.

It's going to be difficult to make myself last. I'm tempted beyond reason with this virgin, looking so pure and innocent before me. I'd chosen her clothes with care, now I wished I'd dressed her as a slut. Every item she's wearing screams she's untouched, and that I'll be the first man to pleasure her. The first to touch her, the first to taste her. The number of firsts cause a growl of possessiveness to escape from my throat, breaking the kiss.

I roll my head back, trying to restrain my base desire to throw her down and ravish her without finesse. She tilts her head, I don't try to explain, unable to understand how much her innocence is turning me on.

After a few deep breaths, I use my unsteady fingers to start undoing the laces which hold the corset tight. As it loosens she sighs with relief. "It wasn't conducive to running," she says with a smile.

"I didn't choose it so you could run in it," I reply gruffly, showing no remorse.

"*You* chose it?"

"I dressed you for me."

She laughs quietly at my admission, her amusement animating her face. As I expose her breasts, her mirth fades, her breathing deepens, and she flutters her hands as if not knowing what to do with them.

"Just let me look." The corset's undone, and I slide it off her shoulders. Her tits are small, but large enough for me, topped with the most delectable nipples I've ever seen. Rosy pink and large in comparison, making me itch to touch. To pinch. To bite. As I stare at them intently, a tremor runs through her.

"Jasim," she gasps out. Just the caress of my eyes is heating her blood.

My fingers touch the sides of her breasts, and she jumps as I trace them. Then, unable to resist any longer, my hands move and I'm touching her nipples, circling their outline, watching them harden in front of my eyes.

Her breathing becomes erratic, and a small unsummoned smile appears on my lips as I home in on my target, pinching those already hard peaks between my forefinger and thumb.

"Jasim." Again, she cries out my name, this time with more urgency.

I apply more pressure, and she staggers but doesn't pull back. "Do you caress yourself, here? Pinch your own nipples?"

"No," she replies, shaking her head. "I've never done that."

Immediately I release her, "Do it now."

With a look of surprise, her fingers take the place of mine, and she copies my actions.

"Harder."

She complies, her mouth gapes open, and I'm driven to the edge of insanity watching her pleasure herself.

Breathing in deep, I smell her arousal, almost able to taste it in the air, I've no doubt if I touch her she'll be wet. It's not difficult to imagine my hard cock sliding into her tight untried depths. Plundering where no man has ever gone before. Stealing her virtue like the warriors of my past.

Eager now, I want no more delay. I step toward her again, and remove her hands, then turn her around so she's facing the divan. With my palm gently resting against her back, I encourage her over to it. When she's there, I swing her up into my arms, then kneel, and gently place her in the middle of the low surface. Releasing her, I stand and take a moment to study her. She looks so right, so beautiful, lying on the bed that's been provided for us. Placed here for the sole reason of divesting her of her innocence. My body trembles as I watch her lying there, my desire and need almost too strong to keep myself in check.

Shrugging off my headdress and tunic, I stand in front of her in my loose cotton trousers, my cock visibly straining, tenting the material as it bobs against my stomach, desperate for release. But for her it's all new, and I must be sure she's ready. Slowly, for the second time, I sink to my knees. Reaching for the scrap of silk that barely hides her from me, I pull it down slowly, sliding it off her feet, slipping off her shoes she'd worn in the desert along with it. A red flush spreads across her body as she's completely naked before me. Completely naked, for the first time before any man.

I need to be sure, to test how innocent I believe she is. I touch her mound, cupping my hand over it. "Has a man had his fingers here before?"

She huffs a laugh, "The guys would have killed him."

I'm glad she had men looking out for her, I owe them a debt for saving her for me.

"They won't be pleased with you," she adds, smiling.

"I'm more than a match for them." I could take any of them with one hand tied behind my back.

Her eyes take in my muscular frame, "Yes, you are," she agrees, and her tongue flicks out, moistening her lips.

Her guileless action makes me groan. Fuck taking this slow. With more urgency, I take hold of her legs and pull them apart. She makes a token resistance, and blushes.

She's not consciously fighting me; her reaction is automatic as this is so new and strange. She wants this, she just doesn't know what I'm going to do.

I slide my hands up her thighs, unwittingly tickling her. She tenses and draws up her legs, but relaxes as I firm my touch. Continuing my journey, my hands touch her bare shaven labia, *yes, Lamis has made sure she did everything I asked,* and I slide one finger into her very wet slit. She's completely dripping for me. *She's ready.* But still I need to go slow. I add another finger to the first. *Fuck, she's so tight, she's going to strangle my cock.* Pulling out my fingers, I put them in my mouth. *Yes, she tastes every bit as good as I thought she would, and that perfume?* My balls churn as I inhale, my breathing unsteady.

I pause, undecided, desperate to put my mouth on her, but knowing if I do, more of her exquisite flavour would cause me to risk losing it before I'm inside her. My restraint being so sorely tried.

Circling my fingers around her clit, I flick it, then strum gently, watching her every reaction, trying to learn her body, what pressure and stroke she likes. I'm a quick study and it doesn't take long before her muscles start to go taut. Once more she tries to close her legs, I shuffle until I'm between her thighs to prevent her. Her eyes are rolling up, her teeth closing on her bottom lip, her back starts to bow and then she starts trembling. As I'd done to her nipple, I pinch her clit and that does it, shooting her over the top as she comes with a scream. And I feel a slice of heaven, knowing I'm the first man to have given her that.

She's so fucking beautiful as she comes down from her peak, her eyes open in wonder, the flush on her cheeks. I can't wait any longer. Standing, I divest myself of my trousers by untying the belt and letting them drop to the floor. Underneath I'm commando.

She's eyeing me up, and that tongue's licking her lips again. Oh, fuck, woman, you don't know what invitation you're sending there. But I'll teach you. *I can teach her anything I want.*

As her eyes blaze in appreciation, I ask, "Have you seen a man naked before?"

A soft laugh. "Plenty of times. I travel with five men, remember, and they're not exactly shy. But not normally in quite that state." As she points at my erection I understand what she's saying. I don't particularly like knowing she's seen even a man's flaccid dick, though for a moment I'm surprised she didn't turn any of them on. Until I remember, they treated her like a sister. And thank Allah for that. Otherwise she wouldn't be mine to deflower.

Reaching around to the drawer I know will have been stocked, I pull out a condom, smoothing it down my cock quickly, just the touch of my own hands requiring me to give the base another squeeze. I'm going to come before I get inside her if I don't take care. The thought is astounding, surely I've trained myself to have more control than that?

Her eyes widen, and she swallows, "We're really going to do this?" It's an unnecessary question, and I don't bother answering. Just stare at her intently, alert for any sign that she might have changed her mind. But apart from the not unexpected nervousness, I can only read fervour on her face.

In one smooth move, I fall to the bed, and pull up her knees for easier access, and then position myself. I'd told her it would hurt, and she recalls my words, her body tensing even before I've begun pressing in.

I fondle her clit, she gasps. I circle around it with my fingers, and her head falls back. Still aroused from her previous release, she's already close. I strum harder and faster, then try pinching again, and that takes her over. While she's still convulsing, I push into the tissues made soft by her orgasm. For a second she doesn't notice, then her eyes catch mine. Her hands come out to my arms, clutching and holding me, fingernails jabbing into my skin.

I don't mean to intentionally hurt her, but I'm a big man. I gain a little more ground, and she makes a small sound of protest.

"Try and relax, let me in."

"Easy for you to say," she rasps out, as her brow furrows and her eyes close.

Sometimes it's better just to rip that band-aid right off. I thrust in hard, and then stop.

She's breathing in pants, moisture glistening in her eyes. "Is that it?"

"No." I tell her honestly, and pull back a little. Then in one strong push I'm there, my balls up against her arse.

She screams and bends forward, her hands clench at me in pain and now the tears are running down her face. Tears which make my cock swell inside her and my balls draw up. Her fear and uncertainty like an elixir on my dark, black soul. I throw my head back, feeling my eyes roll back in their sockets. I'm hanging on by a thread.

Again, I touch her clit, she tries to push me away, but I take hold of her hands in one of mine so she can't stop me. Leaning over her, her arms held tight over her head I toy with her clit, ramping up her arousal despite her discomfort. It doesn't take long before she's starting to tense, but this time it's not with pain.

Knowing I've very little control left, I start to move, pulling out and then pushing back in, enough to stimulate me while trying not to hurt her. Her muscles massage me, as they clench and release. As soon as I know she's reached the peak, as her mouth opens in a scream I hammer in sharply, and then buck once, twice, and that's all it takes for me to start to empty inside.

And oh, fuck, the sensation. The blood drains from my brain, the stars we saw outside nothing to the display in my head, I can feel little spurts of cum continuing to escape from the end of my dick as her movements completely drain me.

At last I stop coming, and open my eyes. She's lying still, the corners of her mouth turned up with a very satisfied smile.

"You good?" I question, when I'm at last able to speak coherently, even if not quite ready to string any thoughts together.

"Good?" her smile broadens. "Yeah, I'm good."

CHAPTER 18
Janna

My chest is heaving as I attempt to top up my oxygen levels, unable to believe how incredible he'd made me feel, or exactly how good making love with Jasim had been. Sensations that I'd never have thought possible had I not experienced them. I'd given myself orgasms before, or I thought I had. But they were little quakes compared to the earthshattering ones Jasim had summoned.

He'd told me when I gave my virginity away, it should be something special, not just something rushed to get over and done with. *Special?* He'd managed to make it beyond my wildest dreams. Starting with the chase through the desert, I could never have envisaged Jasim would quite literally sweep me off my feet, nor have arranged to have this tent set up in the middle of nowhere. *What kind of man would even think of that?*

My eyes start leaking as it dawns on me how completely amazing he had made my first time. Nothing, nothing would ever have been able to top it.

He's lying propped up on his elbow beside me, I feel his fingers wipe at the moisture in my eyes, and turn my head to face him.

"I said I wanted your tears, but not like this. What's the matter, Janna?" His mouth drops as he frowns, "Did I really hurt you? Are you already regretting what we did?"

Placing my fingers against his cheek, I deny both questions, "Only a little, and definitely not. I'm just feeling emotional, Jasim. I'm overwhelmed by everything you've done for me." I pause, and indicate the richly decorated tent, "Setting up all this. You've made it into the most incredible experience for me, and one I'll never forget for as long as I live."

Now a small smile, "That was my aim. I'm glad that it worked."

I continue to stroke his skin, "Just you being the one would have been enough."

He gives a laugh, "You could have told me that before I went to all this trouble."

"I believe I did," I smirk.

He chuckles and then gives me an instruction. "Wait here."

Well I'm not going anywhere. In fact, I can't move. My limbs feel leaden, and for once my orgasms have left me sated. I feel almost sleepy, but force my eyes to stay open, not wanting to waste a moment or to miss a thing about this night. He crosses the tent and goes into a curtained off area, then returns minus condom but with a small bowl. As he brings out a flannel, I put out my hand. He brushes it away, and proceeds to clean me himself.

I try to close my legs, but he holds them apart. "There's a little blood, not too much," he says matter of factly, then grins up at me, "Just enough to satisfy a man."

"Proof of my virginity?" I huff, concerned he hadn't believed me.

"Janna, I knew you were innocent before you told me. It wouldn't have mattered if you hadn't bled at all. But…" he gives a self-deprecating smile, and doesn't need to finish his thought. "Are you sore?"

Experimentally I try my limbs, they all seem to be working, but there's a slight discomfort between my legs, "Not much," I reply.

"Good," he responds, in a voice full of satisfaction.

"Good? I thought, being a sadist, that you'd have wanted me to hurt."

He sits down beside me, there's an assessing look in his eyes. "I tried to be gentle." His hand comes down and smooths over my face, "I kept my inner beast chained tonight."

I wriggle as if to taunt him, "Does it want to come out and play now?"

His eyes rapidly darken, "Be careful how you tempt me."

But I don't want to be cautious. My fatigue disappears, and I try to sit up. Try, because as soon as I start to move, one of his hands whips over my head and grabs something from behind me, the other takes both of mine and his body squashes me to the bed. There are snicking sounds behind me, and when he moves away I find my wrists are securely handcuffed to the tent pole behind my head.

Without saying a word, but keeping his eyes on me, he reaches to the side of the bed and pulls something up. When he shows it to me, my brow rises in question.

"It's a spreader bar," he answers. "I have to thank my brother for putting ideas in my head."

Okay, so what's he going to do with that? And what's his brother got to do with it?

But I don't have time to ask him, he's taken one ankle and cuffed it to one end, then my other is cuffed to the opposite side. He bends my knees up and a ratcheting noise sounds as my ankles are pulled further apart.

Now he stands back, one side of his mouth turned up, "Now I've got you exactly where I want you."

I feel so exposed, unable to move, and completely under his control. *He can do anything he wants to me.* Oh my God. My nipples feel tight, as though begging for attention, and my clit's beating in time with my rapidly pounding heart.

He starts to walk around me, his fingers trailing over my skin, goosebumps following in their wake. "Here, I'm a prince," his voice has dropped an octave, "There are men outside, but they are under my command. You can cry for help, you can scream. But no one will come running. I can do anything I want to you. You are completely at my mercy *alttuyur alssaghira*."

Oh my. His words, the position I'm in, and his deliberation are meant to frighten me, and he's succeeding, but my nerves are turning me on. Wondering what he will do causes a new rush of arousal to dampen my thighs, and in this position, held so open to him, I can hide nothing from him. He must see the evidence of how he affects me glistening in the light from the lamps.

His hand stops moving, "I can torture you, clip your wings. Keep you on edge for hours. Mark you." He's looking into deeply into my eyes, and I shiver. "Your safe word is *ahmar*." He stops and shakes his head, laughing as he corrects himself and gives me the interpretation, "Red. You understand?"

"I'm not going to have to say it."

"You dare to challenge me now?" He pulls himself up. His cock, no longer flaccid, is jutting out and leaking pre-cum, the sight causing my tongue flick out and moisten my lips. He notices, "You want to taste me?"

Eagerly I nod.

His hands come out and pull my head round. It's a rough action, surprising, but one which doesn't hurt, aimed to intimidate not to cause pain, "You suck my cock when I want you to. Not when you decide."

I go to nod, but he's holding me too firmly.

His hands touch my breasts, his fingers rolling my nipples, I try to push up. He slaps my breast lightly, and pulls away. "Bad *alttuyur alssaghira*." His voice is sharp. Without his hands on me, I feel bereft. But soon his palms are back, smoothing over my flesh, and now his mouth is there, sucking at one of my nipples. He uses his teeth, it's enough to bring my back off the bed, his bite staying only the right side of pleasure. *He knows exactly how much I can take.*

As he moves to the other, I feel myself tighten. I open my mouth to plead or to beg and he bites again. Arousal shoots from my nipple to my clit, a stream of electric current making me throb. He lifts his head, and he smiles a knowing smile. My nipples tingle and sting, aftershocks shoot through my pussy. Then, again he lowers his mouth, this time to my stomach, and once more he bites with his teeth. And then he moves up, a bite under my right breast, and now under my left. Little nips that are surprising rather than painful. Until he reaches the top of my breast just over my heart. Now when his teeth descend, he sucks hard and I gasp. When he pulls away I suspect that he's marked me, I'm proven correct when he traces where he's marred the skin, a look of satisfaction on his face.

I didn't know it was possible to be this turned on, there's not one part of me that doesn't feeling alive, no nerve left without stimulus.

He's moving down the bed, lifting the spreader bar and slipping underneath so my legs are over his shoulders. Raising my head, I see him staring at that most private part of me, and my whole body flushes. As he lowers his mouth I flop back on the pillows, and as his tongue explores my slit I shudder with delight. Now I can only be grateful I've waited so long, knowing I've been keeping myself for him. He's not offering me a future, but wow, there could be no better way to have lost my virginity than with such an experienced man. I don't need to wonder, nor ask what I'm expected to do. He's taken all decisions away from me. There's nothing to do but lie back and take all he wants to give. Let him use me for his pleasure. My skin feels electrified at the idea.

Now he's using his hands, holding me apart, stretching me open, then his fingers start to explore. His tongue probes inside me, and I jerk from the bed. Already my desire is ramping up and my muscles are starting to tighten.

"Don't come."

What? He must be joking, there's no way I'm going to be able to stop this. *Owh!* He's slapped my clit, and moved his mouth away. I'm throbbing, my pussy clenching at air.

"Jasim… please." He's got to give me relief, he just has too.

He chuckles, the sound reverberating against my tender parts, "You're mine to torture, I told you that."

And torment me he does, licking me again, and the threat of the orgasm which had started to fade returns in full force. This time I fight to hide it, but as my thigh muscles go tight he laughs again, "I can read you, *alttuyur alssaghira*. Every reaction of your body. *I* control your orgasms. They're mine to give, not for you to steal."

Oh my God, he's killing me. I've never been so aroused, nor felt so frustrated. My hands test their bindings, I try to move my legs. With so little movement I can only squirm and take what he's prepared to give. And he's doing it again, bringing me to the peak but not letting me go over.

I scream in vexation, and he chuckles again. I feel light-headed, the stimulation with no relief almost too much to bear. *He must let me come soon.*

When he pulls out from under the bar and takes my body in his strong arms I gasp with dismay, *he's leaving me hanging.* My clit is beyond sensitive, I feel as though a puff of air would take me over the top. *Just breathe on me. Touch me.* "Jasim…" I wail out his name.

He lifts and turns me, supporting me easily as he pulls the pillows down the bed, then lays me down gently, my stomach held up by the cushions, my forehead lowered. He repositions the spreader bar so my bum's in the air. And makes me wait, aching with need.

I'm unable to stop trembling, so close to the edge. There's nothing in my mind except a dire need to come. Over the sound of blood rushing through my ears, I can hear him inhaling and exhaling. Opening my eyes, which I hadn't realised were closed, I turn my head to the side and can see him behind me, kneeling on the bed, his cock hard and protruding so proudly from his muscular loins. *I need him inside me.* But I've already learned he'll show no pity even if I beg.

Just do something, anything. I need him to assuage this hunger that I'm feeling bone deep. I'm starting to hate him, when at last he moves. His hand finally touches me, swiping my dripping essence from my slit and moving it to my tight hole. He circles his fingers around and starts to push one in. At the foreign and unwelcome invasion, I try to evade him, but his other hand holds me tight.

When I stop moving he slaps my backside hard, "Let me in," he instructs tersely, "Bear down and let me in that tight arse."

Stunned that he's smacked me, my body obeys his command. As the sting fades to warmth his finger sinks in, a burning, uncomfortable feeling.

"Fuck, you're so tight." Almost talking to himself he continues, "You'll wear a butt plug for me, loosen you up. When you're prepared I'll be taking you there."

The naughtiness of the thought thrills me, but that's going to hurt, I tense, "Jasim, no."

Another slap which makes me jump, and then a voice by my ear, "No? You think you've got a say in this? Your body's mine, you belong to me now."

Oh. My. God. It shouldn't turn me on, the thought I'm completely at his mercy, but as new moisture floods out, I admit that it does.

He adds another finger to the one in my arse, pushing up inside me and oh, sweet God in heaven I'm going to come from the feeling. But of course, he doesn't let me, as the feeling of ecstasy rises, it's then he pulls out. "I'm going to mark you now."

What?

And then he starts to really spank me. I try to protest, surely I shouldn't want this. But as his hand hits me, a glow starts spreading through me, my clit feels so swollen, pulsating as though the touch of a feather could set me off. His palm connects again and again, my heart's beating fast, my lungs gulp in air. The smarting of my skin is nothing in comparison to the throbbing need in my clit.

He stops all contact, and I hear a rustling behind me, I'm shaking my head against the bed, unable to process all the sensations of my body.

His hands hold me open, and I feel a prodding at my arsehole. *He's doing that now?* Then the warmth of his body as he lies over me, once again he speaks into my ear, "Not tonight." It's not said to reassure me, but as a promise, or a threat.

Then his condom covered cock is in my already tender slit, and he pushes right in, my copious moisture, his stretching from before, and my intense level of arousal easing his way. Immediately my pussy resumes clamping, as though trying to hold him in. But he's controlling the pace, picking it up and pounding into me, his hand wraps around my braid Lamis had plaited, forcing my head up. I'm completely and utterly under his control.

"Come for me."

I couldn't disobey if I tried. My muscles tauten, and I'm a quivering wreck as instinct takes over and an incredible, earth shattering orgasm floods through me, going on and on and on. As though from a distance, I hear his own shout, and feel jerky movements as he ejects his cum, the feeling making me orgasm all over again. Someone is screaming, I think that it's me. My mind leaves my body.

CHAPTER 19
Jasim

By Allah! It's as if this woman was made to be perfect for me.

Quickly I release her from the spreader bar, massaging her legs to get her circulation going again, and doing the same to her wrists when I remove the cuffs, then pull her to me, holding her close. She's pliant in my arms, her eyes closed. She's deep in subspace, the things I've done to her, the way I tortured her, shooting her there.

Laying my hand over her heart I feel the rapid beating gradually starting to slow, my own mimicking her pace. I'd called her *alttuyur alssaghira*, my little bird, something so fragile I could crush it in my strong hands. But she flew like an eagle, a match for my deepest desires. I'd been wrong to think she wouldn't enjoy my type of play. My mind starts thinking of what else I could do with her, how far I could take her and debase her. Fuck, the way she responded, the strength of her eventual explosion triggering my own out of this world release. While I promised her one night, I already know that won't be enough.

Stretching my arm downwards I run my hands over where I've left bruises, my mark which will soon fade, but for a few hours will remind her of me and this night. Gently, I turn her, and taking a cooling ointment, rub it over her tender skin.

When I'd made the arrangements for this tent, I'd only intended to take her the once, and admit I got carried away. The toys Nijad had sent with me tempting me to do more. But she'd had no need for her safe word, I'd been watching every reaction, every flush on that delectable body. My cock starts to swell as I think about what I could with her back home in my club.

Back in the club? What am I thinking?

As she starts to stir, I shelve the strangely appealing thought, and observe her face as her eyes open. Her pupils remain dilated, letting me know she's not quite back in her head. Reaching down, I take the bottle of water I'd left handy earlier, and twist off the top, bringing it to her lips.

"Drink. You'll be dehydrated."

Still under my command, she does as I suggest, her throat working as she swallows down almost the whole bottle. Her hand comes up to wipe moisture away from her mouth. She's staring at me in amazement.

"How are you feeling?"

Dazed, she shakes her head as though to clear it, "I don't think I can remember my name. What the hell was that, Jasim?"

Pulling her to me, I push her head into my chest and rest my chin on her hair, "You soared into subspace, habiti. It was beautiful to watch."

She snuggles in closer, wincing slightly as her abused body protests. I feel a tinge of guilt as I ask her, "Are you okay?"

"I feel like I've run a marathon." She smiles into my skin, "Oh, Jasim. That was amazing. I never dreamt sex could be anything like that."

"It was good for me too," I admit, "You respond to me so well." Taking hold of her braid, I pull her head up to face me, "Janna, I'm not a man for the long haul, but for my part, I'd like to explore what this is between us for a little longer." I've had more subs than I can remember, but never once have I felt so connected as I do with her.

Her eyes crease as she brings me into focus, and she tilts her head to one side as though testing my sincerity. "You said this would be it. That we'd only have one night."

Brushing back my hair, I gaze at her intently, "I know I did. Janna." I turn slightly away and then back and give a short laugh, "I never expected… The things you let me do to you. Your reactions to me. I thought I'd scare you."

"You did, but in an enjoyable way."

I nod. "That was my aim. And, fuck, you have no idea what that did to me." *Don't ask me to explain.* I don't understand it myself. "I don't know how far we can take this. We'll take each day, each *night* as it comes."

The sides of her mouth turn up as she answers me softly, "I'd like that."

"I'm making no promises." I warn again, "No hopes of anything permanent. You understand that?" I can make no such commitments. To lead her on would be wrong. "I'm never going to settle with one woman, Janna. That's not who I am."

"I understand." She pulls herself up, a rueful grimace as she feels her sore bum, "I've no point of reference, you're the first man to make love to me. I'm not going to make this into more than it is. But I want to learn all you can teach me, before we move on."

Before we move on? The thought that I'll be the man she measures others against causes my body to tighten. Another man touching her? Putting his cock in her? Flogging her?

Quickly, I push those thoughts to the back of my mind. *Concentrate on the now.* And that I'm currently the man who's holding her close. "Was it too much for you? Did I push you too far?" I didn't think I had, but I need, as a Dom, to check.

"No." She follows up the word with a small grin, "But you tormented me. I thought you were never going to let me come."

"But it was better for waiting, wasn't it?"

Her small hand hits my pecs, I cover it with my own, glancing down for a second, noting the contrast in the colour of our skin, my darker olive against the fairness of hers. My mouth turns up at the corners, "If you're not careful, next time I won't."

Now her mouth opens in shock at my threat, another reaction that makes me hug her again.

I provide aftercare to subs, hold them until they recover, providing reassurance as necessary, but this feeling of contentment overtaking me is something I've not felt before. I don't want to move, don't feel suffocated by her closeness. *I feel complete.*

But then I've never initiated a virgin. This strange desire to protect her and keep her near must be down to that. Her. The woman gave me her most precious gift. She's not some nameless sub I've taken responsibility for, just for the scene. The thought should make me uncomfortable, instead it brings peace. A harmony between my body and mind that's been missing in my life. I'm totally relaxed, and reconciled with my world.

"Sleep." My own eyes feel heavy, she must be exhausted as well. As if already programmed, she follows my instruction, her breathing soon evening out. Slipping down the bed I spoon behind her, pulling her close to me, unconsciously repeating how I'd held her that first night.

A loud thundering noise wakes us, she jumps in my arms.

"Good morning, habiti." I place a kiss to the side of her neck.

"Jasim," she turns and then blinks as she looks up at me, "What, where?"

I smile at the dazed look in her eyes, watching as recollection of the night before dawns. Memories confirmed as she stretches and groans, her over-used body protesting her movements. "The helicopter has arrived to take us back to Zalmā."

Her hand touches her bum, "I'm glad we're not riding horses today."

I bark a laugh, "Sore? Let me look." Obediently, she turns over. There's not much to see, but a small area of darkening bruising on each cheek. "You're carrying my marks." And fuck, does that make me hard. But I'm not that much of a bastard, she'll be too sore for another round.

She notices my cock hardening, and licks her lips.

"No, it's too soon. You need time to recover." But her eager eyes glisten, and I refuse her again, "Trust me. It will be better if we wait. You'll be too sore for me now."

She shoots me a cheeky look, "I thought you were a sadist and wouldn't care about that?"

A grin comes to my face, "Oh, I can find ways to torture you without penetration. How about I bring you to the edge and leave you that way?"

Her eyes widen, as she remembers my threat of last night. Her brow creases, "Don't we need to get up and not keep the helicopter waiting?"

"No rush." My smile widens, fueled by the look of horror in her eyes. Yes, there's a million ways I can make her suffer, and I'll enjoy every one. Knowing, of course, her, and my own, eventual reward will be worth it.

She pulls away and sits on the side of the bed, her eyes falling on her discarded dress.

"There are fresh clothes for you, in that chest over there." I point it out, "And behind the curtain, a small shower. Just don't expect much from it, but it's enough to freshen you up." There's a small header tank that's been filled with water which, by now, should have been warmed by the heat of the sun. Functional, if not luxurious.

She washes up first, I follow after, there's not room for both of us at once. But the thought of showering with her in a more adequate cubicle has the unsurprising effect on my cock. Uncomfortable, I try to ignore such thoughts as I make myself ready, dressing for the day in clean robes.

Today I don't fly myself, but sit in the rear two seats with her, as we're piloted over the desert returning to my temporary home. She's nervous at flying, a revelation that fills me with guilt as I remember how I'd ignored her when we'd flown to the desert. Her nerves being the only reason I sit holding her hand. But that doesn't explain the strange reluctance to break our connection when I eventually have to let it go. *She grounds me.*

As the desert palace appears beneath us and we come in to land, I mentally gird myself to return to the real world. The world where I'm the president of a major oil operation, and brother to the emir. My infatuation with the woman beside me must be locked away. At least until tonight. This is good sex between compatible people, nothing more than that.

I start to explain, "Janna, I've work to do when we land."

"I know, you're a busy man." At least she understands me. "And I'm supposed to be flying back with Sally today." A shadow falls over her face as reality hits.

She's given me the perfect out, a way to end this cleanly. I could let her return to the capital and then back to London. Meet up with her when I'm home, and take her to the club. Yes, that's a sensible option. But a twisting feeling in my gut tells me I'm not ready to let her go. "Can you stay a while longer? I wanted to see you tonight."

She thinks for a moment, her manner changing as we come back to reality. "I don't know if I can. How I'll explain that to them."

She means to her protectors, the men who'd take her away from me if they had any inkling of how I want to, have already, corrupted her. But she can't hide forever, and when she sees them, her face will give her away. "Tell them the truth."

She bites her lip, "And what exactly is that, Jasim?"

I take a deep breath, and a leap into unchartered waters, "That we've gotten together, and want to see where this goes."

Her eyes open wide, it wasn't what she'd expected, as if the words I'd uttered in the night were spoken only in the heat of the moment. Little movements on her face, slight changes in her expression shows me she's trying to be sensible, probably remembering how I'd described myself. But then a short laugh accompanies her reply, "They'll kill you."

I shake my head, "You're a woman, now. No longer a girl," I'd made sure of that. "They have to cut you lose sometime."

A bite of her lip, a small nod of her head, "Okay. I'll stay. I don't need to go back straight away, they'll still be wrapping things up. We're not leaving Amahad for another few days. And you're right. It's time I showed my mettle and give it to them straight." Then one of her cheeky grins, "I don't think I'll tell them everything."

And now she makes me chuckle. Hmm. I really do think it's best if some details are kept to ourselves.

The helicopter sets down gently, and I help her out, already half in work mode, thinking of what I've got to do today to catch up on slacking off the day before. Well, really I'm trying to occupy my mind with anything to stop reliving the wonders of last night with the predictable consequence for my libido, which otherwise will have me going through the day with a semi-hard dick. Helping her down, she understands that a blatant display of affection would not be appropriate back at the palace, nonetheless she holds my hand just a little too long, before pulling her fingers from mine…

"Sheikh Jasim! *Ladayna mushkila.*" I turn to see Rais, pacing toward us, his face black as thunder. The fact he's addressed me in Arabic showing the disturbed state of his mind.

"*Mushkilata? Madha hdth?*" I find myself using the same language as I ask what the problem is, then revert back to my preferred English, "What the hell has happened?"

Rais looks down at his feet, and scuffs the sand, a gesture of disgust, "The Englishwoman, the one who filmed in the desert. She's missing."

"What?" I say, almost at the same moment as Janna's hand goes to her mouth.

"Sally?" she squawks. "What do you mean, she's missing?"

My hand goes to her shoulder and I give it a slight squeeze, "Come," I gesture to Rais, "Let's go to the office and you can tell me everything you know."

Ryan's standing waiting, his posture fraught with concern. Whatever has happened, he knows what's going on. Quickly, he takes the lead and we follow him into the palace. Anxious to know what's going on, but aware of discussing business that might be best not overheard, I wait until we're in the more secure location before swinging around, "Talk to me. Rais."

Rais shrugs off his headdress, throwing it onto a chair, "Fadi."

My eyes widen, *Fadi?* Why's he throwing that name out now, Sheikh Fadi leads the Khahri, one of the less progressive tribes who initially threw their backing behind Abdul-Muhsi—may he rot in his grave—when he attempted a coup. Easily led, Fadi, one of the younger desert sheikhs, came to his senses just in time and saw the error of his ways. He'd provided some men and horses yesterday. I'd had a short, amicable conversation with him, and found nothing untoward or suspect.

I glance at Ryan, hoping he can enlighten me, but he's just standing there, his cheeks red with rage. I turn back to Rais, "In the name of Allah, will someone tell me what's going on?"

Rais shakes his head and swears, "He was there, yesterday."

"Yes, I saw him. Some of his men brought horses…"

"Seems Fadi was intrigued by the event. And by the fair-haired woman," Rais continues as if I hadn't interrupted him, "As we were packing up, he spirited the woman away."

Yesterday evening? And he's only thinking of telling me this now? "Why wasn't I informed?"

"At first, I wasn't worried, thought she was doing some extra filming or something. And I didn't want to disturb you, Excellency." The use of my title sounds like a sneer from one of my best friends. And it probably is. He doesn't see me as a desert leader, and, why should he? It's been years since I've been resident in Amahad. "But when she didn't return, we started to make enquiries. He's taken her."

Fuck. This will be the last thing Kadar will want to hear. An Englishwoman kidnapped in the desert? When she should have been under my protection? I'd been so wrapped up in my plans for Janna, I hadn't given a thought to the camerawoman left behind.

"What have you done about it?" I snap.

A shrug from the rugged sheikh, "I've tried to reach out to him, but can't get in contact."

"His phone?"

"Is turned off. Or he hasn't got it with him." Some of the sheikhs are not fans of using satellite phones. Or any modern technology, for that matter.

Shit. "Have you sent out a search party?"

"Of course I have. We've been to the main settlement of the Khahri, but he's not taken her there. There are rumours he's taken her to *alqaleat fi alssama'.*"

The castle in the sky. Not a castle at all, but a fortified ancient building high in the hills, approachable only on horseback. And there's only one reason a man would take a woman there. If he wanted to keep her, and prevent her being taken back.

"What does this mean, Jasim? Why would this Fadi chap take Sally?"

I'd almost forgotten the woman at my side.

Now Ryan steps forward, his hand holding a note. "This was delivered this morning." The Grade A operative looks weary, his anger for the moment contained, but the narrowing of his eyes tells me I'm not going to like what the note says.

Reaching out I take it, unfold it, and rage sweeps through me as I roar, "No. No fucking way. Never." My hand thumps down on the desk, "He's signed his death warrant just by asking for this."

CHAPTER 20
Janna

What on earth is on that piece of paper? Jasim's bellow of protest had made me jump, my concern for my friend escalating in a rush. Looking at the man beside me, I see his body quivering with barely controlled rage. *What is this man, Fadi, asking?* It's clearly something terrible if his death is on the cards.

"Jasim," I start, hesitantly, "What's the matter? What's happened to Sally?" I start to feel sick with worry. I'd been so caught up in last night's glorious activities that I hadn't given a thought to my new friend. Now guilt washes over me. I'd left her alone in the desert. *I never dreamt she wouldn't be safe.*

But Jasim doesn't answer. Instead he ignores me, just staring ahead, his hands clenching into fists at his sides. It's then I realise I know nothing about this man. Oh, I've learned he likes to take control in bed, that he can read my body and knows how to excite me better than I do myself. But what do I know about the man he really is? What makes him happy, sad? And what fires his temper to the extent that it is?

Is he worried for Sally? Would this Fadi person hurt her? Why has she been taken? And what can I do to help?

"Jasim," I try again, "What's going on?"

This time he hears me, and his face looks down, his dark eyes wide and flaring, and I take a step back, bumping up against the hard, muscular chest of the bodyguard, Ryan.

And it's Ryan who speaks to me, "Don't worry, Janna. It will be alright."

"You can't tell her that," Jasim snarls, "Who knows how far this lunatic will take this?"

"He'll see reason." Rais answers him, "What he's done is treason, he'll soon understand that."

The piece of paper Jasim's holding is now crushed in his hand, balled up, and thrown across the room. "I must speak with Kadar."

I'd rather he spoke with me, not knowing what's going on is killing me. But the man who's before me is so different to the person I was with last night, and I don't know how to appeal to him. *His intensity, his rage, scares me.*

"Come with me," Ryan bends to speak into my ear, "You can't help here. I'll take you back to your room."

I round on him, "My friend's been kidnapped. I have to do something."

Again, Jasim's eyes meet mine, his face tightens, then his mouth works, but no words come out. It's as though I'm watching him fight an internal battle. Then, at last, he growls, "Go with Ryan."

Dismissed, my cheeks burn with frustration and anger. Once taking last look at Jasim's unyielding features and know there's no other option. Nodding at Ryan, I let him lead me out through the door, hoping to get some information out of him on the way. But the taciturn bodyguard stays silent until we reach the room Sally and I had stayed in the night before last. On entering, I notice how empty it seems.

Ryan looks like he's just going to leave me, so I grab hold of his arm, "What's going on, Ryan? What's happening? Where's Sally? And what can I do?"

Putting his arm on the door jam, he leans his head on the wood, "Christ, Janna, I wish I could tell you. But Jasim needs to work through it first and decide on a course of action. It's a fucked-up situation. That's all I can say. Look, get in touch with your friends, tell them what's going on. Whatever happens, I doubt you'll be returning to the capital today. Just trust him, Janna. Can you do that?"

Trust a man who just blocked me out, after everything that had happened between us? I feel so frustrated, so angry that he'd ignored me, and so powerless that I didn't know how to comfort him.

"Ryan, please…"

"I can't tell you more. It's Jasim's decision if he wants you to know any more details." Pushing me gently into the room, Ryan pauses before turning to go, "He'll do everything in his power to get Sally back. You can bank on that. Okay? And with Rais and myself beside him, we won't let any harm come to her."

I hate being in the dark, but what's happened today is something completely outside anything I've ever experienced before. While I despise feeling so useless, what help could I possibly offer? I know nothing of the desert, or of their primitive ways. Why did this sheikh take Sally? And how will they get her back? How would I know where to even start to get a kidnapped woman back where she belongs? Knowing I have to leave it to them, even while hating being left out, I shake my head, partly in dismissal of the things Ryan has said, but also because there's nothing I can do. A hand under my chin, soft fingers brushing away tears I didn't even know had escaped. And then a final nod when he sees I've accepted my limitations.

And then Ryan's gone.

And I'm alone.

Rolling my head on my shoulders, I wonder what I should do now. *Ring Mickey.* Whether Jasim had asked me to stay or not, I'm going back to the capital, not until I know Sally's safe. And they need to be told the bad news.

So that makes two reasons why that's going to be a very awkward conversation.

Picking up my phone, I dial and don't have to wait long before it's answered.

"Hey, Janna. We were just talking about you and wondering how the filming went. Hold on, we're all here. I'll put you on speaker."

Oh no. I'd hoped it would just be him at first.

"Hey, girl. How's it going? You survived the horses? You and Sally still coming back today?"

"Yeah, Joe. I did, but…"

"Did you get some good footage? We going to be able to use it? What time are you getting back?"

"Yeah, Ben, but…"

"Did it go to plan?"

"Yes, it did. For goodness sake! Will you let me get a word in edgewise?"

There's laughter and then silence, which I embarrassingly fill by bursting into tears, huge wracking sobs which I can't stop. Now voices all speaking together, "Fuck, Jan, what's going on?" "What's the matter?" and finally, "What HAS that bastard done? I knew we shouldn't have let you go off with him."

"Jasim's done nothing." I sob, realising too late I shouldn't have said his name.

"Janna, speak to me." It's Rory who asks, a little more calmly than the rest. "What's happened? Why are you upset? Have you slept with Jasim?"

As I wonder how they'd known that was even a possible outcome, Mickey takes my silence for assent and snarls into the phone, "Fuck, Janna. We knew you wanted to from the way you looked at him, but never thought he'd be interested."

"Shut it, Joe. He's a man. She offered, he'd take. And by the sound of it he's had enough and…"

"It wasn't like that." I try to stand up for him, fleeting memories of last night reminding me how special he'd made my first time. "Look, I'm not calling about that. Whatever I did or didn't do with Jasim, well, that's my personal business. There's something else." And then quickly, before they can ask me for any more details, continue, "Sally's missing. She might have been kidnapped."

That shuts them up. For a moment. Then they all speak at once, asking me unanswerable questions. Sunny's crying in the background, she'd been her friend too.

"What's Jasim doing? Is he there?"

When I tell Joe he isn't, he swears, "Fuck, girl. He should be comforting you."

"He's organising things, trying to find her and get her back," It's automatic that I come to my lover's defence.

There's mumblings and mutterings, then, "You get your arse back here, Janna. It's obviously not safe down there."

"No, Mickey. I'm not coming back. Not until I know that Sally's safe." And I'm not leaving Jasim until I've had another chance to talk to him once he's calmed down.

It dawns on me this is the first time since I met them I've had distance between us, the miles meaning they can't control me for once. I let their ranting wash over me, ignoring their instructions to return. Disregarding the plans they're making to go back to England and civilisation where women aren't kidnapped by rogue desert sheikhs.

When their protests finally die down, I break into the conversation, reiterating, "I'm staying here."

More unheard conversations, then Joe's on the line, "We're coming to you then. Just as soon as we can. And for fuck's sake, take care, Janna. Stay in the palace and don't go outside. It's clearly not safe down there." I end the call.

I don't need them to tell me. My friend's been stolen away, I won't be putting myself at risk.

A servant enters, and I suspect I'll have to thank Ryan for remembering to feed me, in his current mood I doubt Jasim would think of it. Not that I'm hungry, but the outward sign someone's thinking of me makes me feel slightly less abandoned. I toy with some pastries, which taste like dust in my mouth. At least having to tell them Sally's been kidnapped has taken the heat off of me. For now.

Had I been wrong to give myself to the enigmatic sheikh?

No. Last night is something I will never regret.

CHAPTER 21
Jasim

When I first read the note, I burned with rage, almost unable to speak, not trusting myself to say anything to Janna. The first thought in my head being *Janna's mine*. How dare someone think they had a claim on her? As soon as Ryan had removed her from the room, I rounded on Rais, my fists clenching.

"How did it happen? How did he take Sally without being stopped?"

Rais lets out a loud sigh, "It was partly my fault, I wasn't watching her carefully enough. Hell, I didn't even think that I needed to." He paces away, then turns back, "She had that darn camera with her, wanted to capture some footage of the horses. I've questioned those from my tribe, who said Fadi enticed her away."

"And no one stopped her?"

"No one thought they needed to. We'd gotten back to camp, they were loading the horses. She'd ridden with Fadi, and his tribe were first away. It was only when everyone had left we realised she was missing, and then put together the pieces of how it had happened."

"Fuck it." I drag my hand through my hair. How could this day, that had started so well, end up in such a mess like this? Fleetingly, the thought of Janna in my bed last night goes through my mind. What I wouldn't give to be back there, holding her close, running my hands over her soft skin without a care in the world. The memory of how responsive she'd been to my touch and the demand written on the note causes me to spit out, "He's not getting anywhere near Janna."

"I thought you'd say that." A corner of Rais's mouth turns up, "I assume last night turned out how you'd planned?"

I give a distracted nod, then drop down into a chair, my elbows on my thighs, my hands clasped between my knees. "He's given us three days, Rais." Three days to exchange Janna for her friend. That's who Fadi was really after.

"It will take time to arrange our response."

Yes, it will. The castle in the sky is all but impenetrable. Fadi knew what he was doing, taking the woman there. "He holds all the cards. It's impossible to attack."

A shrug, "And even to try could mean he ends up harming her."

"He's a dead man if he does," I snarl. "He wouldn't really do that, would he? Surely it's just an idle threat."

Another shrug, "What else has he got to bargain with? He's got nothing to lose. He must know he's in serious trouble. How could he think he'd get away with doing what he has?"

"Why Janna?" That's what I don't understand.

Rais seats himself opposite me, "He only saw her yesterday evening, but Jasim, she looked stunning. Running across the sand. It's our heritage, in our blood. To see what we want and take it."

"Centuries ago, perhaps, but not now."

"Fadi's roots are as those of a primitive man of the desert, it's not such a distant past for him."

Rais could be right. "I'll speak to Kadar, he needs to know."

"Of course, my friend. While you do so, I'll check and see if we've discovered anything else. I'll speak to the other sheikhs, they might know him better than I and have views on how he'll play this."

I thank him, and he pats my shoulder on his way out. Fuck, what a mess. Could it have been prevented? Who would have guessed Fadi would go to such extremes, kidnapping one woman to trade for another? But whatever he's planned, he's not taking my Janna. Not until I've had the time I want with her. And no, not even then. How dare Fadi even dream of touching a hair on her head?

I pick up the phone and place my call, needing to hold it away from my ear at the predictable colourful and loud exclamations from my older brother. He contacts Nijad, and soon we're having a three-way call.

"We could let Fadi have this Janna for now." Kadar hears my growl but continues, "He gives up the other woman, and we wait for him to get careless. When he thinks he's won and goes back to his tribe, we swoop in and retrieve Janna."

I'm not having my woman in his hands for a moment. "No."

"It's the old ways of the desert, brother."

And one of the reasons I no longer live in my home country. "I can't agree to that. He could…" My voice breaks off as I try hard not to envision exactly what he could do to her.

Nijad barks a laugh, "She's got to you, hasn't she, brother? You don't want another man's hands on her. I take it my gift came in useful?"

For a response I'm silent, loathe to give myself away. And there's no way I'm going to admit I'd used his hand-cuffs and spreader bar last night.

But I don't need to say anything. Nijad thinks the same way as I, and he cottons on fast, "You did fuck her, didn't you?"

"Is this right, Jasim? Nijad suggested you were taken with her, but I wasn't sure whether to believe him. You're always so careful to avoid complications." Even though I'm hundreds of miles away, I can imagine Kadar's eyebrows rising. "Well, whether or not you've dipped your wick, I don't like this at all. We're trying to promote Amahad as the place foreign tourists will want to come to. Not a place where women are at risk of being abducted. Fuck Fadi, he should know better than this."

"What's Rais's take on how we should play this?" For a second it irks me that Nijad would be asking for the desert sheikh's view rather than my opinion. Another sign I've been away from the country too long.

I swallow down my pride. My two obligatory years doing military service protecting our borders is a long way in my past. "His view is that *alqaleat fi alssama'* is a defensible position, not open to attack."

"We could bomb it from the air…"

"Kind of defeats the point of a rescue," Kadar's dry tones berate my brother.

I ignore the asinine comment from Nijad. "If we try to attack, we put the woman in danger and risk losing the lives of many of our men."

"Has Ryan had anything to say?" Like many of the Grade A team, Ryan's ex-SAS, that elite arm of the British

Military service. And his bosses, Ben Carter and Jon Tharpe, are well versed in hostage extraction.

"He's talking with Jon and Ben now. But it's an unusual situation."

"What have we got to bargain with?" Kadar's thinking like the emir, a contrast to Nijad whose first impulse is to suggest using force. "Apart from giving him what he's asked for."

He's not getting his hands on Janna. "His life?" I counter.

"Unless he harms her, kidnapping a foreign national is not a crime punishable by death. Not anymore. Incarceration, yes." One of Kadar's first actions when he came to the throne was to revise the crimes for which death was the penalty. And at this precise moment, I rather think he's gone too far.

"He's committed treason," I growl.

"Kidnapping a foreign national, yes. Treason, no. Not unless he's taken a woman belonging to a member of the royal family."

In my view, he wants to. "He's taken a hostage but he wants a woman who's under my protection."

"You might have fucked her, Jasim, but that doesn't make her yours." I disagree, I took her virginity, her body, *her soul* belongs to me. For now, anyway.

"There's one option, Jasim. If you married her, she'd become one of us. A royal. No one, not the least Fadi, could argue with that."

Nijad laughs loudly as I gasp. Kadar's suggestion has stunned me into silence. My mouth works but no words come out.

"That's a serious proposition, Kadar. But one which may sway Fadi, if Jas can demonstrate a prior claim to this woman."

"Maybe I spoke hastily. Jasim doesn't want a wife, or any kind of relationship, and there has never been a divorce in the royal family."

I can't believe it when I find myself saying, "Nijad's original marriage contract limited the marriage to five years. There's nothing to say I couldn't have a limited one too." What the hell am I suggesting? Considering tying myself to a woman I hardly know? Even temporarily? I must be going out of my mind.

"Those were exceptional circumstances. And we invoked the old laws." Nevertheless, Kadar's sounding thoughtful, his tone belying his words.

"Those ancient laws still hold sway among the desert tribes," I point out.

Nijad barks a laugh, "You could divorce her by saying 'I divorce you' three times if you're following the primitive ways. And I thought those practices were the very ones you've been running away from." I glare at the phone, unable to deny what he's said is the truth. But as I do, I'm mulling the idea over in my mind. As strange as it may seem, the idea of being wed to Janna isn't immediately distasteful. *She'd belong to me.*

"The marriage would have to be real enough to convince Fadi to give up his demands. And what exactly is it about this woman that Fadi wants her so much, and you're prepared to give up your freedom for her?"

"Not permanently." Hastily, I seek to reassure him. I don't see this as a long-term arrangement. But spending more time with her would not be a hardship. That was my plan anyway. It would just be slightly longer and more a more formal arrangement than I had intended.

"Jasim, you know my views. I want to see you married and settled, but not in this way. We know nothing about her." My older brother would be interested in her pedigree, her suitability to join the family.

"Both you and Nijad married Englishwomen with no breeding," I snap. From first thinking the idea is a joke, now I'm seeking to overcome their objections. *Have I lost my mind?*

After a brief moment of silence, Kadar sounds resigned. "I spoke in haste, brother. This is a step too far. You, as Ni put it so eloquently, have fucked her. You have already got a claim. Just explain that to Fadi."

"And if it isn't sufficient? If he carries out his threats?" Shaking my head, I continue, "With a marriage contract to cement it, there's no argument he could use."

"I'm not convinced that the idea carries merit. There must be something else."

Anything else carries a risk. And this way, I get Janna. "No, Kadar. I don't want to push Fadi into doing something we might all regret. Marrying Janna brings her under the protection of the royal family, as you've just said. It's the simplest way. I'll do it."

"Your determined?"

And suddenly, I know I am. "Yes."

Kadar sighs, "You'll have to persuade her."

Nijad chuckles, "Seems none of us give our women much choice in the matter."

His reference to Cara, who was kidnapped to marry him, and Zoe, who'd ended up as the desert sheikhs' choice of bride for their emir, gives me an idea. "I'll tell her it's the only option and give her no way out. I can marry her by contract. Rais will be one of the witnesses, and his word will stand."

"And the mahr?" Kadar asks about the bride price, the money in our culture traditionally put aside for the bride should the husband desert her. I hadn't thought of that.

But it wouldn't be a problem. "I can sort that out. I'm not exactly penniless."

"Ten million pounds sterling."

"What?" Both Nijad and I exclaim together.

Kadar remains silent for a few seconds, letting the incredibly large amount sink in, before explaining, "It was the amount that the crown put forward for Nijad's marriage. To offer anything less would make her appear less valued."

"And the time period?"

"No time limit," Kadar answers Nijad, and I suspect they're exchanging grins. They're tying me to a woman, something they've long wanted to see.

They're taking advantage. "That's not fair to me, or her."

"Marriage is not to be taken lightly," my older brother's voice booms.

"But surely, in the circumstances… Even our father gave a limit when Nijad was forced to marry."

"At the time, we thought Cara was a thief," Kadar gives the explanation we all know, "He didn't want a criminal tied to the Kassis name for life. Her sole purpose was to provide Nijad with a child." After he's reminded us of the original terms of our younger brother's marriage, he pauses, then, "No, Jasim. The contract will not be for a specific time. As a member of the royal family, you need my permission to take this step. The eyes of the world will be on you once they learn you've taken a wife."

"And if I don't, Sally might die. A woman who came here to work. How would that be viewed internationally?"

"An unfortunate accident, the desert is a wild place."

"That won't work, Janna will have already told her friends that Sally's gone missing."

"But not the rest of the details?"

"No, she hasn't been told." Yet.

"So, we keep that titbit quiet. As you've repeatedly said, Jasim, marriage is not for you. I don't want to force you into it. We'll come up with some story to explain her disappearance, or convince Fadi to give her up, as his plan's not going to work. And you keep your freedom."

And Fadi might follow through with his threat. I can't risk that. "My freedom, as you put it, is not worth a woman's life."

"If you ask her to marry you, do you think she'll agree? I don't like the notion of forcing her hand. That wouldn't look good for us either." Kadar's clearly worried about his country's reputation.

I have no fucking idea. What do I know of her? She plays in a band, she was a virgin. And I'm insanely attracted to her. For now. How long that will last, I don't know. What else do I know of her? Would she agree to a sham of a marriage to protect her friend? Whatever Kadar says, I'm not in the market for a wife, and we will divorce further down what is probably a very short line. But I also understand that my position as a prince of the land means I'd have to make it appear genuine, at least for a while. Any such union would be picked up by the international press. Which means considering living together. *Having her in my bed.*

"Nijad's already brought disrepute on Amahad," Kadar's reading my mind.

"I was cleared." My younger brother sounds angry.

"You were, but people have long memories. And unfortunately, mud sticks. Amahad's good standing is at stake. The people you negotiate with, Jasim, the oil talks. You can't do anything to make them think you're flighty, liable to act on a whim. This marriage must be watertight, no one must suspect we're hiding a reason for why it was so rushed."

"It must appear romantic."

I don't do romance. If Ni was in front of me he'd be able to see my scowl. It's clear the bugger's enjoying this. But I have to concede his point. I'm known as one of the world's richest and most eligible bachelors, it won't be long before any marriage would be picked up by the press. It has to look right. Seem to be authentic, even if it's not.

"If she agrees, I'll make it look real." And until I've had my fill of her, that won't be too difficult.

"She'll have to play her part."

"I'll make sure she understands." But what would that look like? As a sheikh's wife, could she still play in the band? There will be a role expected of her. Could she settle into it? Stand by my side as society would expect?

"Ask her, Jasim," Kadar sounds resigned as he sighs. "Nijad and I will arrange to come down to Z̧almā. To witness your wedding, or to make other plans."

"And speak to Rais before you do, and see if he's come up with any alternative." Again, a reference to my lack of knowledge about the desert and the leaders of the primitive tribes. What other option could there be?

Any alternative could get a lot of our men, and the missing Sally, killed. Ending the phone call, I drop my head into my hands. How can I ask Janna? And will she agree?

CHAPTER 22
Janna

It must be more than an hour later, by which time I've bitten my nails down to the quick, when I hear someone at the door. When it opens, the last person I'd expected, but the first that I'd hoped, appears. Jasim. Following at his heels is Rais, who clearly has difficulty hiding a smirk when Jasim strides across the room, places his hands either side of my face and insistently presses his lips to mine. Automatically I open for him, his tongue drives inside, and I taste a mix of sweet and bitter, the flavour of Arab coffee. The way he moulds to me makes me feel like I'm coming home, and with that one action he wipes all my resentment away.

When he pulls back, his hands still hold me, fingertips gently caressing my skin, "Janna, oh, my Janna. I'm so sorry, can you forgive me?"

My mind blown away by that devastating kiss, for a moment I've forgotten what he's done wrong.

"I couldn't speak to you until I'd calmed down. Oh, Janna. Habiti, forgive me, please?"

Rais standing off to one side, shakes as though he's laughing inwardly. "Forgive him, Janna, please." Then, his mirth disappears. "We need to move this on."

I pull back, holding him at arm's length, "I accept your apology for shutting me out. But tell me what's wrong, please? What's happened to Sally? Where has she gone?" His anger might have disappeared, but he's still tense, "What can I do to help find her?"

He speaks to Rais, but his eyes stare into mine, "How can I tell her, Rais? How can I explain? How do I fucking do this?"

The desert sheikh comes closer, his hand resting supportively on Jasim's shoulder. His face turned to mine, he takes it on himself to enlighten. "Janna, Fadi abducted your friend Sally, but she's not the woman he desires."

That doesn't make any sense. My brow furrows as I look from one to the other, and ask, "So why did he take her? And who does he really want?"

Jasim wipes his hand over his face, as he takes over, his voice trembles as though it's full of emotion. "You. He wants you."

Me? "Me?" my voice comes out as a squeal. "Why on earth would he want *me?*"

With narrowing eyes, Jasim gives me an appraising look, taking me in from head to toe, "We've discussed this, and there's only one reason. The same reason why I wanted you. Because you're beautiful. And, from what he saw, untouched."

I shake my head. Oh, I know I'm quite decent looking, I've had fans for years, but I'm not particularly exceptional. Hell, there must be hundreds, thousands of women more attractive than me. My brow creases as I frown. "What exactly did it say in that note, Jasim?"

As though seeking some help, his eyes flit to Rais before coming back to me. He draws in a sharp breath, "He wants to make an exchange. You, for Sally."

Oh shit. "And? If we don't, he'll keep Sally?" I can't leave her to that fate. But I'm not certain I'm brave enough to offer to take her place.

"He's threatened her if we don't meet his demands."

Fuck! "He'll hurt her?"

The worry on his face increases my concern as Jasim shrugs, "He might do. I don't believe we can afford to take that risk."

My brain's unable to compute all the implications. "Jasim, what are we going to do?" If my voice sounds shaky, I think I can be excused given the circumstances. He couldn't be considering me swapping places with her. *Could he?*

As if reading my mind, immediately his arms encircle me, holding me tightly to him, "I'm not going to let him near you, I promise you that. We're going to get Sally back, without giving you up."

"How? If he's threatened to harm her?" I can feel his fingers gripping me, the tension in him evident. To prompt him I ask again. "How, Jasim? How can we get her back without swapping me for her? He's threatened to hurt her, I can't let him do that." But, on the other hand, *I* don't want to become the plaything of a rough desert sheikh, one who I've never even met, in her stead. As Jasim delays answering, I look down at my interlocked hands, not surprised to find they're visibly trembling. Though the air conditioner is working, sweat comes to my brow. I'd heard the southern desert of Amahad had a troubled reputation, lost in the ways of the ancient world, but coming here to experience it had seemed like it would be a bit of fun. Fun, huh? This is anything but.

Warm hands cover mine, "There is a solution."

For the life of me I can't imagine what it is.

"Habiti, come." Jasim leads me to a low couch, and encourages me to sit. He folds his long limbs, and I feel his leg touching mine. However inappropriate in the current situation, I feel the stirrings of lust, an automatic reaction when his body is close. I try to inch away, his arm comes around me, locking me to him.

I glance up at his face, his eyes are half closed.

"Janna, I've a proposition to put to you. But let me explain first." He nods up at Rais, who turns and leaves us alone. "We know where they're holding Sally, and the problem is, where he's taken her makes it very difficult to attempt a rescue. Even if we go with an army. Fadi's chosen his site well."

"Difficult or impossible, Jasim? And if you attack him, is there a chance he could retaliate and do something to her?"

"Veering towards the impossible I'm afraid. Look, Janna, I don't know Fadi well enough to say whether he'd make good on his threat. But if we make our approach without you, he'll know that he's lost. And he'll be a desperate man."

Desperate men do desperate things. This is all so alien to me. What do I know about soldiers and fighting? Zilch. I could talk thirteen to the dozen about chord progressions but nothing about making preparation for war. All I can do is to listen. Hoping he's got a plan to get Sally back unharmed, and selfishly hoping there'll be no risk to myself, I take a deep breath. "Okay, so what do you propose?"

His hands touch my face as he turns me toward him, despite the seriousness of our discussion, there's a wry grin on his face, "You've hit the nail on the head, habiti."

What? What have I said? My brow creases as I go back over the words I've just spoken, finding nothing jumps out at me. His fingers try to smooth the wrinkles away.

"If we marry, I have a claim on you. One which Fadi will understand and must respect. By our ancient laws, you will be untouchable. A member of, and protected by, the royal family."

My eyes open wide. *Marry? Surely that isn't what he's just suggested?* "What on earth do you mean?"

He shrugs, nonchalantly, his gesture at odds with the seriousness of his words, "I'm proposing to you. Will you marry me?"

What the hell is he talking about? Frowning at the casual way he threw it into the conversation, I think quickly. There's no way I can marry him. I haven't thought about marrying anyone. I'm twenty-two years old, for goodness sake, plenty of time to think about getting hitched in the future. I must be misunderstanding. This has to be some kind of joke.

"You can't mean it. You said yourself you weren't in the market for anything permanent." I state, then reconsider, "Or is it just a pretence to get Sally back?" That must be it. It wouldn't be real.

He takes one of my hands in his, his fingers tracing the veins on the back, "Janna, you know I'm a sheikh, but more than that, I'm a Prince of Amahad."

He's never come over as royal to me, but I know who he is. I don't understand what bearing it has on the situation. My head tilts to one side as I await his explanation.

He squeezes his fingers, "When I marry, habiti, it will be international news. Fadi will expect it. And as a prince of this land, any relationship will be watched very carefully. A marriage will need to look real. But," now a smile comes to his face, "After last night I don't think we'd have any problem in that area. In the short term, at least."

I'm thinking fast, "What about an engagement instead? Then we can break it off when Sally's safe."

"Fadi won't go for that. The idea of a long waiting period once two people agree to be wed is not something familiar to his desert ways."

"You say short term?"

"You'd have to act as my wife, until such a time as we can amicably separate. And ensure it's not in such a way as to discredit the Crown."

I stand, my back to Jasim, my hands wringing together. "I've never considered getting married. And I certainly didn't expect a proposal linked with how soon we could get a divorce." No, if I ever thought about it, it was in far more romantic ways. A candlelit dinner, perhaps, a man getting down on his knees. *But what man could do more for me than Jasim had arranged last night?* Though, that certainly hadn't been with any proposal in mind. Or at the time, a relationship lasting for longer than just the one night.

Hearing a swishing of robes, I'm not surprised to feel him standing behind me, so close his chest is pressed against my back. "You're right. I told you I'm not a man for a permanent relationship. Fuck, Janna. If there was any other way to be certain of getting Sally back, I wouldn't be saying these things." His hands cup my shoulders, "You deserve so much more."

I shrug off his touch, him being so close to me is making me weaken. *What would it be like to belong to this man?* "Surely there must be some other way?"

"None that we can think of. Unless we want to sacrifice men on a mission bound to fail."

"So we sacrifice ourselves." *But would it be so bad?* Last night had been amazing. Then another problem occurs to me, "The band members would kill me."

"No, they wouldn't." Jasim moves to stand in front of me, "I took your virginity last night. And I'm a primitive type of man. With hot desert blood in my veins. Tell them I swept you away, and asked you to marry me."

"Make them believe it's real?"

"Why not?"

They'd certainly have a lot to say about it. But could I convince them? Making them think it was credible might be easier than asking them to accept it was all one big sham. And I expect the least people who know the truth the better.

Now his hands are touching me again, his fingers teasing the sides of my breasts. My nipples peak visibly through the fabric of the tunic I'm wearing. Then he takes hold of my arm, moving my fingers down until they brush against a very hard cock. "It wouldn't be a chore, Janna. I'd make sure you enjoy it."

"What if I'm not enough for you?"

He leans his head down until his forehead is resting against mine, "I think last night showed there are endless possibilities between us. You enjoyed what I did to you. You still carry my marks."

And that reminder is making me wet.

Can I do through with it? How can I not.

"What will happen with me playing in the band?"

"We'll sort all of that out. Take it one step at a time and see what happens."

He pushes in close, his hardness rubbing against my soft stomach, he's not playing fair.

"Okay." Softly, I say the word I hope I'm not going to regret.

"Okay?"

I repeat it more strongly, "Okay, yes. If this is the only way to get Sally home safe." I raise my eyes to look at him,

"But, Jasim, I wouldn't be agreeing to marry you if it wasn't for her."

"And I wouldn't be asking," he counters without missing a beat.

The corners of my lips turn up, "So, a match made in heaven then?"

He grins, "Exactly that." Lowering his head, his mouth comes down on mine, and we seal our bargain, tongues mashing together, lips moving, teeth nipping. Breathless, we break apart. The surprise on his face must match mine.

"We might have pre-empted our wedding night, but I can't wait to have you again. And when I do, you'll be my wife."

I don't understand my reaction, a giddy excitement making me tingle.

We're interrupted by the door opening, it's Rais who's returned. As he enters, Jasim throws him a nod. "It's done. Janna's agreed."

Rais nods in acknowledgement as if he'd never had any doubt about my response. In on the ruse, he doesn't offer insincere congratulations, but comes over to take my hand, "Thank you, Miss Stevens. If there was any way to avoid this we would take it. But I, for one, don't want the blood of your colleague staining the sands."

And like that, a bucket of icy water has been thrown over my arousal. However he's phrased it, Jasim's being coerced in the same way as I am. Neither of us want this. We've just got to survive it.

"So, what happens next?" I shove my disappointment down, and now want to move this charade along so Sally can be safe.

"We're expecting visitors." A new voice enters the conversation, I hadn't seen Ryan come in. "Your band mates are arriving soon, and Jasim, your brothers are flying in too."

"It's time to prepare you." Rais's mouth twitches, as though in amusement. "I've asked Lamis to assist."

Jasim looks serious as he jerks his chin toward the men, "Apart from the three of us in this room, and my brothers, this has got to look genuine. We can't have a sniff of the that the wedding's fake getting to Fadi, neither do we want any news of Sally's abduction getting into the press."

Rais barks a laugh, "Lamis is a romantic. And half the palace knew about your preparations for last night. It will be seen as a natural progression of yesterday's indiscretion. You two just act your parts, and no one will be any the wiser. When the news reaches Fadi, he'll have no doubt it's authentic." He chuckles softly, and points to the two of us, "The very air shimmers with desire when the two of you are together. No one will have difficultly believing you've taken a bride, Jasim."

"What will Fadi do? Are you certain he'll return Sally unharmed?" I want to make sure I'm not tying myself to this man I barely know, however temporarily, for no reason.

And that's when I'm answered with silence. Bloody hell, I could be giving up my freedom and it could all be for nothing.

"We've got to trust it will work. It's our best option." As Rais finishes speaking, he steps aside to let a bubbling and excited Lamis in. She bows deeply to Jasim, delight written all over her face.

Then she comes over to me, "This is wonderful, *kunt 'aerif mataa attabaet alttaelimat alkhassat bik 'ams wa'aeaddatha lak.*" As she lapses into fast Arabic I glance at Jasim, who's wearing an amused expression on his face.

At my raised eyebrow he translates, "She suspected as much, yesterday." Well, it seems Rais had been right in his assessment, and maybe we won't have to try too hard to make people believe we fell sufficiently in love to want to spend the rest of our lives together after just one night. I doubt Mickey and the rest will take it with such understanding.

"Come with me. I help get ready." As Lamis waves toward the door, and Jasim nods to indicate I should go with her, I decide to play my part and shelve my misgivings for now. The maid's excitement is infectious, and I allow it to influence me, knowing how much is weighing on making this appear real.

Lamis takes me through corridors which have me wondering just how old this palace is. The stone beneath our feet is worn away by the thousands, millions of footsteps which must have passed this way. Soon we seem to leave the world of men behind, as I'm taken to an area where women are waiting. A huge bath sunken into the floor, already steaming with water strewn with floating rose petals on the surface. I'm bathed, have makeup put on me, in a similar way to last night. Then, clothed in a robe, they seat me on a chair.

Another woman comes in, this one carrying a box. She opens it, revealing its contents, and takes my hand. At first, I suspect nail varnish, but she gets out a small brush.

"What's she doing, Lamis?"

"Henna," Lamis replies, "She paints hands. New bride do no housework while henna lasts."

Hmm, that sounds a good tradition. But then I remember Jasim has a housekeeper in England, so I doubt I'd be doing much of that in any event. *I'm marrying a sheikh.* The thought makes me pull my hand away, suddenly reluctant to go on with this farce. He's so out of my league, sexually as well as socially. I won't be able to pull this off.

"Let her paint hand." Lamis seems distressed I might not go through with the ritual, but it's more than that. Maybe I won't go through with the wedding at all. *But what about Sally?* I can't leave her to an unknown fate. Taking a deep breath, I start to hold out my hand again. Then narrow my eyes, "You always do this? For a wedding?"

"Yes," Lamis beams, "Is custom."

"How long does it last? Does it wash off?"

"Lasts a full moon."

I take it she means a month. If nothing else, it could be a visible sign that we really are married. Something to convince the rogue sheikh. With a sigh I give in, and watch with intrigue as the delicate pattern is painted on my hands, and then on my feet. As my skin becomes stained with henna, I start to feel like a bride. And, putting aside the enormity of what I'm committing too, think instead of the wedding night and sharing a bed once more with Jasim. *That's something to look forward to at least.*

Then I have doubts. He'd told me about his appetites, will I be able to fulfil them? What if he'd been taking it easy last night? When we're married will he think he owns me? Could he actually hurt me? *Will I be enough for him?* What do I really know about him? His heritage and what he believes? He's a stranger, and has been brought up in a very different way of life. The fact Fadi could just steal a woman, and wanted to exchange her for me... Would Jasim think I belong to him, and not just for play? A shiver runs down my spine, as I realise I have no idea for I'm letting myself in for.

But Sally will be safe. And I'd rather take my chances with Jasim than with the unknown Sheikh Fadi.

315

CHAPTER 23
Jasim

What the fuck has gotten into me? What on earth made me agree to such a preposterous suggestion? Marriage? Me? I could have simply told Fadi I had already made her mine. Would that have worked? *I could at least have tried.*

My reactions are all over the place. It had hurt my pride when she'd scoffed at the idea, and perversely made me try harder to persuade her. And after I'd coaxed her and she's now said yes, I'm a bag of nerves.

As the door closes behind her, taking her from my sight, I rasp out, "How the fuck do I do this?"

"You dress in your best robes." It's a practical suggestion from Rais, but not one I was looking for. "You had no problem bedding her last night."

"Of course I didn't."

"Then, what more is there to marriage?" He would think like that, his own union being short and unremarkable, and taking place when he was little more than a boy himself. He'd been married to an older girl from a neighbouring tribe at just sixteen, a child had quickly followed, his wife dying at the birth. What did he know about the companionship I expected?

I walk into the bedroom and select some clothes, ending up deciding on borrowing Nijad's robes of state. The ceremonial dress, white robes with gold braiding, and a maroon sash which threads over my shoulder and ties around my waist. I put on the ghutra, and a golden agal. Glancing in the mirror, I look every bit a prince. Going back out of the bedroom, Rais looks me up and down, then gives a sharp nod of approval.

There's some irony in getting married in second hand clothes.

"Will I pass muster?"

Rais raises his chin, "You'll pass." And then he leaves me. Needing Dutch courage, I open my brother's convenient liquor cabinet, and pour a shot of whisky. And then, as ready as I can be to face the next hurdle, I make myself comfortable, enjoying the remaining few moments to myself. I don't have to wait long.

"Jasim. Anarchy Rules, and the film crew, have just arrived."

I tap my hand on the back of the couch, coming to a quick decision. "Arrange to bring them here, Ryan. Thank you." Meeting them in the informal sitting room of Nijad's private suite is perhaps less intimidating than meeting them in a state room.

His mouth quirks, "I think I'll stay on hand."

"I think that might be wise." It's quite possible I might shortly need the services of my bodyguard.

Soon, the people I'd last seen in the harem at the Palace of Amahad enter the room, concern written all over their faces. The room becomes crowded with the eight of them there. Waving my hand, I direct them to the dining table, glad it's big enough to seat all of us. One seat remains empty as Ryan stands by the door, his vigilant eyes taking everything in.

"What's going on? Where's Sally?" Joe starts even before he's sat down.

"We know where she is." That's the truthful part.

"Is she alright? Janna told us she'd been kidnapped."

I nod toward Sunny, noticing despite the tan she's acquired, worry has made her look pale, "She's fine." And that may be a lie. "We found out what happened and it's nothing like what we feared. She liked the desert, and went off with a tribe to do more filming. She'll be back in a couple of days." Well, that's what I hope.

"Thank fuck for that!" Joe looks relieved.

"Can't believe she did that." Rory's shaking his head.

Sunny laughs, her spirit seems to be returning. "I can, she's quite an adventurer. And if she's scouting for more locations, I can quite understand."

"We thought the worst when Janna called to say she'd gone missing." Liam's shaking his head, "Women, eh?"

Blake, who I remember is the gaffer, frowns, "She's an independent one. Never thinking to let anyone know when she's got a bee in her bonnet about something. I'll be having words with her when she gets back."

Eli laughs, "You remember that time she wanted to film the Northern Lights? No one knew where she was for hours. Talking to her ain't going to fix it. She'll be up and off on her own again when something else takes her fancy."

I hadn't expected it to be so easy, but though there's an air of suspicion, they seem to be accepting my story for now.

"Well, if that's that, and Sally's fine, where's Janna?" Mickey starts to stand, "I'd like to catch up with her." His eyes narrow suspiciously, "And I'll want to have a chat with you later, once I've spoken to her."

Ah. So Janna's already told them. Well, some of it at least.

And we're at the difficult part already. I raise my hand, "Please sit, Mickey. There's something I need to tell you." How do I explain? How can I describe something even resembling true love when I have no idea what that looks like?

As he grumbles and retakes his seat, it's me who now stands. I walk over to the window, but turn my back on the view, facing them down. "I met Janna, what, six weeks ago now? There was an instant attraction between us."

"Which you told me you weren't going to act on," Mickey snarls and half rises. Ryan's there in a flash, his hand on his shoulder a tactile suggestion the drummer should sit back down. From the size of Mickey's muscles, I think he'd hold his own in a fight. I certainly don't want it to come to that. *Not on my wedding day.* It's bad enough as it is, I don't want to turn up with a blackened eye.

"Let Jasim speak." Ryan tells him, tersely.

"What have you done, Jasim?" Joe's mouth turns down. "Where's Janna?"

I choose my words carefully, "We set up the scene as you wanted it filmed. Only I changed the plan. It was I who stole her away on the horse. And it was for real."

Now the twins stand, "What the fuck have you done with her? What do you mean, you stole her? Did you take her by force?"

I raise my palms, "You misunderstand. It was just for the night. A sheikh and a tent out of the Arabian Nights. If there was any stealing involved, it was all on her part. She stole my heart." Lowering my hands, I cross my fingers behind my back.

Sunny's mouth falls open, and she lets out a sigh, "Sounds romantic."

Nodding my appreciation toward her, I take the offered opening, "It certainly was. And I proposed to her." Well it was several hours later, but I don't have to admit that the timing was off.

Mickey's shaking his head, "Stop right there. It's bloody rubbish coming out of your mouth. I, for one, don't fucking believe it for a minute. You spend one night together and you say you're engaged?" This time he does stand, and Ryan lets him, though he stays hovering close by. "Janna's never even been on a proper date before. No, man, she'd never jump into that. You're forcing her. I've heard tales about Arabs taking women."

Ignoring the slur on my heritage, I keep my voice calm. "I understand how fast it seems, but I assure you when I made the offer, she accepted my proposal. We're getting married." I take a deep breath, and my muscles tense in preparation as I add. "Today."

"What the fuck?" Joe's leapt to his feet. "If she's agreed, she doesn't know what she's doing! Have you drugged her or something?"

If it was anyone else in any other situation, I'd be saying the same thing. How can I convince them? I step forward, my face set as I snarl, "How dare you insult me? I would never stoop as low as that." Though I'd had to use a form of blackmail to get her to agree, the thing is, I'm being forced into it too.

"You love her?"

"Oh Sunny, for fuck's sake, they barely know each other."

And so it starts. For the next fifteen minutes, I try to fabricate a story of two people falling in love under the desert skies. Reaching the conclusion that they can't live without each other after just one night. Some of the words coming out of my mouth make me think I should pursue a career as a write of romance, so outlandish are some of my claims. Behind their backs, Ryan's shooting me looks of disbelief, not at my story, which he knows is pure invention, but at my ability to pull it off. I'm glad I decided it would be me who would break the news, Janna would have folded under the pressure. They want us to wait, I tell them we can't, that the desire for our two lives to become one is too strong. They say she's too young, I tell them she's not. Every argument they throw at me, I come up with a rebuttal.

"You own a fucking BDSM club. And I've seen you in action." Suddenly Mickey's coming toward me, his muscles bunching and he's flexing his hands, "What part does that play in this so-called relationship?"

I raise my shoulders, and shrug them back down, "She'll be my sub."

Mickey roars with rage, Ryan's got a walkie-talkie to his mouth as he steps forward. I block Mickey's punch, he goes to hit me again, but I get in first. Having him on the ground puts him in no better temper. When he rises, Ryan's there fast, holding him back. Then the twins are coming toward me…

The door opens, Kadar and Nijad step in, quickly followed by Rais and some of the palace guard, who take up strategic positions around the room.

"Stop this at once!" My older brother's voice thunders in the room. "Today is a day for celebration. Not for fighting. Jasim. Explain."

No longer under threat, I hold my hands up, "I'm a Dom," I address the group, "I own a kink club. I've seen some of you around, I know you play too. The fact you think I'd ever harm a woman under my care is offensive. Janna will be my wife, and my sub. And I'll take care of her like a Dom should." The disgust that they can consider I'd hurt her, or in any way she wouldn't enjoy, is abhorrent.

Kadar steps up and stands beside me, he addresses the group with distaste on his face, "My brother, Sheikh Jasim, and Miss Janna Stevens will be wed today. I have been persuaded of their relationship and have given my consent. As being akin to her family, you are welcome to be witnesses.

However, I will not permit you to disrupt proceedings. If you continue to act in this manner, I will have you escorted off the premises and returned to London immediately."

A small movement from the guards emphasises the threat behind Kadar's words. Wryly, I note that he hasn't actually lied. Just left much unsaid.

"There's something more to it." Joe rasps out, "She'd never do something like this. Janna's acting totally out of character."

Unseen by the band, Nijad throws me a wink, "My brother too," he tells them earnestly, "But I support him in this."

Mickey's struggling to get free from Ryan's firm hold. "I want to see Janna, make sure she's not being coerced."

"I'm not." The softly, but authoritatively spoken words announce a vision stepping into the room.

Yesterday she was stunning, today she exceeds perfection. So damn beautiful she makes me want to fall to my feet. She's dressed in Arabic style, but the way she carries it off is all her own. She's wearing the clothes of a bride; her mermaid style dress nips in at the waist and hugs her hips tightly before encasing her legs in white satin. Arms covered in lace, her hands holding up a long lace overskirt and train. Glittering jewels sparkle in the light from the windows. The clothes making her look so delicate and feminine, stirs the Dom inside me. There's a glow to her skin, and her eyes are shining, and flowers are braided in her hair. Her hands and feet are adorned with henna. Where they'd gotten the dress from, I have no idea. But the effect is almost regal. *A bride fit for a prince. And she's mine*

I can't stop my feet moving toward her, taking hold of both her hands, gazing into the depths of her dark eyes. It's no pretence that my voice is gruff, she's stolen my air. "You're beautiful." It's an inadequate word, it's all I can think of.

"You scrub up well yourself," she responds, her little hands squeezing mine. As our fingertips touch I feel the callouses she gets from playing the guitar, and my gut clenches as it hits me just how very wrong this is. I'm stealing her away, robbing her of life as she knows it. But another look at my glamourous bride puts paid to my guilt, replacing it with selfishness. Any man would be lucky to have the chance to call her his own. And today, that man is me.

What's she wearing under those clothes? Apart from the marks I left upon her last night. Thank fuck for the robes hiding my lengthening cock. I can't help myself, my hand curls round the back of her neck, pulling her to me. Our mouths meet in a punishing kiss, ignoring everyone else in the room. We break away only when Kadar clears his throat. Wry smiles exchanged between us. We might be marrying out of necessity, but there's no lack of a spark.

Mickey approaches, Ryan close behind, hovering in case I should need him. "Janna, are you sure about this?" He sounds more hesitant, as though our uninhibited display had served to convince him. "It would be sensible to wait."

Her eyes fixed on mine, she addresses herself to him, "We can't wait." Only I'm aware of the double meaning in her words.

My older brother steps forward, "It's time."

Stunned into silence, her friends allow her to leave. Followed by my brothers and hers, hand in hand we walk through the palace, passing across the atrium into one of the state rooms that has been hurriedly prepared. Low stools on a dais for us to seat ourselves, my brothers taking their places to either side.

Bemused, her friends enter, seating themselves on the chairs provided. Rais steps up, and hands two documents over.

My fingers take her left hand, "The contracts bind us together once we sign them," I tell her, "They describe the mahr that I'll provide."

"Mahr?"

"The bride price. Money you will hold in the event that I fail to provide for you." Rais passes me a cheque, and I hand it over.

Her eyes open wide, her hand covers her mouth as she gasps. "Jasim, this is for me? No, it can't be. It's too much."

Kadar interrupts, "It's the Kassis family pledge," he tells her, saving me an explanation.

Nijad laughs softly, "The going rate for brides."

"Accept, habiti. It's part of the formalities."

She looks like she wants to say something different, but is too overawed. She puts her fingers on the cheque; as she takes it, and I give away ten million pounds of my personal fortune. I'm certain to lose it, as we'll be divorcing as soon as we can. It means little to me, I can afford it.

Nijad passes me a ring, I put it on her finger. Kadar puts something in her hand, her eyes widen, and then she places a matching gold ring on mine.

Rais produces a pen, she signs the contract without reading it. I do likewise, Kadar will have had lawyers draw it up, it will do what it's meant to.

I then take hold of her face, my palms cupping her cheeks. "It's done," I tell her softly, "You're mine."

Oh, there should be fanfare, a party, dancing. A celebration shared with my people and hers. But there hadn't been time for me to even think of arranging it. She deserves so much more than I'm offering her today. I make a vow that however long this marriage lasts I'll make her as happy as I can.

"Is that it?" Mickey sounds incredulous. "You'd have had more of a ceremony in a registry office."

But it's Joe who slaps him down, "Don't spoil it for her, Mickey. If this is what she wants, we should let her get on with it."

"Lie on the bed she's fucking made for herself you mean."

My bride stands, sweeps the lacey train around her and goes to her friends. "Can't you just be happy for me for once? No man would have been good enough as far as you're concerned, would he?" Without giving them a chance to answer, or for me to enjoy the feeling of pride I have at that moment, she comes back to me with a flounce and takes my arm. "Husband." Her eyes sparkle with merriment, and I know she's teasing me.

"Don't you forget it," I speak softly into her ear, "Wife. And I'll make tonight I'll make you pay for your taunts."

CHAPTER 24
Janna

Hearing him promise he intends to punish me, my lady parts start tingling. Whatever I think about marriage to his man, there's no doubt with very little effort he can make my body wake up and sing.

As I follow him out of the state room, my mind being mainly on the pleasures the night ahead guarantees to hold, I'm only vaguely conscious of being led across the atrium at the rear of the palace, and emerging on steps leading down into the amazing gardens. An aroma, not unlike barbeques on a summer's day in a park in London assails me. And flashbulbs.

Oh no! Any lingering thoughts I might have had about being able to keep this sham of a marriage quiet disappear when our picture is snapped a hundred times over.

"Smile," a voice suggests in my ear.

"*Qibla, qibla!*" Rings out. I glance at my new husband, who's grinning.

"The photographs are to convince Fadi," he explains in a whisper, "And they're calling out for us to kiss." And we do just that. There on the steps. For a moment, it feels like we've just got married for real. There isn't anything forced or unwanted as Jasim's lips meet mine, our physical attraction to each other undeniable. And affection too, that was there from the beginning when we first met, I liked him, and believed he liked me too. Otherwise why would he have extended the hand of friendship, tended to my wounds and offered to take me home?

But marriage partners, starting a life together, should be in love. And I'm not. And neither is he. Will lust be enough to carry us through? Or will our charade become apparent too fast?

He pulls away, his fingertips taking the place of his lips, "I think Rais has been up to mischief." He turns me to the side where the sheikh is waiting, a wide grin on his face.

"Come, Sheikh, Sheikha. Follow me."

Mystified, at the nod from Jasim, I start walking through the gardens, accepting the congratulations thrown at us by the palace staff. And then we're out in the desert where tents have been hastily erected, and large lumps of meat are slowly turning on spits. Rais leads us to a tent, its big flaps tied open, and settles us down on low cushions. Immediately, a banquet begins to appear in front of our eyes.

Jasim's part amused, part flabbergasted that all this has been set up in such a short time. Soon we're joined by his brothers and the members of Anarchy Rules, along with Blake and Eli. Surprisingly, the lavishness of the spread goes some way to placate my friends, going some way to convince them this is not some rushed and sordid affair. Well, it is, but best they don't know that. The only thing that upsets them is there's no alcohol being served. But at a whispered suggestion from Jasim, they soon solve that problem, finding the supplies in their suites, and sneaking off one or two at a time.

There's entertainment on offer, belly dancing, fire eating, the tribespeople making the most of the impromptu celebration.

Darkness falls, and I'm entranced at the flaming torches lighting the night. If I'd ever given any thought to the subject, this would have surpassed anything I could ever have dreamed or hoped my wedding would entail.

"Happy?" Jasim leans over to speak to me.

And I realise I am.

"Are you having a honeymoon?" Sunny calls out. I don't know how to answer, but Jasim comes to my rescue.

"We are. We're heading into the desert in the morning," he replies, with a surreptitious squeeze of my hand.

It's the one true thing that's been said today.

"You take good fucking care of her," Joe makes his statement, pointing at Jasim with a kebab on a stick. Goodness knows where he's putting all that food, he's been constantly eating since we sat down.

"I will." He accompanies his response with such an intense look into my eyes that Sunny pretends to swoon.

"Just look at that. True love." She fans herself.

A quirk of his lips that only I can see, and then Jasim's kissing me, bending me back over his arm. Sparks fly between us. Nope, nothing to contrive in the attraction department.

"You ready to blow this joint?"

"I…" Suddenly I feel nervous. I might no longer be a virgin, but I don't know what Jasim will expect of me tonight. Beyond the obvious that is.

A breath of warm air in my ear, and I hear him chuckling, "You're already anxious about what I'll do to you. That's making me hard."

"You're cruel."

He brings my fingers to his mouth, and gently kisses them, "Believe me, habiti, I am." But his actions belie his words. I wasn't genuinely scared of him last night, why should I be now? My greatest worry is that my inexperience will disappoint him.

"Come." He stands and pulls me up with him, then, to my surprise, sweeps me up into his arms, carrying me as if I weigh nothing at all. As if someone's given a signal, the crowd parts before us. I might not understand Arabic, but I don't need an interpreter to translate the lewd comments that are thrown at us along our way.

He doesn't put me down while we cross the dry desert, and then through the stark contrast of the flourishing garden. He continues to hold me as we walk through the palace, and on to royal suite. He takes me inside, kicking the door shut behind him, taking me straight into the bedroom and dropping me on the most elaborately decorated bed I've ever seen.

And he doesn't pause before taking out the knife from the scabbard which I thought was ornamental and holding the tip to the top of my dress. I gasp, and freeze.

"I hope you hadn't had thoughts of keeping this."

"Jasim, it must have cost a fortune, you can't…"

But he can. The blade is so sharp the material offers no greater resistance than butter as he slits it from top to bottom, and pushes it to the sides. My bra is severed, now I'm almost naked before him. Then that last scrap of material goes too.

He looks pleased with himself as he holds the knife up for inspection, "Never saw the point in our ceremonial dress before. But there's something to be said for it." Sparing a rueful glance for me he adds, "I've been thinking about getting you naked all night. And I just couldn't wait."

Then his mirth fades, his breathing quickens, his eyes grow dark, and the Dom has entered the room. His arm stretches out, his hand traces my breasts, and then tightens almost to the point of pain, "You're mine, habiti. My sub and my wife. I *own* you."

I inhale sharply, he's too intense. But, immediately he reassures me, he can read my reactions so well.

"You still have your safe word. You'll always have that."

I close my eyes and open them again, relieved he reminded me.

"Habiti, you hold all the power here. I can only do what you allow."

In his free hand he still holds the knife, as I nod indicating my understanding, he touches the tip to my neck, making me gasp again, "Keep very still," he warns me. *Is he going to cut me?*

I know he won't intend to, but if I move… I don't need his instruction, the threat makes me freeze and lay still as stone, holding my breath as he traces the knife down, around my breasts, circling my nipples, then drawing it slowly down my stomach and then further below. I squeeze my eyes shut as he strokes it over that tender part, trying to will my clit not to swell or come out of its protective hood.

Then a sound, and the cold steel is removed from my body to be replaced by his fingers instead. With a sharp inhale, I remember to start breathing again.

"Fuck, you're already dripping wet." I know I am. And I also know it shouldn't have, but the veiled risk of such a sharp blade touching me intimately had turned me on.

He doesn't bother to remove his headdress as he kneels on the bed, pulling my legs apart, and without any delay his mouth is on me. Tonguing my clit, his eyes meet mine, and my body clenches in anticipation, exhilaration increasing my desire at the sight of this fully clothed dark-skinned sheikh intent on his ministrations. He's every girl's wet dream, so handsome, so dominant. *He's mine.* Or, at least, for the moment, and however long this marriage lasts. But it's the present that counts. And I can't imagine a sight more arousing.

As his mouth works, my eyes roll back in my head, then I force them open again, not wanting to miss a moment of the erotic spectacle. I almost regret that I do, as my body gives an involuntary jerk. The vision in front of me, the smell of exotic perfume in the air, the appreciative sounds he's making, every one of my senses is filled by this man. I thought he'd aroused me before. *He hadn't even begun.*

My muscles are out of my control, my thighs closing round him, trapping him to me. The inner walls of my pussy clenching, as though wishing he was there. My hands fist by my sides, fingernails digging into my skin, as my heart rate speeds up and my breath becomes shallow.

His fingers thrust inside, curling around and finding just the right spot.

"Oh, oh…"

What the? He's pulled away. My pussy feels empty and my clit's throbbing so badly.

He's smirking, pushing apart my thighs to free him, and moving up the bed. Taking my hands in one of his, he searches with the other for something behind the bed, and then, *snick*. My hands are cuffed behind me.

"This is Nijad's suite, Nijad's room, and this is his bed. Designed to his specification." He informs me, nodding with satisfaction.

My body's still pulsing, seeking relief. He's not going to leave me like this, is he?

Leaving me hanging and tied to the bed, my—well, for now anyway—handsome sheikh starts to give me a personal striptease, first discarding his headdress and then shrugging off his robes. Standing in his loose cotton trousers, I see the material straining and outlining his stiff cock. I lick my lips, and then bring my gaze higher, settling on his washboard chest, his rich olive skin gleaming with a slight coating of sweat. If I wasn't already on the edge, the sight of him would have taken me there.

"Like what you see?" As I feel blood going to my cheeks, he chuckles at my embarrassment.

After staring at me for a few seconds, his lips curl up, suggesting he's enjoying himself as he opens a drawer beside the bed and takes out a packet. He tears it open, but I can't see what he's got in his hands. Putting my chin on my chest, I peer down for a closer view as he palms something over my breast. He clips something on my nipple and I yelp, and gasp.

"Breathe," his voice is tempered and even.

"It hurts!"

"Give it a moment."

While it still smarts, the pain starts to turn to something else, sending a zing right down to my already throbbing clit. Then he puts the second of, what I now realise, are nipple clamps on my other protruding bud. Again, that bite of pain, followed by the warmth of increased arousal. I squirm against my restraints.

He pulls on a chain connecting the two, making me cry out, "Oh, I'm going to love torturing you." His voice holds no sympathy. "There's a third clamp I can use, but that's not for today."

My brow creases as I try to understand him. "Where does that go?"

He huffs a laugh, "Where do you think?"

Widening my eyes, I look at him, "You can't be serious?" He can't put something so wicked at that tender throbbing nub.

"Want to try it and see?" His eyes are full of amusement then adds, as I rapidly shake my head, "Be a good girl, then."

And then I'm flipped over. With his hands on my inner thighs, he pushes them apart, my legs almost too wide. I try to pull them back, if I can rub them together I might be able to get some relief. The clamps now dangling from my tits, gravity adding more torture, only increase the desperation and the feeling of hanging on to some ledge. *Please let me go over, please.*

"Jasim…"

"Quiet." He pushes my forehead to the bed. Again, he reaches across to the drawer, and I shudder at the thought of what he could be getting out now. He folds his hand around it so I can't see what he's got. Then I jump, as a trickle of something cold slides down my crack. And then his fingers are circling around my puckered hole, and one's pushed inside.

"Jasim!" I all but scream and try to get away.

A hand slaps my arse, "I told you to be quiet. You take what I want to give you." And still his finger probes. "Don't tense, let me in." I know it's Jasim, but the voice that holds no sympathy, makes me feel I'm under a stranger's control.

There's comfort in knowing I could stop this any moment, but also stimulation in believing I can't.

I suffer in silence, but no, *suffering* is not the right word. As my body begins to get used to the invasion, I find it only makes needier, and even more desperate to come. When he moves his finger away, I find I'm mourning the loss of the sensation. But my poor arsehole's not left unabused for long, now he's pushing something inside. Something cold and not as yielding as his finger.

"What…?"

With his hand on the small of my back, he holds me in place. "It's a butt plug. Just a small one," he explains. "Soon it will be my cock, but I need to prepare you first."

I don't think any amount of preparation is going to make that particular part of his anatomy fit inside my small hole, but time later to protest. In fact, I don't think I could come out with any words right now. The pulling on my nipples, my overstimulated clit, the stretch and weird feeling of the butt plug inside, are taking away my ability to think.

He leans over, and whispers into my ear, "Time for your next lesson. Keep in position, I've going to flog you now."

What?

He starts off so gently, leather strands caressing my skin. A gentle massage which ignites all my parts. Embarrassed, I find I'm almost humping the bed in my desperation to get off. Then he starts to work harder, now there's a little sting.

"You should see yourself, your skin's turning the most delightful shade of pink."

The flails hit between my shoulders, then fall on my bum, on lower to my thighs and then start on the return path. The feeling changes from a massage, to setting me on fire.

"Don't come."

What? Doesn't he know how little it would take to push me over? My nipples are tingling, my whole body feeling electrified. My clit's throbbing, begging for relief, and my pussy pulses in time. *And he's telling me to hold back?* Christ, if he so much as breathes there…

Picking up the flogger again, he flicks my clit. I scream at the intensity of the orgasm which goes through me with hardly any warning at all.

"Naughty girl." The words might show his displeasure, but his tone suggests I've played right into his hands. "Naughty girls who come without permission get punished."

What? His words only just filter through as my body is shaking, remnants of my orgasm still causing aftershocks to wrack through my body. Only vaguely aware of what's going on, I hear the sound of a wrapper being opened behind me, and a rubber sheathed cock prodding my pussy.

Then, *whack.* His large hand spanks my butt cheek, and then another blow to the other. Oh, oh. My clit jumps to life again. He continues to spank me, my nipples feel tender, zings rip up and down my body until I'm not certain where they start and end.

"I'm going to fuck you now."

Suddenly he pushes into me, all the way, in one smooth stroke until he's up against my cervix, the plug in my arse making me feel so full. And when he starts moving, there're new sensations, every nerve seems to come alive.

"Fuck, you're so tight, habiti." He picks up the pace and starts hammering inside me. "I'm not going to last long."

Neither am I. And as he continues to push in and pull out in a punishing rhythm, he hits that special spot inside me time after time. When he leans forward and puts his teeth on my neck, I come with a scream, my pussy clenching and releasing, squeezing hard on his cock.

"Fuck, babe. Fuck!"

I'm so sensitive, I feel him swelling to an almost impossible size, I orgasm again and again, until it becomes continual contractions, my vaginal muscles spasming in sweet agony all on their own.

He loses momentum, his body starts jerking, "Janna!" he yells as he comes.

CHAPTER 25
Jasim

I've played with a lot of women, fucked them too. But the reactions of this woman beneath me take me by surprise for the second time. She's no skilled sub with practiced responses, every reaction of her body is unrehearsed and unexpected. She tests my competence as a Dom every step of the way, needing me to watch her, to make sure I'm not pushing her too far, too fast, but her tactile encouragement urges me on to take her to different heights and torture her in any number of deviant ways.

And now, once again, she's drifting in subspace, and I'm finding it hard to fight the urge to get lost in my own head. Quickly, I unfasten the handcuffs, rubbing her arms and wrists to make her comfortable once more. Before I turn her back over, I remove the butt plug, her compliance showing she's got no idea what I'm doing. Going to the bathroom I dispense with the condom, and wash the plug. Then I'm back with her, removing the nipple clamps, using my mouth to relieve the soreness there. She moans as I take them off, but still isn't completely aware.

And then I pull her into my arms, holding her close, my chin resting on the top of her head. *She's mine. We're married.* I could keep her forever.

Damn it.

At this precise moment, I'd give anything to be the right man for her. I've shown her the side of me I thought I'd need to keep hidden, but nothing I've done so far has frightened her off. She could have used her safe word at any time, but she hadn't given any indication she'd wanted to stop me. I begin to wonder where her boundaries might be—the idea of having her under my whip causes my cock to twitch.

I can't afford to pretend this is real, or to let her start believing it. Whether she might be able to match my demands or not, sooner or later I'll get bored and want to move on. I know myself only too well. It's just the newness that is giving me other ideas. Unlike other subs I've played with who already know the score, there's so much I have to show her, and that will take more than just a few nights. The marriage gives me time to play and explore possibilities I never dreamed off, it's not hard to resolve to enjoy it while it lasts. Nevertheless, it can only be a temporary arrangement that meets the needs of the moment. I'm not wired to be a man to be content settling down. At some point in the future, she won't be enough.

But her submissive tendencies are so obvious, having affection for her, I need to consider her future. A vanilla relationship won't work for her, not after the things I've introduced to her. When we're back in London I'll take her to the club, and let her get to know some other Doms, maybe one will take her fancy. There's sufficient confidentiality there that she can perhaps try some out, under my watchful eye, and when the marriage ends, have someone else to lean on. Yes, that's the sensible thing to do.

That's a workable solution, my brain suggests, but my arms automatically tighten around her possessively at just the thought of seeing someone else playing with her.

Time, it's just time, I reassure myself. I'm only naturally greedy and want to keep her for now as my own. Until I've taught her everything I can teach her. I covet her innocence, and once I've destroyed that, I'll be able to move on.

A gentle snore makes me smile, and I slide down the bed, wrapping myself around her, once again spooning in the way we'd done that first night, as thought my body is programmed to protect her. It's not long before I join her in sleep.

I wake before her with a smile of my face as I remember what we did the night before, already planning what I might do when she wakes. But a glance at my phone shows me I've overslept, and already I'm running out of time.

Gently, I shake her shoulder, "Janna, wake up."

She stretches like a cat, her lithe limbs extending, her arms going up over her head, unintentionally offering her breasts for my examination, the tips still slightly reddened from the nipple clamps last night. My cock throbs, I press the heel of my palm to it. We've no time for such pleasure right now.

As her eyes at last open, I speak again. "Good morning, habiti. How are you feeling today?"

Her head turns to face me, "Amazing, Jasim. I feel amazing."

I press my lips to her forehead, "We're compatible in bed," I tell her softly.

"We're married." A crease mars her brow as she remembers.

"It's only a temporary arrangement," I impress on her, "You won't have to be tied to me for long."

A dip of her head shows she understands. A slight frown as she bites her lip, "Jasim, yesterday, the wedding. Last night. I haven't given a thought to Sally and what she's going through." Suddenly she sits up, unaware that she's naked, and her hand comes up to cover her mouth. "Jas, I'm an awful person. While we were making… having sex. She might be suffering…"

"Hush," I replace her hand with mine, feeling the softness of her lips beneath my palm, "We couldn't attempt a rescue last night. There's nothing to feel guilty about." Then I realise she'd used the shortening of my name, which only my brothers have applied to date. And I find that I like it.

"Come. Breakfast will be ready, and I need to go and make plans."

"Are we going to rescue her today?"

Smoothing her hair back with my fingers, I make a promise I hope I'll be able to keep. "Yes."

That gets her moving. Her bag has been brought into my brother's suite which I'm using, and I watch as she selects her clothes and disappears into the bathroom. When I hear the shower running, I grab my robes for the day and use the facilities in the guest bedroom next door, knowing I'll be too tempted to delay our departure if I join her. As I expected, in our absence a breakfast of pastries and coffee has been delivered to the living room. While we were preparing for the day, discreet servants had silently seen to our needs. As I pour a cup of the thick sticky brew, my mind plays over the night before. The consummation of our marriage.

And when she appears, again dressed in the tunic and trousers worn by the people of my country, it's hard not to miss the well-satisfied look on her face. That had been my intention, a visible sign to help convince everyone this marriage is real.

While we both know it's not.

I leave her after breakfast, going to the offices where Kadar, Nijad, and Rais are already waiting.

Nijad stands to greet me, and I grasp the hand he holds out. He examines me carefully, and then barks a laugh, "You had a good night, brother."

Shit. Perhaps it's not just *her* face that will give us away.

I shrug, "I have to thank you for the toys you provided, Nijad. And for the use of your suite."

"Did you go to the dungeon?"

"No." I'm not going to go into details.

Kadar's looking at me strangely, one side of his mouth turned up.

Rais's face is impassive. "Sheikhs, Emir," he starts, "We should go over today's course of action."

I jerk my chin toward him as I take a seat, "You've been planning?" At Nijad's nod, I raise my eyebrow, "And?"

Kadar leans forward, elbows on the table, his hands steepled. "We wanted to leave the girl out of it."

Woman. I correct silently. Very much a woman now. And no, I want Janna kept safe and away from danger.

"But we've reached the conclusion that's sadly impossible. We believe Fadi will want to see her. Will need to see the two of you together to be convinced that the marriage is genuine."

"It needn't be," I refute, raising my chin toward Nijad, letting him know I'm thinking of his first marriage to Cara, "He wanted to force her, he'd understand if I'd used coercion as well." It's one of the primitive practices of our country that I detest. "Surely my word will be sufficient?"

Kadar's shaking his head. "At the very least he'll need to be convinced the marriage has been consummated." Hmm, well it certainly was that. "And I think her behaviour, and yours, will go a long way to persuade him of it. Breaking off, he chuckles, "Your expression is worth more than any picture. It's good, brother, that there's a fire that blazes between the two of you."

"As with any Dom and a new sub." I stare at my older brother, wanting to nip any ideas of a permanent arrangement in the bud.

He doesn't comment.

"I'm not happy involving her."

"If you want to get the other woman back, we need to use everything to convince Fadi. She's going along, brother. We're agreed on that.

I'm not, but can't be certain I'm thinking logically. As I quiet and keep further objection to myself, I realise I'm being asked a question.

"Does she ride?" Rais enquires, "We can't approach other than on horseback."

I frown as I'm reminded how little I know about her. "I have no idea."

Kadar waves dismissively, "She can ride with Jasim if not."

The desert sheikh continues, "Overnight we transported horses and men as far as we could drive. Fadi will have already been warned we're on our way."

"A show of force?" I draw in a breath, hollowing my cheeks, unsure what the rogue sheikh will think about that.

"He must know he's in trouble. Which means he won't be surprised."

"But it's impossible to mount an attack."

"A siege?" Kadar reaches for the coffee pot, and tops up his cup.

"No, brother," Nijad is fast to dismiss his suggestion, "He'll be well stocked up, and we can't leave the woman with him for too long, that will risk him harming her if only to make the point that he's serious. Any rescue will need to be done fast."

My coffee cup is empty, but I don't fill it back up. Raising my eyes, I offer to play my part. "I'll take the lead. Janna with me. We have copies of the documents and photos to prove we are wed."

"You're not going alone," Rais growls, "I'll have my men right behind you. And you're not getting too close. We need to draw him out."

"And take him prisoner." Kadar's not taking this insult to our country lightly. "He must know he's sacrificed his liberty."

"Which makes him dangerous," Nijad states what I'm thinking.

"No harm must come to Janna."

"Or to you, brother. A dead husband leaves her available again." While Nijad might have a point, I hope even Fadi wouldn't be so stupid as to kill a prince of the land. And if he is, hopefully his men will stop him. Retribution would fall on every man of his tribe.

Rais points to a map, and for a moment we study it. The castle in the clouds is reachable only by a single file horse track leading up to a small valley, where ancient accommodation has been built within a natural rock fortress surrounded by buttresses of solid stone.

"Water?"

Rais taps to the rear of the castle, "A spring."

I feel a moment of sympathy for the primitive conditions the innocent videographer is being kept in. "How far have you've been able to take the trucks and horses?"

"They're waiting here." His finger's resting on a plain not too far away.

Examining where Rais is indicating, I query. "And we're flying in? And will meet up with the horses?"

He nods to confirm, "I've been in touch with my men, there's been no movement from the fortress. We had hoped there was a chance, but it seems our presence isn't drawing Fadi out."

No, and it wouldn't me either if I knew my life was on the line. Fadi will stay put, forcing me to go to him.

"Right," Kadar bangs on the table. "Jasim, you go collect your, er, wife, and meet us at the helipad. We've done enough talking. Let's get this mission underway."

"Kadar, you should stay here." My brother's the emir. He shouldn't be risking his life.

"Perhaps," he gives a twisted grin, "But I'm not going to."

Rais looks shocked, "Excellency, I must protest. You are risking the crown if you accompany your brothers."

Kadar stands, sweeping his robes around him, and walks around the room.

"Rais is right, Kadar. We have to consider what will happen if this goes pear-shaped and Fadi gets the upper hand. We don't know how many men he has with him." I'm hoping we can carry out this rescue without bloodshed, but must consider the alternative. "You can't come along."

The emir swears, "Jasim, I feel guilty. If I hadn't have called you back..."

I stop him there, "The wheels were put in motion the night I helped Janna. Allah took it from there. It's not down to you, or me, that this has happened. It's not on you, Kadar."

He stops his pacing and stares at me, then comes over and rests his hand on my shoulder, reaching out he touches Nijad in just the same way, "Brothers, I love you, and would give anything to be by your side. But the fact I cannot is yet another unwanted burden upon the emir." He pauses, and then continues with a growl, "But you both come back, you hear me? You take no unnecessary risks."

"We could forfeit the woman."

I round quickly on Rais at his unacceptable suggestion. Leave Janna with Fadi? Unthinkable. Seeing my face, he raises his hands in supplication.

Once I'm certain he's got the message, I stand, and Kadar pulls me in for a hug, slapping my back, then kissing me on both cheeks. "Be safe," he whispers, and for a second I see a glimmer of moisture in his eyes.

I step back and nod, and then leave to collect my wife.

Remembering that she's not the best flyer, I take Janna's hand as we step onto the helipad and approach the waiting helicopter. My brother has the controls, with Rais seated beside him. That leaves me free to give Janna my full attention. I help her into the back, taking some time to make sure she's comfortable in her harness and has her headset on correctly.

"Okay?"

"Yeah, Ni. We're set."

I hold her hand as we rise, and Nijad expertly turns the craft toward the open desert, leaving the palace of Z̧almā behind.

Once we're flying straight, Janna turns to me, her brow furrowed, "What's the plan, Jas? We turn up, tell Fadi we're married, and he gives Sally back?"

"In a nutshell," I agree.

"Or we hope it will be as simple as that," Nijad adds, rather unhelpfully in my opinion, from the front seat.

"Do you ride, Sheikha?" Rais asks over his shoulder.

I have to give her a nudge, "That's you, habiti."

"What? Oh."

I smile at her look of surprise, "While you're my wife you have a title. You should get used to it and respond to it, habiti. It will help convince Fadi."

She nibbles at her lip, and then remembers she's been asked a question, "No, I don't ride, Sheikh Rais. When I was a child, I was more interested in music than being out in the fresh air."

The fact she'll be in my arms on a horse again makes me recall the chase through the sands. My warrior blood boils, it's the right place for my woman to be. "You'll ride with me."

An almost imperceptible shifting of her body suggests she's remembering it too. Her eyes meet mine, there's a sparkle there. "No tent today," I say softly, cruelly bringing to both our minds the way I divested her of her virginity. Her mouth opens in a delightful O. I grin.

CHAPTER 26

Janna

I'm either getting used to flying in a helicopter, or it's the calming presence of the man sitting beside me, but my stomach doesn't dip and churn as we take off and start flying over the desert. Maybe it's because all my senses were turned upside down last night. Just reminiscing makes me shiver. The things this man does to me, *which I let him do to me.* I had a safeword I could have used at any time. *I just didn't want to.*

And now he's gone and reminded me of that night in the desert, thoughts I really don't need at this serious time. Am I always going to be in a constant state of arousal around him? Or will his effect on me eventually wear off? I hope that it does, and at the same time as his attraction to me. I have to keep reminding myself, I'm not really his wife. Only until we get Sally back, and a short period after that until we'll part and go our different ways. It's so easy to day, but as my gut clenches, it's not because the helicopter is swooping over a dune, already, I'm fear I might never be ready to let him go.

Sally. *Think of Sally.* What is she going through? Is she harmed? Afraid? I turn to look out of the window, but don't take any notice of the sand below us. She'd found the desert romantic, but her delight in it must surely have worn off now. I can't see any pleasure in being held captive. A dreamy idea that must surely have been destroyed by reality.

Frowning, I think back. When Sally had been directing the filming, I don't remember seeing Fadi. I hadn't been introduced to any of the other riders, or taken much notice of the robed men. At the time, my main concern was that the horses they were riding weren't going to run me down. And then, of course, Jasim had come and swept me up into his arms and we'd left everyone else behind.

What kind of man is Sally's kidnapper? He can't be particularly young or attractive, else why would he need to kidnap another woman so he could demand me in her place? My mind conjures up an overweight, heavily bearded, middle-aged man. My nose wrinkles, as I go on to imagine a sweaty, smelly man with a heavy paunch. Cunning and sly, with an unpleasant personality to go along with his looks. My thoughts make me shudder, Jasim squeezes my hand.

What if he doesn't give Sally back? Would I be able I offer myself in exchange? Goosebumps appear just thinking about it and I dismiss the notion fast. Swap the man by my side with the unknown nightmare I've just conjured up in my head? No, I couldn't do it. But how will I feel if he carries out his threat? Can I allow someone to be harmed just so I can enjoy my life? All at once I grow scared. If he's not convinced by our marriage, what could we do then? And what exactly will be expected of me?

"Are you okay?"

I can't lie so give a shake of my head. "I'm just thinking about what will happen. What if Fadi hurts Sally?"

Jasim growls, and his fingers tighten. "He'd be a fool to do that. He knows he's committed a crime against his country by kidnapping a foreign citizen. He won't compound his folly."

"He is facing a prison sentence. We can bargain with that." As Rais breaks in, I jump, having forgotten we were all on the same radio wavelength.

"You'd let him live if he lets Sally go?" Nijad asks.

"Kadar seemed adamant that incarceration would be the penalty. But for how long? The length of his sentence could be used as a starting point for any negotiation," Jasim confirms.

"We're coming up close," Nijad advises. Straining my eyes, up ahead I can see lorries, men, and a corral. "We'll be landing in a minute."

As the helicopter gently settles down, the sound of the rotors makes the horses start. I notice a horse as black as midnight rearing, and Nijad gives a barked laugh of surprise as he shuts down the engine. While the rotors stop turning, Jasim helps me down.

Quickly leaving the pilot's seat, Nijad walks smartly away in the direction of the horses' corral. Jasim gives a little tug at my hand, and we follow behind. The black horse comes thundering over, Nijad stretches out his hand for it to nuzzle.

"Amal, my old friend. It's a long time since I've seen you." With an indulgent smile on his face, Nijad strokes the dark as night horse's face.

Man and horse seem to recognise each other. "Is he yours?"

"Yes, Janna. This is my stallion. Rais, my friend. Thank you for bringing him here."

I hadn't heard Rais approaching, but see him grinning at Jasim's brother. "I knew you'd welcome the chance to ride him. It brings back memories, my old friend, doesn't it?"

As they reminisce, I notice another horse, one who's colour looks familiar, his dark bay coat standing out from the rest. "Is that…?"

"Yes, habiti." A simple confirmation that was the horse Jasim rode to take me to my special surprise night in the Arabian tent.

Rais signals to his men, and soon a pile of tack disappears as horses are bridled and saddled. To my astonishment, Nijad and Jasim jump the fence and start tacking up their own mounts. The ease with which they do so showing a familiarity bred from practice. In no time at all, they're ready and men start to mount up.

Following his brother's example, Jasim is soon astride the dark horse. He holds out his hand, and his strong arm pulls me up so I'm sitting sideways in front of him. My position should feel precarious, but he's holding me tight and makes me feel safe. Nijad's horse is rearing, but he only laughs, and I think, encourages him.

"Show off!" Jasim growls.

There's an army behind us, fifty or so warriors astride their steeds. If I'd come to Amahad wanting adventure, I'd have certainly found it. The thought that Sally would be in her element flits through my head, a salient reminder of just why we're here. Jasim turns the horse, facing it toward what looks like an impenetrable mountain in front of us, and high on the side, I can make out what looks like a fort.

"Is that where we're going?" It looks high up; any path must be steep and dangerous.

"Yes."

Rais, riding a grey, comes alongside us. "Ready?"

Jasim jerks his head, squeezes his legs, and the horse beneath us jumps forward. I clutch at Jasim's arms to keep my balance.

"It's alright, I've got you. I won't let you fall."

As the horses move off, thundering hoof beats sounding behind us, the sun blazes down, and I pull my hijab up over my face to keep the blowing sand out of my face, sparing a thought for the riders following in our wake. Jasim arranges his headdress so only his eyes are visible, transforming him into a dangerous warrior. As my bum slides back into him, I feel his hard cock press into my behind, and I'm glad he can't see my face, and know how much, despite the seriousness of the situation, his closeness and touch is turning me on.

Then my thoughts turn to our destination, and what lies ahead. My brief enjoyment of being held by my man starts to fade, as the uncertainty of what we will find returns. What state will Sally be in? Has Fadi hurt her? How scared will she be, not knowing that help and rescue is on its way? Does she think she's been abandoned? She must feel so alone. Does Fadi even speak English? And what does she know of his plans? Oh God, she must be terrified.

After the brief burst of speed, we slow to a walk, it's the middle of the day, and both horses and men will be wilting. Jasim explains they're conserving their energy in case they need to fight. Fadi must know we're approaching, from his vantage point he won't have missed the lorries and horses, and the small army that's now approaching.

It isn't long before we're travelling over rocky ground, the sound of the hoofbeats echoing around. I start feeling nauseous, and it isn't the rhythm of the horse affecting me. I'm scared.

Rais comes alongside, "He must know we're on our way."

Jasim pulls back on the reins, his horse stops. "Will he come out to meet us?"

Examining the path ahead, holding his hand over his eyes to shield them from sun's rays, Rais studies the route ahead, "I doubt it. He'll expect us to go to him."

Nijad comes up to join us, "Rais. You and I will go ahead. Explain the position and that the woman, sorry," he throws me an apologetic look, "Janna, is no longer available."

"Leave your men here, Rais. I'll go ahead with you. Your word may not be enough, Ni."

"It should be." Nijad's snarl of disagreement reminds me he's the ruling sheikh of the desert.

"Maybe I can convince him?" Tentatively, I offer my suggestion.

"I don't like putting you in danger, habiti, but I don't see any alternative but presenting our relationship to him together."

Yes, our fake marriage. Which must appear anything but false.

Rais calls something out to his men, who start to dismount. He has a quick discussion with a man who seems to be his second-in-command, and they both take out their phones as if checking the batteries or signal.

At my look of confusion, Jasim explains, "The satellite phones should work in the desert."

"Should?"

He waves at the rocky walls which seem to close in over the track. "Unless the signal is blocked."

When Rais finishes his discussion, he's back with us again. "Now, we proceed. Carefully, Sheikhs." His glare suggests while Jasim and Nijad outrank him, here his knowledge of the desert means he rules.

It's a single-track path. Rais takes the lead, Jasim and I behind him, and Nijad brings up the rear. The path is rocky and uneven, and I'm grateful for Jasim holding me tight. The horse stumbles and momentarily loses his footing, then regains it again. My heart's in my mouth as we start up the steep incline.

"Move your weight forward, so we don't overbalance him." As well as I can, I lean down to the horse's neck.

"Are we too heavy for him?"

"Don't worry about that. He can carry both of us, no problem."

But I start having doubts as the track steepens, and hold my breath for what seems like hours until it starts to level out. Up above us the fortress comes nearer, and at last we're entering a plateau. And we're no longer alone.

Emerging from what looks like a solid stone rock face is a man dressed in black robes and headdress, with a dozen warriors behind him. Like their leader, they're all on horseback, and heavily armed. We're outnumbered.

Jasim doesn't falter, he comes up next to Rais, with Nijad on his right. Our horses keep moving, only coming to a halt when we're face to face with the leader.

The man, who I assume is Fadi, moves his horse forward and I notice he is nothing like my imagination had conjured up. He's younger to start with, his features defined making him fairly handsome, intelligent eyes staring out from olive skin much darker than Jasim's. His mouth is full, his chin sharp and clean-shaven. He holds himself regally, and although his robes hide his form, he looks fit like a fighter.

He inclines his head in a polite bow, "Sheikhs. And Miss Stevens. Welcome. You'll come take refreshment before you journey back?" Well, his perfectly spoken English shows he's bilingual, at least.

"Cut the crap, Fadi," Jasim snarls, "We're not here as your guests. We're here to take the Englishwoman home."

"Ah, the lovely Miss Cartwell. I've been enjoying her company." His face twists for a second. "If you come with me, we can make the exchange."

"You do know you're a dead man, don't you?" Nijad's leaning forward, his hands lazily holding loose reins, his stance belying the seriousness of his words.

Fadi laughs, "I've done nothing you haven't done. Both of you," he waves his hand at Jasim, and then toward Nijad, "were involved in a kidnapping. An Englishwoman who you, Nijad, forced to become your bride."

"The circumstances were very different. And it was on the order of the emir. As well you know, Fadi. All the tribal leaders agreed with our actions."

I throw a look toward Nijad, and then remember he'd said Jasim was involved too. But as Jasim's arm tightens around me, I understand it's not the time to ask questions. Feeling eyes burning into me, I stupidly look around and meet the stare of the errant sheikh. He's watching me intently, believing he's so close to his prize. I sink back into my lover's arms.

Jasim must have noticed the direction of his eyes. Possessive arms hold me tight as he turns my head in toward his body, "I'll thank you not to stare at my wife."

Now I can't see him, but I hear the growled exclamation. "What trick are you trying to pull?"

"No trick. We were married yesterday. You have no claim."

There's silence for a moment. Then a rattle of bridles, as summoned horses move closer. "A dead man can't have a wife."

"True words, Fadi," Jasim answers his threat without missing a beat, "If you kill me…"

I gasp, interrupting him, realising what Fadi was suggesting.

"If you kill me," Jasim continues, "You'll be taking the life of a prince of Amahad. Emir Kadar is already insulted by what you've done. There will be no place you can hide if you take up arms against the throne. And your tribe will forfeit their lands."

"Don't be so stupid, man." Rais snarls.

Wriggling in Jasim's arms, I turn around so I can watch the man apparently deliberating on my new husband's fate. I can stay silent no longer, "If you harm Jasim and think you can take me, be warned, I will kill you myself the first chance I get."

Jasim hugs me to him, "I think you can believe my *wife* on that."

Fadi taps his hand against his chin, after a moment he narrows his eyes, "Have you proof you are married?"

"You don't take the word of your sheikh?" Nijad sounds outraged.

Rais reaches into his robes.

"Be very careful," Fadi snarls. "If you kill me, my men's instructions are clear. The woman you've come for will die."

"You asked for proof. I've brought it with us." Rais pulls out some papers, and lets them flutter to the ground.

Jerking his head and spitting out fast words in Arabic, Fadi then waits, as the man he'd addressed slides off his horse and fumbles for the documents lying on the ground. Once he's bundled them up, he passes them into his leader's hands. We all wait in silence as he reads the copies of the contracts, and then looks through the photos.

Finally, he nods, and looks at me. "You make a beautiful bride, but then I knew you would."

"Only for my true husband," I retort.

His head tilts to the side, "This is real? Not an elaborate story you've concocted?"

Jasim snorts, "You can see my signature. Would I have committed on paper had I not given my pledge to this woman?" As he speaks, his hand reaches up, and turns my head toward him. Before I realise what he's doing, his mouth lowers on mine, and he ravishes my lips with a devastating kiss. Knowing we're giving a demonstration, I show I'm a more than willing partner, and if the moan that escapes helps prove my infatuation, it's not intentional.

When Jasim pulls away, my fingers trace the lingering essence of him he left on my lips. Almost forgetting where we are, I gaze into his eyes.

It's only when Fadi speaks again that I return to my senses. "I don't blame you, Sheikh Jasim. I only regret you got there first."

Jasim sighs, "In that case, Sheikh Fadi, let us put an end to this farce. Bring out the woman and we'll take her back. We'll leave it to Emir Kadar to determine your fate."

As a response, Fadi opens his hands and holds them palms up, then raises his chin, "I'm afraid it's not as simple as that."

"What the fuck do you mean?" Rais growls, kicking his horse forward until it's right in the face of Fadi's mount. "Get the woman and bring her here. And you'd better hope she's unharmed."

Now it's Fadi's turn to heave a deep breath, he shrugs, "She's unharmed, I assure you. And I am more than willing to let her go. But she refuses to leave."

What?

Taking care to hold Janna steady, I swing my legs off the horse I've been riding then, realising she probably doesn't want to be left in charge of the beast, lift her off and setting her down behind me as I take a step toward Fadi.

"What the fuck are you talking about?"

He shakes his head, but one corner of his mouth turns up, "She's stubborn. Look, come and see for yourself." He looks and sounds as though he's unwillingly impressed.

Suspecting a trick, I'm reluctant to follow him into the rudimentary castle. And I'm still not going to risk Janna anywhere near him. Not when his plan had been to take her for himself.

"I'll go and check it out." Rais puts himself between us.

"You've no reason to trust me, but I need the girl," he points behind me and then corrects himself, "The Sheikha, to come with us."

Now I'm extremely suspicious. "Why?"

His eyes roll up as though in frustration. "Your wife might be able to talk some sense into Miss Cartwell."

"What's going on?" I glance down at Janna, and pull her so she's beside me, "What have you done to her?"

"*I've* done nothing to her." Fadi says, his phrasing strange. Then he looks down at his feet, and scuffs them on the ground like a little boy. "Look, please, come and talk to her. What would I know about the innermost workings of the female mind?"

I look at Janna, and then at my brother and Rais. To me, Fadi sounds all at once both strange and sincere, but then I don't know him in the same way they do. I've been gone from the country too long. And he'd wanted to steal my woman away, the woman who is, for all current intents and purposes, my wife.

I'm still expecting a trick, but Rais is nodding. "Fadi, I know you well. That you wanted to take the Sheikha for your own must have been some sort of temporary aberration, it's not the normal considered way you act. Though, in the circumstances, I believe you to have some justification." Rais indicates the woman by my side, "In the heat of the desert, the chase across the sands. We have the blood of our ancestors running through our veins, the old ways were to take what they wanted for themselves."

Fadi nods slowly, "Sheikh Jasim, you have a beautiful wife by your side. Had I appreciated the depth of your attraction, and your intention toward her, I never would have made my play. I offer my sincere regrets."

Do I accept his apology?

I raise my eyebrow at Nijad, who's yet to speak his mind. My brother's looking at Fadi carefully, and again I bow to his superior knowledge of this region. What would have been considered unthinkable in London, here doesn't seem so out of place.

"You accept Kadar will want you punished?"

Fadi dips his head, "Sheikh Nijad, I am well aware of my crime."

Nijad touches my arm, "I believe he's being honest, Jas. Let's go inside, and find out what all this is about." Rais nods his agreement.

Remembering I've now got responsibility for someone else, I glance down at Janna. She's staring up at me, defiance in her eyes, "Well, if you're not going in, I will. I want to see Sally and find out what's going on. And if you've hurt her…" She doesn't finish her threat, but spoken as fiercely as any desert warrior. Fadi would be a fool not to heed her warning. I bend down to kiss the top of her head, partly to hide my smile.

Realising we're going to accompany him, Fadi turns and gestures for us to follow him. His men, still on horseback, disappear through the cleft in the rock from which they had come. We go a different way, entering under an ancient arch and into a sparsely furnished room with walls hewn from rock.

"Can I offer you refreshment?" Fadi becomes host as he steps inside.

We all decline, too impatient to meet the person we've come to rescue. "Are you going to bring her to us?"

Fadi shrugs ruefully, "I wish I could, but I can't."

His words don't make sense and a growl comes to my throat. "What have you done with her? You said you hadn't touched her."

"No, no. I said that and it's true." His hands flutter as he rushes to refute the only explanation that I can think of. "Her current predicament is down to her and no one else. Come with me, and I'll show you."

Feeling bemused, I take Janna's hand and follow Fadi down ancient corridors carved out of the rock. We come to a room, Fadi stops outside, seeming reluctant to open the roughly hewn wooden door. "This is my bedroom."

Now it's Rais's turn to scowl, "You had her in your bed while lusting after another?"

Fadi looks like a man defeated, "No, it wasn't like that at all."

As if realising there's nothing else for it, he pushes open the door. And there's Sally, lying on a low divan. She looks up eagerly as we enter, but her expression turns to a scowl when her eyes land on the woman by my side.

"Sally!" Janna exclaims, running across to her friend, seemingly oblivious to the distinct lack of welcome. "We've come to rescue you and take you home." Her arms reach out as if to cuddle her friend, and then waver in mid-air as she comes to an abrupt halt. As she swings back around her eyes are open wide, and her mouth twists, "You bastard! I thought you said you'd hadn't taken advantage of her?"

"I haven't!" Fadi repudiates once again, this time sounding distraught. His hands push at his headdress. At Rais's snarled prompt he starts to explain, "Look, when I brought her here she was struggling, so I used handcuffs. Once we arrived and she knew she would be unable to escape, I took them off as it was impossible for her to escape." He pauses and rakes his hand over his headdress. "Next morning after I'd risen I came back to find her in my bed, and saw she'd handcuffed herself to that old iron pipe."

"Well, unlock her." I eye up the rudimentary plumbing which had been installed at some point.

"I can't!" His voice is almost a wail, "She threw the key out of the window. It's a sheer drop from there. We've searched, but we can't find it."

By Allah! A laugh escapes me. Fuck, she'd turned the tables on him. Nijad and Rais find it hilarious too, both crossing to the window and looking out. Rais turns back shaking his head as his body is wracked with chuckles. "No wonder you couldn't. It must be a hundred feet down."

Janna looks at the woman handcuffed to the bed, "Why on earth did you do that, Sal?"

But Sally glares and looks away, her free hand coming up to wipe away a tear. I try to analyse her reaction. Why would she have done something so senseless in the first place? And why she doesn't seem particularly happy to see the person I thought was her friend? As I watch another none too friendly fleeting glance directed at Janna, the incredible answer comes to me. *She's jealous.* Fadi had his heart set on my woman, now Sally resents the object of his desires. That she'd chosen his bed to chain herself to couldn't be accidental. And from those deductions it's fairly easy to sum it all up. *She wants him.*

The realisation brings a fresh burst of laughter, but I sober fast. *Fadi has to realise.* It's time to find out. While Rais and Nijad are studying the ironwork, trying to work out if there's any way to get her free, I beckon Fadi out of the room. At last having realised Sally isn't in any mood to talk to her, Janna follows us out.

I move a little way along the corridor, and then ask, "Fadi, you must know the reason why she cuffed herself to your bed."

He rolls his eyes, "Well it's fucking obvious, isn't it?"

"What's obvious?" Janna hasn't put it together as quickly as I have. She must have missed or misinterpreted the looks sent her way.

"Habiti, she wants Fadi. And she's jealous that he wanted you."

"It's a bloody mess." Fadi, for once, has gotten something right.

Janna's hand goes to her mouth, "You can't be serious?" A smile appears as she comprehends why we were laughing.

"How else do you explain it? She hardly jumped for joy at her rescue, and chaining herself like that? She doesn't want to leave."

Janna's eyes widen, "She loved the fantasy of Arabia. She must have gotten carried away."

"Yes," I can't resist, pointing at Fadi, "By him."

Now she's laughing too. "Oh Jasim, don't." After her reprimand, she turns sharply to Fadi, "What about you? What are your feelings toward Sally?"

"Apart from her being a royal pain in the arse?" he queries, and then shrugs, "She's okay, I suppose. Pretty enough. If the circumstances were different I wouldn't kick her out of my bed." But under these conditions, it's clear he's wishing that he could. I chuckle again.

As Janna glares at him, a seed of an idea forms in my mind. A fitting punishment, perhaps, for a man who wanted to steal a woman to be his own. To be stolen himself. I point my finger toward him, "An eye for an eye, a tooth for a tooth."

Another shrug as he acknowledges the saying, but it obviously doesn't click why I'm using it now.

"You were going to take Janna and make her your own." I wait for him to admit it, and when he gives a cautious nod, obviously not having an inkling where I'm going with this, I continue, "If Sally wants you, then you will be hers."

His dark skin pales as my words sink in, and his eyes widen in horror, "What? No. She's strong-willed and annoying. Just look what she's done!"

"You're not going to force her?" Janna's worried on Sally's behalf.

"No," I quickly reassure her, "But if that's what Sally wants, her own desert sheikh, then I'm happy to facilitate it. And you," I point my finger toward Fadi, "You'll spend the rest of your life making her happy and fulfilling her every fantasy."

With a start I find I've slipped back into the psyche of my land, where arranged marriages are still not uncommon and are condoned instead of criticised, to imagine for one moment that such an arrangement could be acceptable.

Particularly when Janna gasps, "You can't do that! You can't force him into a loveless marriage."

"He saw nothing wrong in forcing you." I give it to her straight.

"But Sally doesn't deserve it."

But Sally might be getting exactly what she wants. Fadi's a sheikh of the desert, but much of his time he'll spend in the capital, particularly when he's part of Kadar's government. He's a wealthy man, and well educated. And sentenced to the woman must be better than losing his liberty. My mouth quirks as I think how the bargain might appeal to my older brother.

I set out the details, "You spend a month together. Never apart. Take her to your desert encampment and woo her under the stars. You take her to Al Qur'ah, and show her the sights. If, at the end of the month, she doesn't want you anymore, then you are released from the agreement. If, however, she wants to become yours, you marry her. And," remembering Muslim laws which, while not nowadays commonly observed in Amahad, could allow him to take more than one spouse, "She will be the only wife you have."

"She'd be too much of a handful by herself, for me to take another as well," he grumbles. But there's a light in his eyes, whether it's the reprieve from a prison sentence, or a genuine interest in the woman, it's hard to tell.

"It's down to her Fadi. It's her choice. That's the punishment for wanting something that wasn't yours to take."

It's only then I realise Nijad and Rais are behind me. And they've heard every word by the grins on their faces. "A fitting solution, brother," Nijad says as he slaps his hand on my back, "We'll make a desert sheikh of you yet." And that, from my brother, is probably meant as a compliment.

Rais nods his appreciation, and then jerks his chin over his shoulder, "Good pair of handcuffs there. And a fucking strong iron drainage pipe. No chance of removing them without a hacksaw. I've tried to call Nasir, but there's no signal in here. I'll go outside and get him to send for one."

"While you're gone, we'll have a talk with Sally. You wait here, Fadi." At his distracted nod, I take Janna's arm, and lead her back into the bedroom. Sally's sitting with one arm across her chest, looking about as fed up as I've ever seen anyone. While it might have seemed an excellent idea at the time, she's probably regretting her impulsive action now.

"We're having to get some tools," I tell her.

"Sheikh Rais told me that."

As Janna approaches her, she turns her head away. "Sally," Janna starts tentatively, "I've got something to tell you." Her eyes flit to mine, I agree with a nod. Although our marriage isn't real, I can understand knowing about it might comfort her friend if she believes it is. "Jasim and I got married yesterday."

Sally looks at her sharply, "*Married?*"

"Yes." Janna shows her the ring, and gestures toward my hand. I flash mine toward the bed, feeling a strange glimmer of pride.

"He's the only man for me," I think she's laying it on a bit thick, but it will do for now. "And Fadi had an infatuation, though heaven knows why. He only saw me for a moment, and I wouldn't say that was at my best." I have to disagree, she'd looked fantastic running over the sand, casting frightened glimpses back over her shoulder. Her palpable fear stirring my loins. Maybe Fadi has similar appetites? No, fuck, I'm not going there. I've no similarities with that man.

"Sally, you like him, don't you?"

Sally shrugs.

"Oh come on," Janna teases, "You chained yourself to his bed. What else are we to think?"

She humphs, then admits it. "Oh alright, yes. I like him. But he likes you, so nothing can come of it."

"It might do." I butt in, then go on to explain the deal I'd just made with him. "He's yours if you want him."

Her eyes open wider than I would have thought they could, and her fingers cover her mouth. "Oh my. He's mine?"

"If, after a month, you want him to be. Yes."

And now she's flushing red, and her free hand reaches out to grasp Janna's. "Oh my God. A month with a sheikh?" Her excitement is tangible.

"I'll send a man with you. He'll make sure you're treated right. And at any time, if you want to leave, he'll arrange to get you back to England."

Even though I'll do it whether she wants the protection or not, my practical proposition seems to pass her by. Whatever she thinks she feels for Fadi, or whether it's the fantasy or the man, it certainly runs deep.

CHAPTER 28
Janna

I just don't know what to say to you." Joe shakes his head, and reaches into his pocket but pulls his hand out empty. We're in Amahad, he's left the makings of his joint behind in England. He gives a rueful glance then pulls out a cigarette instead. I make no objection as he lights it, having more than a bit of smoke to be concerned about today. "You get married to a goddamn sheikh, for fuck's sake, then disappear into the desert with no word as to where you are?"

"A sheikh who's much older than you. Fuck girl, when you decide to muck your life up, you do it right, don't you?" Mickey's disappointment is rolling off him in waves.

"And what about the band? You can't just walk away." Rory gets in his two pennies worth.

"Go on Liam, Ben. You've probably got something to say, too." I raise an eyebrow and wait for their condemnation. I'll give them all the opportunity to get it off their chests.

Ben is staring at me, then he shakes his head, "Your life, your bed. But I'm not going to kid you and say that I like it." He pauses for a second, "And now you're suggesting you're leaving us in the lurch?"

"You're just as good as me, Ben. You can carry the lead."

"Not before we get a new rhythm guitarist, he can't." Mickey stands and balls some rubbish, chucking into a nearby bin. "You can't just walk out on us. Fuck, Janna, half our audience comes to see you. We've got gigs lined up, and an obligation to fulfil them." But they've got Joe, he's a crowd puller too. Although, while I'm not being modest, I admit he's got a point. The vocalist doesn't have the same attraction for men.

"We've just completed the music vid. Blake's added in the filming in the desert and it looks pretty good. Be a bit stupid to go on with the band minus its star."

I nod at Liam. The video that was supposed to consolidate our future. I stand and pace to the windows, looking out over the gardens of the desert palace. For the past half-hour, I've been trying to persuade them to let me take time off from the band. As far as they all know, my marriage is the real thing. They have no idea it's a ticking time bomb. Or that everything between Jasim and I is fake. The only person with a hope of getting her own personal sheikh out of this has turned out to be Sally. And how fucked up is that? My hands come to my face, my fingers touching lips that so recently felt Jasim's caress. He'd been extremely apologetic, but had explained he had no option other than to leave this morning to make a pre-arranged visit to the oil fields which meant he'd be gone for a few days. I'd wanted to be here when he got back, to spend all the time I can with him, to explore his particular brand of sex, which I doubt I'd find anywhere else. If I leave now, a voice in the back of my head warns me, although I might see him again, it would probably just to keep up pretences, he might prefer to go back to his subs.

I'm not going to kid myself. The only reason this affirmed bachelor married me was because it seemed the easiest way to avoid bloodshed when we went up against Fadi, there was for no other reason. And while I'd agreed to do my part so we didn't cause embarrassment to his country, a fake marriage doesn't necessarily prevent us living apart. Anyone would understand my prior commitment to the band, a duty, as Mickey and the others have said, I'm wrong to feel like breaking.

The sight of flowers blooming in the heat of the desert sun, swaying in the warm breeze, doesn't calm me. Deep down I know if I were to leave now and go back to London with the rest of Anarchy Rules, I'll probably only see Jasim again when it's necessary to keep up the sham. And then, when the time's right, we'll quietly get a divorce. He'll find someone else to torture. The nausea in my stomach lets me know just how much I'll care.

He warned me, repeatedly, that his brand of sex didn't lead to a relationship. *But I want more.*

Anarchy Rules needs me to return with them, they've been telling me all morning how selfish I am to want to stay. But I know, if I go with them, Jasim will take the opportunity to start winding our marriage down.

If I wait for him to return, will it only to snatch a few more nights with him before saying goodbye? How long will it be before he decides it's time to move on? Is he, even now, using the time apart to come to his senses? Remembering all the reasons why any bond between us isn't going to last very long? Will our glorious lovemaking slowly become a half-hearted affair? What would it feel like to gradually be pushed aside? Would it really do any good just to postpone the inevitable? How often had he told me he wasn't going to commit to one woman? It's only a matter of time.

The flowers bend in the warm breeze. While they look at their best today, they'll start dying before long, decaying before they outstay their welcome, to be replaced in time by even finer blooms. Unlike the flowers, I don't want to wither away.

But to leave without speaking to him? *He'll probably be relieved.* If I stay longer, I'll risk losing more of my heart, already I'll already be leaving a big enough piece of it behind. Despite my best intentions, I've fallen for him.

So, there are my choices. Leave of my own volition, or wait to be politely turned away. He's never led me to believe things could be any different. He's never lied.

Mickey's crossing and uncrossing his arms, his patience wearing thin. "Well?" he snaps, "You're still fucking married to the man. Returning and fulfilling your obligations won't have an effect on that."

Oh, but it will. Jasim will have an easy out.

"And it might give you some space to decide if that is really what you want, Janna." Joe, as so often, is the voice of reason. "It happened so fast. Too fast if you ask me. He'll understand you need to come home. Has he insisted you to leave the band?"

I shake my head, no, in fact he said we'd work the logistics out. He wouldn't want me to upset my life for a temporary fling. And while playing on stage holds none of its previous attraction right at this moment, I'd be a fool to give up what I've worked so hard for so long.

"He'll understand you've got responsibilities, girl." *That's the point, Mickey.* He probably will.

My heart feels so heavy, but my mind knows what's right. Even as I make the decision, I already feel empty inside, like part of me is missing.

"I'll come back." I take a deep breath and one last glance at the blossoms, swaying in the breeze. Just like those flowers, I've only a transient place in Jasim's life.

"Thank fuck for that." Mickey strides over, puts his arms around me, and kisses the top of my head. "If your sheikh's worth anything, he'll accept it and want to support you. And he'll be coming back himself in a few weeks, you can pick up from there."

What the drummer doesn't know is that Jasim will be grateful to find I'm gone when he returns. Thankful that he doesn't need to be the one to force the break. And I won't have to listen again when he explains he doesn't do relationships, and while the sex was good—out of this world amazing—everything else between us was an illusion.

Joe starts to gather our bags, already packed and waiting. He glances across at me, and shakes his head. "Sooner we get home the better. Must be something in the air here making people do ridiculous things. You getting married, and Sally staying on to stay with a godforsaken tribe to get more experience of the desert. You'll see this in a different perspective once we get home."

At least everyone bought the story of why Sally wasn't coming back. But then she'd rung them herself using a satellite phone, on loudspeaker I'd heard the excitement in her voice. I was happy for her, though wished it was me who could stay with my sheikh. Joe's voiced my fear, once I'm away from this magical place, my own dream will be over. But I can't tell them the truth.

Liam touches my shoulder as I walk toward the door, and Rory stops me to give me a hug. "It won't be forever. Jasim's based in London, you'll see him again soon. And you know what they say, absence makes the heart grow fonder."

They don't understand. I might never see him again. Or at least, never to be intimate with him. Which helps me accept leaving is the right thing to do. My reluctance to return to England, my desperation to have more time with him… If I don't go now, I'll be risking what's left of my heart.

Without Jasim beside me, the helicopter makes me feel ill and I'm relieved when we finally land at the airport where we meet up with Blake and Eli, and soon find ourselves on a commercial flight back to the UK. All the arrangements had been made on the assumption I'd come to my senses.

It's sleeting when we land, the dark clouds overhead unleashing their load. The onset of winter letting me know my Amahadian tan will soon start to fade. I hope my infatuation with Jasim will dwindle along with it. To live with this emptiness is more than I can bear.

Everything is the same as I left it as I walk into our flat. Apart from the stuffiness from being shut up, the lingering stale cigarette smoke tainting the air makes it seem as if I've never been away. Carrying my bag into my bedroom, I sink down onto the bed, lie back, and stare at the ceiling. The last two weeks already seem like a dream. A wonderful, glorious fantasy, and now it's time I awake.

"Hey, we're getting takeaway." Sunny walks in without even knocking. "Want some?"

I don't feel hungry at all, but I suppose I've got to eat. "Yeah, what're you getting?"

"Chinese?"

"Fine by me." Suddenly I pull myself up, and in an effort to forget my Arabian dream, try to think about somebody else, "Sunny, what's the latest with you and Rory?" And Liam, I add in my head. "I don't want to put my foot in it."

She comes over and sits down beside me, her fingers toy with the duvet cover, "It's all one big fuck up."

Jasim's opened my eyes to the world of sex, giving me experiences I've never had before. Who am I to criticise what anyone else does? What Jasim did, and probably wanted to do to me, what I enjoyed, what we'd done in private, might not make much sense to another person. "It's your life."

Looking at me intently, she shakes her head. "I'm going to end it, Jan. I can't carry on. Neither of them can give me what I really want. It's just become comfortable, you know?" This time she meets my eye, "I know Rory's not faithful to me, Liam keeps me occupied when Rory wants to go out." She looks at the ground, the tip of one shoe brushing up against the other. "To begin with, he just sort of came around when Rory disappeared for the night. Then, one day, we got to kissing. I was reaching for the remote—we were watching a film—and I sort of fell on him. It was an accident. And then, exciting, you know? But wrong."

I don't know, but I keep silent.

"A couple more times, and he wanted to take it further. And that's when Rory admitted he hadn't been faithful. And suggested I go with his brother. What did you call it? A consolation prize? Yeah, that's exactly what it was."

"That must have really hurt." I feel sorry for her.

A shrug, "Writing was on the wall even then, wasn't it? It didn't bother me much at the time. But it's not healthy, and I want more. So, I'm going to end it. With both."

All the anger and disappointment I'd felt toward her disappears at her admission. I reach for her hand and squeeze it.

"I'm sorry the boys made you come back. You must be missing your sheikh. But you'll see him soon enough, won't you? Will you be leaving the flat? Moving in with him?"

Moisture starts to form at the back of my eyes, tears pricking, threatening to fall. Sunny's shared my hopes and dreams for so long. And she's just shared something personal and painful with me. Knowing I'd appreciate someone on my side, I take a deep breath and let it all out, "Don't tell the others. Not yet. I couldn't stand it."

"Tell them, what?"

"It was all fake, Sunny. I knew what I was getting into, okay? Sex. Good sex." *Tremendously great sex.*

She's looking at me wide-eyed. "Go on."

"I didn't fall head over heels for him," *Are you sure about that?* "And neither did he for me. The marriage wasn't real, Sunny."

"Tell me the rest, Janna. You know I'll keep your secret." I know she will. In the seven years that I've known her, never once has she betrayed a confidence, as I have kept hers.

I have no trouble sharing the truth. "Sheikh Fadi had kidnapped Sally, she didn't just run off with him." It was the story we'd told everyone, and her flightiness had meant they'd had little trouble accepting it. "Fadi wanted me, he took Sally so I'd be exchanged for her. Jasim stepped up and, by putting a prior claim on me, Fadi's plans were foiled."

"But Sally's still with him."

I smile at that, "Fadi's punishment for taking her. She wanted to stay." Suddenly I'm telling her everything, the whole story about her handcuffing herself to his bed. Soon we're both rolling around with laughter at the thought of the predicament Fadi's now in.

"Do you think she'll stay with him?"

"Apparently, it's her choice. We'll have to see what happens in the next month."

"Food's here!" Mickey's voice floats up the stairs.

"We'll be there in a sec." Sunny yells back, and then turns to me, "So, you and Jasim?"

I huff, "There's no me and Jasim. We'll be getting a divorce."

"Oh, hon, that's bad." Pulling me in for a hug, she tries to give me some comfort. "But now you've dipped your toe in the water, you know what you want. We'll find someone else for you. Hey, we're both on the lookout now."

CHAPTER 29
Jasim

After the failed attempt to liberate Sally from Fadi, my already planned arrangements meant the very next day I'd been plunged into a tour of the oil fields, leaving me precious little time to spend with my wife. Unable to alter engagements which involved a heavy press presence, along with meetings with oil company reps, I'd had no choice but to leave her, my reluctance down to the ideas in my head of a variety of scenes I wanted to try with her.

Cutting short as much as I could, I'd rushed through my initial tour of the oil fields, managing to shave a day off the time I was meant to be away, eager to return to Z̧almā and see Janna again. And to put some of those ideas into practice.

We needed to talk, to work out the boundaries of our forced relationship, how it would work and how we'd present it to other people. I was thinking of temporarily moving her into my apartment, giving her everything money could buy. Dressing her in lavish designer clothes. And having her in my bed. Every fucking night until our attraction to each other started to wane. On the helicopter flight back from the oilfield, the thought of taking her into Nijad's dungeon, trying out all the equipment I'd originally installed for his use, had the predictable result of my cock swelling against my thigh. Though, in time, it would undoubtedly fade, for now my attraction to her remained as strong as ever.

I'd rushed into the palace, only to find her gone. She'd left without a word. The absence of even a note, showing she'd gone back to her old life, her loyalty stronger to Anarchy Rules than to her temporary husband.

The sudden burst of anger took me by surprise, a vase was thrown and smashed against the wall. But even before the pieces had reached the ground, I'd started to calm. I'd promised her nothing, and what's more, had nothing to give. I couldn't commit to a relationship, she was right to disappear. I would have ended it after a short while, if she hadn't initiated the break herself.

After issuing a short press release announcing to the world Janna had returned to England to continue her career, and a resolve on my part to keep up some sort of pretense when I eventually returned home, I then had to explain our swift separation to my brothers. I was short when I spoke to them, and, after simply exchanging glances, they probed no further. The marriage had served its purpose, no blood had been spilt on Amahadian sands.

But she was still under my skin. Inexplicably missing her, and fearing further rejection, I didn't go back to England immediately, wanting time and distance to get her out of my head. I spent longer than planned revisiting the oil fields, riding the length of some of the pipe line, encouraging the workers, and gaining an understanding of the trials they were facing on a daily basis. I gave interviews confirming the estimated amounts of oil that we'd found, putting paid to the rumours that they had been over reported. I threw myself into my work.

Ryan told me I was becoming reckless, I disagreed. I making sure I was a visible presence in the region. Never admitting any risks I was taking were only trying to fill the vast hole left inside by the woman who'd gotten away. The woman, who, by some quirk of fate, I remained officially tied too.

"How much longer are you going to grace us with your presence?" Nijad, having just flown back in from Al Qur'ah, enters the sitting room of his suite, the suite I'm still staying in. The one that reminds me of my wedding night, but which I'm loathe to move out of. He throws off his headdress, and sinks onto the low cushions in front of the table where I've got maps spread out.

I glare across at him, "I'm doing exactly what you and Kadar wanted me to do."

"I appreciate that, brother, but aren't you needed to wheel some deals? Not much point extracting oil if we've no one to sell it to."

My eyes narrow, to think that I was once afraid when they'd got me here, they'd force me to stay. Now they want to get shot of me. "I said I'd give you two months."

"It's coming up to that now. You should go home to your wife."

"She's not my wife. Not in any real sense."

He shrugs, "Kadar wanted you to keep up appearances, you can't do that from three thousand miles away."

"Butt out of my life, brother." I stand, unwilling to face him, "Tell Kadar he can stick what he wants up his arse. When I get back to London, I'll be seeking a divorce."

"You can't until a year's up. Either under the marriage contract or English law."

"I can get it annulled."

Nijad laughs, "I suppose you could try. It would be entertaining to see. Let's see, what reason will you choose? I suppose you could try to say you were forced into it, but I doubt Kadar would agree to that story coming out. You didn't drug her, or get her drunk. Or are you going to say she did that to you?" As I scowl at him, he continues, "I've got it! You can get her to say you had an STD that you hadn't disclosed."

"Club records won't support that." Like all members, I have regular check-ups and it will be on record that I'm clean.

"Say she had the clap."

"She was a virgin!"

Now he starts chuckling, "Was. That there was your admission the marriage was consummated. Seems you're out of options, brother. You'll have to wait until the year is out."

And have the thought of her hanging over me for twelve months? Without being able to reap the benefits of being married to her?

"You're enjoying this too much, Nijad."

He beckons me back to my seat, "You went into this with your eyes open. You knew what it would mean."

Slumping down, I put my head in my hands, "That was before she left me without a word. I thought we could have fun for a time until whatever it was between us wore itself out. But it ended up she didn't want that. I didn't have a chance to work her out of my system." Yeah, it must be that.

His piercing eyes see everything, "You still want her."

I shrug, the gesture indicating I don't really know what I want.

"Have you even spoken to her?"

I answer with a shake of my head, "I'm leaving her alone. She's made no move to contact me so that's obviously what she wants.."

"Does she? Or is she just waiting for you to make the first approach?" All mirth gone, he's watching me intently, "Why don't you?" He taps his fingers against his mouth, and then gives a nod, "Ah, you're afraid she'll reject you."

How can I talk to him about it, when I don't understand what's in my own mind? When I've spent lonely sleepless nights trying to convince myself the only reason I can't get her out of my head is because she left me before I was ready to let her go? What good could come of me re-opening the wound? She'd only brought forward the end which would have come in time. Is it only because there's a legal document tying us together that I feel responsibility toward her?

Tapping the map in front of us, I point to a spot, "There's a delay with the pipeline, here. I'm heading out tomorrow to see what it is." I hope changing the subject will get him onto something else.

"It's not your job, brother."

But I've made up my mind, "You wanted me to get involved, to get my hands dirty. Smooth things along. That's exactly what I'm doing."

His eyes sharpen, "What does Ryan say?"

My bodyguard has told me visiting that particular spot is a bad idea, "He's got nothing to do with my plans."

"He'll be going with you?"

I nod at that. Not that I particularly want him to, but he wouldn't let me go off alone.

Nijad's brow furrows, "I know this girl has got you twisted in knots, brother, and don't try to deny it. But you haven't a death wish, have you?"

"Oh, for fucks sake, Ni. It's not that dangerous."

"You forget." He pulls his back up straight. "I know the desert."

I don't need the reminder that he thinks I don't. Forcing down my annoyance, I make a conciliatory gesture. "This one last inspection, and then I'll go home."

"Back to your wife?"

I open my hands, palms facing toward him, "Who knows what the fuck I'll find. She could have moved on."

"Or she could be waiting for you."

Having made the decision that this is to be my last day in Amahad, the next morning, I join Ryan at the helipad as we wait for our ride to one of the areas where construction of a pipeline has stalled. Laying hundreds of miles of pipe to take oil from underground to the port where it can be shipped is the major part of this project, and currently the one giving us the most headaches. Where we're headed today is an area where the sand has a particularly high chloride level, which is highly corrosive to the metal pipe. There have been couple of options proposed, and the method chosen could affect the financial viability of the project as a whole. Valid enough reason to justify me being present for the discussion, though in truth, that could have just has easily taken place in my office.

An hour later we arrive, and are greeted by Sheikh Ghalib, one of the older rulers in the desert, and members of the Hagra, his tribe. They're all heavily armed, reminding me of the dangers that are always lurking anywhere near the pipeline construction sites. But there's nothing of concern I can see at the moment, just a range of mountains to our rear, and in front of us, the vast expanse of the sand that's causing us the problems.

We're joined by a couple of engineers, their skin leathered and weather-beaten from spending so much time in the sun. They'd arrived by Jeep, coming down from one of their other sites further along the pipeline. After making introductions and exchanging greetings, I make a start, getting straight down to business.

"Tell me our options again?"

The engineer who seems to be taking the lead taps his pen against his teeth and begins, "The cheapest is raising the pipe on a platform. But it will be at risk of exposure to the elements. A sandstorm could easily cover it. And our problem would return."

Though there's only a slight breeze now, sand is already building up against my shoes. I tilt my head toward Ghalib, "Will the Hagra be able to monitor any damage?"

He doesn't look convinced, "It's an isolated spot here. No oasis to make it a base. I can send out patrols, but how frequently, I can't say. Certainly not enough to keep sand off the pipeline." I know his tribe are farmers, eking a meagre living from what fertile land there is. Taking the men away for these extra duties would hit him hard.

"What else could we do?" I nod toward the lead engineer.

"There is a way to set up electronic protection. But we'd need a generator, and a monitoring operation to ensure that it functioned at all times." And a way to get a qualified person here quickly to fix the fault if anything went wrong. The last thing we'd want is the pipeline to split, spilling precious oil onto the sand.

As I begin to comprehend the difficulties involved in the construction, digging the wells themselves seems to be the simplest part. The engineer clears his throat, getting my attention.

"There's another option. It's expensive."

"Go on."

"There's a new type of polyethylene coating that could protect the metal from corrosion caused by the chloride. It's costly though."

"You're proposing we use some specially coated pipeline for this section?"

"Given the environment, I think it would be wise."

I nod, "Get me some figures."

The engineer smiles and nods, and I think I was right to sweep aside objections for me to come here today. Seeing the isolation of this particular spot, meeting Ghalib, who'd be providing the manpower for whatever is necessary for protection and maintenance for this area, and speaking to the experts on site gives me a much clearer idea of the issues than reading a dry report from my desk back in London. As the wind blows, whipping up sand around us, I get a better impression than I would from afar. And a greater desire to be involved in discussing the solutions. Already, I'm working out how to divert funds from another part of the project to enable the extra expense here. If it isn't too much.

"The polyethylene coated pipes sound the best way to go. But if the cost is prohibitive, we'll have to work out some way of maintaining the electronics solution. Ghalib?"

The elderly sheikh shrugs, "We will have to make it work. We've ventured too much to let it fail now." The desert tribes, wanting to cash in on the liquid gold running under their sands, had each made a hefty investment. Which means all tribes will commit to making it a success.

Just as I turn to thank him, gun shots ring out. The firing coming from the mountains to our rear. We're out in the open with nowhere to run. The only option is to make a hasty retreat.

Ryan races up to cover me, a semi-automatic in his hands.

"Get back to the helicopter, Jasim."

The pilot's not stupid, the rotors are already turning.

"Ghalib?" Fearing for the older man, I see him gun already in hand, surrounded by the men from his tribe with automatic rifles in theirs. They lay covering fire as the sheikh is bundled toward his transport.

"Jasim, get moving. You're the fucking target!"

I know that, but the engineers will be as well. "W*ade 'asfal tughatti alnnar lilmuhundisin.*" I call out my instruction for the engineers to be given protection. Making my way toward the helicopter, I watch them as they race for their Jeeps, breathing a sigh of relief as they safely get away, dust blown up by the spinning tires helping to hide their escape.

"Jasim! Move!" Ryan's screaming at me, as bullets hit the ground all around. Seeing everyone else is safe, I start to run. My guard tries to put his body between me and the shooters, hidden like cowards in the mountain rocks. I've just time to admit it may have been a mistake coming here today, when Ryan falls to the ground, taken down by a bullet to his chest.

Automatically, I turn my body to protect him, devastated by the amount of blood already escaping from the wound. My medic instincts kick in, trying to assess him without causing extra damage. I'm vaguely conscious Ghalib's signaling his men to come back to help, as I feel a sharp pain in my back, then I stumble and fall, hitting my head hard on a rock.

CHAPTER 30
Janna

As the days pass, I'm glad I confided in Sunny. Now her twisted relationship had ended, and without causing ructions with the band, we've returned to sharing everything with each other again. The only one to know the precise state of my relationship with Jasim, she has my back. When I zone out, my thoughts returning to the desert, she covers my slips and diverts attention from me.

When the video is posted on YouTube, it becomes a massive hit, generating new interest in Anarchy Rules. Our gigs are full to bursting, and we start to attract serious attention from wannabe agents and managers. A record contract is offered, and we jump at the chance. Arena gigs follow, and slowly days turn into weeks, and weeks into months. And still, no word from Jasim. Before I know it, almost quarter of the year has gone by.

I play like I used to, but my heart isn't in it. Sometimes the only way I can perform is to imagine he's out there in the audience, and every note and riff is for him. I encourage Ben to fly on his own, stepping more into the background as he takes the lead. I'm pulling away from the band, and I think everyone knows it, but no one wants to mention it aloud. Neither do they gloat on the fact my husband seems to have abandoned me, apparently putting the marriage down to a temporary aberration caused by the desert heat.

Three months and one day later—not that I'm counting—when I'm starting at last to move forward, my phone rings.

"Hello," I answer cautiously, not recognising the number, ready to end the call as soon as I'm questioned about a non-existent, not-my-fault accident that I'd apparently had.

"Janna?" The deep velvety voice stuns me.

"Um, hang on." Taking this call when everyone's sitting around listening is not what I want. I get to my feet and hurry to the privacy of my own room. "Jasim! I didn't expect you to call."

"I'm sorry to bother you after all this time. I hope you are well?"

After I murmur something non-comital, he continues, "I need to ask if you'll to do a favour for me." Even though he can't see me, I nod for him to go on. Just the sound of his voice makes memories slam into me. His scent, his touch. I shiver. At the other end of the line, he clears his throat, "I've been following Anarchy Rules. You've got an amazing number of hits on that video. It came out well, didn't it?"

"Yeah, the band's doing great." I'm surprised I can get words out of my mouth, I'm so stunned to be talking to him. As he hadn't kept in touch, I just expected divorce papers to arrive in the post.

"Look, the thing is, I hate to bring it up, but we are still married and Kadar's up in my business, reminding me of my promise. That we make this look real, at least for a reasonable time."

Really? I thought he'd forgotten and had just let matters drop. What's he going to suggest? "Jasim. I've picked up my life, I can't walk out on the band." And the last thing I want to do is to see him. To re-open the wound that's only just started healing.

"I got that message when you left without talking to me. Don't worry, Janna. I'm not going to interrupt your life. It's only a small favour. I just need to ask if you'll come to an embassy function with me. People are asking questions why my wife's not around. Janna, will, can you, come and put on a show? Just be my escort for the night, to stop tongues wagging? I'm not going to ask you to move in with me or anything. Just be seen by my side for a few hours."

Could I do that? Pretend he's my loving husband just for the night? War waging inside me, I recall exactly what I'd agreed to when it was a ruse to rescue Sally, but can I do it all these weeks later, when I've begun to get him out of my mind? *Have I? Have I really?* It's not actually possible, is it?

I've been silent too long, he fills in the gap, "I'm sorry, I'll tell Kadar to go fuck himself. Not like I haven't done it before." He laughs, then the mirth disappears and his voice deepens again. "You've moved on, haven't you, Janna? Have you found a new man? Do you want me to initiate the divorce?"

There's no one else. Despite Sunny's machinations to set me up, I've not had the faintest interest in anyone else I've met.

"No," I deny it. "I'm still a free woman."

"Not a free woman, not when you're tied to me."

His words hover in the air for a moment, they could be taken in any number of ways. The fact he'd expected me to get on with my life without him probably means he already has. I wonder how many women he's tortured since I last saw him. The thought makes me feel ill.

I shouldn't see him. I should let him move on, and then do so myself. My mind's blocking out what I don't want to accept.

"It's alright, Janna. I'll start the divorce."

"No." The word comes out before I have second thoughts, "No, I'll come to the embassy do."

I hear a sigh of relief, "Are you sure?"

"Yes. What should I wear?" A woman's perennial problem.

"Just a cocktail dress would be fine. You have something like that?"

I'll have to go shopping. "Yes, I can find something. When is it, Jasim?"

"Next Tuesday. I'll come pick you up. You're still at the same address?"

"I am. What time?"

We finalise the arrangements, and then end the call.

Finding a suitable cocktail dress isn't difficult. Getting one that fits me is. I end up buying a size larger than normal, one that's still snug over my breasts but a little too loose over my flat stomach and hips, making me recall how my appetite seems to have fled since I returned from Amahad. If I'm going to lose weight, why can't the loss be equal all over?

Surprisingly, the boys took it in their stride that I'm going out with Jasim tonight. I'd expected an argument, but they seemed more relieved he's contacted me at long last. I'd told them to butt out of what I described as our complicated relationship, explaining if they wanted me in the band, my sacrifice was living apart from my husband while he performed the duties his country required of him. As Mickey sighed and gave me a hug, I saw a twinge of guilt in his eyes, as if he believed he and the rest of Anarchy Rules were the only reason for Jasim and I being apart.

Sunny fusses over me, doing my hair and what I've got to pass for nails—long on my right hand, short on my left, the hazards of playing guitar. She evens them out as best she can, and paints them a discreet pink. She helps me with my make-up, a lot less than I'd wear on stage. The end result, as I look in the mirror, is someone I think would pass for a diplomat's wife.

"There!" she says with a flourish, presenting me with an evening bag she's dug out of her wardrobe, "You look perfect."

I think I'm far from perfection, but hopefully have done enough that I won't embarrass my husband. The nerves churning inside me seem to leach blood from my complexion, and I'm biting my lips, making them red.

"You'll be fine." Sunny assures me, and I reply with a little nod. I'm not worried about going to the embassy, I'm wondering how the hell I can pretend to play the part of a loving partner, and not risk being deceived into thinking it's real.

At seven on the dot, the limo arrives and Jasim gets out of the back. Dressed in a tuxedo, he takes my breath away, making me realise all over again that this is a mistake. But it's too late to back out now. We don't say a word as he stretches out his hand. I take it, and soon I'm seated beside him. The awkwardness stretches out between us.

"You are well?" It's a polite enquiry, a million miles away from the way he'd addressed me in the heat of the desert.

"Yes." It's a small lie, but one which will do for now. "And you?" I'm equally well-mannered.

"I'm doing okay."

There's something in his voice that makes me turn to look at him, to really see him for the first time in three months. I draw in a breath, and can't stop reaching out my hand to touch a still healing scar marring the side of his cheek. "You've been hurt."

He captures my hand, and holds it tight, "Got into some trouble in the desert when I was inspecting the pipeline. It's nothing."

"What happened?" I gasp, horrified at the thought. He'd been injured and nobody told me.

His eyes stare into mine, as if divining whether I really want to know, or I'm just making conversation. To show I really am interested, I phrase it slightly differently, "Please, tell me what happened? I don't like the idea of you being hurt."

He jerks his chin and sits forward, his hands clasped between his knees, "Ah, my habiti. Always with a soft heart." A quick glance at me, and then back down toward his hands. "The attack came out of nowhere. First, Ryan was shot."

"Attack? Shot? Ryan? Is he alright? He's not…"

"No," his hand reaches for mine again, "It was touch and go for a while as he'd lost so much blood, but he'll make a full recovery."

"What about you?" I stare at him as though there are injuries I can't see. Something tells me there's more than he's telling me.

"I took a bullet too. In my back." He pauses and laughs, "Knocked me off my feet and against a rock," he points to his face, "Split my cheek open."

I go cold, realizing that all the time he'd been in my thoughts, I'd never for a moment imagined him in danger. "Jasim…"

"I'm alright, Janna. Nothing vital was hit." His fingers wipe a tear from my eye that I hadn't known had escaped. "I'm well, now, habiti." When he adds the Arabic endearment for the second time, I admit how much missed hearing that word.

Sitting up straighter, I watch the streets of London go by, wet roads flashing under the streetlamps, missing the stars of the desert and the easy companionship that had been between us there. Despite his slip up in calling me 'my love', which I knew from having looked the Arab word up on Google, he seems as distant as he'd been that night we'd first met. This man isn't my husband. He's a stranger. His life since we last met, is outside of my comprehension. *He'd been hurt and I hadn't known.* It can't have been serious. He seems alright now.

He's dismissed my concern as unnecessary, so I turn to a more immediate worry. "What do you need me to do tonight?"

A shrug, "Just be yourself. You will be by my side."

"What if I'm asked what I do?"

"Tell them the truth. That you play in a band. There's nothing to hide."

"Except our fake marriage."

He grimaces. "Well, there's that, of course. Janna, I've looked into it. We'll have to stay married a year. But I won't tie you down."

I wish you would. Tamping down my traitorous thoughts, which just prove the time we spent apart has done nothing to dull his effect on my libido, I try to get more information, "Who will be there?"

"Diplomats, people from the oil industry. And it won't be for long, it's a reception, not a dinner. Drinks and canapes. We'll leave as soon as we can." He pauses and looks at me, "I can't tell you how grateful I am that you're doing this. There's been some gossip about us not being seen together."

"It's hardly a chore." I try to summon a smile. Just being here with him, knowing we've lost that easy intimacy between us, trying to act like it doesn't matter is perhaps one of the hardest things I've ever done. The memory of riding with him in the desert comes into my mind, such a stark contrast to riding in this limousine.

"I haven't heard anything about Sally. Do you know what happened at the end of her month?"

"I do." He grins. And teases me by keeping silent for a moment. When I'm about to prompt him, he continues, "Nijad went to an exhibition in Al Qur'ah. Sally's been busy and was exhibiting some of her photographs there. Fadi set it up for her."

"Was he with her?"

He laughs, "Yes, he was. And completely besotted. Let's just say, Sally has captured her sheikh."

Unlike me. "I'm pleased for her," I manage to say indifferently, while thinking some of the weirdest arrangements have a way of working themselves out.

We pull up outside the doors of the Amahadian Embassy, and wait for the chauffeur to open the doors. Once outside, Jasim links his arm with mine, and leads me inside. His closeness awakens sensations which should stay dormant. *I can do this.* I can pretend, I can have him touch me and still keep my bruised heart intact. I have to.

That Jasim's the guest of honour is apparent when we step inside. Men in smart suits vie for his attention. I stand at his side, doing my best to keep a pleasant smile on my face. To all intents and purposes, I'm ignored by the men, but subjected to various glances from the women around. My facial muscles start hurting after being frozen in place for so long, as I wonder whether any of the females have had the pleasure of being his sub. Oh, I can read their expressions, they're curious about the woman who's managed to snag the bachelor sheikh.

I take a glass of champagne when it's offered but put it down after one sip. And don't partake of the Amahadian delicacies that are offered to me, knowing they'd only form a lump in my already fragile stomach.

I didn't appreciate how hard it would be to pretend as I overhear Jasim's discussions, recognizing what a true diplomat he is. He's committing to nothing, even though it's obvious several people have come to persuade him. Letting them all down gently, with various suggestions of 'I'll consider your proposal' or 'Please contact my office and I'll be happy to look at it'. It soon becomes clear everyone wants a part of him tonight.

And all the time he's touching me. A hand to the small of my back. His fingers on my arm. A touch to my wrist. And each occasion he does so, I get a tingle inside. At one point he turns, checking I'm alright, and there's a flare in his dark eyes as I offer a wan smile back.

It seems like forever, but at last he signals we can leave. A multitude of goodbyes, then we're heading outside. The limousine pulls up in front of us, before I can consider how I'm getting home.

He sits me inside. The car doesn't move.

CHAPTER 31
Janna

I sit waiting for the car to pull off, not certain whether I'm in a rush to get home to restore my equilibrium or if I'd prefer to steal every moment I can with this enigmatic man beside me.

"Janna," his hand comes out and cups my face. "Having you beside me this evening has been torture."

For him, too?

Removing his fingers, he taps both hands on his knees. He looks down at his fingers beating out a rhythm, and when he turns to face me, he looks unsure of himself. "Janna, fuck it. I don't want to simply take you home." Raising one of his hands, he brings it up to caress the side of my face. "I've missed you."

I swallow. Seeing him again, all my thoughts that I was moving on, getting him out of my mind had proved to be so wrong. Unable to find the words to explain, I give a little jerk of my head, hoping the action will convey that I've felt the same.

His eyes stare into mine, so intently I want to turn away, but the touch of his hand has my head held in place. "Janna, our relationship," he breaks off, trying to gather his thoughts. "I don't do relationships, you know that. But there's something between us, something I still want to explore, and I find I'm still not ready to give up on that."

Once again I nod, fearful of saying the wrong thing, waiting to hear what he's going to suggest.

"My club, my lifestyle, it's important to me."

My eyes widen a little, I'm not sure where he's going with this.

He gives a short laugh, "I'm a fucking Dom, Janna, yet I'm find it hard to put this into words. So I'd like to show you instead. What would you say if I wanted to take you to Club Tiacapan? Tonight?"

What would I say?

When I don't immediately answer, he asks me again, "I don't want to let you go, not right now. Will you consider coming to my club?"

Christ! That wasn't what I expected him to say. *His club?* His BDSM club for goodness sake. And if we go there… "Now? Tonight? To play?"

He glances back with a dark look on his face, "Yes." His tone is gruff, as though he's barely keeping himself in check. "You'll be my submissive."

My teeth find my lip and worry at it. What he's asking is a long way from anything I've experienced before, and it scares me a little. "What would I be agreeing to, Jasim? What would you expect?"

"Are you worried I'd hurt you?" When I raise my shoulders, he offers a reassuring smile. "Have you heard of the phrase, mind fuck?"

I haven't, but I can guess what it might be.

He looks at the glass between us and the driver, as though ensuring our conversation will be private. And even then, brings his mouth close to my ear. "I get off on your fear, of you not knowing what to expect, of being able to take you to places you never dreamed of going."

"But that includes pain."

"Have I actually hurt you before? When I spanked you, you liked it."

And I can't deny that that's true.

"In a sexually charged situation, your brain translates what you'd otherwise reject by releasing endorphins. When you're tied up and helpless, leaving yourself open to anything I want to do, your fear of the unknown increases your arousal, and that does the same to me too."

"How do you know what I would and wouldn't like? What if you took it too far?"

"That's why we have safewords. If you had more experience, we'd be discussing your limits, what you do and don't like. But as you're a novice, we'll both be finding our way. And I'll be taking it slow. I'm an experienced Dom, Janna. You'll find me stopping before you think you've had enough, I can read the signs of your body."

Already I'm starting to feel the arousal he's speaking of. I was brave in the desert, I told him I could match him. And nothing he did there took me too far. But the idea of going to his club where experienced people play, both excites and scares me, there would be opportunities and the equipment to do so much more. I feel my cheeks flush, and that's when I know that I'm going to say yes. How could I pass up this chance to learn more about his life?

"So will you try it? Come and be my submissive tonight?" He takes a deep breath, and seems to hold it, waiting for my answer.

As his submissive. *Not as his wife. Not as someone he wants any other relationship with.* But wasn't that all that was ever on offer? I knew that when I gave him my virginity, so nothing has changed. But the chance to give myself to him again, to feel him take charge of my body? For the first time in three months, I feel alive.

"Yes," I breathe, answering him with no hesitation, pushing to the back of my mind any thought of how I might regret it tomorrow.

A quick knock on the glass, a hasty instruction to the driver, and this time, when he takes my hand, Jasim raises it to his lips and kisses it. "Tonight, you're mine, Janna." His deep velvety voice washes over me as he clarifies, "Your body belongs to me. Can you give me that?"

Like a switch being thrown, tingles of anticipation start to run up and down my spine. But it's his club, and we'll presumably be playing in public, and my arousal is tinged with trepidation which the bastard probably knows and likes. "What can I expect? I've never been to a club before."

A smirk and a chuckle shows that I'm right. "It will push you, for sure. But isn't that just what I've always done, habiti?" He has. And everything he's done, I've enjoyed. "If you reached the place where you were so uncomfortable you couldn't take any more, and I'd missed the signs, your safeword will stop everything. I'd be troubled if you held it back. But my aim is not to push you so far."

"I've no idea what to expect."

"That's part of the thrill. Isn't it?"

Not knowing what I'm going into, having to trust him completely. As a delightful shiver overtakes me, I can't deny my underwear is getting soaked.

"Just the thought is turning you on."

Jerking my chin, I admit that my smug sheikh is completely right.

Before long we're turning up a long driveway and coming to a halt in front of massive wooden doors. The chauffeur again does his job opening doors and allowing us out, then the limousine drives away, leaving us standing at the entrance. As Jasim puts his hand to my back, I'm aware I'm shaking. But along with my anxiety is eagerness, and I'm impatient to see what's a very big part of Jasim's life. *He's allowing me to see the real him.*

Wasting no time, he opens the door and encourages me into a reception area, and I'm slightly disappointed there's no intriguing equipment immediately in sight. Apart from the ornate decoration as befits a mansion three hundred years old, there's just a desk that could have been in any foyer in any office building. Except, that is, for the scantily clad woman sitting behind it with her breasts hanging out in full view.

"Jasim! It's good to see you. It's been so long since you've been here. When did you get back?"

"Gloria. Good to see you too. I only returned last week. I was away longer than expected."

My mouth drops open, and a warm glow rises inside as it becomes clear he had contacted me almost as soon as he'd gotten back. I'd been wrong to spend sleepless nights worrying about him playing with beautiful subs in his club. *He hadn't even been in the country.*

"And who's your guest?"

"Let me introduce you to my wife." His words make me start. I didn't expect him to be so open. Though I know it's the role we'll need to play for another nine months, that he's so circumspect about it is surprising. I'm not the only one to be taken aback, his receptionist's jaw almost hits the floor.

She recovers fast. "Well, let's get you set up." When she brings out a box from under her desk, Jasim reaches inside and pulls out two wristbands.

"White for you, so everyone knows you're a novice." I blush at that. After a moment, he reaches up and his fingers trace my neck, "Have we got any training collars handy, Gloria?" he asks over his shoulder.

"Yes, somewhere. Hang on, how's this?"

"That will do fine." Jasim turns back to me, and a narrow band of red leather comes into sight. "If a sub's not collared, she's considered fair game. I'll put this on you for tonight, habiti, so people know you've been claimed."

If a strip of leather protects me from unwelcome advances, who am I to complain? At my nod, he passes it around my neck, locks it, and pockets a key. Surreptitiously, I touch my fingers to the collar. That I can't take it off makes me feel I'm already under his control. *But I'm fooling myself if I believe I haven't been since the moment he picked me up tonight.*

"Have a good night," says the receptionist cheerily, and then I'm being pulled by my hand into the first BDSM club I've ever been in in my life.

At first, I see nothing. This is just an entrance hall, with cloakrooms off to either side. A fleeting glimpse, then he's encouraging me through the next door, which opens into the club proper. And oh, hell. My eyes go so wide I think they've taken up all of my face. The size of the interior, the equipment and stage areas, takes me by surprise. I've never been exposed to anything like this before. Reading about such places is one thing. Seeing it is quite another. It's busy and crowded. So many people, some nearly naked and others completely so. As well as the sights, there's the sounds. The air's tainted with the odour of sex and arousal. My breath leaves my lungs and I want to turn tail and run.

"Er," I pull back on his hand, "I don't think I'm ready for this."

"If you're not, if you really can't try, I'll take you home." He stares into my eyes, and his fingers rise and touch the pulse hammering in my neck, "I know it's a lot to take in, especially as it's your first time." He breaks off and gives a low laugh, "You trusted me with your first time before. Can you trust me now? Try for me?"

I remember this is his environment, he owns the club. This is his lifestyle which he's allowing an insight into. Trying to swallow down my fear, I remember he's done nothing to cause me harm, nor anything I didn't enjoy. He's pushed me, and that's what he's doing now, even though I believe he's skating along the lines of my limit.

But if I want to know him better, understand him, I should at least give him a chance. *This is all he's going to offer me.* If I mess it up now, I might never see him again.

As his fingers squeeze my hand, I give a little jerk of my chin to let him know I'll try.

He points at my wristbands, "There's a two-drink limit per member for anyone wanting to play. We'll go to the bar and you can have something to help steady your nerves. Then, if you're ready, we can try a small scene. If you don't want to play tonight, I'll understand. There's no need to be worried. I appreciate how overwhelming it is." He smiles down at me, "You're not the first new sub who's been terrified at first."

That the club has a similar effect on other newcomers makes me feel slightly better. Nodding nervously, I take my first step into the room. The music isn't loud but it's a thudding rock beat, and screams and shouts of pain and satisfaction mingle to form a cacophony of sound. Almost too afraid to look in any direction, I let him lead me across to a bar, behind which is standing a jovial man.

"Master J!" he calls out as we approach. Then his eyes fall on me, and on my collar. "I heard you got married. Congratulations! Fuck me, never thought I'd see the day. And you've collared a sub?"

The way he says it, he could be talking about two different people. The spouse and the play partner. Is he suggesting Jasim's cheating? Little wifey left at home? Is that what people here would expect?

"This is my wife, Ralph. *And* she's my sub." I'm glad he cleared that up, though the thought of him coming to play with another sub creeps into my mind. I realise he's still speaking to the bartender, "Could you watch her for a moment while I go and get changed. Janna, you'll be quite safe here with Master Ralph. I'll only be a minute."

"Yeah, I'll do my babysitting stint. Off you go, Master J. What do you want to drink, sweetheart?"

My face drops as I see him walk away, I don't want to be left on my own. But Master Ralph is smiling warmly, and I remember my manners. "I'll have an orange juice please." Recalling I'm supposed to give over one of the wristbands, I reach to take one off. A meaty palm stays my hand, "No need for that if you're just having a soft drink."

"Oh, okay. It's my first time."

"I can see that, sweetheart." He gives me a cocky grin then leans his elbows on the bar, "Now, what do we call you?"

"My name's Janna."

"Is that what you want to go by in the club?"

Well, what else would anyone call me? Then it dawns on me, he's giving me the choice of anonymity. I shrug.

"Guess you'll have to think about that."

As someone calls him away to get them a drink, I bravely turn and look out at what's going on behind me. There, on a spanking bench close by, and in full view of everyone, a sub is screaming out her release. I thought I'd be disgusted, instead I feel envious, wishing that was me, rubbing my thighs together to ease the ache inside. Feeling braver, I watch someone else, a sub on her knees serving her Dom. Bloody hell, it's all a real-life porn show. *I didn't appreciate it would turn me on.* No wonder the guys were wary about me being exposed to all this.

Quickly looking away, I scan the large room, but although extreme petting is going on, no one's having full on sex. Or not that I can see. And then my eyes fall on Jasim who, true to his word, hasn't left me for long and is now walking toward me. And, oh, shit. If I needed anything else to arouse me, the sight of him in tight leather trousers and a bare chest covered only by a leather waistcoat hanging open would serve that purpose. He's striding straight for me, another grin on his face.

"Ralph been looking after you?" As I nod yes, he indicates the area behind him, "I should have explained some things before. I had no expectations of bringing you here tonight, I'm doing everything the wrong way around. I've been remiss in not preparing you. You'll only be playing with me, pet. Normally you'd have paperwork to complete, but as I'm the owner I'm vouching for you, okay? Right."

He pauses, scrunching his face, "There's no penetrative sex in the main room. Private rooms are available for people who to go further. You see the people in orange vests?" He points one of them out. "They're dungeon monitors who make sure everything is safe, sane, and consensual. If you ever shout out your safeword, they'll coming running to help."

"Even if I'm with you?"

"I might own the club, but I'm still subject to the rules. Some I might be able to bend, such as letting you in without completing the documentation, but not that." He waits for the information he's given me to sink in, but before he can speak again, another man comes up to us. He's looking paler and less robust than when I last saw him.

"Ryan, mate. Good to see you." Jasim takes his arm and pulls him in for a man hug. "How the fuck are you doing?"

Ryan nods at me, "Hi, Janna," before turning back to Jasim, "I've only got another week or so tied to the desk. I can understand now why Sean was going stir crazy confined to the office."

Jasim's still got hold of his arm, and as I watch I see his face fall, "Man, I'm so sorry."

"What the fuck?" Ryan glares at him. "It's my job. I know what I signed up for. Let's not go through this again."

It sounds like a discussion they've had before. Jasim's worried glance at Ryan signifies he's not convinced, but the scowl on the bodyguard's face stops him from saying anything more. After a few seconds, he shakes his head and turns away. Something catches his eye. "Can you wait here with Janna a sec, Ry? I've got a piece of equipment to reserve."

At Ryan's understanding smirk, Jasim disappears again, and my narrowed eyes follow him, wondering what he's up to.

Ryan touches my arm. I already know he's a man of few words, so I'm surprised when he starts talking. "He's feeling guilty, Janna. But he's got no reason to."

I look up at him, and point to the scar visible on his chest, remembering their conversation and putting two and two together. "Because you got hurt?"

"Yes. When you disappeared, Janna, he started taking risks. Exposing himself when he shouldn't. That day, I warned him not to go to check on the pipeline. I'm his bodyguard, for fuck's sake. Now he thinks he put me in danger by ignoring my advice. But it wasn't a specific threat, just my inclination to keep the person I'm protecting away from any front line. If I'd known for a fact there were insurgents in the area, I wouldn't have let him go. I'd have found some way of stopping him, even if it meant locking him in a room. It wasn't his fault."

I nod to encourage him to continue, it's the most I've ever heard him speak at one time. He's telling me this for a reason. It makes sense, Jasim's an honorable man, and if he thought he was in any way to blame for putting someone's life in danger, it would be bound to hit him hard.

"You said he took risks after I'd left?" I shake my head, not understanding why he's talking like this. *Had my leaving affected him?*

As if to assuage any responsibility I might feel, Ryan shakes his head quickly, "Whether your leaving was the cause, or whether being in Amahad for longer was getting to him, it's impossible to say. But it's undeniable he became more careless. Oh, someone else might not have noticed, I doubt if he knew himself. But I know him too well."

"He didn't like that I left without explaining."

"No man likes that, Janna."

I look down at my feet, and then at Jasim who's doing something across the room. "I didn't think he'd care. We married for a reason."

Ryan's hand touches my chin and raises it so I'm forced to look him in the face, "It was an extreme solution. Just telling Fadi he'd claimed you might well have worked."

If he's right, there was no need for the marriage. Was I put in this position for nothing? I dismiss the idea, "But it might not."

Ryan gives a little jerk of his head, I can't read whether it's in agreement or dismissal.

For a short while my mind's been taken off why Jasim's brought me here. But as he comes back with a knowing smile on his face, my nerves return to me fast. Without saying a word, he puts his arm around my shoulders, and nodding at Ryan, leads me away. We cross the crowded room and approach a stage in the corner. Taking pride of place is a big cross. There's no one else close by, I presume this is the equipment he's reserved for us to play. I swallow a few times as he speaks to confirm my fears.

"It's a St Andrew's Cross, and I want to tie you to it."

Okay. Nervously I ask, "And then what?"

He's standing behind me, my back pulled into his chest. I can feel his arousal, hard and evident, his cock jerking in his leather pants. His mouth nuzzles my neck, and a tingling feeling banishes some of my fear. *Whatever he did to me in the past, it was all for my enjoyment.* Can I trust him to take care of me now? *I'll try.* Taking a deep breath, I try to settle my nerves.

"I want to blindfold you, then you won't be so aware of your surroundings, and hopefully not so worried about being on display."

On display? He's not suggesting what I think he is, is he? I focus on the blindfold. "And I won't be able to see what you're doing."

"Exactly." I feel warm breath on my ear. "You liked the flogger, didn't you?"

"Is that what you're going to do? Flog me?" He's right, I did enjoy it. Just the thought of what he's asking is making me wetter. Around me are cries of pleasure and pain, the music's thumping, my clit throbbing in time. I'm scared and apprehensive, but so bloody turned on. I'm probably going to do whatever he wants.

His hands caress my arms, "You have your safeword. We use the traffic light system at Tiacapan. Red, for stop, green if I check in and you're doing okay, and yellow if you want me to slow down. Got it?"

"Red, stop. Green go. Yellow ease up a bit."

"Good girl." He pauses for a moment, just the light touch of his fingers is making me tingle. "First though, we need to get you out of these clothes."

Naked? "What, all of them?" I turn around, and try to plead with my eyes.

"You'll be facing the cross. All anyone will see is your arse. And that's if they look. Habiti, you'll be just another body to anyone who sees. No one will censure you here. Now, are you going to be brave for me?"

Am I? It's what he wants. Can I take that leap of faith and trust him? I eye up the others in the room, all concentrating on their own play. Apart from my lack of clothes, is it much different than being on stage?

His hands are running up and down my arms, his mouth nuzzling at my neck. "I'm pushing you fast, I know that."

He pauses, and for a second his hands still. "Too much perhaps. Janna, I've dreamed on having you here, but if you'd prefer, I will take you home. Or we can just watch others scening, whatever you want is perfectly fine."

That might be the words that have come out of his mouth, but what will happen if I give up and let him take me home? The way I'd ensnared him was to tell him I could match his appetites, and unless that was a lie, I can't bow out now. This lifestyle means everything to him, my chances of seeing him again, touching him, will probably be nil. "You want me to do this." I know that he does, and how important this is for him.

"I do." His voice tremors with tension, "Will you try?"

CHAPTER 32
Jasim

I stand rigid, waiting for her to refuse, for the word *no* to come out of her mouth. Not wanting to rush her, I give her some time to reach her decision, and then my cock leaps as she gives the answer I hoped for, but didn't dare to expect, knowing how much I'm asking of an inexperienced sub. But this is such a vital part of my life, and I want her to share it with me. I hold my breath.

"Yes." Her voice trembles, she's not certain, but she's giving it a chance. I knew she was brave.

"Good girl." I breathe out my relief.

With any other sub we'd be having a negotiation, she'd tell me what she expects and wants, and I'd translate that into what she needs. But she'll have no idea what to ask for. So I'll be playing this by ear, pushing her into a short scene just to introduce her to a more formal type of play. Easing her in gently. Already I know I won't be satisfied with just the one night, my mind racing ahead on where we could go from here. I smile to myself, while it's much too early for my whip, I'd love to see her tensing at the sound of the crack, not knowing where or when the lash is going to fall. The possibilities between us are endless.

Shutting my thoughts down of the future, I make myself concentrate on the here and now. And with that in mind, I take a deep breath and centre myself, summoning my knowledge of beginner subs, what buttons to push, and what might make it easier for her. To that end, while I want her naked, I'm not going to ask her to do a striptease. Giving her a little push, I move her toward the cross, then undo her zipper and push her dress off her shoulders. I remove her bra and push down her underwear, softly asking her to lift her feet so I can remove them entirely. Goosebumps have risen on her skin, but she can't be cold. The temperature is always carefully controlled in here, making it just right for naked subs. She's being so brave, she makes no protest.

Taking hold of her hand, I snap it into one of the cuffs, then do the same to her other. Gently kicking her legs apart, I fasten first one, then the other ankle to the cross. She's shaking now, and I don't want her terrified. Well, not just yet. Removing the blindfold I had in my pocket, I put it around her eyes, cutting out all light. With her ability to see taken away, it will make her focus on other things. Unable to glimpse anyone who might wander over, hopefully she won't be disturbed about the onlookers we could we attract. As Master Dom and part-owner, there's often people watching how I play. But I'm sensible enough to keep that bit of information to myself.

While we've been apart I've been unable to get out of my head how she had responded to me. That delectable edge of fear which I loved to insert into my play having the exact result I wanted but hadn't anticipated. It had turned her on, increased her arousal and enhanced the outcome for us both. And now I've got her here. In my club. There's so many things I want to do. Once more the thought flits through my head, tonight need only be a start.

Careful to retain tactile assurance, I keep my hand on her as I move around to her front and fasten my mouth over hers. It's been weeks since we kissed, and quickly I discover how much I've missed it. Such an innocent connection which makes my balls tighten. Fuck, her taste, the way her tongue slides against mine… I take a moment to savour how fucking wonderful she is. I'd been convinced I'd never sample her mouth again, and almost managed to persuade myself it wasn't as good as I'd remembered. I'd been so fucking wrong.

Reluctant I pull away, not forgetting to check in. "Are you doing okay?"

"I… I think so." Her voice sounds both tentative and dreamy. The kiss has affected her too.

"I'm right here with you. At no time will I leave you. If you're worried say yellow and if I'm not touching you, I'll come straight back. If you say red you'll have a dungeon monitor here in seconds. You're safe with me."

One side of her mouth turns up.

"What's that half-smile for, habiti?"

"I'm not sure the word safe and you go together."

Reaching my hand around, I give a half-hearted slap on her backside. "Smartarse," I tell her. For the first time in three months, I'm enjoying myself. Brushing her long dark hair over one shoulder, I start braiding the long strands into a plait it so I won't catch it. Now I've got a clear view of her back.

"A hairdresser now?"

"Watch it," I laugh.

I stand back and admire her and am ready to start. "Now I'm going to warm you up," I warn her. Turning, I take two floggers out of my toy bag, and moving to the front of the cross wait for a few seconds before starting to lash her. Her body's tense, and I want to take that tension away. I start gently, getting into a rhythm using the right then the left, my strikes in time with the music. After a few minutes she begins to relax, I increase the intensity, moving up and then down, gradually awakening all her nerve endings. The repetitive activity soothing me as much as her.

When she leans into the cross, I start to lash harder, watching carefully for signs of discomfort. When her body's glowing a delicious shade of pink and I've got her into a state of complete relaxation, I decide to change things up a bit.

Putting down the floggers, I go to my toy bag and take out the most innocuous of objects. In the right hands, however, it could have been invented by the very devil himself. Wooden clothes pegs. I quickly return to her so she doesn't think I've left her, though to be honest, I don't think she's realized the flogging has ended yet. I smooth my hands down her pinkened body, loving the touch of her satin soft skin against my hands. *I've missed her.* Which is a strange admission since, normally, I never had thoughts about a sub once I ended a scene. *But I hadn't finished with her. I hadn't had enough time to get her out of my system.*

"Jasim," she says softly, sounding slightly drunk. Her back, bum, and legs are flushed red from my attentions. She's the most beautiful sight I've ever seen.

"Here you call me Master." A title I've not let anyone call me before. Oh, they can call me Master J, but with just the one word, it signifies a commitment, identifying me as her sole Dom. My hands stop moving involuntarily as I think about any other Dom playing with her. *She's mine.* Another strange claim of ownership that feels right, but is an odd thought to strike me. She's mine, for now, I silently amend.

I shake my head to clear it of all these bizarre thoughts, and continue exploring her body with my fingertips. I hadn't noticed she'd felt bony before, she seems to have lost weight. I'm having trouble finding skin to … ah, there. I attach a clothes peg. She gasps and struggles, trying to detach it.

"Hush, take it for me."

"What the hell is it?" She wriggles again.

Another slap to her arse, "Keep still! Remember the nipple clamps? Breathe into it and relax." I give her a moment, and see when she stills. Undeterred by her protest, I attach another one. And then another. Soon there's a ladder of pegs running down each side of her torso. I run my finger along her slit, she's soaking wet. *She's enjoying this.* The little bites of pain enhancing her arousal. And her suffering certainly increases mine. I take a moment to breathe deeply myself, willing my cock to have patience.

"You look fucking beautiful taking the pain for me." And it's true, she does. My cock lengthens almost uncomfortably.

I move around to her front, unable to prevent myself stealing another kiss and then take advantage of my new position. Her breasts are amazing, I cover them with my hands. *She hasn't lost weight here.* And her nipples are protruding nicely, ready and waiting for my clamps, looking a little larger than I remember. Using my mouth, I tease them even more, adding a little nip which gets her squirm-ing.

Then I take out the clamp and fasten it on.

She squeals and tries to back away.

"It's alright," I try and soothe her, "It's no tighter than you wore before."

"Jasim, no. Yellow. No, Red. Please, take it off," she yelps out.

Taken aback at her vehemence and the unexpected utterance of her safeword, I honour her request quickly, giving a brief nod to the dungeon monitor who'd heard her sharp cry. He lifts his chin, seeing the distraught expression on my face and that I've got it under control. My aim had been to cause a slight pain to arouse her, I have no desire to really hurt her.

What seemed to her to be a device of torture removed, I soothe her sore nipple with my tongue, sucking that hard nub into my mouth. Looks like it's a no to clamps today. Shame, I would have enjoyed taking them off. "It's alright, habiti. We don't have to use them." Gradually tension leaves her again.

Carefully, I examine her. Her breathing is shallow, her skin covered with a light sheen of perspiration, "Give me a colour, habiti."

There's a slight pause while she processes my request, and before she gives me her answer. "Green," she breathes.

"And how are you feeling?"

"Turned on." Comes the reply. "Jasim… Master, I…"

"I'm in charge." I tell her firmly, noticing the rippling of her skin as a shiver runs through her. I touch my hand to her pussy, not surprised to find it's become sopping. I smile, even though she can't see it. Putting my fingers to my mouth, I suck on her sweet essence. "You're so beautiful, pet. So responsive. Just a few moments more. Will you take it for me?" I don't tell her she's got no choice, there's one thing that has to be done, despite any protest she might make. As her head moves up and down, my cock swells even more, knowing she's taking everything for me. Well, everything except nipple clamps that is.

When her muscles loosen, I step around to her back, eyeing the pegs I've placed down her sides. A cruel grin comes to my face. There are two ways to remove them, and either will hurt. The first is to thread a line between them and then pull them off together, or… I pick up the crop I'd gotten ready, and hit my target.

The first peg comes off.

"Ouch!"

Yup, that would smart. "Breathe, habiti, take a deep breath." Without giving her any more warning I start to lash right then left. The clothes pegs ping off, going in alternate directions. Her protests get louder with each one as blood rushes back. Her body will be tingling and throbbing all over, not dissimilar to the painful churning in my balls.

And then the last one hits the ground. I move swiftly to her, my chest pressed against her back. Thrusting my fingers inside her, I curl them around to stroke her g-spot, accurately finding it the first time. Twisting my hand, I press my thumb to her clit, and *gently* massage her breast with my other hand, a very soft tweak to her nipples.

She's wet, swollen, and ready. Her body pulsing with the sharp tingles from having the pegs removed, her brain confusing the signals of arousal and pain. She's still glowing from the flogging. She comes quickly and hard, with a cross between a scream and a wail. I continue my assault on her pussy, wringing a second, then third orgasm from her. Waves ripple through her body, her muscles contracting and releasing, time after time. When she collapses forward, her weight hanging from the cuffs, I quickly support her, releasing her immediately, holding her as I unfasten her ankles and rub rapidly on her skin. Then, grabbing the blanket I'd left ready, wrap her and hold her tightly in my arms. When I remove the blindfold, she doesn't even notice.

"Wow, she reaches subspace so spectacularly. She's beautiful, Jasim."

I hadn't realized Ryan's been watching, and his words send a rush of pride through me.

"I'll clean up. You look after her." He pauses before adding with a grin, "Room three's available."

I thank him profusely, then carry her out of the main club and into the hallway, kicking open the door of the appointed room. Taking her to the bed, I sit down, easily taking her weight as I lean back against the headboard, an almost comatose woman in my arms. *Ryan was right. She responds to me so beautifully. Only to me.*

The room, like all the private rooms, has been well prepared. Bottles of spring water are within easy reach on the bedside table. Taking one, I open it and put it to her mouth. She drinks automatically, then, bottle finished, she snuggles against me, fitting so well in my arms I start to believe I've found the perfect sub. Have I been a fool? Kidding myself this was only temporary? Stupid to ignore what my possessive feelings have trying to tell me? I've shared women before, I'm never going to let another man touch her. Watch another send her into subspace? Or even lay a hand on her soft skin? *I've been conning myself.* An unfamiliar sensation grabs me, an emotion I hesitate to name. *Why didn't I chase after her? Why did I leave it so long?*

Gently, I smooth my hands over her body, rubbing the places where the pegs pinched. As I softly massage her, slowly she comes back to her senses, her face turns up to me, her eyes bright and shining, her lips turning up.

"Jasim, that was incredible."

"How are you feeling?"

"Like my whole body is alive and tingling."

"Here?" I sweep my hand down to her clit, circling it gently.

"Oh, yes… There." She jumps as she's so sensitive.

"Need my cock inside you, habiti."

Her heart beat speeds up, I don't need words to tell me she's ready. Standing, I quickly strip, then reach into the well-stocked drawer and take out a condom, smoothing it on over my rock-hard dick. Turning her over, I press her hands to the headboard and pull up her hips so she's resting on her knees. I can't wait to be inside her, her body might be tingling, mine's tight as a drum, her every reaction to the scene we'd just played ramping up my arousal so I won't be able to string this out.

As my cock probes her entrance, she pushes back against me. Her pussy's so swollen it's difficult to press in.

She gasps at my intrusion, "Jasim, please…"

She doesn't need to beg me. With a sudden thrust, I press home. Home. This is what she feels like to me. *I've missed this*. The feeling of perfection, as though she was made only for me. As though being the one to take her virginity has moulded her only for my cock. The possessive revelation incites me. I withdraw, then plunge in. Christ, this woman! Her muscles are squeezing me, little moans coming from her mouth. She's holding tight to the headboard, following my instructions. *Has anything ever felt this right before?* I drive in again, and again, repositioning her slightly so I hit her sensitive nerves time after time. Her thighs lock, signaling she's close.

"Come for me!" I shout, and as her muscles start contracting, squeezing my cock, I lunge in one last time, pressing tight against her cervix as cum floods the condom. With little stabs, more bursts follow until my balls feel drained and empty.

I'd started this night with no expectations. No hopes we'd end up like this. Yes, the invitation had been a ruse, an excuse to see her again, but as soon as she'd stepped into the limousine my cock had started to harden, and I knew exactly how what I wanted for the evening's finale. I didn't expect her to agree to come to the club, never hoped to see her tied to a cross. And yet it had happened.

And now I admit just how much I've missed her. And that she's making me reevaluate my stance on monogamous relationships. I don't want this to be the last time we play, and my desert blood stirs, telling me any other man who touched her would fast meet his death.

Moving my weight off her, I roll onto my side, pulling her against me, her back to my front. I can't keep my hands off her, they wander over her ribs, feeling her bones protruding more than the last time she was in my arms, again reminding me she's lost weight, and for a second I wonder why. *Has she missed me?* My fingers trace her skin, her breasts do seem larger, but perhaps it's my memory, or the weight loss elsewhere creating the illusion they've increased in size. My palms cover them as if to check them, she wriggles as I squeeze gently, her hands cover mine as though to still them.

"Sensitive?" I ask.

"A bit."

My heart rate which had started slowing, now begins to speed up. I start to tense as I tentatively ask, "You've lost weight, habiti. Have you been ill?"

She stretches her limbs, "I've been a bit out of sorts. The change in the climate, I expect. And the band's working so hard now. We're having to turn gigs down."

"You've been sick?"

"A little."

I'm silent as I think it through, little signs that a man other than a trained and experienced Dom might have missed. I still as things start to add up. As I reach my conclusion I force all emotion out of my voice. As casually as possible, I ask, "Are you pregnant?"

Her body goes rigid, "What? No." She replies firmly. "Of course I'm not."

But her denial has come too quickly.

"Janna, habiti. Your breasts are bigger and more sensitive, and you've lost weight. And you've just admitted you've been nauseous." I glide my hand across her still flat belly. "Are you close to your period? Have you been on a diet?" I reach for explanations which aren't so extreme.

She struggles as though to pull herself up, but I imprison her to me. "I've just had no appetite." She shrugs my observations off.

I'm a Dom, I can read her. I sit up, pulling her around so I can look straight into her eyes. As I get her full attention, I ask again, "Could you be pregnant?"

She stares at me, then her eyes flick away. Again, she tries to evade my hold.

"Janna," I start.

But she interrupts me, "There's been no one else. And you always used condoms. It's not possible, Jasim."

I close my eyes briefly, and take a deep breath, "Condoms are not always one hundred percent effective." I know she's telling the truth and she's not been with another man. She's not the kind of woman who'd rush from my bed to another's. And if she had been, there would have been tell-tale signs, a slight difference in the way she reacted to me if she'd been taught to respond to another man's touch. No cock has been where mine has been. I would have known it. And I remember everything. I've been with no other woman since her.

"I can't be pregnant, Jasim. I can't." There's moisture leaking from her eyes.

I try to think rationally, and keep my voice calm, betraying none of my feelings. "Janna, have you had a period since we've been together?"

"Yes!" A pause, then, "Well, a light one but…"

She could be, but she's in denial. If she is, she'll already be three months along. The weight-loss concerns me, she's not been looking after herself. That my first reaction is concern for her health, and that of the possible baby, surprises me. I have none of the adverse feelings I would have expected, I'm not dismayed I could be caught in a trap. If she's having my child, there'll be no divorce. *And she'll be mine. Forever.*

I grasp her arms, "Janna, look at me." Those glorious dark eyes turn to meet mine, but the sparkle is missing. "We need to find out. We'll find out for sure in the morning."

She frowns and shakes her head, "I'm certain I'm not."

We could go around in circles all night. "Come, get dressed. You're coming back to my place tonight." Telling myself it's just because I'm concerned she might be pregnant, but knowing I'm inviting her back for a myriad of reasons I don't want to think about right now. First and foremost, that I'm unwilling to let her out of my sight.

Huffing, she pulls away and starts collecting her clothes, "You want me with you because you've got this stupid notion. Jasim, I'm not pregnant. I can't be. It's best you just let me go home." She slides on her knickers and squeezes her oversized boobs into her bra. "Please, Jasim. This," she points her hand around the room and then toward the door, "Coming to the club tonight was a onetime thing. I know that."

Was I too emphatic when I explained the limitations of our relationship? Does she not believe I could have changed?

"I want you with me and I want you in my bed. I want to hold you." And, I want to find out whether we've got a problem to deal with or not. If I let her out of my sight, I don't trust her not to continue ignoring what's happening to her body. She's right, it should be impossible, but I wouldn't be the first man to be let down by a faulty strip of latex. "I've missed you, Janna. I'm not ready to let you go." And there. I've told her the truth.

CHAPTER 33
Janna

I'd felt utterly overwhelmed from the moment I stepped into the limousine with Jasim. Just being back in his presence reminded me of why I left him, and why I shouldn't have allowed him back into my life. His aura, his presence. He lights up my body, even when he's not touching me. No other man could ever come close to affecting me the way that he does.

I'd played the part of dutiful wife at the embassy, being polite and staying by his side, finding it easier than I'd expected to settle into my role. I thought he'd take me straight home afterwards, leave me to minister to myself in my own lonely bed. But completely unexpected, he'd allowed me this insight into his lifestyle and what makes him tick by bringing me to his club.

My emotions tied to the cross, swinging like a pendulum between elation and fear, while knowing he would never really hurt me or force me beyond what I could take, had only served to increase my arousal. And those orgasms? My body still burns from his touch.

I can't be pregnant. His question out of the blue, asked in my post-orgasmic haze, forced me to think about something I hadn't wanted to consider. *It's not possible.* There must be another reason why the smell of coffee makes me feel sick. I've had mild food poisoning since I returned from Amahad, which I can't seem to shake off. That must account for the nausea I've felt. I can't possibly have a child growing inside me, an alien predator leeching life out of me. I refuse to believe it. He always used protection.

I know my breasts have grown heavy and painful, but it must be down to something else. My trip abroad simply upset my cycle, I'm probably due for a period anytime now.

Automatically, I reach for my clothing, knowing that Jasim must be as horrified as me at the idea. But he's acting so calmly. *If I am…* No. I'm not.

If I continue to refuse to go back to his apartment I know he'll take me home. But he's dangling that carrot I can't quite refuse, the chance to sleep in his arms once again. And it might be the last time. Once this night has ended, and tomorrow we put an end to his crazy speculation, who knows when or if I might see him again? Will he call me up requesting I show my face at another diplomatic function? Or invite me back to his club, just to play? Or, having had this scare, will he stay as far away as he possibly can? *Does he think I'm trying to trap him?* But there's no way I could have become pregnant. He took charge of protection. *Oh, stop it. I'm not.* But the risk raising its head might be sufficient to keep him away. No man wants to be trapped. Particularly him. He's made that very clear on any number of occasions.

I'll take a few more hours in his company while berating myself, knowing it's stupid to accept his invitation. Now I've had another taste and it's even better than I remembered, I'll be like an addict, just hanging around for my next fix. And every time when, if, he calls, I'll drop everything to be with him. I'm stupid, I should be hardening my heart and staying away. What an imbecile I've turned out to be, just another woman desperate for any attention from her man.

I make no further argument as he leads me through the now much quieter club. Scenes seem to be over, people cuddled together, soft voices speaking by the bar. I tuck myself into his side as he crosses the room and out through the door to where the limousine's waiting.

I remember his impressive home, and he takes me to the same bedroom. Totally drained and exhausted, I barely notice as he helps me undress, folds back the duvet and encourages me to slip into the bed. As he slides in behind me, it seems all too familiar. The only difference to the last time I was here is that this time he's naked and under the covers.

With too much to contemplate, my brain seems to shut down, and with warm arms surrounding me, I sleep like the dead, having the best night's rest since I returned to England.

I didn't notice Jasim leaving the bed, but something alerts me and I start to stir. I open my eyes to see Jasim staring down at me with a mug in his hand.

"Coffee?"

Violently I shake my head. As my hand goes up to cover my mouth, I wave him away, get up, and run to the en-suite bathroom. As I'm leaning over the bowl, I feel hands at my back, smoothing my hair away from my face, and then a tissue is passed to me. As I wipe my mouth I feel myself flushing, from the nausea and embarrassment.

"I've made an appointment," he tells me emotionlessly.

"What?" My brain hasn't started functioning yet.

"Janna. We've got to find out. We're seeing a doctor at eleven. She's a friend of mine." His voice gives nothing away. Surely he must be feeling something? Dread at the least.

Tears come to my eyes, and I can't turn around to face him. *I don't want to know. It's easier to pretend that nothing is wrong.*

I come up with excuses, "I can't go in my little black dress."

"It's only just gone nine. I'll take you home to get changed, and we'll go from there. We've plenty of time."

I start shaking, and it's not that I'm naked and cold, and hanging my head over the toilet. It's the thought of facing my friends in the state I'm in. Or the state I'm possibly in. "I don't want to see anyone."

He strokes my back, I lean into his soothing touch. "Leave it with me." He passes me a robe, "Put this on for now. Are you feeling better? Can you eat some toast or something?"

Suddenly I'm feeling hungry, my stomach growls as I make my response. "Toast would be good."

"Come to the kitchen when you're ready."

He leaves me alone. I splash water on my face, use the toilet for its proper purpose, and run my fingers through my hair. As I did last time, I find a spare toothbrush in the cabinet. Having stolen a few moments to myself, I meet him in the kitchen, and put a small amount of butter on the piece of dry toast. My hand is not at all steady as I bring it to my mouth.

"Good girl, eat it all up." Under his watchful stare I manage to finish the slice, then, suddenly feeling hungry, reach for another.

He grins, I seem to have pleased him. Then he leans up against the counter and crosses his arms, "If you're pregnant," he starts, but I interrupt him.

"I'm not."

"Janna…"

My eyes plead with him not to talk about this. I can't bear to think about it. We'll have *the discussion* if my nightmare comes true.

He looks frustrated, his hands running through his dark hair. But he respects my wishes, indicating my plate. "Have you had enough?"

I nod, and push it toward him. He takes it and places it in the dishwasher. "My housekeeper will be here soon. She'll take care of cleaning up." It's another sign of the gulf between us, I always have to clear up after myself. And usually after the rest of Anarchy Rules as well. How could I have ever dreamed I'd fit into his world?

When he holds out his hand, I clasp his fingers, and he leads me through to the lounge. I hesitate before sitting down and tell him defiantly, "Look Jasim, I don't want to go to a doctor. There's no need." Not with him. I'll go buy a test at the chemist and then make any necessary decision depending on the result. He doesn't have to be involved. He did what he could to avoid such a situation. It would be my mess to sort out.

But I should have known he wouldn't agree. Swinging around fast he cups my face, "Janna. Do this for me. The doctor we're going to see does a lot of health testing for the club. If for nothing else, we can get those tests completed. You do want to go to Tiacapan again with me, don't you?"

I can't do anything but nod. *Of course I do.* If that's all he's offering me, I'll jump in with both feet. I'm just terrified that by going to the doctor I'm going to discover a truth that I don't want to admit. And where would we go from there? How will that affect Jasim? And our non-relationship? Or playing in the band? *I can't be pregnant.*

"I don't want to know," I admit, my eyes filling with tears.

He hugs me to him, rocks me like a baby as I sob in his arms.

I don't know how long we sit there, him trying to imbibe his strength into me, neither of us saying anything. We're disturbed by the sound of a doorbell ringing. Jasim pulls away, and after telling me to stay put, goes to answer it. He returns with several bags in his hands. He places them on a couch, then beckons me over.

"Hopefully there's something in here you can use."

Curious, I flick my eyes to him, but he's looking impassive. Gingerly, I reach down and open one of the bags. It's full of brand new clothes, jeans, t-shirts. Again I glance up, puzzled, and open another bag. A smart looking leather jacket is there. And in another, a couple of bags and accessories. And the final one has a selection of underwear. My mouth drops open.

"How the hell?"

He shrugs, "I called a personal shopper. You didn't want to get your own clothes, you couldn't wear last night's dress. Take what you want, if you don't like something, I can send it back."

"I can't afford any of this. It's all designer." I pick at the labels.

He smirks, "I can afford it, and you are my wife."

"In name only." I dismiss it.

He frowns for a moment, then quickly recovers. "Look, you need clothes. Just choose something for today. You don't need to keep it all if you don't want to."

It must be nice to be so rich. Snap your fingers and things get done.

He pats my shoulder, "Take it into the bedroom and try it on. Find something to wear this morning." His eyes pointedly go to an ornate clock hanging on the wall, "We're running out of time."

And that's how I find myself dressed in new bra and knickers, designer jeans which are butter soft and fit like a glove, a pretty blouse with lace inset and a new leather jacket, and walking into a doctor's office just an hour later.

I might be dressed up, but it doesn't alter my mood. Especially after I have to pee in a cup, and then wait for the results.

Jasim sits beside me in the comfortable leather chairs, a far cry from the hard, plastic seats in my normal surgery. In the background, soothing music plays, but it doesn't help calm my nerves. As I feel a squeeze on my hand, I realise I'm trembling.

"It will be alright," Jasim tries to calm me. "Whatever happens."

If my fears come true, I feel nothing will ever be right again. I'm picking at my nails and biting my lip, with Jasim now silent beside me, when the nurse calls me in.

"Sheikha Janna Kassis? The doctor will see you now." I need Jasim's tug at my hand to get me moving. I didn't even recognize my married name.

But that's the least of my worries as we enter a surgery, and an older woman stands and holds out her hand. Not only does Jasim take it, but he kisses her cheek, "Mary, thank you for fitting us in this morning."

"For you, Jasim, I'll always make time. You know that." There's twinkle in her eye, and then she turns to me. "It's nice to meet you, Sheikha."

I nod distractedly, still amazed he's booked me in as his wife.

"Take a seat, both of you." She waves us to chairs placed in front of a desk, and sits behind it. She picks up a piece of paper. "Right, so the good news is that you're pregnant. Congratulations."

As she taps something into her computer, I feel the blood drain from my face. *No. I can't be.* "Are you certain?" I ask her, not even daring to look at Jasim. Suddenly, I don't want him here. "Um, can I speak to you alone?"

"No."

Wide eyed, I turn swiftly to Jasim and then look back at the doctor who's shaking her head.

"I'm your Dom and husband," Jasim continues firmly. "And, the father of your child."

Mary leans on the desk, her hands clasped in front of her, "I take it you're fairly new to the lifestyle? You do understand you will have made a commitment to your Dom that he owns your body?"

"We haven't signed a contract, Mary." Jasim explains while my eyes open wider.

She frowns, "In that case…"

"But I'm going to stay." His hand touches my face, "Janna, this is a shock. To you and to me. Let's deal with it together, okay?"

I don't know what I'm thinking, let alone what he is. I want to curl into a ball and cry. In the scheme of things, it probably makes no difference whether he's here or not. Reluctantly, I nod.

"Let's get to practicalities. Do you know how far along you are?" The doctor draws my attention.

Jasim answers for me, "We were married twelve weeks ago."

"And you've had intercourse during that time?"

Jasim answers unerringly, "No. The last time was three months ago. And we always used condoms."

Mary's eyes widen, but she makes no comment. I flush, wondering what the hell she's thinking about what seems to be a celibate marriage. But she asks no questions, and simply states, "Condoms have been known to be unreliable, but it's rare."

Jasim shakes his head, "I know that, Mary."

She looks at me, "And you haven't been with anyone else in the meantime?"

My mouth drops open, "Of course not!"

"In that case, you're probably into your second trimester. And you haven't taken a test or seen a doctor before?"

Jasim interjects for me, "No." His eyes seem to challenge the doctor.

As the news starts to sink in, I think of my options, "What if I want an abortion?"

Jasim growls softly, Mary looks up impassively, "We can talk about the courses of action open to you in a minute. For a start, we'll do an ultrasound to see confirm your dates and see what we're dealing with. Go behind the screen, pet, and get undressed. Just remove your jacket and top.

You can leave your jeans and bra on. Lie on the bed and I'll be in in a moment.

Oh no. Not quite sure how I'm going to do this, I wait a second too long before complying. Obviously mistaking the reason for my delay, Jasim stretches out his hand.

"Come on, habiti. We need to know what we're dealing with."

Yeah, and the doctor's going to get an eyeful of something she doesn't expect. But knowing I can't refuse, I get up, surprised when Jasim clearly intends to accompany me. His expression is unreadable. *Is he in as much shock as me?* He nods at my top, but as my hands go to remove it, he pushes them away, taking hold of it himself and slipping it over my head. A twisted grin comes to my face as he sees me pull my arms into my sides. Awkwardly I lie down, keeping my body rigid and my hands tight to my hips.

"Move your arms a little, give me some room." My eyes flick to Jasim's face, and he nods reassuringly. Doing as Mary asked, I cringe, knowing I'm revealing six tiny bruises down each side of my torso.

Leaning down, Jasim plants a kiss to my mouth. "My marks," he breathes into his ear.

Mary notices them, but instead of reacting as though she's seeing an example of abuse, she gives what strangely looks like a nod of approval to Jasim.

And then comes the moment of truth. As the doctor puts cold gel all over my stomach, I begin to shake, hoping beyond hope the test was wrong and there'll be nothing for her to find. I begin to shake, and embarrassment about my bruises becomes the last thing on my mind.

"Relax, pet. This isn't invasive. I'm just going to run this probe over your stomach." She points to a screen by the side of the bed, and switches it on. "Just watch this and we'll see how far along he or she is."

Oh please, don't talk about it like that. It's just a bundle of cells, a foreign body which shouldn't be there.

But she's quick and efficient, and soon the probe finds its target. An image appears on the screen, and a loud fast thumping sound fills the air.

"That's baby's heartbeat. And see, here it is. There's the head, the spine…" She continues to point out body parts, and I can make out a hand and a foot, even fingers and toes. A lump comes into my throat. *It's a baby. Inside me. Jasim's baby.*

She starts to take measurements. "Well, I think I can confirm you're about fourteen weeks along which ties in nicely with what you told me, Jasim."

As she mentions his name, I turn my head to see such a look of amazement on his face. An expression I didn't expect to see. His eyes are glistening with moisture. As if he feels me watching him, he tears his gaze away from the screen, then his lips close on mine. When he lifts them away, he smiles at me, "Our baby. Look, habiti. Our baby. We made that between us."

"An accident, Jasim."

Brushing a stray strand of hair away from my face, he grows serious, "I've always used condoms, never gone without. Never had one not work before. This is Allah's work, Janna. It has to be."

Mary coughs to get our attention. "I'll just wipe this gel off." And without wasting a moment, she efficiently does. "Get dressed and we'll talk through your options."

Jasim hands me my jeans, he's looking concerned. "Janna, it's your body, your choice."

"What do you want, Jasim?"

He shakes his head, "I'm not going to influence you."

"But you just said it was God's will!"

His face twists, "How we go forward from here will be the challenge Allah has sent to us."

That doesn't tell me anything. "I want to know what you think."

"Come," he holds out his hand, "Mary's a busy woman. Let's finish up here, and then we can talk."

Walking out from behind the curtain, we take our seats again. Mary is watching us carefully, then she addresses me. "Do you still want to talk about your alternatives to going through with this? This pregnancy wasn't planned. I take it it's a shock."

A shock. Something so life changing described in two simple words. I started the morning with no other thought in mind but to end this alien life growing inside me if the pregnancy was confirmed. But I hadn't been prepared to see what I'd thought of as a malignant entity looking anything but. My hand goes to my stomach, already feeling a strange protective instinct for the life growing inside me. The baby looked like a miracle, not a mistake.

I glance at Jasim, he's not giving anything away. And then back to the doctor, "No. I'm going ahead with the pregnancy." Now the decision is made, suddenly something hits me, "Did everything, um, did it all look okay?" Already I'm concerned. "I haven't done anything different, or looked after myself very well."

Mary nods, "You didn't know. Some women don't have many symptoms." And some, like me, ignored those that were there. "I assure you I saw nothing missing and nothing that shouldn't be there. Have you drunk much alcohol? Smoked? Taken drugs?"

I shake my head, "Very little alcohol. I've lost the taste for it, and coffee."

Mary gives a half-smile, "Sometimes your body knows what you need, even if your mind hasn't quite accepted it. Now, I'll just take some blood. If you need extra treatment, iron or the like I'll be in touch. Just make sure you eat a balanced diet. I'll give you a diet sheet so you know what you should be eating, and what to avoid." She looks sympathetic, "I won't go into too much now, as it's a lot to take in. Especially as you didn't expect it."

"What about sex? And play?" Jasim puts in. His comment surprises me as I'd been assuming he'd run from his responsibilities, and half expecting I wouldn't see him after today. Maybe he's simply covering all bases.

"Sex as long as it's comfortable. Avoid impact play, and nothing too strenuous." She breaks off and winks, "Clothes pegs will be fine."

How does the doctor know how I got the marks?

Jasim doesn't notice my curious glance his way, he's looking down at his hands, then back at the doctor, "I flogged her last night."

She grins, "Not too hard, I would hope? But babies are well protected in the womb, and are more resilient than you would think. I doubt you did any damage, but just take it easy from here on in, okay? You can keep a tally of any punishments earned for after the birth."

She's in the lifestyle. She must be. And why does the thought of Jasim punishing me cause a totally inappropriate reaction from my libido? *But he won't be around after the birth.* I'm trying hard not to get my hopes up, telling myself I don't want him to stay close just because of the baby.

Blood's taken from my arm, I hardly notice with all the thoughts spinning through my head.

"I play in a band." It occurs to me, I ought to ask.

"Just keep on with life as normal and do whatever you feel like doing as long as you're comfortable. Listen to your body, it will tell you if you need to stop or slow down a bit."

She wants to see me in a month. While I nod my head, it's another thing I'll need to discuss. She's in a private practice, I won't be able to afford the appointments, even now Anarchy Rules is making more money. I really should make arrangements to go to my own GP and take advantage of the National Health.

CHAPTER 34
Jasim

Janna's so quiet, I know she's in shock as I take her hand and walk her out of Mary's office. And I don't speak, giving her time to process the life changing, shattering, news she's just been given.

I was glad Mary could fit us in at such short notice; she's a Domme, and a popular choice of doctor for myself and many members of Club Tiacapan. Her no-nonsense approach and understanding of the lifestyle a benefit for all involved. I smile to myself, not sure whether a vanilla doctor wouldn't have turned a hair when I admitted to beating my wife the previous night. And Janna was unable to hide the marks I'd left on her. Just seeing them made me start to get hard in a very inappropriate situation. Then what I saw on the screen wiped all thoughts of arousal out of my mind.

Janna's pregnant. With my child. The child I saw on the screen. I've never wanted children, they were for other people, never for me. But when faced with the reality, I was completely blindsided by the heartbeat I'd heard and the infant I'd seen. It wasn't something abstract, and surprisingly, it looked totally formed. If Janna had continued to say she wanted to abort it, despite my views that it was her decision, I would have been devastated. If it had been only a bundle of cells, that might have been different. But this looked like, was, a complete human being.

Mine to protect, cherish, and love. Just like its mother. Walking to the car and unlocking the door, I feel like falling to my knees and thanking whichever god had spun the wheel letting such odds to fall in my favour. Slapping me around the head with a situation I couldn't avoid. Making me come to my senses and admit I didn't want to let this woman walk out of my life. All at once giving a name to that emotion I'd felt but failed to recognize last night. And now I'm going to look after her. Care for her and my child. *My child.* I'm walking on air.

I open her door and help her inside.

"I'm not an invalid, Jasim," she grumbles. I smirk to myself, no she's not, but I'm going to make her life as easy as I possibly can.

Going around to the driver's side, I get in myself. The car starts with hardly a sound.

"Why, when you're in the oil business, do you drive an electric car? Wouldn't a gas guzzler be more appropriate?"

Suspecting her question is a distraction from the conversation we must have, I shrug, "Hey, I respect the environment. Fossil fuels have their place, but that doesn't mean I have to use them all the time. If it makes you feel better, I also have a Ferrari." I put the car in gear and start to pull away. "Are you hungry? I thought we could get lunch."

"No." She replies quickly, then corrects herself, "Well, yes. I'm going to eat, Jasim. I know I need to look after myself. But can you just take me home? I need time to think."

To think about what? I'm not worried she's going to consider ending the pregnancy as she'd been so adamant in front of Mary. Which only leaves her to contemplate us. Our marriage. Of bringing up a child alone. I don't want her to think about any of that. Not before she understands how I feel. Reaching out my hand, I rest it on hers, disheartened when she pulls it away. "We've got a lot to talk about. This involves the two of us. We shouldn't try to make far reaching decisions without discussing it together."

She throws me a sharp look, "There's nothing for you to decide."

"No?" I reverse back into the space, put the gear into neutral and pull up the handbrake. "I think it was me that was wearing the condom that failed. I know that is my child that you're carrying in your womb. It's my responsibility as well as yours."

"And it's my body. As you said. I can do what I like with my body."

"But it's my child. If you're keeping the baby, it's mine too."

I notice my voice has grown harsh. This is not the place for such a conversation. Around us cars are pulling in or out of spaces, people walking around. It's off-putting. We need somewhere relaxing for this. And I know just the place. Restarting the engine, for the second time I put it into gear.

"Where are we going?"

"We need to talk, Janna," I tell her for the second time since we left Mary's office. "I'm taking you somewhere we can do that. Without distractions." As she opens her mouth to protest, "I'll take you home, but not until after we've talked. If you don't want to hear what I'm going to explain, just ignore me. If you don't want to speak to me, keep your mouth shut. But I'm not letting you go back to your flat to sit and stew until I've at least had a chance to have my say."

She closes her lips, pursing them to show her disapproval. I play my winning card. "As soon as you go home, you'll have the rest of the band wanting to know where you've been and what you've been doing. You'll want to tell them what's happened, I know you will. And then you'll spend the time listening to advice thrown at you from all different directions. Come with me, and I'll let you have space to get things clear in your own mind before you bring in anyone else."

I pause, throwing a glance in her direction in time to see her nod. Breathing a sigh of relief that she's not cutting me out completely, or not just yet, I press my foot on the accelerator and the car starts to move. I've one destination in mind, and luckily, it's not too far.

As we turn into the drive way leading to Club Tiacapan, she cries out, "No, Jasim. This isn't what I want."

Knowing she thinks I'm going to pressure her through sex, I nip her protests in the bud, "Janna, relax. Trust me. This isn't what you think."

"I thought you were taking me to some neutral ground."

"I am. You didn't want to go back to your place, or come to mine. I didn't want to have this dialogue in a crowded restaurant. *Trust* me."

She humphs and goes quiet. I park around the back in the almost empty carpark, and bring her around to a side door. Using my key, I open it and step aside so she can precede me. I lead her down some corridors and then into the main room. It looks totally different than it does at night. Lights blaze down illuminating everything, and a small team of cleaners are working hard making sure every crevice is free of dirt and dust, and every piece of equipment is disinfected. Instead of sex and sweat the place smells of polish, instead of the noise of screaming and shouts of ecstasy, the sounds are of the vacuum and quiet conversation. I nod at the staff as we make our way through to the VIP area, and from there to the back stairs.

"It's different," she remarks. "It looks so innocent by day."

I smile my agreement. At the top of the stairway I unlock and open another door. This leads into a small, brightly lit apartment. It's furnished with a small kitchenette, a sitting/dining area, and another door leads to a bedroom. It's the flat I use on the nights I don't want to go home. I've never brought another woman here, it's my own private sanctuary.

She gives me a curious look. "Whose is this?"

"It's mine."

"Why didn't we come here last night, instead of one of the private rooms?"

"Because it's mine. If I sleep here, I sleep alone. You're the first woman, apart from the cleaners, who's ever stepped foot inside."

"Why?" She sounds puzzled.

I throw myself down on the sofa, stretching out my arm as an invitation for her to join me. "It was never a conscious decision, but it just became my own space. Somewhere I can escape, and if I don't want to, needn't be found."

"You keep it secret?"

"The staff know, of course, and the other owners. But I've never brought a sub here."

"But you've brought me."

"You're not just my sub. You're my wife."

"Not really." She's said that before, and the dismissal makes my gut clench.

At last she sits down. When my arm moves down onto her shoulder, she doesn't resist. After giving her a quick hug, I pull my arm back and sit forward, my elbows on my thighs. I interlock my fingers together. "I forced you into this marriage."

Looking sideways, I see her head shake. "We were both forced."

Now I stare at my feet. "That isn't quite true. I didn't have to marry you. Just claiming you in front of Fadi could have been enough. Just explaining I'd already taken your innocence."

She sucks in a breath. "But you said that wouldn't work?"

Shrugging I tell her, "We could have tried." At the time, I didn't understand why I took the more extreme route. Sure, it was the one most guaranteed to work, but it was a big step and commitment. Now I'm realising, even then, I felt more than I'd admitted.

Her eyes narrow, her voice sharpens. "Then, why? I don't understand."

I sigh and try to find an excuse she'll accept. "Kadar and Nijad have long wanted to see me married, to share in the marital bliss that they'd found. And although I didn't consciously own it right then, something inside me must have wanted that too. I didn't put up much of an argument before I agreed to their suggestion, and followed it through. Marriage should have been an antipathy for me, instead I went into it with my eyes open, and willingly."

"Help me here, Jasim. I'm really having difficulty processing this."

Reaching into my pocket I draw out my wallet, and extract two photographs and hand them to her. As she takes them from me, I know what she's seeing. They are both pictures of our wedding. One where we're sharing a kiss, one where we're looking at each other. And the same expression of desire is on each of our faces.

I tap the second one, "I've carried these with me since the day of our wedding."

She glances at me, her mouth wide open.

"That trip I left on, the day after our marriage. I was already starting to grasp that you were something special. I found it so fucking hard to stay away from you. I returned a day early, as I couldn't wait to get back. And when I did, I found you gone." I give it a moment before uttering my next admission. "I was a fool not to follow you back to England."

She gasps, and her hand covers her lips. "You didn't let me know. I thought you'd have been happy. It wasn't meant to be real, Jasim. You told me that enough times."

"No." And how I regretted that now. "You'd gone home, and I took that as a sign. Fuck, Janna. I've spent all my life running from relationships. Convincing myself getting involved was the last thing I wanted. I forced you into a marriage that you obviously didn't want, otherwise you wouldn't have left me that way. I convinced myself I was pleased you'd made the decision, and tried to dismiss my other thoughts as a temporary aberration. I reminded myself I never wanted to tie myself to one woman."

"Are you saying that's now changed? Why?" She's looking confused, and I don't blame her.

I address her valid question. The answer's simple. "You."

"Me?" Her voice rises almost to a squeak. "Why me?"

I gesture around me. "This is a major part of my life, Janna. I started the club as a safe place to play for *me*, as much as anyone else. A place where I could be myself. Where I could practice my depravity without condemnation, finding likeminded people to play with."

She snorts a laugh. "If you're depraved, Jasim, then I must be too. I *like* what you do. I worry I'd never find another man to satisfy me in the same way. Or at all."

I grimace. "I'd want to kill any man who even thought to try. You'll never be in another's arms ever again, Janna." As

I make my vow, I glance up see her looking confused. "I didn't think that I could find what I needed in a life partner, a woman whose needs matched mine. And when we met, I thought you'd run as soon as you knew what I am. You're a dark horse, Janna."

"And you're a dark horse too. I didn't know who, what you were. Just knew how much I was attracted to you. And that I wanted you."

"You hounded me until I gave in." I chuckle at the memory of how hard I'd tried to stay away from her. And how unsuccessful I'd been. Now it's time for full disclosure, "I didn't need your company last night. Marriages fail all the time. Kadar wouldn't have been impressed, but I could have concocted some story good enough to satisfy others why ours didn't work out. But I couldn't do it. I'd stayed away, but then just couldn't anymore. As soon as I landed in England, I looked for an excuse to get in touch. And then I played on your better nature to get you to agree to go to the embassy with me."

She's biting her lip and doesn't look convinced. I need to tell her the rest. "I'd have come back sooner, but I was injured. In hospital. I told you I was shot." At the quizzical rise of her eyebrows I continue, "It was worse than I led you to believe. The bullet went into my back."

"You said it was nothing. Her eyes narrow, "I didn't see any injury last night."

"I didn't let you see. I kept my clothes on, then fucked you from behind. You couldn't touch or see the scar." I don't really know why, it had seemed important not to play on her sympathy.

"Can I see it now?"

No longer wanting secrets between us, I turn around and raise my shirt. There on my back, the still angry looking scar where the bullet went in. A couple of inches higher it would have gone through my heart. Two inches to the left and it would have shattered my spine. I'd come face to face with my mortality. "I no longer have a spleen. But I'm alive."

"You've told me a little." She purses her lips. "Tell me the rest, Jasim."

"When Ryan was injured, I acted like a fool. I'd been trained in the army as a medic. My first reaction was to turn to see to his wound. Hence, when I went to him, they got me in my back. It was my fault we were there, Janna. I insisted on going when Ryan advised me it was too dangerous."

"He spoke about that to me last night. He said there was no specific threat, just the normal volatility of the region he was warning about."

"He's being too generous. That I stuck to my guns and wouldn't listen got us both wounded. It was all I could think about when I was in hospital. I spent the long days re-evaluating my views on life. That's when I realized what a fool I'd been to just let you go. And when I knew I had to do everything I could to get you back."

"Ryan had said you'd grown reckless."

She's got a point, "I had. When I returned to the palace and found you were gone, I didn't understand my reaction, but now it's clear that I was devastated, and not thinking straight. Even then I was denying you mattered to me. I tried to push you out of my thoughts by throwing myself into everything. It's down to me Ryan got hurt."

"If anything, it's on me." As my eyes flick to her in astonishment, she continues, "I thought I was making it easy for you. A clean break. You were gone, and I wasn't sure how I could bear to say goodbye if I'd waited until you returned. We'd have had a few more nights, and then you'd have wanted me to go. And…"

I guess what she's going to say. "I'm not stupid, well, not all the time," I smirk at myself, "I know the rest of Anarchy Rules would have put pressure on you."

"They said you'd return to London."

"I would have if I could."

She wipes away a tear. "I wish I'd known you'd been hurt."

"I came as soon as I was able to." It had been my heart that had driven me, even though it had taken me almost being fatally injured to realise what was missing from my life. "As soon as I was fit enough, I came back and reached out to you."

Breaking off, I look down to my fists, bunched tightly together as I struggle to express emotions I had been denying I even owned. "I tried to convince myself I'd be happy with you as just my sub. I still had a notion I could fuck you out of my system. I've been a fool, Janna."

She touches my hand, the first touch she's initiated since we left the surgery. "No more than me. I was denying there being any possibility I was pregnant, but I'd have to have admitted it soon. If you hadn't have reached out to me, I wouldn't have known what to do, whether to contact you."

And it's come around to our current predicament. "I'm over the moon, Janna. Last night, while you were sleeping, I went through every emotion in my head. Fuck, I couldn't even remember why I'd never wanted a child. To see your belly swell with my seed? I don't deserve you, or this. But from the depth of my heart I'm now admitting the truth. I came back to see if you'd give our marriage a chance. The fact you're pregnant is a bonus I don't deserve. I want you in my life. I want to live with you, be everything for you. I want to be your husband. For real this time."

She's biting her lip.

"Spit it out, what's the matter?" I frown, wondering if, now I've laid it on the line, she's going to tell me it isn't what she wants.

"You're older than me. You're a Dom. You're controlling. I've been controlled and directed all my life. I don't want to swap one kind of prison for another. I want to have some freedom…"

"I'm a Dom in the bedroom. I won't control your life outside of it." How can I explain it to her, "The reason I left Amahad was due to my overbearing father, I needed to get out from under his thumb. I understand your fears only too well, and know exactly how you're feeling. I promise you, if I ever come on too strong, well, your safeword will work in our everyday life as well as in bed or in the dungeon."

Her lips turn up at the thought of her safewording out.

"You've met Cara and Zoe? Do they seem like they're cowed? Ruled by their men?"

She grins at this, "Certainly not."

"They're both married to Doms. Huh, it runs in the family." I want her to know I'll be behind her, encouraging her, not directing her life. "I'll support you in the band."

"I'm leaving Anarchy Rules. They know it already. Oh, there isn't a date set yet, but I've been pulling away."

My eyes widen, I didn't expect that.

"It's not just about you. I just feel I need something else, I've been dissatisfied for a long time now. Even before we went to Amahad. I'd felt something was missing. Something for me, which I've never had." She moves her hands across her stomach, and I wonder whether she even knows she's doing it. "Maybe write music, or even teach. I don't know. I just want more in my life than to live it out on a stage."

"You play a good Domme." I chuckle.

She laughs, "I'm acting a part." Her face grows serious again, "Only you, Jasim. It was only you who saw the real person I am. I don't think even the other band members know how much of an act I was putting on. And certainly, none of the other men who tried to flirt with me ever did."

"You allowed me to see you, Janna. And I'm so fucking grateful for that." I pause, thinking, "And I've shown you me. There are no secrets kept hidden."

"How's this going to work? You're a sheikh, a diplomat...."

"We're us, Janna. Two people who'll work it out together." I break off, as a previously unthinkable notion comes to me. If she has no ties here, there's nothing holding me back. Just the excuses of years past that no longer seem valid. I take a deep breath, "If you leave the band, and, if you want to, we could go back to Amahad. Make it our home." I can't quite believe the words that have just come out of my mouth. But the thought of living near my brothers, going *home* with my wife and child seems to plug an empty space inside of me where I didn't even know there was a hole.

She's quiet as she thinks. And then turns with a gorgeous smile that engages her eyes, "Jasim, I think I'd like that."

CHAPTER 35
Janna

The warm breeze of the evening stirs the air, making fragrant flowers bend and release their heady perfume. Up above me the sky glimmers with a million stars and the full moon hangs proud in all its glory. I take a deep breath, inhaling the aroma of the place which has become my home.

"Janna!" Turning I greet Cara, noticing the animation on her face.

"Zorah's used the potty for the first time. Can you believe that? My little girl's growing so fast."

As she draws close I reach out and hug her. "She's grown so much even in the time I've been here." I've grown to love Zorah and little Ra'id.

Cara smiles, "She's already getting into everything. I long for the days she stayed put."

I join in as Cara laughs, and link my arm with hers as we walk through the garden, pausing a moment to enjoy the tinkling of a fountain playing. Well, she walks, and I wad-dle. I'm eight and a half months pregnant now, and can't wait to meet my baby, fed up of being unable to see my toes. In the time since I've been here, Cara's become such a good friend, along with Zoe.

"How's Kadar's plans progressing?"

"The elections will be held next month. Wow, it's so exciting, Janna. The country's going to be so much better off. With a democratic form of government on the horizon our currency is soaring. And AmaOil's shares are zooming up."

Far from being a subservient wife, Cara holds a senior position in government, advising the Finance Minister. A position she'd be holding were it not for her desire to spend time with her child and husband.

"Is Zoe back?"

"Yes, she's just got in." Zoe, another highly independent woman has directed her creativity toward setting up mobile schools and teachers to bring education to the desert tribes. She's loved by all the sheikhs, though when she disappears on one of her extended trips to the more sparsely populated regions, I swear I see more grey hair peppering Kadar's head. But he doesn't prevent her doing what she loves.

I haven't found my place quite yet, but then I'm doing an important job. Incubating the next prince or princess of the realm.

"Come, let's join the men."

Nodding, I agree, and follow my sister-in-law into the palace, taking the opulence in my stride. Making our way to an informal dining room I hear voices inside, and a smile spreads across my face. Cara eyes roll, and even before I see it, I can picture the scene.

"You're talking crap, Kadar."

We push open the door. The man I was initially in awe of glares at his brother. Nijad chuckles and Jasim directs his next comment to him, "For fuck's sake, Ni. It was the only reasonable thing to do."

"You're talking out of your arse again, brother. Something drew you. Whether or not you had any obligation to her, she owned you from that point on."

Jasim looks thoughtful, but as he sees me enter, he rises out of his seat. I'm trying to stifle a laugh like I normally do when the three highly educated sheikhs let down their hair. They behave no differently than the band members I used to spend my time with. The easy relationship between them had soon put me at my ease. Mind you, they could change to become brooding sheikhs at the drop of a hat.

My personal sheikh looks resplendent in his desert robes, and I can barely remember what he looks like wearing a suit. And currently his dark gold flecked eyes are staring down at me, concern written over his face, "Are you feeling alright, habiti?"

I've had twinges in my back all day, but don't want to worry him. Just another drawback of carrying a large baby around. "I'm good." Which is an understatement. I'm happier than I ever expected to be. Once Jasim decided to commit he was all in. I couldn't ask for a more devoted husband.

"You look tired, habiti." And this is where the Dom comes out. "Kadar, Ni. My wife needs rest. We'll continue our discussions tomorrow." He gives me no choice, but I wouldn't contradict him, he reads me so well he knows just how fatigued I've become.

The other men bow their heads, but that doesn't hide the identical smirks on their faces. Cara comes over and kisses my cheek and wishes me goodnight. This is my family now, as well as a husband I've gained two brothers and sisters.

Jasim doesn't need to lead the way as he walks through the palace that I've come to know like the back of my hand. The guards are greeted as friends, and I try out my Arabic and as usual my tortuous accent raises an indulgent smile. We come to our suite, a glorious set of rooms almost the size of Jasim's apartment back in England, and going inside, my husband throws off his headdress, allowing his now longer hair to hang free.

He turns and opens his arms. Though my huge belly prevents us getting too close, he pulls me to him. He's already aroused. "Are you too tired, habiti?"

Not in the least. Being pregnant seems to have made me even more randy, though we need to be inventive as the time's getting close. "I need you, Jasim."

Although I must weight a ton, he picks me up and carries me into our bedroom. He stands me by the bed, and slowly undresses me, making me feel like that special present being unwrapped on Christmas Day. Naked, I slide onto the bed, turning onto my side. The bed dips behind me, and warm hands snake around and caress my breasts, oh, so gently he weighs them, and then flicks his fingers over my nipples. It's all I can stand, and he knows he need to use the softest of touches.

I push my arse back, feeling his hard length prodding at my behind. Already my clit is begging for his touch. "I'm not going to last long," I warn him.

A soft chuckle, the vibration shooting up my spine, "Neither will I. Fuck, I never thought it could get better, but knowing that's my baby in there…" As his hand snakes to my stomach, the baby gives a massive kick. "It's such a turn on, knowing I'm going to be meeting him soon."

"Or her."

"Or her," he echoes. Uncaring what sex it is so long as it's healthy, we hadn't bothered to find out.

Then he's moving his fingers to where I need them, probing inside while his thumb touches my clit. It's all I need; a massive explosion starts to rise as my thighs trap his arm. The orgasm so powerful, every part of my swollen uterus tensing with waves of ecstasy. His fingers keep moving, I come again. My heart's beating wildly, my breathing frantic.

"Another good one?"

"Oh yeah." It's as much as I can say.

And now he's pushing inside me, slowly and methodically stretching my vagina, and I welcome the intrusion.

"I. Love. You." He rasps out, as he struggles to get inside. He lifts my leg, putting it over his arm, making more space. He pulls out and pushes in, a glorious feeling.

"Love you too," I respond, having to gasp the words out.

Finally, he's fully in, and waits for a moment. "Best fucking feeling in all the world. I love my cock inside you. Only you."

I can't even answer him, I'm feeling so full, so overwhelmed. Pregnancy hormones make tears leak from my eyes.

"I'm going to fuck you now." I moan at the familiar warning which always affects me, and as he starts thrusting I hang on for the ride. It's not long before my muscles start contracting, a wail comes from my mouth as it's almost too intense for me to bear. I suck in a breath reaching, reaching… He unerringly hits that spot over and over until I momentarily see stars in front of my eyes and I'm screaming, going over the top.

Simultaneously he starts jerking, short strokes as his cock swells and I swear I feel jets of warm cum discharging inside me.

"Fuck, it just keeps getting better. Every. Single. Time."

I'm taking deep breaths, well, as deep as I can with a baby pushing up against my lungs. It seems to take forever until my breathing begins to even. I feel him leave the bed, and return with a washcloth, and gently he cleans me up. I allow him to do it, the little service for me, giving him pleasure.

Then his hand stills. "Er, Janna. Either you squirted quite a lot or…"

Still lost in the aftermath of my rapturous experience, it takes a second or two for his words to sink in. "Help me up." He gives me his hand and pulls me into a sitting position. Looking down I can see what he means. My eyes widen. "I think my waters have broken."

He stands, closing his eyes briefly before opening again, and I see him take a deep breath as he brings himself under control. In a measured voice he asks, "Shall I drive you to hospital, or do you want an ambulance?"

Though I don't relish the hours of labour I suspect lie in front of me, I doubt the baby will be coming anytime soon. "You drive."

"Wait there. I'll get you some clothes."

"Don't forget my bag," I remind him, even though I know he won't. He's such an organised man.

A contraction hits me, it's harder than the Braxton Hicks I've been experiencing, and instinctively I know this is the start of the real thing. He's by my side in seconds, and rubbing my back. "Breathe, habiti. Breathe."

"I'm not tied up now, Jasim." I attempt to joke with him, hearing the Dom in his voice. "I expect you'll thrive on my pain."

"No," he starts seriously, "I'd never ask you to suffer pain beyond which you can bear. But today I can't stop it or take it away. If I could do this for you, I would. But I'll be beside you, every step of the way. Now let's get you dressed. The sooner we're at the hospital, the happier I'll be."

The journey passes in a blur. Jasim summoned a driver so he can be with me in the back. Mindful of his precious cargo, we've got outriders with us, guards on motorbikes clearing the way. I'm wracked with pain, the contractions getting closer and closer.

With one hand on mine, the other holding his phone to his ear, Jasim alerts the medical staff, and contacts his brothers. On his final call, he yanks the device away from his ear and the excited scream I hear makes me grin through the pain.

"Aiza?"

"Aiza," he confirms. "She's flying back."

I've only met his sister once, but immediately got on with her like a house on fire. We're the same age, after all.

At the hospital, I'm bundled into a wheelchair and taken to the royal suite. If it wasn't so clean and smelling of antiseptic, it would look more like a hotel room. Necessary equipment discreetly placed so as to not look overbearing.

Almost immediately, I have an examination that seems invasive, I squeeze Jasim's hand hard.

"This baby is impatient." The doctor looks at me and smiles. "You can have gas and air, but it's too late for an epidural."

"You can take it." Jasim says, his eyebrow arched as though in challenge. I bark a laugh, and as he gives a wry smile he knows exactly what I'm thinking. *He's said that before too.*

An eternity of pain later, which I'm told was *only* a few hours and during which I wished I was able to say 'red' more than once, Ati is born. Our son. His name meaning gift. Considering the way he was conceived, how he brought us back together and to our senses, it's seemed a fitting moniker to give him. Once I'm ready, and Ati swathed in a blanket, the door to the suite opens and Jasim's brothers rush in, along with their wives.

Tired and exhausted, I rest back on the pillows, allowing my son, *my son*, to be passed around his doting uncles and aunts. Jasim hovers anxiously, as though worried someone might drop him. Then he comes over, *our son* in his arms, holding him gingerly as though he could break. He gives him to me, the others leave to give us some privacy, and I hold him to my breast and try to make him latch on.

As he's rooting for my nipple, Jasim gives a wry smile, "Guess I'm going to have to share you now." He brushes his hair back, then leans down and kisses Ati on the head, then me on the lips, "The words are inadequate, but thank you from the very bottom of my heart. You've given me something I never thought I'd have. A wife and a family."

With one hand on my baby, I reach out the other to him, "I love you, Jasim." I swallow a couple of times before continuing, "It's me who should be grateful, you've given me so much." I grin, "I'm glad I chased you and didn't give up."

He draws in a breath as if imagining what would have happened if I hadn't, then tells me in a voice full of emotion, "So am I, habiti. So am I."

They say if you save a life you're forever responsible for that person.

I might not have literally saved her life, but she certainly saved mine.

"So, the eternal bachelor has well and truly been caught." Nijad barks a laugh, "You've got a son and wife now."

"And you're home in Amahad." Kadar can't resist poking the sleeping bear.

Yes. And yes. And doesn't it feel right? Looking down at the sleeping bundle in my arms, I'm overwhelmed by the love I feel for my son, let alone how much I care for his mother. The woman I tried to evade, because from the beginning she'd tied me up in knots, pulling me to her as though she held the end of an invisible piece of string.

Life's turned full circle now. Once I couldn't wait to get away, now I view my necessary visits to London and living in that gray dreary city with distaste. "I'm selling my share of Club Tiacapan," I tell my brothers, to identical looks of disbelief. "Oh, I'll retain membership, I'm not giving up playing. But the reasons I started it aren't there anymore."

Kadar nods his head, "When you find the *one*, you don't need anyone else."

"Add a child into the mix, you don't have time for play." Nijad gives a small frown, and I shake my head, his warning causing no consternation. I might have less freedom to play with my wife, but I'll not mind spending time with my son.

"Or the energy," my older brother adds laughing, pointing to the baby sleeping peacefully in my arms.

I smile ruefully, he might only be a week old, but already he's got his mother and I wrapped around his little finger, bringing all my protective and caring instincts to the fore. Already I can't imagine being without him. And if I lost her, I'd lose my soul. Staring down into his face, and not for the first time, cataloguing his precious features which seem to be a combination of both mine and hers, I say softly, "I get it now. What you were telling me. I thought I'd been avoiding a trap, but instead I was living in one of my own making."

Nijad appears at my side, his hand falls on my shoulder, "Janna's going to make a great mother, a great wife, and a great sub."

"She already is," I tell him. And I mean every word.

"Well, that's that then."

I glance at Kadar, "What's what?"

He points to Nijad, and then at me, and then back at himself. "No more machinations, no more searching. We've all been caught now. Three bachelor brothers, now with their wives."

"No more kidnappings or arranged marriages?" Nijad grins.

"Hmm," Kadar steeples his hands under his chin, "There's still one sibling left."

Aiza.

OTHER WORKS BY MANDA MELLETT

Blood Brothers

- *Stolen Lives* (#1 – Nijad & Cara)
- *Close Protection* (#2 – Jon & Mia)
- *Second Chances* (#3 – Kadar & Zoe)
- *Identity Crisis* (#4 – Sean & Vanessa)
- *Dark Horses* (#5 – Jasim & Janna)

SATAN'S DEVILS MC

- *Turning Wheels* (Blood Brothers #3.5, Satan's Devils #1 – Wraith & Sophie)
- *Drummer's Beat* (#2 – Drummer & Sam)

Coming in 2017:
- *Slick Running* (#3 – Slick & Ella)
- *Targeting Dart* (#4)

Sign up for my newsletter to hear about new releases:
http://eepurl.com/b1PXO5

Slick

Running

SATAN'S DEVILS #3

Slick

I'm devastated when disaster hits the Satan's Devils MC. Shocked and angry, there couldn't be a worse time to be contacted by the woman I'd briefly made my old lady, only for her to run the moment things got too tough. She'd left me with no explanation, and in my book that was enough to cut her out for good. But when she explains her situation, it's difficult to refuse to offer my help. But it has to be on the condition she knows what was once between us will stay dead and buried. There had been no good reason for her to run, had there?

Ella

I didn't run from Slick, I ran from his club, only to find the world outside their protection can be just as dangerous. And now, to protect my little sister, I've no alternative other than to go to Slick for help. It's not good timing, the Satan's Devils have just lost one of their own.

I understand why Slick wants to keep his distance, I'd hurt him when he'd put everything on the line, acting out of character and claiming me as his old lady. A gesture I'd thrown back in his face. But I'm not the same woman he first met. There are things he doesn't know.

SATAN'S DEVILS #3: Slick Running

Brothers protecting their own

ACKNOWLEDGEMENTS

When I started writing the Blood Brothers series it was Jasim's story that was foremost in my mind. But I needed to set the groundwork first, and that's how it came about that his brothers got their books, along with some of the bodyguards from Grade A, before I could start work on the intriguing man who owns a BDSM club.

I've had so much support and encouragement for this series, reviews and messages letting me know that my readers are as in love with the Kassis brothers and the men from Grade A as I am. I thank everyone who's bought and read the Blood Brothers books, and especially those who've let me know how much they enjoy the series. You don't know how much those comments spur me on to keep writing.

Alex, you're my number one fan, and you encourage me all the time. I can't wait to hear what you think of *Dark Horses*.

Once again, I must thank Lia Rees who brings the men alive with her brilliant cover design.

This is my second time working with editor, Elizabeth Wright, who I seem to owe new pairs of panties too as she tells me editing the book set hers on fire. I very much enjoyed working with you, Elizabeth, and I appreciated your enthusiasm for *Dark Horses*.

Finally, thanks to my husband who as always supports me in my writing, and doesn't seem to mind when I zone out and live in a different world. And, of course, my son, who's always there to support me.

If you enjoy *Dark Horses*, or even if you don't, I'd love to hear from you. Authors love to read reviews of their books.

ABOUT THE AUTHOR

After commuting for too many years to London working in various senior management roles, Manda Mellett left the rat race and now fulfils her dream and writes full time. She draws on her background in psychology, the experience of working in different disciplines and personal life experiences in her books.

Manda lives in the beautiful countryside of North Essex with her husband and two slightly nutty Irish Setters. Walking her dogs gives her the thinking time to come up with plots for her novels, and she often dictates ideas onto her phone on the move, while looking over her shoulder hoping no one is around to listen to her. Manda's other main hobby is reading, and she devours as many books as she can.

Her biggest fan is her gay son (every mother should have one!). Her favourite pastime when he is home is the late night chatting sessions they enjoy, where no topic is taboo, and usually accompanied by a bottle of wine or two.

Email: manda@mandamellett.com

Website: www.mandamellett.com

Connect with me on Facebook:

https://www.facebook.com/mandamellett

Sign up for my newsletter to hear about new releases in the Blood Brothers and Satan's Devils series: http://eepurl.com/b1PXO5

Photo by Carmel Jane Photography